Charley's Flying School

Charley's Flying School

Rosa B. Lane

Copyright ©2018 Rosa B. Lane
All rights reserved.
ISBN:9798649640855

DEDICATION

I dedicate this book to my late beloved husband, Bob, for the support and help he gave me. He flew IFR and I flew VFR. Together we had a glorious life flying together in good weather and above the rain and clouds in sunshine.

Table of Contents

DEDICATION v
ACKNOWLEDGMENTS xi
Chapter 1 1
Chapter 2 27
Chapter 3 45
Chapter 4 65
Chapter 5 79
Chapter 6 101
Chapter 7 113
Chapter 8 121
Chapter 9 129
Chapter 10 135
Chapter 11 139
Chapter 12 147
Chapter 13 171
Chapter 14 183
Chapter 15 187
Chapter 16 203
Chapter 17 209
Chapter 18 215
Chapter 19 229
Chapter 20 233
Chapter 21 237
Chapter 22 243
Chapter 23 247

Chapter 24 253
Chapter 25 263
Chapter 26 271
Chapter 27 275
Chapter 28 281
Chapter 29 291
Chapter 30 299
ABOUT THE AUTHOR 305

ACKNOWLEDGMENTS

I want to thank my daughter, Diana Grunloh for her art work on the cover design and her help in editing. I also want to thank my daughter-in-law, Mary Lane, and my son, Bruce Lane for the assistance they provided in proof reading, editing and formatting "Connie." I also want to thank all of the readers who have read my writings and have encouraged me to keep writing. Thank you!

Chapter 1

The stranger stood quietly in the partial shade of the hangar door watching the quick efficient movements of the mechanic changing the tire on a small high wing training plane. The mechanic's back was toward the door, and no apparent sign was given that the tall tanned man had even been noticed. In spite of the shapeless olive cover-all and grease stained hat, there was a grace of movement and precision which held the attention of the man. It was several minutes before he spoke.

"I'm looking for the owner of the training school." His voice was tossed against the hangar walls, and it echoed across the large room. The mechanic did not look up but continued to tighten a final nut.

"I'm the owner."

"There must be some mistake. I'm looking for Charley Jackson, the owner of Charley's Flying School."

The mechanic stiffened, hesitated as if fighting for control, then slowly stood up and turned toward the stranger. A silence enveloped the hangar as the stranger found himself looking into two large sapphire blue eyes. Their gazes met and held clinging in the hot summer air. For just an instant it seemed as if time stopped. Silence fell over the hangar. A buzzing wasp settled on the hangar door. The brown eyes of the man opened in surprise.

"You're a -"

"Woman," she spoke clearly and defensively. "What can I do for you?"

"I'm Calvin Morris. Friends call me Cal. You must be Jerry Jackson. I've come to see Charley Jackson about our business. We talked at the Southwest Fly-in."

The grease smeared face paled. The young woman struggled for control. Would it never stop? Would ghosts always be intruding?

"My father never returned home from the fly-in." The voice quivered. She turned her head fighting the pain so new and strange.

The man frowned. "Never returned? What happened?"

The girl breathed deeply. "He was driving home from the airport and was hit head on by a drunken driver. Just five miles from home." She stopped, gained some control and added, "What did you wish to see him about?"

"He didn't tell you about me?" The stranger raised his eyebrows in surprise.

"No. Should he have? He called before he left the air show and said he had a surprise for me that's all." She spoke the last words so softly they were almost inaudible. She looked up at him and continued, "Let me clean these tools, and we'll go inside and talk."

She began picking up the tools. The man bent to help her. They both ducked under the wing of the plane and walked to the long work table which stood against the hangar's back wall. Behind the table a large panel had been hung on the wall where shining tools were neatly placed in labeled positions. They placed the tools on the table and the girl busied herself cleaning and oiling them. She worked quietly. Calvin returned and brought the worn tire back laying it on the floor by the table.

"Thank you." She spoke softly as if afraid her voice would give away her inner turmoil.

"You keep a clean hangar. I like that, Jerry. May I call you Jerry? Charley told me all about you. He was mighty proud of you. Somehow I didn't quite expect you to be so-." His face reddened as if he suddenly realized he was talking too much. "So lovely." he added to himself.

Jerry looked at him. Who was he? He talked as if she were a hired hand and he the owner. Irritation flooded her. "Let's go to the office."

They walked from the hangar into the hot summer air, blinking at the sun's assault upon their eyes. A two-room trailer had been permanently installed for office use next to the hangar. A few flowers had thrived along a stone walk and along the front of the trailer in spite of the Texas heat. Jerry led Calvin up the walk and into the air-conditioned trailer. The cool air of the office enveloped them bringing a sigh of relief from the man.

"Feels good." He brushed his damp forehead with the back of his hand.

"There's cool water in the cooler and soft drinks in the ice box. I'll clean up. Won't be but a minute." Jerry disappeared into the second room of the trailer leaving the stranger to take stock of the office. She needed the time to get the ache in her heart under control.

The trailer was large with one room converted to an office and the other a teaching room. The office windows were draped with novelty cotton curtains showing old time airplanes. Along the wall under the window was a table containing an empty coffee-maker and the accessories. On the left stood a water cooler and cup dispenser with a waste basket in the corner. A vinyl covered sofa stood against the back wall facing a low coffee table holding several current flying magazines. On the other side of the room under the windows were several chairs. The door to the classroom stood open showing one long table with chairs. He glimpsed a bulletin board at the back of the room on which was pinned squares of torn shirt tails. The shirt tails had printed on them in large black letters the names and dates of the students who had experienced the victory of their first solo flight.

Calvin glanced at the plaster novelty planes zooming at each other above the sofa. He was studying the certificates on the wall above the office desk when the door opened and Jerry appeared. Her sleeveless cotton shirt was tucked into her jeans revealing a too slim waist. Her long blond hair was caught up into a pony tail emphasizing high cheekbones and a determined chin. She did not notice the quick intake of Calvin's breath. She stood there with a half-smile for a moment, then walked with long graceful strides to his side and looked up at the certificates.

"Charley could make an airplane dance. He was an aerobatic

champ once. He flew with some of the greats." Her voice broke, and she clenched her jaws for a second before continuing. "He had bought the Aerobat and was planning to give lessons. Now I'll have to sell the Aerobat."

"Why? I'm an aerobatic instructor." Calvin's voice was quiet and sounded puzzled.

Again, the possessiveness of this stranger irritated her. "I can't hire you." Jerry walked to the coffee maker and carried the glass pot quietly into the other room returning with it filled with water. As she started the coffee brewing, she was unaware of the gaze the stranger was giving her.

"What kind of business did you have with my father?" Jerry sat down at the cluttered desk wearily and looked at the tall man.

"I'm your new partner," he said quietly not quite knowing what to expect.

Jerry looked at him in disbelief. "So you think you can just walk in here and take over MY flying school by informing me you're my partner? What kind of a vulture are you to try to take advantage of someone's tragedy?" She stood and looked up at him angrily. "I don't know who you are but you had better leave. Just because I'm a woman and alone you think you can walk in here and steal my business. I'm in trouble, but I'll survive without the likes of you. Get out!" Color had flooded her face and the sapphire eyes sparkled with flecks of fire. "Get out!"

"And leave you to sell everything to pay the bills? You can't run the school alone." He had a half-smile, and amusement filled his brown eyes. Jerry felt as if an older brother was laughing and teasing her. "You can't throw me out. I own half of this school."

"Liar! Charley would never do that. Not without talking to me."

"He did." His voice was firm and allowed no argument.

Jerry felt as if she had been slapped. For the first time Jerry noticed that the man had brought a leather flight bag in with him. From it he pulled a large brown envelope. He held it out to her, watching her closely as she took it with trembling fingers. Jerry looked up at the man, fighting tears. Then she pushed them back behind the dam she had built to contain her grief.

"How could he!" She felt anger at Charley, at the stranger, and at the world. "How could he?" She pulled the sheets from the envelope and read them. "How could he?" All the loneliness, the hours of worry, the working every night till midnight, all of this to save the school for this arrogant stranger. "How could he?" For the first time in her life she felt defeated, numb.

"Charley had a copy and my check. Surely you found it in his things." Jerry looked up at him feeling light headed and strange at his statement. She had not opened Charley's bag or his flight bag. The pain had been so great; she had put them in his closet and closed the door to his room. It had not been opened since. She had not been able to bring herself to go back into his room. It was as if by not opening his bags, he would be back.

"I'll go home and look." She felt numb physically and emotionally; and, like a robot, she started for the door. A pair of strong hands stopped her. Calvin held her shoulders in his hands so tightly it hurt her.

"It's not necessary right now. Sit down." He led her to the couch and pushed her down gently then poured her a cup of coffee. "Here, drink this. Charley tried to call you. I was with him. But you didn't answer at home or here. So he went ahead with the sale. I'm so sorry I shocked you." He poured himself a cup of coffee and sat down on one of the chairs opposite Jerry.

Jerry let Calvin push her gently onto the sofa and put a cup of coffee into her hands. She made no protest. A great heaviness invaded her body and her spirit. It was like a nightmare unreal and impossible. She would wake up soon and it would be gone. The coffee in the cup reflected the light, and Jerry looked into its depths seeing ghosts of the past.

Jerry could not remember a time when she was not around airplanes. Always her father had been with her. In the early years there had been her mother; but she had died when Jerry was eight and the memory of her was faded and blurred. She remembered a tall beautiful woman bending to tie her sash on Sunday morning and taking her hand when they were shopping. But the real thing she remembered was the perfume her mother always wore. After all these years, there was still a partly used bottle on the dresser in the bedroom her parents had shared. Jerry had gone into the room many times and tried to remember, but it always was the brief blurred memory of a beautiful, laughing woman. Aunt Molly and Uncle Art, close friends of the family, had come to stay a while and help with the agony of adjusting to a motherless home. They had been strong friends to the aching hearts.

Jerry remembered her mother trying to fly the Uncle Art's World War I Curtiss Jenny biplane the first time. The plane bounced on landing. Jerry had laughed and cried out, "Jenny's jumpin'! Jumpin' Jenny, Daddy." Jumpin' Jenny had stuck to Uncle Art's World War I biplane. She remembered the first clumsy attempt at screwing a bolt and Charley's laughter at her failure. "I'll make you my partner yet," he had told her. How proud those words had made her. It had always been her hope that someday Charley would make it legal. She knew if she had been a son–. Slowly Jerry became aware of a gentle hand on her shoulder as if she were a breakable doll. The voice was condescending and sympathetic.

"I know a shock like this coming on top of Charley's death is difficult for a-." Calvin forced himself to say the words that he knew would make her hate him, "- a woman."

Jerry stiffened. The numbness gave way to anger. She placed the coffee cup on the table then violently brushed his hand from her shoulder and stood facing him.

"Don't worry, I'll handle everything, and-." Calvin never finished his sentence.

"How dare you use my sex as an excuse to steal my business!" Jerry was alive, the heaviness gone, the grief buried for the moment. "I know men who have broken under less. I'm quite capable of handling MY business. I don't need you or any other man. Who are you anyway?"

"I'm your partner and you might as well get used to me. WE have a flying school to run and had better get at it. No point in wasting time in self-pity and anger. I have a lot to do to get settled. You don't happen to know where I can find a decent rooming house or a motel?"

Jerry glared at him. He was right and she hated him for it. "There's a hotel in Trenten about ten miles from here. Ma Brown's boarding house is about five miles south."

"How many students do you have today?"

"None. Officially we're closed. I don't have classes on Monday. I use that day to catch up on my mechanical work and paper work or at least try. The paper work suffers. Sometimes I have fire patrol. But mostly it's just catching up. We-I mean I do rent planes to qualified students."

Calvin smiled inwardly at the change. The hurt was still there, deep in her eyes, but a new determination and a new fire sparkled. When she looked at him he could feel the resentment and anger he had deliberately kindled. Time, he thought, will change that. I'll make it change somehow.

But there was something else there. Something that drew them together into one being; yet, kept them separated into two individuals. They stood looking at each other while the waves of a new and strange feeling held them. Jerry saw deep in his eyes a need for her that she felt for him. Both felt breathless and a little confused at this unexpected turn of events.

"I'll -I'll go find a place to stay at least temporary. I'll be back to go over things with you". Calvin trembled as he picked up the flight bag and walked to the door. He hesitated as if he was going to speak then opened the door and left.

Jerry stood staring after him feeling helpless and suddenly alone. Silence descended once more, and she felt as if it had been a bad dream. Who was this man? No one had ever made her have such feelings. Where did he come from? Why had Charley sold half of the business? Why to a stranger? Calvin Morris had a lot of explaining to do.

She thought of the closed room at home. She knew she had to go home, enter it, search the baggage and locate the missing check and the second copy of the sale --if there was one. Shaking and confused she unplugged the coffee maker, retrieved her purse and the keys from a drawer and turned the sign in the window to "Closed".

Driving home she felt that she was a robot, doing what had to be done automatically, without thought. Oh God! Have I been repairing the planes without thought? Suppose I've missed something? She tortured herself with all the possibilities. The car in front of her flashed red brake lights, and she slowed. It was then she realized she had gone past her turn. She had lived here all her life and she had driven right past it! Angry at herself she pulled over to the side of the road, waited for the traffic to clear, then turned around and drove back to her street.

Jerry lived in a modest neighborhood of middle-class houses. Her home was a two-story brick built long ago when brick was the vogue. The large front yard was shaded with a holly tree and bordered with shrubs. The driveway ran to a double garage connected to the house by a breeze-way. The shrubbery, normally well cared for, now showed neglect. She parked in the driveway under the shade of a large sweet-gum tree and got out.

Jerry hurried up the back steps and across the screened porch to the door, unlocked it and walked through the utility room into the roomy kitchen and breakfast room. Without stopping, she hurried across the family room, into the hall and to the master bedroom. She stopped before the door trembling. Again, tears pushed their way into her eyes; and again, she dammed them back. Slowly, she turned the knob and opened the door.

She stood in the door way feeling more surprised than grief stricken. Somehow she had expected a dramatic change, ghosts of the past to haunt her, but the room was just as it had always been. Dust lay over the furniture now, the closed white and lavender drapes and matching spread that her mother had made gave the room a quiet peaceful feeling. Jerry turned on the light and walked to the closet.

From the bottom of the closet she pulled the unopened suitcase and flight bag. She paused, then carried them to the double bed. "Well, I knew it had to come, but not like this." Taking a deep breath as if the extra oxygen could give her emotional strength, she opened the suitcase. She carefully lifted the clean garments from the bag and separated them from the soiled ones. She had been meticulous at putting a change for each day when she packed for Charley. As usual, he used only half of the clothes she packed. Dear Charley. He was like a boy on a camping trip. She brushed her hand across her eyes and swallowed hard forcing herself to search for the papers. There was nothing but clothes and his shaving kit.

Next, she opened the flight bag and removed the contents one by one. I.F.R. charts, V.F.R. sectionals, plotter, log book, and a large brown envelope. Jerry knew without opening it that it held the papers. She pulled the contents out and read the signed sales contract then looked at the check. The amount startled her. Charley was a better business man than she had thought. She could pay for the Aerobat, pay the taxes, and have enough left to keep the school going at least for a while. And she wouldn't have to sell the house. To save the school and her home she would put up with Calvin Morris if it killed her.

Gathering up her courage, she walked into the master bathroom and to the bathtub. In the soap dish was the new bar of soap she had placed there for Charley. He had always hated tiny half used bars so her mother, and now she, always put out a new bar for him. Jerry had always felt proud and grown up to finish the bar for her father. A smile played over her lips. Jerry had never had a brand-new bar of soap for her own. She reached down and touched the soap knowing Charley would never use it.

She walked back into the bedroom and sat down on the bed by the luggage. Jerry picked up Charley's log book and hugged it to her. He would never fill out another line. The dam she had built bent and broke. All the grief and pain she had held back swept over the wall. "Charley, Charley," she sobbed. "Daddy, Daddy, Daddy." Rocking back and forth on the bed hugging his log book to her, Jerry cried.

When Jerry pulled up to the hangar, she was dismayed to realize she had left the hangar doors open. She drove around to the side of the trailer and parked by a strange red station wagon sporting Illinois license plates. Calvin Morris had beaten her back! She had not even thought of that possibility. She walked to the hangar and found Calvin looking over the tools.

"Pretty careless to leave the hangar open," he scolded as if she were a naughty child.

Jerry stood quietly saying nothing. Calvin turned and looked at her. Her eyes were red and swollen and her face pale. She had been crying. Shame flooded him at his harshness. His heart went out to her.

"Jerry, I'm sorry. Can't we forget business for today and just be friends. I expected to find a friend here, not an enemy. Let's fight tomorrow. Let us be friends today." His voice was gentle and soft. Jerry looked up at him and saw his forehead creased. His brown eyes filled with sorrow. Once more they drew her into them. He held out his hands to her. "We all need a friend sometimes. You don't have to cry alone."

Without thinking she took his hands and let him draw her to him. He surrounded her with strong arms and held her comforting her silently. Jerry felt his strength filling her, quieting her and she wiped her eyes with the back of her hand.

"Friends for a day." She managed a smile.

"For a day," he answered wanting to kiss her but only smiled a little friendly smile and stepped back.

"Did you find a room?" she asked.

"As a matter of fact, I got a room with Ma Brown. She's quite a gal."

"She has a reputation of the best cook around here. She spoils her boarders something fierce. She's particular to whom she lets her rooms."

"I told her I was your partner. That seemed to be a magic word. Have you known her long?"

"All my life she used to babysit me before she started her boarding house. When her husband died she refused to go home to her parents with her teenagers. She opened a spare room to a boarder. As her kids left home she rented the others. Her kids want her to live with them but she refuses. She's a wonderful woman." Jerry had a special place in her heart for Ma Brown. She wondered why she had referred this stranger to Ma's. "Shall we go over the supplies?"

"I thought perhaps we could have lunch first. I haven't eaten all day."

Jerry was aware she had not eaten either but did not feel hungry. "I'm not hungry," she said.

"I'll see you later then," he said. He turned and walked away without another word.

Jerry was in the office before she realized the door had not been locked and the light on the coffee pot was on. She knew she had turned it off and locked the door. Jerry walked to the small refrigerator by the classroom door. It was freshly stocked with soft drinks and a small carton of coffee cream. She reached inside and pulled out a carton of yogurt which was moldy. Anger started to flood her but she reminded herself "friends for a day".

How did he get in? Slowly she remembered Charley had a spare set of keys he always carried. They had not been among his belongings the police had given her and were not in his bag. Before things went any farther she would have this Calvin Morris, whoever he was, explain this. She took the yogurt into the bathroom and washed it down the drain, rinsed the carton, then threw it into the waste basket. Jerry was at the desk going through the bills when the door opened and Calvin appeared. He was carrying two paper bags.

"Hamburgers and malts," he announced setting the bags on the table. "The yogurt was spoiled. I thought you might not know." Jerry did not understand why this thoughtful gesture made her uncomfortable and resentful. She managed a clumsy thank you and walked over to the table.

"How did you get in?" Her voice a bit sharper than intended. Jerry had to know if he had Charley's keys.

"Charley gave me a set of keys when we were at the fly-in. At the time I was planning to fly down. Then I decided I would need my car, so I drove down. Charley said there was a couch in the office I could use if I got in late and didn't want to hunt a room."

"I missed the keys among his things. Where do you want to start?" Jerry picked up the wrappers and cleared the coffee table. "I was going over the bills. I found the check and the paper in Charley's flight bag. I'll have to leave early to deposit the check today." Her voice had a forced friendliness. She did not know how to divide the money but decided to put half of it in her personal account and the rest in the flying school's account. She would decide later what to do. She picked up the bills and began to go through them with Calvin. When they finished, Calvin looked at the stack of correspondence.

"How did things get into such a mess?" He said it more to himself than to Jerry. At once he regretted it.

Jerry swung around to him wanting to strike out at him physically but instead struck verbally.

"I've been instructor, mechanic, and ground school instructor and tried to keep up the bills. I've done the best I could to keep things going. What did you think I've been doing since Charley died? I've been fighting to get my inheritance straightened out. I'm a pilot, a mechanic not a secretary! If you're so great, you take care of them." Jerry was nearing the end of her self- control. The truce was on dangerous ground. Yesterday morning she had never seen this man; now he was pushing his way into her business and declaring her incompetent. She wished she could turn the clock back and erase him from her life.

"I'm sorry. I always seem to say the wrong thing." His voice was soft and apologetic. "Look, Jerry, it was thoughtless of me." Calvin stood looking down at her, his brown eyes filled with anxiety, his face like a little boy who has been rejected. "I'll take over the ground school. I've taught before. How many students are there?"

Jerry looked up at the man. In spite of her distrust of men, she felt he was honest. For the sake of the school she would honor the truce. But she'd never trust him. Who was he anyway?

"There's only eight in ground school now. I have six others in the air who've finished ground school and passed their written test. Half the ground school students were Charley's. They decided to stay on and finish ground school even though I just couldn't take them on the flying end. I had to spend time on the mechanics. The rest of Charley's students went elsewhere."

"I'll take the eight in ground school if it's ok with you. I can take them though to their license. We'll try to find a secretary as soon as we can. Meanwhile we'll work together on the bills. What teaching equipment do you have?"

"Only books and a blackboard and the student's individual supplies. We were considering one of the visual screens with tapes but hadn't decided. Charley preferred the teacher student relationship instead of the electronic teaching devices. He always said a student couldn't ask questions of a video tape. I thought it would be a supplement for the students to use to emphasize the class work if they needed to go over the lesson again."

It was hard for Jerry to explain the ground school. For Charley it was a fun time. A time to take fresh minds full of the awe and excitement of flying and teach them what years of experience had shown him to be true. It was the time to make them think in terms of obeying the FAA regulations and of safety. They had never had a student fail the FAA written test. Charley was a born teacher. Jerry knew when she first took the class over that she could never take his place in the classroom. She was anyone's equal in the air; but somehow, when it came to face a classroom she could not quite get through.

It was best that Calvin wanted to teach. Jerry had admitted long ago that she was better in the hangar with the planes and engines than trying to teach density altitude to students. "Ground school is on Wednesday 7 p.m. till 9. But it usually runs over. They are a good group and work hard."

"Let's go out and check the hangar. You have a well-organized shop there. How much of the work can you do?"

"Most of it. I studied it in college. My degree is in aeronautical engineering, but I like it here better."

The two of them left the office and went to the hanger. Two Cessna 150 trainers, a shining new 150 Aerobat, and a four passenger 182 Skylane made up the Cessna team of airplanes. Jerry began to explain the inventory of equipment and supplies.

"The 182 has full IFR panel. We also have one 150 with instrument capabilities. Most students prefer the 150 because it's cheaper. N20236 has to have its hundred-hour inspection before it can be flown. I was preparing to begin work on it this afternoon. I want to have it ready for the FAA inspector by Friday, if possible." Jerry led him to one of the planes which had N20236 painted in large letters on its side. Calvin followed her and looked over the plane. He was starting to look at the Aerobat when a distant drone of an engine made him stop.

Jerry lifted her head listening. The sound became louder and a smile spread across Jerry's face. Calvin had not seen her smile. His heart leaped. She was as beautiful as Charley had said. She turned and hurried from the hangar with Calvin close behind her. He had never heard that sound before. They walked into the sunny afternoon and peered into the cloudless blue sky toward the end of the active runway.

"Am I seeing things?" Calvin stood staring unbelieving at the antique biplane gliding onto the runway. "I could swear that is a Curtis Jenny. Where in the world did a Jenny come from?"

"Uncle Art," said Jerry. "He found it in his barn when he bought his ranch. Spent years getting it flying again. I remember-" Jerry stopped. She could not share the precious memories with this stranger. "You'll like Uncle Art. He and Charley flew together in an aerobatic show."

"Is that Arthur Swenson?" Calvin's voice was excited.

"Yes. How did you know?" Jerry was surprised and irritated that he should know Uncle Art's name.

"My father was one of the aerobatic team." Cal's eyes sparkled in anticipation of seeing his father's old friend.

Jerry looked up at the tall broad-shouldered man absorbed in the biplane taxiing clear of the runway. THAT Morris! Charley had told many tales of the years they had spent together. Rex Morris's son! No wonder Charley had sold the partnership so quickly. He would trust anyone related to Rex Morris.

"I have to get one of the 150s out of the hangar to make room for Jumpin' Jenny. Can't let her stay outside." Jerry hurried toward the hangar and placed a tow bar on one of the planes. She started to pull the plane out of the hangar.

"I'll do that," Cal offered reaching for the tow bar.

"I'm capable of doing it myself." Jerry was aware of her rudeness, but irrational anger momentarily flooded her. She would show him she was not a helpless female. Calvin turned quietly and walked from the hangar and stood watching the Jenny taxiing. At least he could push it, Jerry thought unreasonably as she pulled the plane to a special tie-down Charley had fixed years ago so Art could have hangar space for Jumpin' Jenny. She finished tying the plane down just as the ancient plane taxied to the hangar.

The pilot who climbed from the cockpit seemed to belong to the same past as the antique plane. He pulled off his helmet and goggles revealing a tousled head of snow white hair.

"Jerry, my girl," he cried holding out his arms for her.

"Uncle Art! I'm so glad to see you!" Jerry flew into his arm just like she had done since she was a child. "What brings you to town?"

"My flight physical is due." Momentarily the sparkle in his sky blue eyes disappeared then it flared again. "How's things with you, my dear?"

Calvin approached the Jenny. "I don't believe it!" He touched the ancient airplane reverently as if it were a holy shrine. "Oh, I'm Calvin Morris," said Cal reaching his hand to Uncle Art.

Uncle Art took Cal's hand. "Arthur Swenson. I see you like my Jenny."

Jerry threw a dark angry look at Cal and explained, "Mr. Morris bought half of the school from Charley at the fly-in."

"Well- "Uncle Art's quick glance at Jerry and Cal seemed to understand the strained situation instinctively, "Charley mentioned he needed another instructor. But a partner?" He frowned a second as if trying to think, then asked, "Any relation to Rex Morris?"

"He's my father."

"Rex's boy! We flew together!" Art's face lit up in a broad smile and he held out his hand to Calvin. Cal gripped the hand, happy that someone was glad to see him.

"I know. I feel as if I've always known you and Charley. I've heard the tales so often." Calvin stopped, suddenly aware of Jerry's presence.

"I know what really brought you to town," Jerry interrupted feeling the pain of Cal's last remark. "You want a charcoal broiled steak Jerry Jackson style." She forced a laugh. "I have to leave early so I'll pick up a couple of giant steaks."

Uncle Art looked surprised at Jerry's deliberate exclusion of her partner. "I've a better idea," he said, "Let's celebrate and I'll take you two to dinner." Jerry flushed as she realized Uncle Art was scolding her for her rudeness.

"I just arrived and have a lot to do-," Cal said, but he didn't know Art's persistence.

"Nonsense, you've got to eat." Uncle Art said. Jerry started to say he was staying at Ma Brown's but something stopped her.

Cal grinned a lopsided grin. "You've got me there. But I insist dinner is on me." He turned to Jerry. "You pick the place," he started, but stopped as she spun around and walked to the office. Cal watched her go, angry at her behavior, yet sorry for her. "She didn't know Charley sold me the partnership. She's angry and hurt," he told Uncle Art as if apologizing for Jerry's behavior.

"I guessed it was something like that. You have to realize Jerry worshiped her father and all this has been a blow. And she also distrusts handsome men."

Cal grinned, and then looked serious. "I don't know about handsome, but I am a man." Uncle Art chuckled. Cal shook his head. "She hated me the minute she realized Charley had sold half of the school and had not talked it over with her."

"She's headstrong, stubborn, independent and a thoroughly wonderful girl. She's like my own daughter. I guess I'm all she has now that Charley's gone." Tears tried to obscure Art's eyes at the thought of his old friend and he added quickly, "We'd better get Jenny inside."

The two men had finished putting Jenny in the hangar when Jerry came out of the office. She was calmer now but walked determined.

"I guess you know how to lock up," she said sarcastically to Cal in spite of her determination to be nice. "I have to get to the bank before it closes. Uncle Art, do you want to come along?"

Uncle Art rubbed his chin then answered, "Calvin can bring me over. We'll meet you at your house."

"All right. I guess I could get three steaks." It was a strange apology for her, but it took a lot of effort. She did it for Uncle Art, she told herself.

"Thank you, but I'd be honored to escort you to dinner," said Cal. "I guess I got off on the wrong foot. Perhaps we could start over?

Friends for today, Jerry."

Jerry looked up at the tall stranger standing in the partial shade of the hangar. A ray of sunlight touched his hair and reflected all the shades of brown and red, then leaped to his eyes and touched off an inner tenderness that made Jerry feel like a clumsy child. "Sorry," she said trying to smile convincingly.

"Truce," he offered holding out his hand. Jerry took his hand. Again the shock of his touch made her heart pound. She withdrew her hand too quickly and mumbled that she had better hurry, turned and nearly ran to her small yellow car. The two men watched her go in silence.

Uncle Art noticed a quiet little smile on Calvin's lips and a fresh sparkle in his eyes.

"I-I guess we'd better lock up," Cal said suddenly and turned to the task of pulling the huge sliding doors to the hangar closed. The task done, they walked to the office. "It's going to take some getting used to this humidity," Cal sighed mopping his damp forehead.

"Humidity and bugs, the common complaint of northerners," grinned Uncle Art. "But wait till they're shoveling snow up north and you're still in your shirt sleeves. That's when the complaints stop."

"Can't say that I'll miss preheating my planes in winter."

"Oh, we get some freezing weather in this area but not a lot. It snows a little once every five or ten years."

Jerry got into her car and started the engine. Soon she was driving down the airport road passing parked planes. She always caught herself looking carefully out the car windows unconsciously checking her "wing tips" for clearance, which made her feel slightly foolish.

She took care of her business and returned home. At a touch of her finger to the automatic garage door opener, the doors rolled upwards. Jerry drove the car into place being careful not to get too close to the sixteen-foot boat parked on its trailer. Jerry had not thought about the boat. "What shall I do with it?", she wondered. She did not want to sell it, but it was too big for her to pull with her car. The truck was destroyed with Charley. She shook her head and left it for later.

She walked slowly up the back steps noting the lawn needed mowing and pulled open the screen door. The screened in porch was furnished with a table of flowers which were wilting in the heat. Jerry picked up the watering can and sprinkled them feeling guilty at her neglect. The begonia was blooming profusely and she touched it tenderly. Charley had brought it home for her just before-. She turned abruptly and walked into the house curling her nose at the scent of mustiness which always greeted her before she flipped on the air-conditioner. How did people live here without air-conditioning? But people can adjust to anything otherwise the human race would not exist. And she could, somehow, adjust to Calvin Morris.

Jerry walked to the stairs, paused a moment and glanced toward the master bedroom, then slowly with aching heart she climbed the stairs and went to her room. The house seemed so empty. She crushed the memories of Charley coming home laughing and planning the next days' work. With misty eyes blurring her vision, she stumbled to her bed and tossed her purse on it. She had better hurry, she reminded herself. Uncle Art's room needed dusting. She collected the dust cloth and polish from the hall closet and hurried to his room. As long as she could remember, there had been the room at the end of the hall ready for Uncle Art. He had his own key so he could come and go as he wished when he had to come to town for business. She finished his room and hurried to shower and dress.

The cool shower felt good after the heat of the hangar and she tarried longer than she realized. She washed her long blond hair and toweled it leaving it still damp. As she stood trying to untangle it she swore again to get it cut. She had barely finished fastening her skirt when the back door bell rang and Uncle Art yelled his usual greeting, "Are you decent?" Jerry walked to the stairs and called down "Yes" then returned to finish dressing.

She looked at herself in the full-length mirror. Her denim gathered western square dance style skirt was loose about her waist in spite of its elastic. She wrapped a sash of scarlet around her and decided scarlet was not her mood. From the belt rack she pulled a dark blue plastic belt and fastened it over the light blue skirt. Her beige sandals and blouse accented her tanned skin. Her hair hung freely down her back held back from her face by a blue scarf tied at the side so that its trailing ends and her hair became tangled in an orderly fashion. She picked up her worn shoulder bag and stared at its ugliness. But it was all she had. She had not thought of clothes since college and her tragic love affair. She must go shopping. For reasons she could not explain, she felt it suddenly important to look nice.

She heard Uncle Art in his shower singing as always in his fine baritone. He had turned down a promising career as a singer for the uncertain future of the sky and never regretted it. Smiling as she ran down the stairs, she felt the care of today disappear for a while and felt the presence of Charley almost like it used to be. Then she brought in the mail. Junk mail for Charley. Her light heartedness had vanished.

Uncle Art came down the stairs in a sport shirt and slacks looking like a school boy. He'll never grow old, Jerry thought.

"Cal is going to pick us up. I never thought I'd be having dinner with Rex Morris's son. I've got to get together with Rex."

"When we get back, why don't you and Cal call them?" Jerry could have bitten her tongue. She had invited that man in after dinner not meaning to!

"That's a fine idea, my dear. I'm sure they're anxious about Cal. Where shall we go to eat? The Steak House, OK?"

"That sounds good. I haven't been there for ages. I guess the last time was when Charley, you and I went." Jerry walked to the window saw her reflection and wondered if she looked too childish. "How do I look Uncle Art?" She turned with a whirl of cotton skirt.

"You look beautiful, my dear," he answered around the unlit pipe he held in his mouth. He watched Jerry pacing and thought, - "If I didn't know differently, I'd swear she was waiting for a boyfriend. Well, it's about time." He chuckled silently.

Jerry saw the car pull up the drive and stop. "He's here," she said. She picked up her purse and hung it over her shoulder. "Shall we go meet him?"

"Oh, let him come and get us," grinned Uncle Art. "Exercise will do him good." He pulled the pipe from his mouth and put it in the ash tray Jerry kept for him.

"You're a meanie," giggled Jerry as she went to the door.

The Steak House was a family restaurant with good food for a moderate price. They were lucky to be early and were seated quickly.

"I'll have the T-bone," decided Art. "Always have the T-bone well done and a beer."

Jerry and Calvin looked over their menus. The waitress asked if they wanted drinks. Jerry drank very little. Flying and alcohol do not mix, but tonight she decided to order a glass of wine with her filet medium rare. Cal ordered a beer and a porterhouse steak medium rare with the baked potato.

"I don't drink anything much but Molly, she was my late wife, and I used to enjoy one in the evening," Uncle Art added with a smile.

The drinks arrived and Uncle Art proposed a toast to the new comer. Then Calvin offered one to his new partner. Jerry could think of nothing except, "Here's to Charley."

"To Charley," toasted Art and Cal.

"Uncle Art wants you to call your folks so he can talk to your Dad," she told Cal casually.

"I called earlier, but they'd love to hear from Art and to meet you, Jerry."

"I've got a lot of shopping to do next Monday. I sent a check in for the Aerobat. The taxes are paid, and tomorrow I'll take my house off the market."

"How did you happen to buy into Charley's school?" Uncle Art asked Cal.

"Well, it's a long story, but you asked for it. We had a nice private air field. No control tower, just small. When my grandfather first opened it, it was a sod strip in the middle of nowhere. By the time Dad inherited it, subdivisions were blooming everywhere. It was okay until about ten years ago they built real close to the field, too close. Then people started to complain."

Uncle Art and Jerry nodded. Uncle Art added, "It is being enacted all over the country. Builders knowing there is an airport next door build subdivisions for speculation anyway. The buyers ignore the airport when they buy, but later complain about the airport. The politics begin; and, the airport is forced out of business. Everyone loses."

"In our case it seems a developer had a relative in the right place and a scare campaign began," Cal continued. "They never mentioned the life-flight helicopter based at our field or the sheriff's helicopter stationed there. They only focused on the one fatal accident we ever had. A pilot was landing a high wing plane when a low wing plane with no radio landed on top of him. Neither could see the other but the high wing plane had been on Unicom frequency warning traffic. He could not avoid the other plane since he was landing. Both pilots were killed. That's when the 'no tower' dangerous to houses' started.

The truth was the developer had tried to buy us out and when we refused to sell warned us we'd be sorry. We were condemned and forced to sell. The reason was low income public housing. There now stands VIP condominiums on our airport. The people got their way but now have no Life-Flight helicopter and must depend on ambulance service thirty miles away and no sheriff's chopper either. I wonder if they really won." Cal swirled the beer around in his glass then took a drink. "In the last two years we could have saved at least three lives with the life-flight. They couldn't get an ambulance in time."

Jerry was finishing her steak. "Suppose they did that to Memorial Field?" she thought. She doubted it. Mr. Trenton's father who owned the airport had dedicated it as a memorial for the pilots in the area who died in World War II and had established a museum in their honor. She doubted anyone could close it. Yet his son Jeffrey who inherited it seemed different from him. She did not really know him she thought as the waitress appeared and cleared the dishes asking if they wanted desert. They ordered cheesecake and coffee.

"Where did your parents go?" Jerry asked.

"Back to the farm. Got a little farm in Illinois raising wheat and soybeans. There's some dairy cows. They inherited it from my grandfather. It's been in the hands of an overseer all these years. My parents like the country. There's a small airport about fifty miles north and they go up there week-ends and give lessons. Dad put in a landing strip at the farm twenty years ago. I've been crop dusting for him." Cal sipped the last of his coffee. "This is a good place to eat. We must do it again."

"I'm stuffed," said Jerry. In fact, it was the first real meal she had eaten since Charley died. She had been living on quick snacks, yogurt, and sandwiches. They left the coolness of the air-conditioned restaurant and braved the heat and humidity as they hurried to the air-conditioned car.

"I imagine they'll call for fire patrol tomorrow. It's been so dry this week. If there's any wind at all it could be a high-risk day." Jerry settled into the back seat. "I guess I'd better teach you the ropes. I had to cancel all lessons after two o'clock so I could fly patrol."

"Can't they get someone else?" asked Cal.

"We bid for contracts, and Charley won. I usually fly while he holds- I mean- he used to stay at the school." Jerry's voice quivered for a moment.

"Where do you live?" inquired Cal looking at Art.

"I own a small ranch west of here. Nice little place. Got my own landing strip. Had to with Jenny. Couldn't trust her at an airport. You'll have to fly over and visit."

They pulled into Jerry's driveway. "Come in for coffee, and we'll call your folks. Uncle Art is anxious to talk to your father."

"It's late," said Cal not really wanting to go to the boarding house but not wanting to impose. He knew Jerry still resented him.

"Nonsense," answered Uncle Art. "Come on it's only eight."

"Just a quick call", he relented. As they entered the house he was already regretting the acceptance. He suddenly realized how tired he was.

"Uncle Art, why don't you go to my room and use the extension? Then both of you can talk." Jerry escorted Cal to the breakfast room and showed him the neat built in desk which was accented with a red telephone. Uncle Art disappeared up the stairs and Cal settled himself at the desk and began dialing. Jerry put the teakettle on to heat water for instant coffee. She had not brewed coffee since Charley's death. It seemed so much trouble just for one person.

From where she stood getting cups, she could see Calvin

listening at the phone. His hair was tumbled like a little boy's. His arms were relaxed on the desk. Jerry found herself studying the profile of this stranger who had so suddenly appeared in her life. A little smile turned the corner of his mouth as he greeted his father. Jerry noticed a scar on Cal's arm and caught herself totally absorbed in wondering about it. She was startled when she heard her name.

"My folks want to meet you, Jerry." Cal was holding out the phone. Jerry felt her face flush, wondering if he knew she had been watching him. With quick strides, she was at the desk and took the phone.

"Hello," she said feeling a little uncomfortable.

"Hello, I'm Cal's father," boomed a voice.

"And I'm his mother," came a quiet one. "I hope you don't let my son bully you. You know these men!" The laugh at the other end of the line was secret and knowing causing Jerry to laugh in response.

"Don't worry," she said making a face at Cal. "I've grown up at the airport and I can handle him."

"Hey, what's going on here?" Cal reached for the phone and Jerry dodged away pulling the cradle across the desk.

"I'm anxious to meet you," said Jerry. "I only wish Charley was here," she added softly.

There was a silence on the other end. "Cal told us earlier. I'm still trying to believe it," said Cal's father. "If there is anything we can do, let us know."

Jerry knew he meant it. "It's all right now. Thank you."

"We'll be bringing Cal's plane down to him in a few weeks," said Mrs. Morris. "We'll be looking forward to meeting you." The booming voice of Rex reminding them it was costing a fortune brought the conversation to an end. By the time she said goodbye, Uncle Art had joined them in the kitchen-breakfast room.

"Sure good to hear Rex again!" he exclaimed. "Coffee ready?"

"It's instant and no cream. I forgot." Jerry stirred instant the coffee into the cups of hot water. The three of them carried their cups into the family room and settled onto the worn but comfortable sofa and an ancient overstuffed chair.

"Your parents are real nice. When they come, they'll have to stay here. I've plenty of room."

"That's considerate of you. They'd like that."

"What time is your doctor's appointment?" Jerry asked Art.

"Ten. I'll run you to the airport, and breakfast is on me," he answered. "Then I'll steal the car as always."

"Fine." It had always been that way. Uncle Art took Jerry to work and then her car was his for the day. Of course, before they always had Charley's pickup if she or Charley needed transportation.

"I'll come by and pick you up if you wish," offered Cal.

"No. I don't get to bum a breakfast very often, but thanks." Jerry suddenly felt tense and wary of Calvin. She must not become dependent upon any man again.

"Well, it has been a long day and I'm bushed. I'll see you tomorrow. Thanks, Jerry, for the phone call." He wanted to say it was sweet, but he set down his cup and got up to leave.

After he was gone Jerry was startled at how empty the room seemed. She carried the cups into the kitchen and put them in the dishwasher.

"Don't be too hard on him, my dear." Uncle Art spoke from the kitchen doorway.

"What do you mean? Jerry flushed as she dried her hands on a paper towel.

"He's a fine man. Don't push him too far."

"I don't know what you're talking about. How can I push him anywhere? He's already trying to take over." She remembered the morning and felt both resentment and anger at the same time. The school is mine. I earned it, she told herself.

"Well, now you can take a day off and get some rest. You have a partner now. You've lost weight."

Jerry turned and walked over to him. Putting her arms around him she hugged him. "I love you. I'll be all right. And things will work out. It-it's such a shock."

Uncle Art patted her hair like he used to when she was a little girl. "I know, honey. Charley didn't mean it to hurt you. I know he had a reason for such sudden decision. I believe he always thought you were his partner. Maybe we'll never know, but don't be hurt."

"What would I do without you?" Jerry fought the tears. I will not cry.

"If I don't let you get to bed, you might take that back. I'll check the doors and you go on to bed." Uncle Art gently shooed her toward the stairs and turned to check the doors to be sure they were locked.

Jerry hurried up the stairs. It had been a strange day. One that she knew would change her life forever. She pondered on how it might change as she stretched out in her bed. Little did she imagine all the lives that would be changed forever with this new partnership. She closed her eyes to try to think of all the things that must be done, but a strange feeling of security invaded her. A feeling that she could not understand. She closed her eyes and drifted into a deep peaceful sleep for the first time since Charley died.

Pilot's Day

Today is a day God gave to Pilots.
It's a day saved special to fly
Ceiling unlimited, visibility same,
Nothing but calm blue sky.
The windsock hangs limp,
The planes restlessly wait through
Pre-flight inspection
To race for the blue.
It would be nice to go upward
And never come down.
But the flying day ends.
I'm once more on the ground
Still my heart and my soul
Are five thousand feet high,
My feet on the ground,
My heart in the sky.

Chapter 2

When Jerry awakened the next morning she felt refreshed and calm. She found Uncle Art in the living room reading the morning paper and smoking his pipe. For an instant she felt as if time had rolled back and the tragedy had never happened.

"Good morning," said Jerry kissing him on the cheek. "I'm ready when you are."

He smiled. "Good morning, my dear. Let's go." He laid down the paper and stood up. "It says no rain again today. Won't have any crops if it keeps this up," he added.

"We're nine inches behind, and I know they'll call fire patrol. There have been a number of small fires it's so dry. One careless cigarette or neglected trash fire and we could have a big one. Come on, race you to the car. Jerry trotted from the house as she used to when she was a child.

"I'm too old for that," laughed Uncle Art. It was good to see her smile again.

They were still laughing when they arrived at the airport restaurant. A large round table nearly filled one end of the long dining room. This was where the pilots and others who worked at the airport gathered each morning. The group greeted them but not with the usual cheerfulness.

"Why the long faces?" asked Uncle Art as they settled at the table.

"It's Jimmy Cole. Had a heart attack while flying pipeline

inspection. He managed to set her down on a country road. He sat there a while then took off and came back." Carla Wright answered drawing her dark eyebrows together as if pained.

"Not Jimmy!" Jerry was shocked. She knew it meant he would never fly again. What does a man whose whole life is flying do when he can no longer fly? Jimmy Cole had been flying pipeline inspection as long as Jerry could remember.

"How's he doing?" Asked Uncle Art accepting the menu the waitress handed him.

"He's still in the hospital getting tests."

Uncle Art insisted Jerry have ham and eggs along with him. Her protests were ignored with a shake of his head. "You're too thin. Gotta put some meat on your bones," he told her.

"How's things with you?" asked Carla. "It's rumored you have a new partner. Any truth?" Carla Wright was a middle-aged helicopter flight instructor who had fought her way into aviation, losing her husband and children in the process. She was blunt, honest, and one of kindest persons Jerry had ever met. Jerry flushed with surprise and a mild irritation. She was always amazed at the airport grapevine and how news traveled.

"Yes, it's true." Jerry answered. "He arrived yesterday morning. Charley sold him half of the school when he was at the fly-in." As usual with mention of Charley, Jerry had to force self-control to keep the ache away.

"Is he that tall good looking dude that was asking for Charley's Flying School yesterday?" This was asked by Bob Hardy, the owner of the airport's charter helicopter service. He grinned mischievously at Jerry, his white teeth flashing between his graying moustache and beard.

Jerry nodded and was saved from further questions by the arrival of the waitress with their breakfast. The savory odor of the ham and eggs, hash brown potatoes with hot biscuits, gravy, and coffee made Jerry glad Uncle Art had ordered for her. As they ate, the conversation drifted to students' antics, price of fuel, government restrictions, and other pilot talk. The partnership seemed forgotten for the moment, and Jerry was glad. It gave her a warm comfortable feeling to talk to the others in the business. They had helped her enormously when Charley died, and she would never forget their kindness. One by one the group dispersed. Uncle Art finished his coffee and picked up their check. Jerry took a final gulp of coffee and joined him at the cashier's desk as he paid for their breakfast.

"Thanks, Uncle Art. You serve up a good meal." said Jerry with an impish grin as they went to the car. The wind had picked up and was gusting through the trees making the air feel a little less humid. Jerry by habit searched the sky for weather and found not a cloud in sight. "It's going to be another hot one." She sighed as she climbed into the car. They drove slowly to the office keeping alert for aircraft taxiing across the road.

At the office Jerry got out of the car. "Coming in?' she asked Uncle Art as she started up the steps. He nodded. Jerry fished for her keys to open the door and was startled to find it was unlocked. She pushed the door open and stepped inside. At the desk sat Calvin absorbed in the piles of bill, schedules, and other papers. He looked up and grinned.

"Good morning." His greeting was warm and friendly. Jerry stopped, frozen, staring at him. No one had the right to go through her desk! Then she reminded herself that he had bought that right. His eyes teased as he added, "Friends for a day is over. Now it's time to fight."

"I see you've made yourself at home," she said icily trying not to allow herself to be drawn into those brown magnetic eyes.

Cal raised his eyebrows perplexed and then looked down at the desk trying to keep the disappointment from his face. "Just trying to see what's going on. I see you have an 8:30 student, a rental for 9AM and a 10:30 student. Who handles the rental of the planes while you're out?"

"The plane rental is to a private pilot who is also a minister. I use the honor system I leave the key at the front office and put the plane out front before I go up. He's quite trustworthy," she retorted defensively.

"Oh, sorry. I just wanted to know. No need for battle stations."

"Reverend Mitchell flies every Tuesday at this time. He takes underprivileged children for rides. He takes some supplies to a mission up north a ways. Too far to drive in one day. We- I never charge for the plane, he buys the gas. Anything else?"

"Hey. How about letting me in? It's hot out here!" Uncle Art gently nudged Jerry from the doorway. "You two can hold off the conversation till I get into the air-conditioning." Uncle Art closed the door. "Good morning, Cal. How was Ma Brown's cooking?"

Cal's face lit up. "She is one fantastic lady! She said you and Jerry are to have dinner with the gang tonight, or she'll skin you alive. She sent a gallon jug of lemonade. Said that soda and coffee aren't fit for man or beast. She's quite a woman!"

"I've never turned down a meal at Sarah Brown's," replied Art laughing. "Best cook I ever knew. Except for my Molly."

"Oh, Jerry she said to tell you quote, 'I'm baking apple cinnamon pie for dinner. Please bring a gallon of Blue Bell Homemade vanilla,' unquote. What's Blue Bell Homemade vanilla?"

"Sure can tell that you're a stranger. Only the best ice cream in the world. Made in Texas," explained Art.

"Sorry to break up the talk, but I've got work to do," said Jerry. "Are you coming back here after your doctor's appointment? If you are, I'll put you to work I expect they'll be calling fire patrol and I'd like you to watch the office. Otherwise I'll have to lock up as usual."

"I can hold down the fort," said Cal.

"Cal, you're coming with me on fire patrol. You may as well learn how. You may have to take it someday."

"Sounds fine with me. I thought I'd try to get acquainted with the accounts and the shop this morning. Do you have a key to this drawer that's locked?" Asked Calvin.

"There's only my private things in there. Nothing you'd be interested in." Jerry pulled a key from her purse and unlocked the drawer dropped her purse into it then locked it and turned and walked out of the office. Cal tried to hide a smile. He had grown up with a mother and a sister. In the drawer his quick glance saw hand lotion, personal female products and her purse. No matter how hard you try to be a man, my love, you are a woman, Cal thought.

Jerry walked to the hangar and unlocked the doors. She started to push them open. Cal and Uncle Art were both at her side and took over the job. Jerry was both annoyed and pleased with their help. She put the tow bar on a Cessna 150 trainer with large black numbers N30316 on the side and started to pull it out of the hangar. Uncle Art and Cal pushed on each wing and the plane rolled easily onto the blacktop in front of the hangar.

"Thanks," said Jerry gruffly. She removed the tow bar and returned it to the hangar. "If you're going to be here," she said to Cal, "you can get the Aerobat for Rev. Mitchell. 236 is down for its inspection so we can't use it. The Aerobat's ok on fuel. I always make sure the tanks are full each night." Jerry gave the orders without thinking and did not see the tightening of his jaw and an angry flash in his eyes, but Uncle Art did and turned away stifling a grin.

"Yes, sir!" said Cal with a salute. "Glad you keep the tanks full. I'd hate condensation to cause water in the fuel." The sarcastic salute was not lost on Jerry. She turned silently and walked back to the office.

The phone was ringing as she entered. It was the expected call for fire patrol. She sat looking at the papers Calvin had placed on the desk. It was the confusion of receipts and bills which she had tried to sort out late Sunday night and had, in a moment of despair thrown them in a heap into one of the drawers. Calvin had smoothed them out and organized them into neat piles according to dates with bills and receipts in separate piles. What a dunce he must think I am, she told herself. But I'm a pilot not a book-keeper.

The voices of Cal and Uncle Art penetrated her thoughts. They were talking about the Jenny. As she started to go through the bills, Uncle Art popped into the room, called goodbye and disappeared. Cal came into the office no longer cheerful. He crossed to the desk and looked down at Jerry.

"So you do the accounting?" He towered above her making her feel like a small child.

"Only since Charley died. He took care of everything. I don't like to sit at a desk"

"Obviously." Cal's words were biting. "Let's see if we can at least get the bills paid."

"There's not enough in the bank to pay them. I can't write checks until your check clears. Until then we need to discuss money. I can't put all my money into the school. I have to pay my back mortgage and taxes on my house. That's why they were such a mess. I-I just was so -". Jerry stopped and took a deep breath. Cal's heart went out to her.

"Let's see what we need." Cal's anger had dissolved as quickly as it had come. He picked up the stack of bills and was sorting through them when the door opened. The two of them looked up. Silhouetted against the bright morning sun stood a young girl. She stepped into the room and closed the door. The sun from the windows reflected golden red from her short-cropped curls. Her face was pale and the freckles stood out across her nose like a holiday parade. Two large blue frightened eyes looked at them for a moment. The girl bit her lower lip, took a deep breath as if she was getting ready to leap off a high dive, and spoke.

"I'm Maggie Dawson. I've heard that sometimes a person can work in exchange for flying lessons. My friend, Hermon Jolly, he was a student here, said maybe you would hire me. I'll do anything. I can wash airplanes or anything." She ran out of breath, stopped staring at Jerry and Cal and took a deep breath.

In unison Cal and Jerry asked, "Can you keep books?"

A big smile crossed her face and her eyes brightened. "I made straight 'A's in my business classes. I thought you already probably had a secretary."

Jerry looked up at Cal. His eyes met hers and she felt a ripple of excitement We think alike, she realized with surprise. "When can you start?" she asked the girl.

The girl looked startled. "You mean it? Really? Wow! I -I was so sure you would say no I almost didn't come. I can start now, today- just need to call Mom and tell her. She thinks I'm nuts."

Jerry laughed. "Here's the phone. I have a student in a few minutes, but Cal can introduce you-. Oh, by the way, I'm Jerry Jackson and this is Calvin Morris. Cal will be your instructor-," Jerry looked up questioningly at Cal who nodded in approval.

"Oh, I know all about you Miss Jackson," gushed Maggie. "I

mean about your being an instructor and mechanic. Gee-" Maggie picked up the phone, her hands shaking with excitement and dialed home.

While Maggie talked to her mother, Jerry handed Cal the check book she used for the flying school. He pursed his lips a moment, then said quietly, "I'll see to it there's enough money to pay the current bills. I need to transfer cash from my account in Illinois to a local bank anyway. I have traveler's checks I can cash. Today we will sort things out. Any chance to cancel this lesson?"

"No. He's almost ready for his check ride. He's passed his written exam and all he needs is to work out a few rough spots and he'll be ready for the flight exam. I think today will probably do it for instruction. I can't cancel. You understand."

"Only too well. Would you believe I got the measles two days before my check ride?"

"Oh, no!" Jerry shook her head and laughed. "What tough luck! I guess I had a guardian angel or something."

"Look," Cal told her. "I'll get Maggie started on some sort of filing system and let her answer the phone. I'll explain about scheduling. Okay?"

"Great," sighed Jerry. Like a puzzle, things at last seemed to be falling into the right places. The door opened and her student arrived. She took a clipboard holding the aircraft's number on a sheet of paper and columns for the student to fill in the time of rental and number of hours flown along with his signature. The keys were clipped to the board. Jerry handed the clipboard to the young man and they left together.

When Jerry returned from the lesson she found her 10:30 student had canceled. Reverend Mitchell had picked up the plane and would return about one. Jerry made a call and arranged for the F.A.A. inspector to give a check ride to her excited student the following week on Wednesday. Then she turned to the new secretary.

"Have you been able to make any order out of this mess?" She asked.

Maggie grinned and said, "Sure. I've got it all worked out. Mr.-er-Cal has gone to buy a filing cabinet and do some business. He said he'd be back about 1:30 with some chicken. Your Uncle Art called and said he'd be in about 3:00. He wants to see a sick friend. I guess that's all. Here's the mail. Do you want me to open it or do you?"

"I'd better. At least for now. It's probably more bills." Jerry took the half dozen letters and walked into the second room of the trailer. It was set up for teaching. She sat down at the long table which was in the center of the room surrounded with chairs and looked at the mail. The light bill and junk mail. She gave the bill to Maggie and told her she would be in the hangar working.

At twelve-fifteen Cal returned with three chicken dinners. Jerry had put the radio equipment needed for fire patrol into the plane and was draining the oil from the trainer N20236 tied down in front of the hangar.

"Lunch," called Cal as he entered the trailer. Jerry left the plane and wiped her hands.

"You're going to make me fat," she exclaimed when she had changed from her coveralls and washed. "I never eat lunch!"

"No wonder you're so thin," grinned Cal.

"Don't you know you can get a vitamin deficiency? You should eat three good meals a day with very little red meat and lots of green vegetables, fish and yogurt," Maggie told her.

"Don't tell me we've hired a health nut," sighed Jerry. "Between you two and Uncle Art you'll make me healthy or kill me trying."

"Oh, I'm not a health nut. I just believe there's a way to keep healthy through nutrition," said Maggie as she carefully pulled the spicy crisp skin from her chicken. "All the fat is under the skin," she explained. "I'll bring my lunch from now on. I'm used to nuts and seeds and a salad. Mother thinks I'm abnormal and Dad thinks it's a fad. Really though I feel much better. I've eliminated most of the sugar, all the coffee, tea, soft drinks and junk foods. My hair is softer and shinier, and I've a lot more energy."

Jerry looked at the healthy young woman so full of life and vitality. "I may join you if I thought it would give me dimples like yours."

"You're joshing me. But I'll bet you'd feel better, really." Cal broke into the conversation to inquire about fire patrol.

"I'll explain it briefly before we take off. The plane is refueled and ready to go. I've done the pre-flight. I can't eat all this!"

"I'll take your extra piece and the roll," said Cal.

"Have the mashed potatoes too. The slaw is all I need. It's going to be hot flying today. I was afraid the wind would come but it's stayed pretty calm. A strong wind in weather like this makes an extreme fire hazard."

"You want this leg?" Maggie asked Cal offering him her box.

"No, thanks. I've had enough. Put it in the refrigerator. I'll eat it when we get back."

"Do you always eat so much?" asked Jerry laughing.

"No. I usually eat more. I am a growing boy," answered Cal with a lopsided grin Jerry would grow to know.

"I'll clean up," said Maggie starting to gather the boxes. "Did you get the filing cabinet?"

"In the station wagon. I'll bring it in." Cal wiped his hands on a napkin and went to get the cabinet.

"He's real nice. He said you're partners. Herman told me about your father. I'm real sorry," Maggie said, as she placed the trash in the waste basket.

"Yes, we're partners." Jerry went to the desk and pulled a clipboard containing the maps and the grid for the fire patrol. "I need to empty the waste baskets. Today is trash day."

"Is that the big covered can in the hangar? Do you set it by the road? I'll be glad to do it."

"You're a secretary not a trash carrier."

"Oh, that's all right. Just show me where to put it. Oh!" Maggie hurried to open the door for Cal and the file cabinet. "That's a nice one!"

"Where do you want this, Jerry?"

"Wherever Maggie needs it. How about right at the end of the desk? Okay?" Jerry looked at Maggie for her consent.

"That's fine. I'll just take the trash out now. I'll get the other basket from the class room." Maggie disappeared into the class room and returned with the other basket.

"I'll go with you. This isn't required, Maggie." The two of them went out into the scorching afternoon air. Jerry showed Maggie where to set the large can from the hangar for trash pickup.

"I'm going to like this. I can't wait. Cal said we could start my lessons Monday unless he could work me in sooner. And I'll start ground school with the next class!"

When they got back to the office Jerry got out the sectionals and grids for the fire patrol. "I'll show you briefly about fire patrol," she told Cal.

Cal nodded, then turned to Maggie handing her his checkbook. "If you will make out checks for those bills, I'll sign them." Jerry looked at him in surprise. "I couldn't get my funds transferred to a joint account for the school without your signature, so I'll take care of these and we can sort things out later," he explained as they walked into the class room.

"I guess a joint account is best. We should decide who signs the checks to be sure there's no mix up, though."

"I thought you should," replied Cal

Suddenly Jerry felt suspicious again. Was he patronizing her? Was this another creeping infiltration to get complete control? Charley! Charley! She cried within her heart. How could you have done this to me? She would watch him very closely and never trust him completely. She was confused at her illogical anger at this stranger who had done nothing wrong, only saving the school with his own money. That was what bothered her. That and the feelings he stirred deep inside her. Jerry pushed her confusion behind her as she sat down at the long table. She removed the sectional from the clipboard and spread it on the table.

"This is my area. It is laid out in blocks. There are nine blocks per page. They are each numbered." She picked up a transparent plastic overlay gridded in squares and laid it over a block. "The grids cover 40 acres. We pin point the fire as accurately as possible within the forty acres. If there's a road we give the ground crews the location. I guess that's confusing but you'll understand better after we fly it."

"How many acres are in a mile?" asked Cal.

"Six-hundred and forty acres. Each block is equivalent to twenty-five miles. Say there's a fire here," she pointed to a spot. "That's block four six-seven; grid C-Charley. The grids are numbered A-b-etc. and each of the sixteen blocks is numbered. The fire would be radioed to the dispatcher as block 467; grid C-Charley, Number 15." Cal was looking at the map with a thoughtful frown. "It's much like a road map."

"Each sectional," he murmured referring to the aerial maps. "Nine blocks." He rubbed his chin.

At last I can tell him something he doesn't know, Jerry thought. A warm surge of superiority which flowed through her made her feel more generous toward Cal.

"It will clear up after you fly it. It's really easy. The main thing is to really know the territory. Today we are to fly the high hazard patrol. Normally I fly the whole area. I start here at the east side fly a zig zag pattern," she showed the path on the maps, "covering the entire area in a north - south path. But in high hazard I take only half of the area. Another pilot flies the other half. We will zig -zag in a more compact pattern. This way a closer check is made on all points. Understand?" Cal nodded. "I'll show you where to expect smoke like the lumber yards and how to tell if it's controlled. You look for people, vehicles and other signs. If there are none, then look for a road to direct the crew as closely as possible to the fire. We'll leave in 15 minutes. The flight will take two hours unless we are asked to double check an area. Sometimes we have to make a second flight over certain areas." Jerry gathered up the maps and replaced them and the grid on the clipboard. "I'll see you at the plane in a few minutes."

The plane was like a steam room when Jerry opened the doors. Cal joined her and shook his head. "Sure is humid and hot."

"Humid? It's dry for this area. It's only about 74% humidity. Wait till it's 90% or 100% and still not raining. Do you want to fly? I'll tell you where to go. I've done the pre-flight."

"Sure. Guess today is as good as any for you to check me out as a pilot." Cal immediately walked around the plane doing his own pre-flight. Then he entered the plane on the pilot's side adjusting the seat for his six-foot height.

Jerry flushed feeling foolish. How could he read my mind? Jerry did not know if she should be angry that he did not trust her pre-flight or admire him for doing his own pre-flight as every responsible pilot should do. She walked around the plane and climbed into the passenger side. She quietly adjusted the seat belt and shoulder harness. When the doors were closed and locked, Jerry was startled at how Cal seemed to fill the cockpit. It was not just his body, but something undefinable, the feeling of his presence. As if the plane had always been missing something and now it was complete. She hid her discomposure by talking.

"These are special radios to contact the dispatcher at the ranger station." She handed him the earphones with attached mike. While they put them on she continued, "They are separate from our regular navigation radios. We'd better get going. The tower ground-control frequency is dialed in. Can you hear me ok?"

Calvin nodded answering her "Yes."

Jerry stopped talking as Cal called out through the open window, "Clear Prop" and started the engine. He checked the instruments. Turned on the radios, and called the tower's ground control. In a few minutes they had taxied to the active runway and Cal had finished the run-up check of the engine. The tower cleared them to take off. Cal taxied onto the runway and pushed in the throttle. The plane rolled forward, faster and faster. When the airspeed reached sixty mph Cal gently eased the control wheel back. They were airborne. Beautiful, thought Jerry grudgingly as the excitement of becoming airborne filled her soul.

Once out of the traffic pattern Jerry directed Cal north toward her patrol area. She then radioed the dispatcher at the ranger station that her patrol had started. Cal started flying the zig-zag path according to Jerry's instructions. Pointing beneath them Jerry showed Cal a sawmill and other industries which always had smoke. At intervals she reported her position to the coordinator. The flight went smoothly for an hour, and then Cal spotted smoke near a small lake. Jerry directed him to fly to it putting the smoke on the right side of the plane. As they approached it she searched the area for trucks, cars or any machinery or people to indicate it was a controlled fire. She saw none.

Cal slowed the plane, put the flaps down, flying the plane at the slowest possible speed. Jerry was busy locating the fire on the grid. She spotted a country road leading to the lake. Satisfied she had her information all correct she called the ranger station, identified herself and told them, "I have a wildfire."

At the station Jerry knew the coordinator had a map and grid identical to hers. He would spot the fire and call the fire team located nearest to the fire. The two-man team would find the fire on their maps. They were equipped with a flatbed truck containing a tractor with a fire plow. The team would proceed to the fire, make a fire break and start a back fire. Most fires were contained within fifteen acres. Once she had reported, Jerry told Cal to continue the patrol. The rest of the patrol was routine.

Flying home was relaxing and enjoyable. The sky was clear and the wind was calm. Cal looked around the area and said, "What a day for flying. You can see forever today. CAVU."

"Yes. Clear and visibility unlimited. I don't know what I'd do without flying. Don't you feel sorry for those who don't fly?" Jerry asked. Cal looked at her. Jerry had the smile that she unconsciously wore when she flew. She looked at him. He nodded his heart filled with warmth at her smile that swept over him like a summer breeze.

"I've loved flying as long as I can remember," he said. "Maybe it's because I was almost born in a plane. They landed after Mom had gone into labor. An ambulance met them at the airport and she barely made it. But I'm patient. I waited." Jerry laughed.

"I'm just normal. Hospital and all. I had lots of time so I just fiddled around all day nearly drove Charley and Mom mad." They were nearing the airport now and Cal called the controller for landing instructions.

Back in the office, Jerry drank a glass of cool water then sipped on a second. Cal mopped his face with a wet towel and poured himself a glass of water. He sat down at the table and began filling out his pilot's log book.

"You did real well," said Jerry. "Are you sure you've never flown patrol before?"

"Nope. Just a natural flare, I guess." He said grinning.

Jerry was smiling in spite of herself. In the air they had been two professional pilots. They had worked as a team smoothly and efficiently. She could not help being excited to find someone who complimented her so completely. A feeling of contentment stole over her drawing her into a satisfied lethargy she had never before felt.

Maggie broke the spell by reminding her that Uncle Art was coming back in a few minutes and it was after four o'clock. Jerry jerked back to reality so fast she spilled her water.

"I nearly forgot! Ma Brown's dinner! I have to shower and change yet! Maggie, you can leave any time. I'll see you tomorrow."

"Okay. Thanks, Jerry." Maggie collected her purse and left. It seemed as if a ray of sunshine had parted from the room with her.

"She's a nice girl," observed Cal watching the youngster so full of life and dreams. "I hope she finds all her dreams."

"I believe she will," answered Jerry. "I guess we were lucky she came in. Where could Uncle Art have gone? He knows how Ma is, and we still have to stop at the store." Jerry was pacing the floor feeling irritable at being delayed. But more irritable at the strange disturbing feeling she had towards Cal. When she was away from him her mind and senses were alert to the way he wanted to take over the school. But somehow when she was with him she felt so-so blasted feminine! I won't let him seduce me she told herself fiercely.

"Why don't you take my car?," Cal was saying. "I'll ride back with Art."

Jerry looked at him startled. "Oh, I-." The door opened and Uncle Art came into the office.

"Sorry, the time slipped by. Have you seen the Spitfire they're salvaging? A really fine plane." Uncle Art was full of excitement and apology.

Jerry sighed. "Let's go. Thanks for the offer, Cal." They turned off the air-conditioner and left.

Uncle Art and Jerry arrived at Ma Brown's at 6:00 p.m. Ma Brown greeted them with a hearty hug.

"Art, you old scallywag. You don't come around near often enough." Ma's soft brown eyes twinkled with delight. She was medium height, broad shoulders, and stocky build. Her brown straight hair was cut in a short saucy style matching the lively sparkle of her smile. One would find it hard to believe Ma had four grown sons. She had married at sixteen and was widowed at twenty-eight. Now at fifty-five she looked forty in spite of working hard her whole life. She's ageless, Jerry thought. I can't remember her ever looking different.

Aloud Jerry said, "I'll put the ice-cream in the freezer," and headed for the kitchen. "Hi, Maria. How's everything with you and your family?" Jerry greeted the plump Mexican woman who was getting an arm full of plates and silverware to carry to the dining room.

"Ah, Jerry." Maria flashed Jerry a warm smile. "My Rosita starts to business school next fall, and Johnny is looking more like Pedro all the time. He's as mischievous as his father, too." Maria spoke only English and insisted her family do the same. "Soon we will all be American citizens," she added in her heavily accented English.

Jerry put the ice-cream into the freezer and took some of Maria's dishes. "I'll help you. Has it been five years since you started studying?" Jerry had known Maria and her family since Ma Brown had given them a home in a trailer on the back of her large lot-and a job. She had somehow persuaded the immigration officials to give them temporary legal status. So much has happened in five years, thought Jerry. What will happen now with Cal? She tried to put him out of her thoughts as she placed the plates on the white table cloth delicately embroidered around the edges with flowers and birds.

"This is new! How beautiful. Where did Ma get this?" Jerry lifted the edge of the table cloth to look more closely at the design.

Maria's eyes sparkled with pride. "Rosita and I made it for Ma. Our little surprise for her being so nice."

"Maria, it's so beautiful. It's almost a shame to get it soiled."

"Thank you, Jerry. We do embroidered skirts and blouses and sell them to make extra money to save for Johnny's college. When my Johnny is an American citizen, he must have a college education."

"I'm sure he will. He's twelve now, isn't he?" The two women walked back to the kitchen and began dishing up the food while they discussed Johnny's abilities.

"There you are!" Ma Brown joined them. "I wondered if you'd got lost, Jerry." Ma prepared a glass of ice water and handed it to Jerry. "Take this to Cal, please. He says he's as thirsty as a cactus." She handed the glass to Jerry smiling in a knowing way.

Automatically Jerry took the water feeling the coolness of its glass container contrasting with the warm flush she felt creeping up her neck. Why did Ma look at her like that-as if -! Jerry forced a "will do," and started to leave the kitchen. As she stepped through the door she nearly collided with Cal. "Oops! Here's your water." She handed him the glass. As his hand closed around it Jerry's fingers were captured beneath his. She started, a slight hardly noticeable jerk as the shock of his warm rough hand burned its way into her blood. She looked up at him. Their eyes met and locked. Jerry saw in the brown depths of his eyes that pulled her into his soul that he too had felt the shock. The second they shared seemed an eternity before Jerry said, "May I have my hand?"

"Sorry," he whispered hoarsely. Jerry was surprised to realize he was so shaken. Could it be Cal was human after all?

Cal turned back to the living room forgetting to thank Jerry. Jerry went back to the kitchen filled with confusion from the brief encounter. With the three women working together soon the table was loaded family style with tossed salad, golden brown chicken fried steak piled high on a large platter, mashed potatoes, pan gravy, green beans cooked with bacon, mushrooms and onions, a large tray of fresh vegetables, and mounds of hot biscuits that completed the plain cooking. For dessert there was hot apple pie and ice cream. The coffee was plentiful and freshly ground.

They were a strange assortment, but like all of Ma's boarders they got along well. Bonnie Williams sat at Ma's right. A retired school teacher, she spent her time doing volunteer work with special needs children and writing children's books. She was thin, petite and greying but possessed unending humor and energy. Tonight Uncle Art sat on Ma's left. Next to him Paul Snyder, a thirty-five-year-old city employee who was trying to put his life back together after a divorce.

Cal sat between him and Hershel Olson, a big blond truck driver who had the end of the table. He was a widower with no family and had adopted Ma. Jerry was across from Cal next to Miss Bonnie. The chatter was continuous.

Jerry ate quietly, insisting on waiting on the table so Ma could sit down and eat for a change. Maria always left when dinner was on the table so she could eat with her own family. Rosita came over and cleaned up after dinner. Too soon the evening was over. Jerry had made an effort to avoid talking or looking at Cal. She found herself afraid of encountering those smoldering eyes. Even her favorite dessert lost some of its flavor as she felt Cal's eyes on her. That night she lay in bed trying to forget those eyes, but even in her sleep they kept drawing her into their depths.

Rosa B. Lane

Chapter 3

Wednesday dawned clear and hot. Jerry was up early talking to FAA flight service to check the weather. She had just hung up the phone when Uncle Art appeared. "My treat today," said Jerry. "There's a front coming in from the west. Sounds like a bad storm with it." Jerry walked to the car with Uncle Art.

"Better get Jenny home. Planned to stay another day but you'll need to tuck your plane away, and I need to be at the ranch if it's a bad storm." Art rubbed his chin thoughtfully. "Jerry it's none of my business but-."

"Uncle Art, you're all the family I have. Whatever concerns me is your business but Calvin Morris and I are partners only. Nothing else."

Jerry pulled into the restaurant parking lot. The news at the pilot's round table was that Jimmy Cole was ok but was grounded. A front was coming in, expected in two days.

"What's that storm out by Cuba doing?" Uncle Art asked. "I haven't checked the big picture weather today." Breakfast came and the usual pilot talk went around the table. Jerry could feel the repressed desire to ask about her new partner from sentences started and stopped with a shake of someone's head. Finally, she could stand it no longer.

"Calvin Morris, my partner, is a good pilot. No, there is no romance." So stating she got up and went to the cashier to pay the bill. Behind her she heard Carla's voice teasingly say, "Me thinks the lady protesteth too much." It was followed by suppressed laughter. Why does everyone try to get me involved, thought Jerry. Pilots!

Jerry and Art got to the office shortly before Jerry's first student had arrived. By the time the student arrived she had the plane ready and waiting outside. While the student did his pre-flight she went into the office to get the plane's key and clipboard that showed the plane's flight information. Maggie arrived at the same time and headed for the desk at once.

Maggie looked up from the desk where she was sorting papers to file. She grinned showing dimples. "He's cute!"

"He's a good student but lacks feeling. He's very precise and technical but no warmth. I don't know why he's flying. I'm not sure he even likes it." Jerry added, "But he's very capable."

Jerry walked out to the plane. Her student was a nice looking, neatly attired young man. She handed him the key and the clipboard and watched with critical eye as he efficiently did his pre-flight. He should be ready to take his flight test after this final check out.

As they went through the maneuvers Kevin was precise as always but a glance at his face made Jerry wonder. His expression appeared totally empty of warmth; but, he was totally sure of himself. As they taxied back to the ramp, Jerry told him she would set up a date for his flight exam. He showed no elation, only acceptance. Most students were on cloud nine but it was just another item to Kevin.

"Kevin," she asked as they tied the plane down. "Don't you like to fly? I have the feeling you don't really care."

"Why should I? My dad's getting me a plane, so I have to fly it. It's just transportation. Like cars or motorcycles."

"You never seem excited. I guess it's none of my business, but aren't you ever glad about anything?"

"Jerry, I stopped being glad about anything when I was five and my parents divorced. Fought over me for custody, but only to spite each other. No one cared about me. Who's that cute red head?"

"Leave her alone!" The words slipped out from Jerry before she realized she spoke her thoughts out loud.

"I guess that's up to her," Kevin answered coldly and walked to the office. Jerry cursed herself. He'd see Maggie now for spite; of that she was certain. Jerry returned the clipboard to Maggie to register his time and charges while she filled out Kevin's log book. A telephone call got him an appointment for his FAA exam. Then Jerry went out to see Cal.

He was unscrewing inspection caps and preparing a plane for its periodic inspection. He felt Jerry's presence and spoke without looking up. "I've a friend who's an excellent mechanic. He's willing to come here and work if it's ok with you. He's got a wife and six kids."

"It sounds like you've hired him," Jerry retorted once again feeling angry and left out of the decision.

"I have. But I need a house for him. He's black."

"So? You hired him. You house hunt!" She turned and walked away with long angry strides. Cal continued to work, but he shook his head and sighed. He would ask Ma Brown. She would help him.

When Jerry entered the office Maggie was talking to a little grey haired lady wearing slacks and a tee shirt that showed an airplane on the back and a slogan "Never Too Old" in blazing letters. Maggie introduced her as Abby Norman. Abby smiled and her blue eyes sparkled behind her glasses.

"I just want to solo once around the field to show those old ladies at the garden club," she explained. "I like gardening, but I'm only sixty-five. I need to give them something new to talk about," Jerry laughed. Suddenly her anger was gone as she saw this petite, plump grand-motherly lady who wanted to give her friends something to gossip about.

"Well, Mrs. Norman-"

The woman interrupted, "Abby, my dear. I've been a widow for ten years."

"You will have to pass a flight physical."

"I already have." Abby fished into the depths of her oversized purse and brought out an envelope and handed it to Jerry. "I've been asking my nephew about this. He's a commercial pilot. He told me all about it. I've studied his books. I used to be a teacher."

"Well, all is in order. You need a radio license and I'll help you there. But we can start right now if you like. I'm free until eleven.

Or you can make an appointment."

"Now," said Abby quickly. "Here's my logbook. My nephew got it for me," she added proudly.

They walked out to the plane with the clipboard. Jerry started to explain the pre-flight. "Since the plane has just flown you would not normally check the fuel for water in the tanks. Only first flight and after fill-up." Jerry took the small cup and showed Abby how to drain the gas from each wing tank and look for bubbles of water which could spell trouble in an engine. She then showed her how to make sure everything was in order step by step. Then they climbed into the cockpit.

Jerry handed Abby the starting check list and went through it and the instrument panel with Abby. "Make sure all avionics are off," she told Abby. "Only then turn on the Master switch, beacons and radios. Be sure to call "Clear Prop" loudly so anyone around will know the engine is going to be turned on. I'll handle the radio today. All you need to do is to follow the list and I'll show you each step. I'll show you how the controls work and you follow to get the feel. Most students have mike fright at first."

"Oh, radios don't bother me," said Abby. "My late husband, Henry J. was a ham operator so I got my ham license shortly after we were married. I'm used to the radio. It's what they're talking about that is foreign to me." Abby leaned out the window and called surprising loudly, "CLEAR PROP!" She turned to Jerry and asked if her earphones and mike were working ok.

"I can hear you. You should be able to hear yourself. You'll learn to understand the tower as we go along." Jerry told her to turn the key, the engine started and she flicked the radio on calling ground control. "We're cleared to taxi to the active runway so you follow the rudder pedals and feel what I do. In an airplane the stick or wheel is used only in the air. On the ground the rudder controls the plane. The brakes are the top pedals and the rudder is the lower." Jerry pushed the throttle forward enough to start the plane rolling down the ramp onto the taxi-way. Abbie's eyes grew wide with excitement. A big smile spread across her plump face.

At the active runway Jerry switched to air control and did the final engine run-up. She explained each step to Abby as they followed the check list for before takeoff. Control cleared them to take off. The plane taxied into place and Jerry gently pushed in the throttle bringing the man-made bird to life. It raced faster and faster down the runway until with a gentle pull back on the control wheel they were airborne. Abby looked down at the earth falling away below them. Never had she felt such elation. Never such freedom. Was she too old for this? She had passed the FAA physical so she must not be too old. Physically and emotionally she felt sixteen!

When they were over the official practice field for students, Jerry told Abby to take the controls. With a big smile Abby took the controls while Jerry followed each movement on the other control wheel in front of her as she looked for traffic and watched Abby carefully. Abby took the controls easily and flew straight and level for a while then made a gentle bank to the left followed by one to the right. All the time she was smiling as if she were in another world. Jerry saw she was climbing higher and told her to correct it and stay at two-thousand feet. Abby looked at the altimeter and dropped the nose down slightly until the level was reached and then leveled out with a little difficulty due to the wind picking up. Jerry was surprised at the unexpected skill Abby showed and wondered if she had flown before. Everything Abby was shown she seemed to do reasonably well. Soon the flight was over and they returned to the field. Jerry called the tower, got instructions for landing and lined up for the landing. When they taxied to the ramp, Abbie was chattering with excitement and asking questions non-stop.

"We have a procedure to shut down the plane," Jerry told her to check the list. All avionics were turned off first before the Master switch was turned off and the engine shut down. Abbie's knowledge surprised Jerry. Furthermore, Abby's skill at the controls puzzled Jerry. They returned to the office and Jerry offered Abby a soda while Maggie wrote up the bill.

"Where did you learn to handle the controls? You say you've never flown but you do it as if you've had some practice," she asked as they sipped the cool drinks.

"My nephew, the pilot, has one of those practice machines to learn how to fly. I play with it every chance I get. And I have flown with him. He rents a plane when I visit and we have a ball. I'm going to like flying. Maybe I'll even get my license. What the Garden Club would say about that!" She giggled like a school girl. Maggie handed her the bill laughing with her.

"If you go to ground school, Mrs. Norman, we'll be in the same class," Maggie told her. "I'm working here for my instruction. I haven't started yet. I start Monday."

"Wouldn't that be nice! I'll do it!" Abby turned to Jerry. "Can you take me in a regular class?"

"I think we can make room for one more." So it was settled. Abby was going the whole way. Jerry's eleven o'clock student was waiting so she left, their excited voices following her to the plane.

By the time she returned the wind had picked up and clouds were rolling in from the Gulf. She barely got the plane refueled and in the hangar before the puffy white clouds had turned to black thunder-heads. Rain was much needed. Jerry retired to the hangar to work on the plane shut down for inspection. Cal went to the class room to review his notes for the class.

She was so intent that she was only vaguely aware that the rain had stopped. She was bending over the engine when Cal came into the hangar. He stood watching her smiling at her baggy coveralls with a greasy hand print on the rear where she had wiped her hand unthinking. She brushed the sweat from her forehead knocking her protective hat askew. A long golden braid slipped out of its prison and fell over her shoulder onto the grease of the engine.

"Damn," she muttered trying to brush the grease covered braid away. A strong hand reached over and plucked it to safety. Jerry froze. Charlie use to do that. Cal grinned as he wiped the end off with a clean shop towel.

"Such unlady like language! Hold still I'll tuck it in," he chuckled. "There. Is that OK?" When she nodded and mumbled thanks he added, "I came out to see if I could help. I've a while before class. You looked just like the picture."

Jerry straightened up and looked at him startled. "Picture?" Cal reached into his pocket for his billfold and produced a well-worn picture of her with oil dripping from her pigtail. The picture Charley had taken when she was sixteen and carried with him for years.

"Where did you get that? Charley always carried it," she demanded.

"He gave it to me at the fly-in." He was surprised at her attack. "Where did you think I got it?" For a moment they stared at each other. Cal, surprised, a little hurt and angry; Jerry confused and her heart aching for Charley.

"I'm sorry. I guess- I was startled." She started to turn back to her work.

"And you're always willing to believe the worst about me." He turned and walked away emotionally running from the mixture of his feelings he had for this girl. Even though he came here to meet her, he did not expect this.

Jerry turned and watched him go. His strides long and firm. Why did Charley give him her photo? What was there about him that upset her so and made her say things she would never have said to anyone else? Why was she angry unfairly? She shook her head as if to clear her mind and concentrated again on her work.

Maggie had left at 5:00. It was now 7:00. Jerry went into the office to introduce Cal to the pre-flight class. He seemed to fit in easily. Just like Charley she thought. She left the room and finished the sandwich Maggie brought them before she left. Suddenly she felt so alone. So useless. So out of place. In my own school I feel left out, she thought. When Charley was alive she usually worked on planes and they went home together. Now there was no one with whom to discuss the students. No one with whom to laugh at the funny antics of students or groan at the beating the airplanes were given on new student landings. The house was musty, hot and so very empty.

She sighed and prepared the coffee and donuts for the students' break. Students needed time to stretch between sessions. By the time the coffee was ready they came trooping out laughing with each other and asking Cal a myriad of questions. Cal saw Jerry looking at him. A pang cut his heart at the lonely girl trying to smile. She was lonely. He could feel it. How he wanted to take her-. He made himself stop thinking.

"How's it going?" Jerry asked above the din.

"Fine. And you? Why don't you go home and get some sleep?" The moment it came out he regretted it. "But it would be nice to have you here in case I need something I can't find," he added too quickly.

"I am tired," said Jerry suddenly feeling exhausted. "I think I will go home. A hot shower and bed sounds good." She started to get her purse but Cal caught her arm.

"Jerry," he started. "Nothing." What could he say? Jerry looked at him feeling that he needed to say something important but could not. A loud laugh broke the moment reminding them where they were and whatever it was, he left unsaid.

"Good night," she told him as he went back to the class room.

"Good night, Jer," he said. It was becoming a habit for him to shorten her nickname. And it sounded nice coming from him. Anyway she just wanted to leave.

Leaving did no good. Even a warm shower and shampoo did not stem the lonely restless feeling. She drew her robe around her and went downstairs barefoot. For a long time after she watered and fed the plants she stood on the back porch looking at the sky. The clouds had returned. That was the Houston area, drought or flood, seldom a happy medium. She watched the lightning flicker from cloud to cloud and felt the wind get stronger as the storm built. The lights of a car pulling into her drive startled her and sent her scrambling to the front door. Who in the world at this hour? When she opened the door, Cal stood there his hair blowing in the wind.

"Cal?" Why wasn't she surprised? "What's wrong?"

"Nothing. I saw your lights on. Well -may I come in?" He stood there cursing himself for letting an impulse bring him here. Feeling like a school boy he stepped inside at Jerry's gesture. "You looked like you didn't feel well and I was concerned."

Jerry looked at him and smiled. Somehow when he entered the house it felt as if everything was all right. She could not explain it. She did not care. He stood there looking down at her, smiling an embarrassed little smile. For the first time he seemed lost and uncertain. She should have heard the danger signal, but tonight she needed to be with someone and she did not listen.

"Come in. Have a seat. I'll make coffee."

"No. I just wanted to be sure you were OK."

"I'm fine. But sit a while. Tell me about your class. We haven't had much time to discuss things."

Cal walked into the family room behind her and took a seat on the sofa. She curled up at the other end tucking her long legs under her. For a long while he talked about the class and their responses. They discussed the planes.

"The FAA inspector will be here at 8 for the plane. I'm not qualified for the final inspection. Well, I can't sign the papers. He takes my word. Usually he makes no suggestions for any additional repairs. Maggie is working out great, isn't she? If I'd ever had a kid sister, I'd have liked one like her."

"She's a good secretary. Things seem to be shaping up. I found a house for my mechanic. When he gets settled in you can get back to flying. We need you in the air. And I'll take you through aerobatic certificate if you wish."

"I'd like that. Sure you don't want coffee?"

"No. I'd best be going I feel better knowing you're not ill." Cal got up to leave. They walked to the door and said good night. Cal left feeling the emptiness of his arms knowing she should be in them; not knowing how to bring her there.

Jerry watched him walk to the car. It had started to rain again leaving wet drops on his back. She wanted to call him back but could not. He still seemed to be taking over her life and she would never let it happen again. She closed the door and leaned against it fighting her feelings. Yet having seen him again seemed to soothe her restlessness. She knew she could sleep now. And she did.

Once the bills were paid and desk work sorted out, everything else fell into place. All the planes were flying now. By the end of the week the word was out and new students began to come. The rain had cancelled fire patrol for the time being, and Jerry was once again free to fly. It was decided she would take Mondays off, and Cal would take Tuesday their least busy day.

By Monday Jerry decided to go to the mall. It had been a long time since she had gone shopping. Jerry felt lost. She had awakened as usual at five a.m. only to realize it was her day off. Cal was taking charge of the flying school on Monday's now. She had awaken early for so long that now she could not sleep past five.

She got out of bed, stretched, breathed deeply and crawled back into bed. It was no use. Sleep would not come. Finally, she gave up. She showered, put a load of laundry in to wash and ate breakfast. It was 6:30 a.m. Her braids kept slipping over her shoulders and she started to push them back for the umpteenth time when in anger she cursed the long hair she detested. Suddenly she realized she no longer needed to wear her hair long. A feeling of guilt swept over her. Charley had loved her long unruly hair and thought it was charming and feminine. Jerry had worn it long to please him. Now her reason for braids was gone. Tears stung her eyes and she felt disloyal and guilty, but the seed was planted and it took shape as she did a few odd jobs.

When the large shopping mall opened, Jerry parked her car near the entrance to the stores. Her plans had been made. She pushed her way into the mall and checked the map at the entrance. The beauty shop was on the second floor just above her. She took the escalator feeling a little giddy at what she was going to do. When she walked into the shop, the beautician looked at her hair and sighed.

"I want my hair cut short and styled," she announced. "I'd like an appointment this morning if possible."

The beautician's eyes sparkled with anticipation. "I can take you now if you have time. Or Betty can take you at two."

"Now," said Jerry. By two she might get cold feet and change her mind.

She was ushered to a chair and after a short conference a style was decided upon. At the first snip of the scissors, Jerry cringed. She watched in the mirror as her golden hair fell away. When the stylist was finished Jerry felt cool and naked. To her surprise her hair now fell into soft waves Jerry had never before seen.

"The weight of your hair pulled it straight," explained the stylist. "You look lovely."

Jerry stared at the stranger in the mirror. She no longer looked like a pig-tailed little girl. Before her was a woman with short fashionably styled hair. She was a little dazed as she paid the cashier. Now for the next step.

Her neighbor, Cynthia, worked in a dress shop on the third floor. Jerry headed there. It was an expensive shop which catered to exclusive customers. Jerry had never even considered paying their prices but she could look and get ideas. There were no other customers at this hour, and Cynthia saw Jerry as she entered the shop.

"Jerry! Don't tell me you finally took a day off?" Cynthia came around the counter and gave Jerry a friendly hug. "The kids want Ned and me to go somewhere so Auntie Jerry can babysit. You're more fun than we are." Jerry laughed as she always did at Cynthia's bubbling good humor. "You've cut your hair! It looks great!"

"Auntie Jerry came to spend money today. I need some decent clothes. It has been so long I need help."

Cynthia looked at Jerry wide eyed and then grinned. That must be some man that she has for a partner, she thought. Out loud she said "We've got some sales, but I want you to see some of the new stock. Your size is over there." While Jerry browsed through the sale rack, Cynthia disappeared into the back room returning in a few minutes with several items for Jerry to see. Jerry had selected a couple of dresses from the sale rack to try on and followed Cynthia to the dressing room. The sale dresses never got off the hanger. For the next two hours Jerry tried on the dresses Cynthia brought to her. It was the mix and match out fits which fascinated Jerry. Jackets, pants, skirts, blouses, vests, and belts of many colors which could be combined in dozens of ways. Surrounded by so many beautiful clothes Jerry felt totally lost. She stood in front of the mirror and saw a tall slim girl in pants, vest jacket and blouse. It could not be her. It was a stranger she saw in a slim skirt, shirt, vest and purse in a shade of green she had never thought she could wear. There were two coordinating pairs of slacks with it. But the price tag! Ninety dollars for one blouse! But Jerry felt wild and carefree today.

Before Jerry could make up her mind which outfits she preferred, Cynthia entered the dressing room with a flowing chiffon dress which made Jerry gasp. The kind of dress she had dreamed about when she was in college. When she stood in front of the mirror she knew she had to have it no matter what it cost. The very simplicity of the design gave the beautiful blue print a chance to be noticed with no interruptions from ruffles or fancy trim. It had a sweetheart neckline low enough but not too low. The bodice was form fitting and swept into a full circular skirt just the right length to show off her slim legs. A matching Jacket of solid blue covered the sleeveless dress. Decorating the jacket were long silver beads sewn into swirling leaf design around the edges. A matching blue beaded bag was available. Jerry looked at the price tag and her heart sank. She could have two mix and match outfits, shoes and purse for less than this one dress. She thought of her checking account and knew she could afford both. Still, she was used to getting the cheapest, and it was strange to do otherwise. The phone rang and Cynthia left to answer it. Jerry stepped out of the dressing room into the store and found the three-way mirror and whirled in front of it. As she turned she saw a young man standing in the door grinning.

"Buy it," he said softly and he walked away.

"No," Cynthia said as she replaced the phone, "we do not hire him to tell our ladies they are beautiful. I knew that was your kind of dress when I unpacked it."

"I'll take it, the bag and the green and beige outfits. Also, the green purse and all three shirts. What is the damage? Can I still buy lunch?"

Jerry's hand actually shook as she wrote the check for more money than she had spent on clothes in the last ten years. But she had never had clothes that fit so well and made her feel so at ease. She decided to wear her green pantsuit to lunch and to finish her shopping. Just having a new shoulder bag made her feel good. She left the rest of her purchases and her old jeans and tee shirt with Cynthia.

The mall was crowded with people carrying bags of assorted sizes and shapes. Several were eating ice cream cones or other snacks and Jerry realized she was very hungry. There was a very nice restaurant somewhere in the mall but she could not remember where. She found an information plaque and planned her path through the maze of corridors up to the beautifully decorated restaurant on the fourth floor. As she expected, there were no seats so she put her name on the waiting list. Too excited to sit quietly like another woman was doing, she walked over to a painting. It was a reproduction of Venus rising from the sea. She felt that she too was rising to a new life. So engrossed did she become in trying to remember the story behind the picture, she did not see the man who stopped behind her until he spoke.

"Don't you wish it was the real thing?" Jerry turned and looked up into the smiling eyes of the young man who had watched her in the dress shop. "Did you buy it?" Jerry flushed and nodded. "What is the occasion?"

"You ask a lot of questions for a stranger," she replied.

"I would say a man who picks a dress for a lady is not considered a stranger." His brown eyes crinkled with a smile. "I would say the lady should have lunch with him."

"I shouldn't but I will. No point in both of us eating alone. Dutch of course."

"The Lambert party" came the call from a loudspeaker. Mr. Lambert took Jerry's arm and ushered her to the desk just inside the dining room.

"Miss -" he raised an eyebrow and looked at Jerry, "Miss Jackson will join me. Please cancel her table." He supplied the missing information when Jerry gave him her name. "You're not married or anything are you? I don't want an irate husband chasing me."

Jerry laughed and shook her newly styled hair. "And you? Irate wives and girlfriends chase people too."

"No commitments," he replied. Jerry followed the hostess to a table for two in a corner. When they were seated Mr. Lambert looked at the beautiful young woman across the table from him. "Well, Miss Jackson, what is the occasion?"

"Well, Mr. Lambert, none. I just felt like shopping today. Women do that you know."

"So I've heard. I think I know a good way to justify the purchase. Have dinner with me."

"Oh? You are that important?" Jerry said in mock sarcasm.

"Definitely."

"I think you should fill me in on the reason."

"My father is THE Lambert of the lumber industry."

"Not your father. You."

"My, you are persistent." He frowned as if he were trying very hard to think. Shaking his head, he sighed. "I guess that's it. I am not important except for my grandfather's inheritance he left me."

"I'm afraid having dinner with a non-important person is impossible."

"You're looking for a rich, famous husband with a year to live?"

"As a matter of fact, I am not looking for a husband at all. If I were, his wealth would have nothing to do with it. I am too busy to go out in the evening."

"What could a beautiful young woman like you do to keep her too busy to have dinner with a handsome young rich man like me?" He looked taken aback while trying to suppress a grin.

"I own a flying school. I teach flying and some of it is night flying. Some students can come only after work. Of course, there is the night flying part of the training." She spoke calmly and was amused as the mock shock was replaced by the real thing.

"You, a flying instructor? You belong in a castle!"

"Come, let's not get carried away." Jerry was laughing. "I belong in an airplane or in a hangar repairing one. This is my day off."

"You have tonight then?" he asked.

"Yes, but I also have laundry to do. Even beautiful but poor flying instructors have to have clean clothes."

"I guess you can cook and sew and care for kids."

"Some, sort of, and yes. How can you, a handsome eligible bachelor, have so much time away from your work?"

"I don't work. I play." He was looking at her intently when the waitress came to take their order. "Do you like sirloin tips? They have a very good sauce here. Their chef salad is good too."

"I'll have the chef salad with house dressing and a glass of milk please."

"Make mine the sirloin tips and bring lots of bread sticks. I'll have a glass of burgundy."

The waitress took the menus and he added, "My name is Richard. And yours is Jackson what?"

"My friends call me Jerry. I was named Geraldine after my grandmother. Richard is a nice name. Do they call you Rick?"

"Actually, no. Mother insisted I must be called Richard Allen Lambert the third. No nick names. But- at college I was Rick. Mother never knew. I'm only Richard around her. If someone slips up, they get told about it." He said it with a forced laugh. Jerry did not know whether to think he was a mama's boy or was just trying to please a tyrannical mother. At any rate, she doubted she would like her. "About dinner. Saturday and Sunday there's a dinner dance at the country club. Please come with me."

"I can't. I just don't pick up men at malls. I shouldn't even have lunch with you without knowing you." Jerry saw a doubtful look on his face and added, "Besides I told you I'm a working girl." The waitress brought their food and the conversation stopped for a while. "This salad is very good," Jerry added to break the awkward silence.

"Where is this airport you work at?"

"It's Memorial Airport. I'm half owner of Charley's Flying School. It's a lot of work, and I love it."

"Well, I'll have to take flying lessons, if that's the only way I can see you again."

"You have kissed the Blarney Stone. But I like it. Cal, my partner, is a good instructor. He will take you. I'm full up."

"Cal. Competition?"

"Oh I don't think so. He's getting bald and is sixty with a little poochy tummy." Jerry said teasingly, not knowing why.

"You, too, seem to have kissed the stone. Ever been to Ireland?"

"No. I've never been anywhere except to college. Never thought about it. I guess I never had time. I really love flying and when Dad died I inherited the school and haven't had time for anything. Until a few days ago when I got a partner. I may have some time now. We'll get a mechanic soon, and I can get back to flying. We hired a secretary who is working out great."

"You're really serious about being a flying instructor, aren't you? I thought it was a come on. I never met a working girl before. Just society players like me. Nothing to do but have fun and gossip about each other." The waitress came to clear the dishes and asked if they wanted dessert. "I'll have a piece of cherry pie and coffee. How about you?"

"None for me. Just coffee." Jerry wondered why she ordered coffee. She should pay her bill and leave now. But this totally lazy man intrigued her. At least that's what she thought when men just lived off the money someone else earned. She could not imagine a life with no reason to get up in the morning except to play. How boring.

"Richard, are you teasing me about not working? Everyone has to work. Someone has to make the money you spend." She sipped her coffee and waited for and answer.

"I don't need to. My grandfather left me a sizable inheritance which I will get when I turn 25 a few hours from now and my parents are wealthy. I would shock them both if I attempted to work."

"What did you study in college? Surely you majored in something." Jerry drank the last of her coffee.

"Actually, I was on the rowing team, debating team, and took English Lit. as my major. There was some math and business stuff because Dad insisted I learn something useful. I hated it. I boxed a little. Never was good at sports. There hasn't been anything I am really interested in, and since I don't have to work, I just travel and have fun. Isn't that what it's all about?"

"I thought it was about leaving the world a little better than when you came into it."

"I guess I do that. I make jobs for travel agents, tailors, car builders and everything I do to have fun. Someone has to be on the job to take care of things. Yes, I make lots of work for people." Richard finished his pie and took a last drink of coffee. "How about the dance? At least dinner Sunday since you have Monday off."

"I'll go with you to dinner Sunday, but I must get home by midnight or I'll fall asleep."

"If it's in my arms, I won't mind." He looked at her with a grin.

"Keep that up and the dinner is off. I've got to go. I've more shopping to do. If you have a pen and paper I'll give you my address. What time Sunday?" Even as she spoke she was thinking she was out of her mind. At least she had none of the confusion she felt with Cal. Just a dinner could not hurt. "Do we pay on the way out? Where is the waitress?"

"It's taken care of. You are my guest. I'll pick you up Sunday at seven. You said Dutch, not me. I'll see you then." He did not let Jerry protest. She picked up her purse and said goodbye. I must be out of my mind! But what kind of life is it to play all the time? It might be interesting to find out.

Jerry finished her shopping for jeans and new coveralls then went up to retrieve her purchases from Cynthia. She was exhausted when she got home. Flying all day was not as tiring as shopping all day. And she had behaved very badly. Picking up a man! She began to have second thoughts about the dinner but had neglected to get his phone number. She knew Uncle Art would disapprove. So would Cal; and, that made it all right, she rationalized.

Tuesday rolled around very quickly. When Jerry got to work she opened the hangar and started to work feeling very stiff in her new coveralls. Maggie had the day off, so once again she was alone. That is until Arnie Shepherd showed up. He was a medium sized man who looked like he worked out every day. He had a big smile as he introduced himself. Jerry had not been happy to find out Cal had hired him without her consent, but after meeting him she liked him at once.

"How much flying time do you have, Arnie?"

"None. I fix 'em, but you won't catch me flying one. I got family," said Arnie grinning from ear to ear.

Jerry showed him around the hangar and the planes. She started to explain the maintenance when he interrupted. "Ma'am, just show 'em to me and I'll do the rest. I was born fixin' airplanes." Before Jerry could answer he looked at the engines and planes one by one taking notes and told her exactly what needed to be done including some suggestions to make the work easier. Jerry realized that once again Cal had been right and she resented it.

"Well, Arnie, if you need anything I'll be in the office until nine when my student arrives." She started to leave then turned and added, "Arnie, if you want to get cool come on in the office. There's cool water and soda in the fridge. If there is no coffee, we'll make some for you. Any time you want something from the restaurant feel free to go. Just let us know. We don't punch time clocks here. We have a certain amount of work to be done, sometimes a schedule to keep, and we all work together."

"Yes, ma'am. Cal already told me that and that you were the boss in the hangar. He said you were the best pilot he had ever flown with except maybe Mr. Rex. OOPS! I wasn't supposed to tell you that."

"Your secret is safe with me. Cal is very good, too. Whether he is up to Charley's ability I'll have to wait and see. Don't tell him I said so. My name is Jerry, Arnie. We're not formal here either."

"Yes, ma'am-Jerry." As Jerry left the hangar Arnie shook his head. He knew Cal was smitten with this girl, but she seemed totally indifferent. Yet they seemed a perfect match. He sighed and went to work.

Jerry went to the office feeling free and at the same time oddly out of place. Was this another way to ease her out of her school? She had a hard time trying to convince herself that Cal was not sincere. She knew Arnie was everything Cal had said he was. And she had to admit they needed a mechanic. She still had the feeling that he was slowly taking away her jobs and putting her as just another instructor by increasing her flying time. A tiny voice said she was unfair but she ignored it.

Charley's Flying School

Chapter 4

For a while Jerry and Cal had a truce. They worked together surprisingly well. Cal proved a good pupil at understanding the system of fire patrol. Jerry felt he could be trusted to fly a patrol alone. The Texas heat and humidity were stifling. Jerry worried about Arnie working in the hangar and saw to it he had plenty of cool water and frequent breaks when he would take them. On Friday a cold front came through. The bad weather was made worse by the front going to the Gulf and coming back as a warm front bringing more bad weather. As Charley used to say, it turned into a see-saw front closing the student flying down and grounding all planes. Maggie had the desk cleared up like magic. Everything was filed neatly and she was given the week-end off. Cal and Jerry took the down time to help Arnie to spruce up all the planes and get them in tip-top order. By Sunday Jerry decided to leave early. She had told no one about her date. Cal and Arnie stayed on in the hangar doing odds and ends.

Jerry stood in her bedroom freshly showered and shampooed looking at the beautiful dress she had bought. She laid it out on the bed with the accessories. She was surprised at the excitement she felt. She had not dressed for a dance since she had been jilted by her fiancée three months before their wedding. He had married his boss's daughter and his rise in the company was swift and profitable. Jerry had been devastated and swore never to trust a man with her emotions again. A swift thought of Cal swept through her thoughts and she shoved it away.

She was ready early and was sitting in the family room when the doorbell rang. She wondered who it could be. Richard did not seem the kind to be early. She went to the door and there stood Cal. He looked at her totally shocked. What Cal saw was Jerry with her blond hair neatly styled, a soft make up and delicate perfume wearing the most beautiful dress he had ever seen off the movie screen. She was the most captivating woman he had ever known. The way Cal looked at her made Jerry feel like a woman for the first time since she was jilted.

"I did not know you had plans. Oh, this letter got misplaced with the bills and I thought I'd bring it over. Jerry, you look beautiful. What's the occasion?" He could have bit his tongue when he asked.

"I have a date," she answered. "I met him while shopping. We're going to his country club to a dinner dance." She didn't know why she told him she had picked up a man. "Come in. I'm ready early."

Cal started to refuse then decided to find out who this man was. She was playing with fire going out with strange men. Surely she knew that. He followed her into the family room and handed her the letter.

"Thank you. He is Richard Lambert of the Lambert lumber empire. I'm sure I'll be all right." Cal knew she was teasing him and he felt his face flush. She could read him so easily.

"I'm sure you know what you are doing, but be careful. I'd better go before he gets here. It might spoil things." He got up to leave.

"Thank you, Cal. I'll be fine." Jerry walked to the door with him and as he left he wanted to go back and take her in his arms and- . He hurried to his car. Jerry watched Cal as he drove away. Suddenly she wished it was Cal she was going dancing with, then shook it out of her mind. All she needed was to become involved with him of all men. Richard was harmless. He wasn't interested in anything except a pretty woman to be his escort and to show off. She would play his game. It might even be fun pretending she belonged to the rich and famous.

It was only a few minutes before the bell rang again. She

opened it and Richard stood there with a box containing a white orchid. "Come in," she invited. He stepped into the room, and she closed the door. "My humble home. Unlike the mansion you probably come from."

He handed her the orchid. "You are beautiful." She took the corsage from the box and started to pin it to her jacket. He took it from her and expertly attached it. "The old experienced corsage fixer." He placed the empty box on the table by the door. "You are right. It's not like the Piney Woods Estate. It looks comfortable and warm."

"Piney Woods Estate! That gorgeous house in the forest about ten miles from the lumber mill? I fly over it all the time when I'm on fire patrol. I tell my students that your runway is a good emergency landing field if they need one. I hope you don't mind."

"That's the one. I must confess we have a helicopter and a twin-engine business jet. I don't fly. We have our hired pilots for the company. Shall we go?" He escorted her to the waiting chauffeured limousine. Jerry got into the limousine and looked around.

"This is a first for me. I could get used to this," she noted as she settled back in the luxurious seat. Richard settled close to her.

"Stick with me, baby, and you can have it all," he said mimicking a tough guy. Jerry laughed.

"You must have spent a long time kissing the Blarney Stone. I can't imagine having someone driving me everywhere. Don't you drive at all?"

"Of course. I have a lovely gold convertible I play with. I just wanted to impress you. I confess."

"Well, you have. Is this the club? I won't know anyone here." Jerry was nervous at the thought of actually facing the rich and famous.

"You will have me." Richard helped her from the limo when the chauffeur opened the door. They walked to the door and were greeted by the door man. Jerry felt like Cinderella and would not have been surprised if her gown had turned into coveralls at the stroke of twelve.

Richard escorted Jerry graciously into the large hall filled with women in beautiful gowns and men dressed like him in white jackets and dark trousers. For once Jerry knew her dress fit into the social costumes of the others. It felt unreal. Richard held out his arm. She tucked hers through his and walked through the crowd with him. He was greeted by both men and women young and old. Then the music started, and he asked if she wanted to dance.

"I haven't danced since I was in college. I wasn't very good then," she warned him as he escorted her to the dance floor.

"I'll have to remedy that," and he whirled her across the floor to a lively waltz. As they whirled to the tune Jerry found she was having fun for the first time in a long time. It had been four years since that bum had dumped her. This was the first real date. She was here because she knew Richard was never going to be serious. It was then she saw him. She felt the blood drain from her face and she missed a step.

"Are you all right? You look like you've seen a ghost."

"I have. Over there. The tall man with the dark-haired pregnant wife. She is very lovely."

Richard led her so he could see them. "Do you know him?"

"Yes. He's the one that dumped me without bothering to let me know he was getting married to his boss's daughter. Three months before our wedding." She chuckled. "He didn't give me a chance to return his engagement ring before the wedding. I was hurt and angry." Jerry stopped and wondered how she had even thought of her revenge.

"What did you do with it?" asked Richard looking at her vacant finger.

"I went back to the jeweler where he bought it and asked if he would buy it back. He agreed to give me nine-thousand dollars for it. I had him make out the check to the Salvation Army and asked for a sales receipt. Made copies of the check and sales receipt. I sent the check to the charity next day in his name giving his address to them requesting a thank you note be sent to him. Then I waited. He did exactly what I thought he would do. Wrote me a letter asking for his ring back." The music stopped and they walked from the dance floor.

"Don't keep me in suspense. What next?" Richard led her to a small table and motioned for one the waiter carrying drinks on a tray. "Do you want a glass of wine?"

"I don't drink much. Is there a diet coke?" The waiter left.

"Okay, what did you do?"

"I sent him the receipt copy and a copy of the check. I sent a note that I had made a donation to the Salvation Army in his name. I did not think he wanted the ring back since he had not notified me of his coming marriage. Of course I didn't want it, so I knew he would agree to give it to charity. He could take it off his income tax as a charity donation. I never heard from him again. I wish I could have been a fly on the wall when he read the letter." Jerry laughed and Richard joined her.

"Jerry, you have a devious mind and I love it. When we get our drinks I'll take you over and introduce you. Face your enemy and get it over with." He said it joking but it hit Jerry like a bolt of lightning.

"I don't know," she started feeling her hands starting to shake at the prospects of speaking to Angus Hampton again.

"Come on. Let him know you have not withered away. Indeed, you have not."

"I did not look like this in college. I had long hair I braided or wore in a ponytail to keep it out of the way, and I was a teenager of nineteen. Totally in love with a man that all the girls wanted. At least that's what I thought. The only thing I would not do for him was sleep with him. I said marriage first. He was not happy but didn't push it. I guess his sudden marriage explains why." The drinks were delivered and Richard stood up.

"Come on, Jerry. This will be the most fun I've had for a long time. Now remember we are old friends in fact a bit more. I'll make him regret he treated you so badly."

"What are you up to?" Jerry joined him smiling.

"Just act like we are lovers." Jerry shook her head and let him escort her to where Angus and his wife stood.

"Hello, Angus. It's been a long time. This is Richard Lambert of the lumber Lamberts. You must be Angus's wife." Jerry could see that Angus did not recognize her at first. "I'm Jerry Jackson. Angus and I were friends in college" The expression on Angus face was shock. "Angus, you did get the letter I sent you several years ago?"

Angus recovered himself and nodded. "Yes, I got it." The pallor of his face slowly turned to an angry flush.

"Good," Jerry said. She felt her hand on Richard's arm trembling, and Richard put his drink on a passing tray so he could cover her shaking hand with his.

"Isn't she a beauty?" Richard said to Angus. "Well dear, we must go or Mother will be unhappy."

"Of course, honey." To Angus she added, "Mother doesn't like to be kept waiting. It was nice seeing you again. I hope you have a safe pregnancy, my dear."

Richard said in a reminder voice, "Oh, I arranged the African safari for the winter. How about Alaska next month? Get away from this heat. Or would you rather go diving?" As they walked away Jerry told him anywhere was fine with her. Richard glanced back and Angus was staring at them. Feeling the warmth and encouragement of Richard's hand, Jerry felt she had faced the cause her fear and had destroyed it. Angus had been literally speechless.

Richard escorted Jerry into the dining room. He walked to a large table. "Mother, this is Jerry Jackson, my guest." The woman he addressed was about fifty. Her hair was upswept into stylish waves. It was dark brown streaked by a beautician with platinum blond streaks. She wore a matronly high-necked dress of beige that complimented her coloring exactly. The large diamonds she wore did the job they were bought for- a way to show how wealthy she was. He then introduced her to each of the other guests at the table. He led her to the two empty seats and assisted her to sit down. Well, thought Jerry, I've gotten this far. Now what?

"Are you from the railroad Jacksons?" asked Mrs. Lambert.

"Mother, the aviation Jacksons," inserted Richard. "They have airplanes."

"Commercial?" This came from Mr. Lambert. "I'm in lumber and oil myself."

"I guess you could say that," answered Jerry. "I own a flying school. We fly fire patrol and pest patrol. We teach students how to fly a small single engine plane and have a flight school to teach the basics needed to pass the FAA written exam."

"A flying school? You teach flying? Could you teach me?" This came from a young blond girl in a rather low-cut gown and too much makeup.

"Of course, Estelle isn't it? You have to know something of math and pass a physical. There's a lot of hard work and studying. Are you interested?"

"My daughter will never fly one of those things," Estelle's Mother declared. "And I would never permit her to go to an airport. It's not fit for young women." She had dyed platinum blond hair in an up-sweep and too much eye shadow on for Jerry's taste. Jerry saw that Richard was waiting for her to defend herself.

"I guess not everyone has the courage or ability to be a pilot. But I've never seen a drunk at the airport. I think it is somewhat more decent than some of the night clubs I've read about in the paper. In fact, I've seen a few 'beautiful people' here tonight that have over indulged. It's all in the point of view one has as to what is decent or not. Now I don't think it is decent to have an affair with other people's spouse. Or to put marriage on and off like a glove. I feel each person should work for the money they spend and not live off someone else's hard work." Jerry looked with calm anger at Richard. Silence fell at the table.

Estelle was laughing. "Bravo. I agree! What airport are you flying out of?"

"Memorial Airport." The conversation was interrupted by the more wine. Jerry felt she had perhaps been rude but she would never let anyone insult her profession. The insult had been extremely rude of the other woman. She looked down the table and a young man raised his glass to her with a smile. The shrimp cocktail appetizer came. Jerry became aware of not so subtle glances at her as she picked up the seafood fork. The women were hoping she would be confused at all the silverware. They looked disappointed. The men started talking about the economy and the women gossiped. Estelle sat quietly and smiled and nodded to Jerry. At least there seemed to be one human at the table. She wondered about Richard. He seemed to enjoy her discomfort. The next course of salad came and went and no one spoke to her. Richard was talking to the man next to him. With the main course he looked up at her.

"Jerry we're going to the Florida Keys to do some diving and I'd like to take you. Will you come?"

"No. I have a business to run. I can't just pick up and go when I please. I have what is called responsibilities. You may not understand that." She felt eyes turn toward Richard. The man who toasted her was laughing. A slightly plump young woman sitting across from him sent him a scorching look. Mrs. Lambert looked relieved.

"Just what kind of flying do you do?" Mrs. Lambert asked with a tone of voice of a superior talking down to her inferior.

"I instruct students how to fly. When it is very dry, I fly fire patrol over your beautiful estate to look for fires that might destroy your home and lumber mill. I cover a lot of the piney woods. I have spotted four potential disasters so far this summer. One about three miles from the mill and one about five miles from your home. Had it been windy the rangers might not have been able to put them out so fast. You were lucky. I guess you might say I'm one of the guardian angels of the forest."

"You mean you fly the ranger patrol? I see your planes from the mill. We're all grateful for such service. I can't imagine a beautiful woman like you doing such a dangerous work." Mr. Lambert looked at her with respect. Mrs. Lambert glared at him.

"A lot of women do dangerous jobs. There are soldiers, nurses, doctors, firefighters, policewomen and many others. I knew a woman that worked for the utility company and fixed downed wires in all kinds of weather. Talk about danger!"

"I've heard of flying doctors and nurses. My uncle who lives Australia is a doctor and flies to people who live too far to get to a hospital. I've always thought I'd like that except all I can do is be a social butterfly. My finishing school did not teach me how to live," Estelle said wistfully.

"You do not have to do anything but find a husband of my choice," said her Mother. "It's socially unacceptable for people in our class to work."

"It's a good thing every one doesn't feel that way, Mother.

You would be cooking and cleaning and sewing and doing all the work you now hire done so you can sit around and feel superior," Estelle said knowing it would anger her mother. "I respect working people. They leave the world a better place."

"Not another crusader!" Richard sighed, "I say if you can afford to spend your life playing why not play?"

"To avoid work," called a young man sporting a neatly trimmed beard and moustache. "Cheers," he added and downed the rest of his wine. The wine glass was refilled quickly.

The dessert was brought and Jerry looked at the chocolate cake with raspberry sauce around the plate in a decorative design and wondered why it was not put on the cake so one could eat it. She liked chocolate and raspberry together. The cake, along with the coffee that was brought, was very good. It was some of the company that made the meal unpleasant. So this is the social life she always saw in the movies. Useless.

When the meal was finished, Richard escorted her back to the ball room. She excused herself to go to the powder room. He said he would meet her at the bar. The dancing was still going strong. In the ladies lounge, she sighed. It was a relief to get away from the snobs. Well, she wanted to know, and now she did.

"Hello." It was Estelle. "I'm so glad you came. You're a breath of fresh air. All the girls can talk about is men and each other interspersed with styles of hair and clothes. They are uneducated in anything else. Too bad for some of them are really bright. I wish you would come with us to dive."

"Thank you, Estelle. You seem to be the only one with manners. The gentleman who toasted me seems nice."

"He's married to the dark-haired woman who watched him like a hawk. He fancies himself irresistible. They were married to put the two fortunes together. I will not marry like that. It's what Mother wants, but not what I want."

"You're old enough. Why don't you do what you want? You have the money, don't you?"

"Yes and no. I'm on an allowance until I'm 21. And I just never had the courage to face Mother. I hope you change your mind.

The diving is really better than this. Excuse me. I've got to go find the others."

"I'd better get back to Richard. Thanks Estelle. I needed a friend tonight. I think I disappointed the women by knowing what fork to use." They both laughed as they parted.

Richard was at the bar. He was looking across the room when Jerry walked up. "Come. I want you to meet Senator Stone. He's a good man to know." He whirled Jerry through the dancers to the other side of the room and introduced her to a man slightly overweight who greeted them warmly. "I want you to meet Jerry Jackson. Jerry, Senator Stone."

"I believe we've met. Oh, I remember. Your father was the pilot who flew us to Austin last year. I can't believe you are the pig tailed kid at the hangar getting the plane ready." He took Jerry's hand in a firm friendly shake. "How is Charley?"

"Charley was killed in an auto accident by a drunk. The man had been arrested on numerous times for drinking but only fined. His license should have been revoked a long time ago. There ought to be a law."

"As a matter of fact, some of us are hounding our representatives to pass such a law. I'm real sorry about Charley. He was a fine pilot and a nice person. If there's anything I can do let me know."

"Thank you. I'll call on you if I need to."

"Would you excuse us for a minute, Jerry? I have some business to discuss with the Senator." Jerry said yes, and the two walked away. Jerry stood waiting, people watching. She saw Angus approaching alone.

"That was a dirty stunt you pulled on me. Giving my money to charity," he accused angrily.

"Oh, I thought the engagement ring was a gift from you since you didn't have the decency to break our engagement like a man. If you had, I would have given it to you. I had to find out from my roommate who read about your wedding in her paper. Talk about dirty tricks. I feel sorry for your poor wife. Does she know you married her for her father's money and a position in his firm?" Jerry turned around and walked away.

"Was Angus bothering you?" Richard joined Jerry as she walked away.

"I think I bothered him. He said I played a dirty trick on him by giving his money away. It did just what I hoped it would. Hit him in his purse. Did you settle your business?"

"Oh, yes. It is a parking ticket I want erased. Even if he's not a Senator now he still has clout. Do you want to dance?" Jerry nodded and they joined the dancers.

"That's not the right thing to do, Richard. We all have to pay our fines."

"Life is full of fines people pay and don't deserve." Richard spoke bitterly. Before Jerry could answer, he whirled her into the crowd of dancers and changed the subject.

As they were driving home, Jerry was silent. "Richard, why did you bring me? I had the feeling it was to show off a lowly peasant and hope to outrage your mother. Sorry to disappoint you. I actually knew which fork to use."

"I'm sorry if I gave that impression. You're only partly right. It was to show you off but because you are so lovely. You're different from the women I know, and I like talking to you. It never occurred to me you would be other than what you are. Forgive me. I hope you will change your mind, and come diving with us."

"I won't."

When they arrived at Jerry's home, Richard saw her to the door. "Jerry, it's been an enjoyable evening for me. May I see you again?"

"I don't think so. It was interesting to see how the rich and famous live but I don't fit in. Thank you for this evening. Good night, Richard." She started to turn, and Richard pulled her to him and kissed her softly.

"Good night, Jerry. Thank you for going with me. You're not going to get rid of me so easily. Remember, I'm a spoiled playboy and all I have to do is to haunt you until you say 'yes'." He turned and walked to the limousine. Jerry watched him go with mixed feelings.

Richard's kiss lingered like a butterfly on her lips, and she laughed as she locked the door. He's a teaser. But he's wasting it on me, she thought. From nowhere the thought slid through her mind "How would Cal kiss?" She shook her head. She knew it would not be a butterfly kiss. It was getting harder to be angry with Cal. He was so nice and such a hard worker. Besides, everyone liked him. She turned off the lights and went upstairs. As she got ready for bed, she smiled. She had finally had the opportunity to tell Angus off. Somehow it was not the good feeling she had thought it would be. She could not help but feel sorry for his wife. That could have been her married to that scum. It was after two a.m. when she finally fell asleep.

The phone was ringing. Jerry, drugged with sleep, tried to wake up. She reached for it and woke up enough to say, "Hello. Who is this at this hour?"

"Jerry, it's Cal. Can you come in today? My mother was in a car accident. She's in surgery now, and I have to go to her." Cal's voice was too calm. It sounded forced and controlled with an effort.

Jerry sat up wide awake. "Of course, I had some wine at dinner. What time is it? Six? I won't be able to fly until later this morning. I'll be there as quickly as I can. Are you going to fly? Should you fly emotionally stressed?"

Cal smiled into the phone. "I've flown air rescue when it was my friends who needed to be rescued. I'm fine. Thanks for asking. I'm taking the Skylane."

I'll be there as soon as I can. Take care, Cal. If I miss you, call me when you can and I'll send her flowers."

"I'll do that. Thanks." Cal looked at the phone in surprise as he hung up. Did she really care?

Charley's Flying School

Rosa B. Lane

Chapter 5

Jerry showered to try to wake up. She was not hungry but she grabbed a roll and instant coffee and rushed to the airport. Cal was just finishing a flight plan. The weather was CAVU all the way, but there was a line of storms was to the West headed their way. Otherwise, it was a perfect day to fly. He turned and smiled at her as she entered the office.

"Thanks, Jerry. I owe you one. I've got the plane ready and I'm on my way."

"No problem. It's what partners do. You're sure you're ok to fly? We teach our students never to fly under stress or illness."

"I'm sure. Goodbye." He hesitated as he turned and looked at her. Their eyes met and for and instant Jerry thought he was going to kiss her. Or did she hope he would?

"Goodbye, Cal. Don't forget to call. I hope your mother is all right." Cal left the office and walked to the plane.

Maggie came in and stood looking at the two wondering how long it would be before they realized they really liked each other a lot. "What's going on? This is your day off."

"Cal's mother was in an accident and is seriously hurt. He's taking the 182 back to Illinois. I'll be here until he gets back. No day off for a while. I'm going to call Uncle Art." Jerry picked up the phone. Uncle Art insisted he come and help for a few days while Cal was gone. Art still had his teaching license. Jerry was relieved for since Cal had come their business had picked up. They were both flying full time now. They needed the four-passenger plane for pest patrol and fire patrol. Jerry would have to arrange for someone else to take it. Jerry had barely hung up the phone when the door opened, and Richard entered.

"May I help you?" asked Maggie. Jerry turned around and was surprised to see him this early. It was barely eight a.m.

"I'm looking for Jerry," he said smiling at Jerry. "I thought this was your day off. I told you I was persistent."

"Richard. What are you doing here? I did have today off, but my partner has a family emergency and will be gone a few days. No time off until he gets back."

"I came to take you for breakfast. Or lunch. Or dinner. You have to eat."

"Maggie runs down to the restaurant and brings me a sandwich. Look, Richard, I'm very busy. I can't talk now. Please go."

Richard walked over to Jerry and said, "All right. But I'll be back." He placed his hands on her shoulders and pulled her to him giving her a hard demanding kiss. Jerry pulled back and before he could move slapped him across the face with a resounding "whack." He looked surprised then he smiled and left laughing softly. Jerry shut the door behind him and stood against it rubbing her hand. She had never slapped anyone before, but he needed to know that kind of conduct would not be tolerated.

"I think he thought you were challenging him," observed Maggie. "I don't like him."

"He's a spoiled little rich boy. But can be quite charming, if he wants to be. Did Cal have any students booked for today?"

Maggie looked at the schedule and answered, "Not 'til eleven. That's all. One is finished and is ready for his flight test. Cal was going to start me if he had time."

"Would you like me to start you? I can after lunch. If there's a patrols call I'll have to find someone to replace me. I can't fly until ten. I had some wine late last night and have to wait several hours. We can rent one of the 150s if a qualified student wants to practice solo. Call me. I'm going out to the hangar and see if Arnie needs help."

Maggie's eyes sparkled. "Would you? Thank you."

"Maggie, Cal and I talked and we feel that what you do here

is so valuable to us that we are putting you on a small salary as well as the ground school and flying. I don't know what we would have done without you."

"Gosh! I don't know what to say. Thank you! I do need the money for gas."

"When you get your license you will have a full time job here if you wish. I hope you decide to stay."

Maggie watched her leave breathless with surprise and joy. These were the best people to work for. Of course she would stay and save the money for her nursing school if she didn't get a scholarship. Today was a good day. Her parents would be happy.

Jerry walked to the hangar. Arnie was inspecting tires as he always did each day. There was not a bolt or screw he did not know by heart, at least it seemed that way. Today Arnie stood examining a wrench, shaking his head. He looked up as Jerry came in.

"Miss Jerry," he started.

"Arnie, please it's just Jerry. We're friends working together to make our school a success. What is it?" She walked over to him.

"There's some tools that need to be replaced with modern designs that work better and faster. I'm not complaining, but I can do a better job." He looked apologetic.

Jerry stood looking at the wrench and her eyes flooded. She fought it back. "Charley was planning to go over all the tools when he got back," she said softly. "Will you do it? He has a new catalogue in the office. I just- that wrench was Charley's father's. It's antique given to his grandpa when he was a boy. Charley treasured it. I'll put it where it will be safe."

"I understand Miss - er- Jerry. I'll let you know when I'm finished."

"I'll bring you a notebook and you can make a list. We can look at the catalogue together. Anything I can do to help? I've got a couple of hours 'til my student." Arnie shook his head. Jerry went back to the office for the notebook, pen and the catalogue.

When she returned Kevin was talking to Maggie. "Kevin. How was your check ride?" Jerry asked.

"I passed," he answered totally without emotion. "I came to

rent a plane for a couple of hours. The Aerobat"

"I'm sorry Kevin. You're not qualified to fly the Aerobat. A 150 is available."

"It can be flown as a straight plane." Kevin was angry.

"I know. But I also know you. I'll rent you a 150 but not the Aerobat"

"I'm done with 150s. I can do stunts if I want to."

"Not in my plane. You need special training to fly aerobatics. You can kill yourself if you don't have proper training. It takes lots of practice with a skilled instructor. Is there anything else?"

"I know all the instructions by heart. I'm good and you know it," Kevin glared angrily at her and turned to leave. He looked at Maggie as if to speak, then went out the door.

"Well, how about that?" Maggie was surprised. "I thought better of him. We do seem to be having men problems today."

"Be careful of him, Maggie. I didn't like the way he looked at you. He's cold. I've never seen a student who has passed his flight test who didn't come back walking on air and let us cut off his shirt tail to place on the board." Jerry shook her head. She wondered why he was flying. "He is too sure of himself, and that spells disaster. If I rented him the Aerobat he would try to do something he has no business doing. I know his attitude."

"He sure is handsome." Maggie went back to her work. Jerry took the notebook and catalogue back to Arnie. She wished she knew more about Kevin. He looked like trouble. Maggie needed to watch her step.

Jerry spent the time waiting for her student going over the studies for the flight class. At eleven the student arrived. It was Abby Norman. She was all smiles. Jerry had pulled N30316 trainer out and inspected it.

"Hello, Abby. The plane is ready. You need to do the pre-flight. Shall we go?"

"I need the ladies' room. Here is something I wrote for you. I'll be right back" Abby disappeared into the other room. Jerry took the envelope and pulled out a sheet of paper. She started reading it, then laughed.

She handed it to Maggie who read it out loud.

"Me–I Can Fly!
I'm learning to fly! I'm so happy, so gay!
I've got the plane ready. We're on our way!
I roar down the runway, my instructor turns pale.
I lift the plane off. I missed the fence rail!
We do touch and goes, my approach is -well fair,
But when I flare out I'm fifty feet in the air.
My instructor keeps mumbling, then one sunny day,
I hear what she's saying, she's starting to pray!
My heart is so happy, I look at the sky.
My airspeed gets lower-she's yelling "Fly-fly-FLY!"
I'm glued to the airspeed, it's just right again.
My instructor is trembling-"Turn -miss that plane!"
She's nervous, poor lady, I can't understand why.
She's the instructor. It's ME learning to fly."

Maggie was laughing when Abby arrived to start her lesson. "Abby, that's great. Shall I put it on the bulletin board?" She handed it back to Jerry.

"Yes, please do. Thank you, Abby. Let's go." They walked to the waiting plane.

Abby got the cup and checked for water in the fuel. She did the walk around check under Jerry's watchful eye. Her hands ran over the prop edges to be sure there were no nicks that could cause trouble, checked for wasps' nests, looked at the tires, all the leading edges, she raised the hood and checked the oil and looked for anything unusual. They then got into the plane. Today Jerry let Abby call the tower for directions. Abby looked lost when the controller quickly gave her the information. Jerry smiled and took the mike.

"The wind is 6 knots and we use runway one-seven," she told Abby and directed her to the correct taxiway. Abby taxied to the active runway under Jerry's direction.

"Get the check list for the engine run-up." Abby took the list and sighed realizing how much she had to know just to get into the air. "I'll do it and you watch. Next time you can do it." The engine run-up complete, Jerry called the tower to tell them they were ready to take off. "All right, Abby now you follow me and we're off." Abby was a good student and a joy to teach.

When they returned to the airport a message was waiting from Uncle Art. A line of thunderstorms had formed to the west of his ranch moving at sixty miles an hour and he would have to wait to come. Jerry thought if they were near his ranch then they would be in the area in about two hours. She dialed Flight Service for an update.

"Maggie, I'm sorry we'll have to postpone your lesson. There's a line of thunderstorms, very dangerous ones, headed this way and will be here sooner than was expected in about an hour and a half. They are moving very fast. Possible hail. They'll pass through quickly but will be damaging. It's no go for flying small planes."

"That's all right, Jerry. Maybe it won't last long. I've some work to catch up on from Saturday. I got a 150 handbook. I'll be more ready after I read about the plane. I'll go get some lunch for you."

"No, I'll run down myself as soon as I take care of the plane. It's fast moving so perhaps we can still get an hour in later." Jerry went to the hangar and with Arnie's help pulled the plane into the hangar.

"Arnie, what's wrong? You seem restless. Anything worrying you?" Jerry asked. It was unlike Arnie to be so quiet. He seemed as if he was thinking of something else.

"My missus is expecting any day now. It's number seven and she's not been well. She's alone with the other six. I worry about her. All alone in a strange town. My wife is awful homesick for her family in St. Louis." He looked at Jerry his brow wrinkled with concern.

"We're grounded for a while. Why don't you go home and take care of her? There's nothing of importance to do right now. Call me and let me know how she is. There's a bad thunderstorm headed this way. She should have you with her."

"Thank you, Miss-er–Jerry. You're just like Cal said you'd be. I appreciate this."

"Take care. Do you have the money for her hospital and doctor? If not, I can write a check. We don't have insurance yet. Just too many things for me to do since Charley died."

"Cal has already taken care of that before I came down here. He's a real good man."

"I know." Jerry was surprised that she said that. But deep inside she knew it was the truth. He was a better man than she had realized but would not admit it even to herself.

Arnie gathered his tools together and took them to the table. Jerry returned to the office, collected her purse and left for lunch. She headed for the pilots' table which was nearly empty. Carla was there eating one of the airport's famous hamburgers. Bob Hardy was just leaving. He smiled hello to her as he left.

Jerry found a seat near Carla and they exchanged greetings. Jerry took the menu the waitress handed her. She didn't know why because she knew it by heart. She ordered a cup of the homemade beef stew. The owner of the airport had the food ordered direct from a local farm. Everything was fresh and homegrown, including the beef.

"You grounded too?" she asked to make conversation.

"Yes. I really think there should be some way to take these losses of income off our taxes. There's no way to get the income back that we lose in bad weather. This storm is costing me at least $500. Where's that partner of yours?"

"His mother had an accident and he took the 182 back to Illinois early this morning. She was in surgery when he left. He should be there about now. I hope he didn't run into this storm."

"How's he working out? I understand you have a secretary and a mechanic now. You look better. Got some color finally. We were all concerned. You were working day and night." Carla smiled. Jerry had known Carla all her life. Many times she had stayed at Carla's school when Charley had to fly fire patrol.

"Thanks, Carla. You have all been wonderful. Charley sold the partnership at the fly-in. Cal is the son of an old friend of his. His father flew with Uncle Art and Charley for years. I've heard a lot of tales about them."

"I remember Charley and Art talking about them. They must have been quite the team. Stayed together until they all got married and had to settle down." Carla stopped as the memories of her own love of flying cost her. "My son came by last week. He joined the Air Force and is learning to fly fighters. His dad objected just as strongly as he objected to my flying. George could never understand anyone's passion to do something special. My daughter wants to be an artist and is fighting him. I told her I'd send her to college when her dad refused to let her study art. George called me and started on the same old theme that caused our divorce. I just told him she was my kid too and she had a right to reach for the rainbow if she felt she had to. He didn't understand a word. But she is going to study art. I won that by paying for her college myself. Poor guy. A good man. Just can't understand." Carla shook her head and sighed.

"I won't marry anyone who doesn't have a passion for flying. I don't know what I would do if I was permanently grounded. How's Jimmy taking it?"

"Right now he's just trying to get his health back. He was over here Sunday with his wife. She's a wonderful woman. Doesn't fly herself but supports him all the way. She's a strong shoulder for him to lean on. He is pretty devastated. I guess it's like the death of a loved one."

"Well, I'd better get back before I get wet. Supposed to be hail in this storm. See you around." Jerry left stopping at the candy counter to collect a few candy bars. The wind had picked up and clouds were coming in from the west.

Jerry found Maggie finishing up her filing. "Maggie, this is supposed to be a bad storm. You can leave if you want to. We can't fly till it's passed. The wind is picking up now."

"If it's all right with you, I'll stay. I would like to study some of the books if I may. I called Mom. I assured her it's fine here." They both stopped talking and looked at the door. A sound Jerry knew only too well came bursting in on the conversation. "What's a plane doing with this weather coming in?"

"He's got problems." Jerry stepped outside and looked at the active runway. "He's coming in too fast." The wind had shifted and was now a tailwind. The two women watched as the small aircraft struggled to keep on course to the runway.

"His engine has stopped!" cried Maggie staring in panic at the small plane. "He's losing control!"

The sky was getting dark from the storm that was nearly upon them. A gust of wind appeared to push the plane out of control and the sound of metal grating on the runway was followed by silence. The plane had crashed landed tipping one wing onto the concrete as it slid to a halt swinging half onto the grass.

"Come on, he may be hurt. Get the first aid kit. I'll grab the fire extinguisher," Jerry told Maggie as she ran to the car. Maggie grabbed the first aid kit from the classroom and followed her. Jerry sped down the taxiway to the runway and to the crash site. Maggie was out of the car and at the plane with Jerry on her heels. The pilot was slumped over the controls. As Maggie pulled open the door he moaned and looked up. Blood was running down his face. The young man looked at Maggie, her face pale and red curls whipping about her cheeks.

"Have I died and gone to Heaven?" he asked looking into her eyes.

"No. I'm glad you followed the emergency procedure and unlocked the door. That's gasoline I smell and if you don't get out of there we all may be in Heaven." Jerry reached over and unfastened the seatbelt and shoulder harness. Can you move all right?"

He nodded and painfully tried to get out of the seat. Maggie reached for one arm and Jerry the other. The pilot cried out with pain. They helped him to the ground as the sirens of the fire trucks and police summoned by the control tower announced that help had arrived. The police drove up to the crash and the officer stepped out of the patrol car. He took Jerry's place.

"Let's get him to my office. He'll need an ambulance, Jed. I'd best get the ignition turned off and his luggage." As she turned the fire truck arrived and a young woman leaped out.

"I'll do that Jerry." Jerry turned and smiled at Sue. Sue had been one of her best students and knew exactly what to do. She had followed her mother's footsteps and become a firefighter as well as a pilot.

"It's all yours, Sue. Bring the bags to my office. I'll take care of them until things are sorted out. He'll be at the office 'til the ambulance gets here." Sue nodded as she reached into the plane to shut off the engine and retrieved the keys. Jerry joined Maggie and Jed who had put the victim into the back seat and Maggie was holding a pressure bandage on his cut. The young man was smiling in wonder at Maggie who was sitting close to him. Jed turned and grinned at Jerry.

"I'll have to ask some questions. I'll meet you at your office." Jerry nodded and got into her car and headed back to the office silently smiling. The young man was nice looking and Maggie was taking very good care of his cut. The rain started to fall.

After Jed had placed the pilot on the sofa, Maggie had found a pillow and gently placed it under his head. She washed the blood from his face being very careful to not disturb the pressure bandage she had placed securely on the cut and tied in place. Jed and Jerry watched them quietly for a few minutes. Then Jed said he was going to have to disturb them and get some information. Jerry turned away to keep her smile from showing. Maggie was showing a bit more concern for a 'patient' than absolutely necessary. Sue had brought in his duffle bag and flight bag and left them. She told them the fire danger was over and a crew had moved the plane off the runway onto the grass. The runway was cleared and safe. Jerry thanked her and placed the bags in the classroom out of the way.

The pilot was Mike O'Hara, a theology student who was coming in to visit his family in Spring Texas. His engine had developed trouble and a tailwind hit him as he was trying to land. He lost control just before touching down. A wild gust of cross-wind had finished things and sent him onto the grass. He was lucky. He was dizzy and had a headache, a cut on his head and his right arm was painful. Maggie had placed his arm in a precautionary sling. He groaned when he thought of his hard earned, beautiful plane piled up on the grass. The ambulance arrived to take him to the hospital. Maggie handed him her phone number and name and he gave her his parent's phone number and promised to call her. Jed then said he needed them to answer some questions as witnesses.

Jerry pulled some cold drinks from the fridge and they told their stories. When Jed had gone, Jerry looked at Maggie. "I'm sure he'll be all right. You were superb."

"He's real nice. I hope his arm is all right. I don't think it's broken. I never thought my high school first aid class would be used at the airport. One never can tell. He wants to see me again when he's released from the hospital. Should I?"

"I'm afraid I'm not the right one to give that kind of advice. I don't seem to have much luck with new men." Jerry was thinking of Richard and the way he had been the first time and the way he had acted when he was here. Quite different! The phone was ringing and Maggie answered.

"It's for you. It's Cal." She handed the phone to Jerry.

"Hello, Cal. How is your Mother?" Somehow hearing his voice telling her everything was fine made Jerry feel better after the excitement of the crash. His mother would go home in a few days, and he wanted to stay and help get her settled into home care. Her leg would be in a cast for a while. "Stay as long as she needs you. Our families come first. I sent Arnie home. His wife is ready to have her baby any time, and with the storm I had to cancel classes. It's raining harder now. Art will come as soon as he can and help out."

"Are you saying I'm not needed?" Cal's voice was steady but defensive.

"You are needed. But you need to help your folks. If Charley was here he'd tell you the same thing." She could hear a sigh of relief. Was he afraid he was dispensable? "We are stuck with this storm and changed plans for today that's all. We had an emergency landing here about an hour ago. The pilot will be okay, but the plane is a mess. Give your Mother my best. I'll send some flowers to her home. I-" Jerry almost said "I need you" and was horrified at the slip. "Let us know when you're on the way back. Goodbye to you too."

Cal had caught the "I" and the hesitation. He had the feeling she had almost said that she missed him. He hoped as much as he missed her. Someday maybe it would be all right to say he loved her very much. For now, it was patience and struggling to keep it. He hung up the phone gently, wondering if that would ever be.

The storm hit with all its fury now. They could hear hail on the trailer, and Jerry cursed herself for not parking their cars in the hangar. Cal's station wagon would be caught as well as her's and Maggie's. She just didn't think about it. If Cal was angry, she deserved it. Maggie was in the classroom studying, and Jerry sipped a bottle of cola. She stared out at the storm. The rain was coming down making the windows look like they were under a waterfall. A gust of wind rocked the trailer and Maggie cried out. Jerry went in to her. She sat by her and started teaching her from the books to try to soothe both of their nerves. It was late afternoon before the storm passed. It was supposed to be fast moving. Once again Jerry was impressed by how the weather so often ignored the predictions.

"Maggie, I'm going to check on the cars. I'm almost afraid to look. That hail could do a lot of damage." She opened the door and stepped out into the hot humid air feeling as if she had stepped into a greenhouse. Maggie joined her. She shook her head sadly, and Maggie gave out a little moan. The hail had broken all of Jerry's windows and some of Maggie's. Cal had parked on the far side so his car was not hit so badly but still had most of the windows destroyed. The sides and top of Jerry's car were dented from the hail. Maggie's car had been partly saved by Jerry's but still had many dents. Cal's wagon got little bad damage on the sides but the roof was a mess. "It's my fault for not thinking to put them away." Jerry was mentally cursing herself. "I'm so sorry Maggie. I'll pay your deductible."

"It's not your fault. We were both kind of busy. He's real cute." Jerry looked at her puzzled then laughed. Maggie was still with her patient.

"We'd better see if they will start. I couldn't have put Cal's away anyhow. I don't have any keys." Jerry turned to go get her keys.

"Oh, are these them? They were on the desk. I didn't know whose they were. I guess he left them just in case." Maggie spoke guiltily as she looked at Jerry.

"Well, we'll just have to face his wrath." Then Jerry smiled. She couldn't picture Cal being angry under the circumstances. Why did she feel that? She shook her head confused. She seemed to have uncontrolled thoughts today.

Once they cleaned up, the glass the cars started with no

problems. By the time they cleared the parking place of bits of glass that might puncture a tire it was quite late. Jerry offered to buy Maggie dinner but Maggie said no. She had better get home. Later they learned that every car in the storm's path that was sitting outside had all the windows broken and the same damage they had suffered. Maggie left and Jerry was starting to lock up when the phone rang.

"Charley's Flying School, Jerry speaking."

"Uncle Art here. Everything okay there?"

"Our cars were battered. I forgot to put them in the hangar. Since the 182 is gone I think we could have gotten all three in. Haven't looked at the trailer yet. I'm afraid to. Cal is going to be mad when he sees his car. How about you?"

"The men are out now to assess the damage. Barn's okay. Your horse is fine, so is Jenny. Hobo tried to bolt but we caught her. She's sure sprightly for a horse her age. The house lost some shingles and the worker's cars got clobbered. We're still taking inventory. Heard from Cal?"

"Yes. His mother is doing well. He will be gone a few more days. Her leg was bad enough to need surgery. He's going to help his dad get her settled in and find some help before coming back. We'll have to cancel some classes, I guess. At least there will be no fire patrol but if pest control is called I'll have to get someone to fly it. Cal has the 182. Oh, we had an emergency landing just about the time the storm hit." She told him about the accident. "Maggie is still enchanted by the young man." She could hear Art laugh.

"I'll fly over as soon as I take care of matters here." Art hung up just as the door opened.

Jerry looked up and a young man followed by a child of about six entered. "How can I help you? We are closed."

"I'm Shaun O'Hara and this is Laurie my daughter who did not stay in the car as she was told. I'm Mike's brother. The police said Mike's luggage was here."

"Of course. It's in the other room. I'll get it. How's Mike?"

"Well, he insists he was saved by a red-haired angel and I have a message for her. All of our family thanks you for getting help so fast. He will have to keep his arm quiet for a while and he had some stitches on his head, but since it's hard he'll be fine."

Jerry returned with the duffle bag and flight bag laughing. "I'm afraid the angel has gone home. I'll be glad to relay any message. I'm Jerry Jackson. I'm half owner of this school. Maggie, the angel, is our secretary. She did a great job. In fact, a bit more than the first aid book says." Jerry grinned as she set down the bags. "She was quite impressed by Mike."

Shaun reached into his pocket and removed an envelope. "He could only remember 'Maggie' with red hair and a smile to make heaven itself look dull. You must have some secretary. That's all he talked about. He did say there was a blond and a policeman too."

"I must say the officer was almost embarrassed to interrupt them to get the police report filled out. I think they both forgot we were in the room. That's all the bags the firefighter brought over. Did you see his plane? Mike was very lucky."

"Just from the road. He really worked hard to get that plane. Do you think it will fly again?"

"I haven't looked at it. The FAA inspectors will be inquiring, and he has a million forms to fill out. If he needs any help, I will be glad to help. I'm afraid Maggie is too new to help, so he's stuck with me. And I don't have red hair." They both laughed. Shaun carried the luggage out to the car. Laurie hesitated.

"Lady, do you fly an airplane? I want to be an astronaut when I grow up."

"Yes, Laurie I do. I teach people how to fly. Good luck to you. Remember you will have to study hard and learn a lot of math and science to be an astronaut. Have your dad and mom call me and we can arrange to take you for a ride. Free. Just because we girls need to stick together." She held out her hand, and Laurie solemnly shook it. Then Laurie turned and ran to the car. Jerry smiled. She was like that once. But she had been lucky enough to be raised in an airplane.

Jerry found Cal's keys and opened the hangar and put his car away. Then she locked the school and headed for home. She was very tired and was concerned about damage to her house. When she arrived, the damage was less than she had feared. It was mostly small limbs from trees and shingles from the roof that were in her yard.

Upon inspection there did not seem to be any leaks upstairs. She would inspect the attic later. Now she had to call Ma Brown and see if she was all right, something Charley and she had always done. Ma assured her all was fine. The cars got some damage and the roof but not serious. Jerry told her about the emergency landing. She knew the boarders would have a great topic of gossip at dinner tonight. She was about to go upstairs to take a hot soaking bath, then have a sandwich when the doorbell rang.

Jerry answered the door and there stood Richard. Behind him were several men in the uniform of waiters carrying metal carriers for hot food. "I brought some dinner," he announced. "I thought you might like something special after the storm. And to apologize for my bad behavior today. May we come in?" Caught off guard, Jerry nodded them to come in.

"A phone call would have been enough. Why all this? I'm very tired, Richard." In spite of herself she showed the way to the kitchen. "Sorry, but the meal might be fancy but the dining room isn't." The waiters placed the food on the counter and proceeded to unpack the containers they had brought with them.

"Lobster, salad, baked potatoes, rolls and wine. I hope it pleases you." Richard managed to sound contrite. Jerry shook her head and laughed.

"The Blarney Stone again. I just got in from the airport. We had an accident and I'm afraid I'm not dressed for a formal dinner." She noticed for the first time that there was blood on her blouse, and she smelled of gasoline. "I really need to wash up."

"You're hurt!" Richard seemed genuinely alarmed.

"Not mine. The accident victim's. Sit down while I go wash up." She turned and went upstairs irritated at his presumptuousness and at the same time flattered. He was wrong if he thought she could be bought with dinner delivered in such style. But it did smell good and she had to admit Richard had flair.

She took a quick shower and deliberately pulled on jeans and a tee shirt. She did not feel like dressing for dinner no matter what it was or how it was served. When she returned the kitchen was empty, but the door to the dining room was open and the beautiful antique dining table that had been her grandmother's was set with a spotless white linen cloth. Her mother's silver candlesticks had fresh candles lit. The food had been served in the china that had been brought and the wine poured. It was beautiful. Richard in his stylish dinner jacket escorted Jerry in her tee shirt and jeans to the table. She could not help feeling like a queen as he assisted her into her seated. She smiled at him.

"It's beautiful, and I do admit better than the bologna sandwich I had planned. Thanks, Richard."

"Did the storm do much damage?" Richard asked taking a sip of wine. Before she could answer the phone rang. Jerry excused herself and went into the kitchen.

"Hello." The voice on the other end made her heart leap. It was Cal. "Cal. Is everything all right?"

"I just wanted to know how you weathered the storm. It sounded like a monster. Are you okay?"

"I'm okay but the cars outside got banged up. I'm sorry I forgot to put them inside. The windows are smashed and the cars dented. I told Maggie we would pay for her deductible. Art is checking out his damage. He's concerned for the livestock, but the house and barn and Jenny are all safe. Did it get you? It looked like it was a line all the way north"

"We got some rain but nothing much. I-" Cal hesitated a moment. "I miss you."

"I miss you too. You say it will be another week?"

"Actually, my aunt is on her way. She said she would stay so I could go back to work. She hates to see people idle. She's getting here Wednesday so I'll try to be in Thursday. I'll call." There was a silence between them that seemed to say what neither would admit. "Goodbye. I'm glad everyone is ok."

"Goodbye, Cal. We need you." Jerry hung up the phone.

Jerry returned to the dining room. "Sorry, Richard. That was my partner. His aunt is coming so he'll be back Thursday. He was concerned about things here."

"You mean the middle-aged partner who is balding and has a poochy tummy. He must have some very old relatives in great condition." Richard's eyes were sparkling with mischief.

Jerry laughed. "All right. He's six feet tall with brown hair and eyes. His father and mine flew together with Uncle Art for years until they all met the right girls and got married. If you're wondering, yes, he is nice looking and a very nice man. But that is all. Period. He is the best pilot I've ever flown with except Charley and Uncle Art."

"I didn't realize that you were so serious about flying. It IS your life isn't it?"

"I'm as serious about flying as you are about being a playboy and only living for fun. How boring it must get to have no reason to get up in the morning except more of the same. Flying and teaching people how to fly is never dull. You always know you will be waited on hand and foot. I have to take care of myself. I also have to get up at 6 a.m. Thank you for the lovely dinner. It is nice to be spoiled once in a while."

"You could be all the time if you wanted to be."

"You mean be your mistress? What happens to me if I get pregnant? Do you buy me off? No Richard. Marriage, love, a church wedding, the whole thing for me. Money doesn't mean that much. A good man to love me does." Jerry looked at Richard. His face had drained of color. He looked faint. "Richard? What is it? Are you ill?" Richard shook his head, clenched his jaws and took a deep breath.

"Does your dinner please you? More wine?" He spoke with forced control and a smile.

"I'm fine. It's all very good." They finished the meal in silence. Jerry got up and started to clear the dishes from the table.

"I'll do that Miss." A waiter came from the kitchen and took them from her.

"I'll wash them before you return them. I can't have it said I send dirty dishes back to where ever they came from." Jerry smiled and carried the wine glasses to the kitchen. She rinsed the dishes in spite of Richard's protests and then washed them. The waiter dried them smiling.

"You're just like my wife," said the waiter. "I can hear her say the same thing." Richard stood by helplessly looking at them.

"This was supposed to be a surprise," he said when the dishes were clean and the waiters were packing up.

"It was Richard. I just have my pride and a clean house is part of it. I was raised differently than you. That's all. Your pride is not to raise your finger to do any work to help yourself. Mine is not to have anyone do my work as long as I can raise a finger to do it. Total opposites. It's really late and it's been a long day and will be longer one tomorrow. I have to get to the airport, call the insurance for my car and find a rental while it's being fixed and somehow run the school alone. By the way do you know a Kevin Roberts? I believe he comes from one of the wealthy families."

"Kevin Roberts. No, but I can inquire. Why?"

"Well it's really none of my business, but he seems interested in Maggie and she's such an innocent. There's something so cold and ruthless about him. He's an excellent technical pilot, but doesn't like to fly. I'm concerned about her. That's all. She just nineteen."

"But you like her and don't want to see her hurt. I'll inquire and give you a call. I have enjoyed seeing you again. I hope the next time will be longer." Richard walked behind the hired men who carried the food containers and stopped at the door. "I won't kiss you. I don't want to be slapped again." Richard spoke with forced levity. He was pale and looked completely shaken.

"Richard come in and sit a while. You look like you have seen a ghost. Was it something I said? I'm sorry if I was too blunt." Richard went with her to the family room and sat down on the sofa. He was visibly shaken. "Do you want to talk about it?"

"I've wanted someone to talk about it with for eight years. My child would be seven if it lived or was adopted or whatever happened."

"Child!" Jerry realized that she had triggered some terrible pain when she had asked if he would buy her off if she got pregnant.

"I was seventeen, only a few days from my 18th birthday, and had just graduated from high school. Lilly was a junior just sixteen. We fell in love and planned to get married when she graduated. But she got pregnant. When my parents found out, against my protests, they shipped me to relatives in England to go to college and gave her father a check for $50,000 and sent her away. I was under age and so was she. I did not get my inheritance until I was twenty-five and did not know how to fight my parents. I wasn't much of a man I guess. I wrote to Lilly but she never answered. When I came home I went to her house, the whole area had been turned into a mall and I could find nothing about her folks. I did find a woman who said it was pitiful. Her folks kicked her out. It seems they took the money and threw her out with nowhere to go. I searched everywhere I could and I found nothing.

I had no money of my own to search until my birthday yesterday. I now have my inheritance. Forty million dollars. Jerry, I've never stopped loving her. How could my parents do this to their grandchild? When you spoke, I pictured her alone, hungry sick, my child hungry and me with millions. I have to find her if it's the last thing I do."

"But you have been such a playboy." Jerry was puzzled.

"It was all I knew to do to try to forget. But I never could. Then two years ago my brother, Dale had the same thing happen to him. I was on one of my wild trips and didn't know about it until it was too late. If only I had been at home. My parents made them an offer. Get married and lose everything or Sadie could have a $100,000. Dale said he would give his inheritance up, but Sadie took the money and disappeared. Dale went wild. He started racing sports cars and was killed three months later because he no longer cared to live. I want to find my brother's child too. Where do I start? I'm lost."

Jerry could hardly comprehend what she was hearing. His family had thrown away two grandchildren because the mothers were not of the right class? They had sacrificed the life of their youngest son in doing so and ruined the youth of the other. She shook her head. Richard was crying now, as if the burden he had carried for so many years had been lightened. She sat beside him and put her arm around his shoulders and held him like a child. He really loves the girl and wants the children. There was a very deep well of manhood in Richard that had been buried and she was seeing it now for the first time. Manhood that his parents did not know existed. They sat for a long time in silence while Richard struggled for control. Finally, he lifted his head.

"Where do I start?" He finally asked taking a deep breath.

"I would begin with a lawyer who specializes in finding lost people. Get a team of detectives to trace the two mothers if they can. You have all the money you need. Start asking about lawyers in that specialty. Homes for unwed mothers. Your detectives should know how to find those in her area eight years ago. If I can help any way I will. Let me know."

Richard stood up and pulled Jerry up before him. "If I had a sister, I would want her to be just like you, Jerry. I'll start tomorrow." He bent and kissed her on the cheek. She walked him to the door and bade him good luck. He was a different person from the playboy who had brought her dinner to her. She respected him for the first time as a person of substance not just a fun boy. She was surprised that a tear fell from her eye unbidden.

"Good-by. I'll call you." Richard walked to the waiting limousine. The waiting chauffeur opened the door for him and they were soon gone. Jerry shut the door. She locked the deadbolt shaking her head.

She went to the dining room to replace the handmade runner only to find it carefully in place with fresh candles in the silver candlesticks. She smiled. They looked lovely on each side of the silver bowl of silk flowers. Jerry started to close the dining room door and stopped. It had been closed since Charley died. Maybe it was time to leave it open again.

Charley's Flying School

Rosa B. Lane

Chapter 6

Jerry was up at six the next morning. Monday was a "day off" she would never forget. She hoped Tuesday would be better. It was seven thirty by the time Jerry got to the office. Maggie had the day off and Arnie called to say his wife had presented him with another girl. Three boys and four girls. He would be in on Wednesday if it was all right. Jerry told him yes. They had named the girl Francis for his grandmother. Jerry couldn't help wondering about the children that Richard was setting out to find.

Jerry felt tired by eight and she had a student and Rev. Mitchell coming. She sighed and pulled open the hangar and pulled the aerobatic plane out and got it ready for the Reverend. Then she pulled a 150 out and prepared for her first student. Rev. Mitchell showed up at eight-thirty and was off to deliver the supplies and medicine to his remote church. Then he would give the children a ride. They had so little to look forward to in their poverty-stricken lives. He is a saint, thought Jerry.

Her student came and they were off. Today he would slow fly. She wanted him to learn s-turns if the wind was right. He was Jefferson Green, a man of about forty, who finally decided to make a little boy's dream come true in spite of his wife's objections. And he was very good, but some reaction time needed work. Last time the wind had been very strong. Jerry had shown him that one could slow-fly the airplane into the wind as slowly as possible just above stalling and if the wind was strong enough could be pushed backward. This never failed to bring awe to the student. He remembered the slow flying exercise. The lesson went well. She let him land the plane by himself today and he was elated. They taxied back to the ramp.

Abby came in just as Mr. Green was leaving. As always, Abby was bubbling with enthusiasm. That night Abby wrote in her diary:

"I forgot to do some of the check list today -oil pressure, mobility of controls and almost turned on the radio before I started the plane. Jerry said to do that might mess up the radios. I had a hard time turning until Jerry finally got me to stop trying to force the plane to turn by turning my body. I tried to relax and as if by magic the plane turned gently and I felt as if I was a part of the plane. It was fantastic. Speaking of fantastic, I wonder how long it's going to be before Jerry realizes how much she misses Cal. The look in her eyes when she speaks of him is -well- adoration or maybe even love. Only she doesn't know it."

Since Tuesday was Cal's day off the student load was light. Abby had done well. Jerry had no more students until 2:00. After lunch she came back to try to locate her insurance agent. He had recommended a body shop and she made an appointment for an estimate. For the first time in her life she felt she would like to go home and take a nap instead of flying. Then her student came in all smiles and eager. The flying lessons were a birthday present from her parents for her eighteenth birthday. The fatigue lifted and Jerry was in the air again and vitally alive.

The rest of the afternoon was spent on getting her car settled in the body shop and obtaining a rental. By the time Jerry arrived home she had little appetite for the chicken dinner she had bought on the way home. She had just gotten out of the tub when the phone rang. Quickly wrapping a bath towel about her, she picked up the phone by her bed. It was Estelle. Jerry started to ask her to call back but something in her voice sounded so urgent she could not.

"Estelle. Is something wrong?"

"Jerry, I need some place to stay where Mother can't find me. I've left home. You're the only one I could think of. I'm on my way to my uncle's in Australia but he's out of town and they can't reach him. He'll be gone for two weeks. Mother will find me in town. I'm scared, Jerry. She's trying to make me marry a man I detest. Help me."

Jerry felt like she was listening to a soap opera. "Estelle. Listen. You are of legal age and have your own money. There's nothing your mother can do to make you marry someone you don't want to."

"That's just it. I won't have anything but an allowance from my trust until I'm twenty-one. I have been saving some of my allowance and I have enough to get to my uncle's but it won't last long in hotels. I've had it with all the fake social snobbery. I want something better. Something like you have. When I don't show up at the Keys to dive, they'll call to see why. You gave me courage to do this. Please help me now."

"You can stay here tonight, and we'll find somewhere for you tomorrow. Let me give you directions." Jerry directed Estelle to her house then finished getting her pajamas and robe on. She tucked her feet into slippers and went downstairs and waited for Estelle. It was nearly an hour before her red convertible pulled into the drive. Jerry switched on the porch lights and went to meet Estelle.

"How can I ever thank you?" Estelle asked as she got out of her car.

"You'd better put the top up. I have no space in the garage for your car. Let me help you with your bags." She helped Estelle carry several bags into the house. "I'll have to put sheets on the guest bed. I had just got out of the tub when you called. Come on in and sit down and tell me about it." Jerry switched off the porch light and guided Estelle into the living room.

Estelle looked around the room surprised. "It's so friendly," she said softly. "Is that your father? He is very handsome. Mine died three years ago. Heart attack. The doctor had told him to quit smoking, but he just laughed. He thought that a lot of nonsense. He chose to smoke and he died. I wonder if it was worth his life. Sorry. I just never really knew him." Her voice was sad. She took the seat offered by Jerry.

"Would you like something cool to drink? Water or soda?" Estelle shook her head. "Tell me what's going on. I'll help if I can."

"I never really thought of how others live. My home- Mother's house - is cold and sterile without feeling. This room is so full of -

love and warmth. It's a happy room. You are lucky. Jerry. Sorry. I left word with the housekeeper that I was going on the dive trip and loaded up my stuff and told her what flight I was on. Then I took off. I headed for Houston. I got a hotel room and tried to get Uncle Andy. They told me he was gone on a tour of the stations and it would be a while before they could get him. They're leaving word at all the places he's going to visit to call me. I gave him your number and the airport number I hope that's okay. I asked them not to call Mother.

"Uncle Andy and I have always been close. He's considered the black sheep of the family because he built a clinic with his own funds and a little from donations and the government. He makes very little money but he has as much as Mother has and doesn't need it. So he's not liked in the family; he does honorable work as a doctor of the poor. I've always wanted to visit him but wasn't allowed to. Now I'm on my way as soon as I can contact him."

"Why are you afraid of your Mother?" Jerry looked at her puzzled at the fear on the young girl's face. Tonight she was wearing no make-up and the natural beauty of her youth showed.

"I ran away last year and she had special officers haul me back. I told them I was legally of age but they virtually kidnaped me and took me back by force. This time I won't go. She has high officials who owe her favors. When she was young she gave them some. My father was a womanizer, so I'm the black sheep. I'm not going to be pushed into that sick life. When you came to the dinner, I saw what kind of woman I want to be. Free of social expectations and to be me. I'm not doing this very well. But you stood up to them in defense of your work and your way of life. I felt ashamed of mine. Is there any place you know of nearby where I could rent an apartment for a while?"

"I'm a little confused. But I don't know of any apartments of the luxury you're used to but I know a special place quiet and peaceful if you like ranches. I'll call Uncle Art and see if he can help. You probably will be put to work helping with the chores, but it won't cost you a cent. How does that sound?"

"It sounds nice. But won't they know he's your uncle?" Estelle looked worried, and she bit her full lips in distress.

"We're not related just close family friends. He and my father along with Cal's father flew together for years. We've always been very close." Jerry smiled and patted Estelle's hand. "Don't worry. He'll keep you safe."

"Where is Richard? He said something strange to me a few days ago. He said he'd soon have the money to find his dream. I don't understand."

"His dream is to find the girl his family separated him from when he was seventeen. He loved her and wanted to marry her but she was from the wrong side of the tracks. They sent him to England to school and she disappeared. She was sixteen, pregnant and alone. He's looking for her now that he has his own money. He wants to find his brother Dale's child if it was ever born. They did the same to Dale. That's why his brother went into wild racing and died. I don't know where he is. I wish him luck. He has become a real man. I'm proud of him."

Estelle stared at Jerry. Then she smiled. "He did it! We were always friends. He often said he wanted to find her. And now he finally has started hunting for her. He was wild because he was hurting so much. I knew that. I knew he had real substance inside him. I do wish him luck."

"We'd better get your bed ready. Get your overnight bag and let's go to bed."

With the tinkling of the music box alarm clock Jerry awakened. At six a.m. the sun was bright and promising to be another hot humid day. Jerry yawned and got out of bed. Wednesday, she thought. It seemed as if this week was playing out in slow motion and months of action had happened since she got up on Monday to Cal's phone call telling of his mother's accident. She got dressed and went down the hall to awaken Estelle. The bed was empty.

"Estelle. We've got to hurry."

"Downstairs," came back the answer. "Sleepy head. I have hot water for coffee and the toast is ready."

Jerry hurried down the stairs and into the kitchen. Estelle stood grinning proudly at the breakfast table set and ready. "Wow! I'm not used to such service. Thank you." Estelle poured the hot water for the instant coffee and served several slices of toast to Jerry.

"I found one jar of jam but no cereal. There's a little milk. Don't you eat at home?"

"Not much since there's only me. It's handy to eat at the airport and I'm usually too tired to cook. Have you had anything?"

"Some toast and coffee. I never eat breakfast at home for I'm rarely up before ten. My bags are in the car. I'm ready when you are." Estelle was beaming with the pride of her efficiency.

"We'll call Uncle Art from the airport. I haven't given Maggie a key yet, and she's coming in this morning." Jerry spread a slice of toast with the last of the strawberry jam and stirred instant coffee into the hot water Estelle poured for her. "I have an early student today. Some of the others had to cancel because of the storm damage to their cars or homes. So it should be a lazy day, but tonight I have to teach the ground school class. So it will be a long day anyway. I'll just brush my teeth and we'll be off."

Estelle followed Jerry to the airport. She had never been to a small airport before. If spite of the early hour there was a lot of activity. They parked at the trailer, and Jerry smiled. Arnie was already at work. After unlocking the trailer and flipping on the air-conditioning Jerry called Art.

"Hello, Jerry." It never ceased to amaze her how Art always knew it was her.

"Good morning, Uncle Art. I need you to do a favor for a friend of mine if you can. She needs a place to stay for a week or two out of sight. She is nineteen and has run away from home. She is on her way to Australia but can't get in touch with her uncle. There's nothing illegal. She just doesn't want to marry the man her mother wants her to. Will you be able to help her?" Art was laughing. Jerry could almost see him shaking his head the way he did when amused.

"Jerry, since when have you started a school for the lovelorn? First, it's Maggie; now another girl. Tell her she is welcome but will have to take care of herself. No service here. Flora has enough to do without extra work."

"Thanks, I knew you would help. Her name is Estelle and she's driving a red convertible." Jerry listened then said, "That is great. I'll tell her. I'll give her instructions." Jerry hung up the phone. "Do you have a map?"

Estelle nodded, "In the car. I'll get it." When she brought it back Jerry took a high-lighter and marked the way.

"Uncle Art will meet you at the fork in the road. It's kind of confusing. He'll have an old blue pickup. If he can't come, then one of his men will be there. There's a service station and restaurant at the fork. Joe's Station it's called. He is about a hundred miles west of here. So get your tank filled before you leave. Oh, let me get you some water. It's going to be hot today." Jerry got a bottle of water from the fridge and handed it to Estelle. "They'll find some place to put your car. Keep your top up and whatever you do don't break any speed limits. They now have a helicopter watching. I know. The hard way. You don't want your picture in the local newspapers." Jerry laughed and bid Estelle goodbye telling her to call if she got lost. Somehow Jerry couldn't feature Estelle getting lost. "Call me when you get there."

Maggie showed up at the same time as Jerry's first student. He was Matthew Henderson, a martial arts instructor. Jerry had the plane ready to go and they were off. Maggie liked Matt. He reminded her of her older brother. Jerry said he was ready for his flight test. This was just practice to iron out a couple of wrinkles. Maggie put a pot of coffee on, checked the soda to be sure there was enough for tonight's class and settled down to catch up on the paper work. It always seemed to grow into a mountain when she was gone a day. It was quiet and pleasant working here. The drone of a plane landing or taking off, but no one disturbed her work. She thought of the office she had worked in after school that was so noisy that it was hard to concentrate. And she wondered about Mike. He was supposed to call her tonight.

She heard the training plane returning to the ramp at the same time the door opened door opened and a man entered. "May I help you?"

"I'm looking for Estelle Parker. I'm a private investigator." He was a big man and looked like a bully to Maggie.

"I'm sorry but there is no one here by that name." Maggie

looked up at him. "You might try one of the other FBO's." At his puzzled looked she added, "Fixed base operators. We have no student here by that name."

The man glared at her and said in a rough voice, "Look girlie, I'll have no-"

"Is there a problem?" Jerry entered with Matt behind her. "Take care of Matt's bill. I'll handle this, Maggie." She turned to the man and asked, "What can I do for you?"

"Where's the owner of this dump? I don't want to talk to a bunch of women." The man wiped his florid forehead with a white handkerchief.

"I'm the owner of this 'dump' so you're stuck with a bunch of women. If that displeases you, please leave." Jerry glared at him.

"Why you little-" He took a threatening step toward Jerry. Matt stopped writing his check and straightened up.

Out in the hangar Arnie looked at the large wrench he was trying to use. It was hopeless. He would have to see Jerry about a replacement. He took the tool and walked to the office. As he opened the door he saw the angry threatening look on the man's face, Jerry's angry look and Matt turning to the stranger. "Do you have a problem, Miss Jerry?" he said shifting the wrench to his right hand.

At the same time Matt stepped close to Jerry and asked, "Is there a problem, Jerry?" Matt towered over the stranger.

"I didn't get your name, Mr.? This is a student. He teaches martial arts. And this is my mechanic, and if you want to tell me what this is all about like a gentleman, okay. If not then please leave. We have work to do."

The investigator looked at Arnie with the huge wrench in his hand and up at the towering six-foot three Matt and turned to leave. "I'll be back. I want Estelle Parker."

"I wouldn't come back if I were you. There's no one here by that name." The man stormed out the door. "Thanks, Matt. You came in just in time, Arnie." They stood and watched him leave. Jerry signed off Matt's log book then reached for the phone. Matt finished his check and Arnie closed the door.

"Thanks, both of you. I have a call to make. I'll be with you in a minute, Arnie. Good luck with your flight test, Matt. You were perfect today."

Jerry dialed Uncle Art's number. Matt nodded goodbye and left. When she got Art on the phone she related the incident. Art said he'd find a perfect hide out for her and laughed. Jerry wondered what he was up to now. She turned to Arnie.

"Miss Jerry this old wrench just doesn't work anymore and I need it to finish the job. Is there one I can borrow from someone today? The order won't be here "til next week-hopefully then."

"When will you stop calling me 'Miss'? It's Jerry. I'll call Carla and see if she has one." She dialed Carla's number and explained the situation. "She said to come on over." Jerry walked over to the coffee pot as Arnie left for Carla's office on the other side of the airport. She fixed a cup and sat down. "Maggie, things used to be so simple when Charley was here." Maggie laughed.

The rest of day was quiet. Two students had cancelled due to the storm damage on their cars or home that had to be taken care of. Jerry went into the classroom to prepare for the ground school class at seven. She didn't know where Cal had left off so she would let the students ask questions for review. They were almost ready for their written exams. She was laying out her notes when Maggie called her to the phone.

Estelle had arrived safely and was being sent to a secret hideout. When Art told her where Estelle was being taken Jerry almost choked. The local convent. Uncle Art had been of great help to the Church even though he was not Catholic. They, like everyone who knew him, loved him. So they were delighted to help him with his problem, especially since it was to stop an unholy marriage. Her car would be put in a barn and covered with tarp and hay.

Estelle had almost forgotten she was Catholic. When she arrived at the convent she told them the complete story and asked if she could go to confession soon. She had a long talk with the Reverend Mother. She told her of her life and how she hated it. She did not want to marry a man thirty years older than she was whom she detested. Her mother had already started to make wedding plans. So Estelle ran away. She was waiting for word from her uncle in

Australia. She wanted to help him in his work with the poor. She hoped to study nursing and flying. Estelle thanked her for the refuge. She would do any work she could while she was there. The Reverend Mother was impressed. She made her welcome and had her escorted to a room. Estelle was given instructions as to meals and prayers. Her bags were stored for her and she was given a uniform. When she was alone she changed into the robes. Even her mother would not know her in the nun's robes. She felt safe and at peace.

Charley's Flying School

Rosa B. Lane

Chapter 7

Jerry took time out for lunch. She had expected to bring back a sandwich but could not resist the Wednesday special of chicken and dumplings. She was sipping at her milk when Carla arrived. "Thanks for the loaner. We have a bunch of things ordered and with luck they'll be here next week."

"No problem. Who's this detective looking for? He's a nasty one. If I knew I'd never tell him."

"He's looking for a girl I met who is escaping an unwanted marriage. She's nineteen but her mother is a tyrant. She's done this before and been kidnapped and returned home." Jerry told her of the incident at the office and how Arnie had just happened to walk in with the huge wrench in his hand and her student had been a six-foot three martial arts instructor. "You should have seen the look on his face when Arnie walked in and Matt walked over by me and glared down at him." They laughed. "But I'll be glad when Cal gets back. I think this man is trouble and a bully. Things like this never happened when Charley was here. I miss him so."

Carla reached across the table and patted Jerry's hand. "We all do. I don't think anyone would get tough with Charley." They both laughed. Charley had been a boxer in college. He was not as tall as Matt but was built like the athlete he always was. Carla's order came and they ate in silence, remembering.

The day proceeded quietly in spite of the wild beginning. It was close to five when Jerry heard a familiar sound. She went to the door and the 182 was taxiing to the ramp. Cal was back early! She went out to meet him. Arnie had gone to return the wrench, and Maggie was preparing to leave. Jerry felt a deep relief. Then Maggie called to her that she was wanted on the phone.

"Jerry speaking," she answered. Cal came in and started for the water. Jerry hit the speaker and the voice was loud and angry. "Mrs. Lambert, would you repeat that? The connection is not too good."

"Where is Richard?" Her voice was loud and full of venom.

"I don't know." Jerry answered. Cal walked over and stood beside her listening to the threatening tone of Mrs. Lambert's voice.

"How much do you want to stop seeing him?"

"Let's see. You got rid of Dale's child with a hundred thousand dollars and Richard's with fifty thousand. How much am I worth?" Cal started to speak. Jerry shook her head. He put his arm around her waist and she smiled up at his support.

"I'll give you a hundred thousand. But you leave town."

"Sorry. I have a business, and I am not for sale. The only way I'll stop seeing Richard is if he tells me himself."

"Listen you little whore. I'll destroy that flying school of yours and you'll never fly again." Cal's arm tightened and his jaws clenched angrily.

"Who are you calling a whore?" Cal asked in voice so controlled that it startled Jerry. The control itself was a threat.

"Who are you?" Mrs. Lambert's voice was surprised

"I'm Jerry's partner and own half of this school. I think you should apologize for what you said. I think you might have a little problem destroying our school. Jerry's not alone."

"No and I'm not a scared sixteen-year-old and I don't want your money. So I think you should do what my partner says and apologize for such bad language. Do you respect your son so little that you think that he shacks up with every woman he meets? Or are you judging him by your own actions? You might as well have killed Dale when you bought off the woman he loved and who was carrying his child. That was why he went wild and raced cars so insanely. You have only one son left. Are you going to destroy all your heirs?" There was silence.

"How dare you talk to me like that! That's family business." Her voice had become shaky with anger.

"You mean she shouldn't tell the truth. It seems you've made it our business with your threats." Cal's voice was not quite so controlled. "You listen to me. Don't you ever talk to Jerry like that again. And if you ever call her or harass her, I'll personally put you behind bars. Do you understand?" Jerry hung up the phone.

"Thanks, Cal. I'm not pregnant. There's never been an affair in my life. We are only friends. Richard said he would like a sister like me. He has gone to find his child and the woman he has loved since he was seventeen. He's also going to try to find his brother's child if it was ever born. He's a fine man." She turned toward Cal. His arm was still around her waist. "Welcome home. How's your mother?" she said and looked up at him. "Hold me, Cal. I'm so tired. Hold me." He gathered her in his arms and hugged her. A warmth swept through him like a gentle breeze. How much he had wanted this since he arrived here for her to come into his arms of her own need. How much he wanted to kiss her but somehow, he felt it was not the right time. "I missed you."

"Mother's fine. I missed you, too. It seems I leave town for three days and the sky falls. Why don't we put the 182 away and grab some dinner before the class.?"

"Oh. We'll have to move your car. I'm so sorry I didn't get it put away. I'll get your keys." Jerry went around the desk and removed the keys from the locked drawer. They walked to the hangar. Arnie had returned and was cleaning up.

"Hi, Cal. Welcome back." he said cheerfully.

"Now you don't call Cal 'Mr.' so why me 'Miss'?" Jerry teased.

"Better drop the 'Miss' or she will nag you to death. You know women."

"Indeed, I do. I have a house full. All right I'll try. Jerry."

Cal backed his station wagon out of the hangar and parked it by Jerry's rental. He shook his head. "You really got clobbered here," he said when he returned and helped Arnie tow the plane into the hangar. "How did you make out, Arnie?"

"My old truck was already so battered it couldn't tell the difference."

"Arnie was busy becoming a father. Will you lock up the hangar Arnie? We're going for dinner before class."

"Yes, Jerry," Arnie said grinning. What a nice girl, he thought. No wonder Cal is in love with her. When is she going to see that she loves him too?

When Jerry got home, she fell into bed exhausted. Even a shower did not make her feel better. She set the alarm and tried to get to sleep. She wondered where Richard was and if he had found any clues to what happened to Lilly. She wondered how Estelle was making out in a convent. Somehow Jerry felt Estelle would be right at home anywhere. She was so glad Cal was back. It had felt so good to have him hold her, to know he was there for her. She fell asleep feeling his arms around her. She no longer felt he was stealing her school, but somewhere deep inside she felt he was stealing her heart.

The routine was getting back to normal. The students were doing well, and Cal said the next class of ground school would start in a week. This group was ready to face the written exam. Maggie was delighted, and when Cal took her up for her first lesson, she came back elated. Jerry felt comfortable again. By the end of the week her car was back and so was Cal's. Maggie had hers repaired, and Jerry reimbursed her for the deductible.

Sunday night Jerry did not set the alarm. She had decided for once in her life to sleep all day Monday. At seven the phone rang. There was a call from Australia person to person for Estelle. Jerry blinked awake. "She isn't here. This is Jerry Jackson, her friend. She said her Uncle Andy would call. I can get a message to her but I don't have her number." The voice on the other end told the operator he would talk to Jerry.

"So, you know Estelle well enough to know who Uncle Andy is. How is she and what was so important that messages have been left over half of Australia for me to call?" Jerry explained. "Tell her to hang on. I'm coming to get her as fast as I can. I have a few things to do but I'll be there as fast as possible. I won't let my sister ruin Estelle's life."

"Thank you. I'll get word to her right away. I'm looking forward to meeting you. Goodbye."

Jerry decided it was no use to go back to bed so she dressed and went downstairs to fix some coffee. While she sipped her coffee, she dialed Art.

"Hello, Jerry," Said Uncle Art cheerfully. "Why so early on your day off?" Jerry explained to him that Estelle's uncle was coming to get her. "I'll get word to her as quickly as I can. She must have some kind of uncle to come all the way from Australia to take her home. I guess I'd best stick around here until Estelle is safely delivered to her uncle. How's Cal's mother?"

"She's doing fine. Her sister came and took control. She sent Cal back yesterday." Jerry caught Art up on the events with Mrs. Lambert and the detective. "Uncle Art, I need a vacation at the ranch."

"Come on out. You know the routine."

"I also know I need to do laundry and clean house. It's a mess here. Thanks for helping us."

"That's what friends are for. Come when you can. Goodbye."

Jerry popped some bread into the toaster and set out the jam and butter. Her bare cupboard had forced her to take time to stop for groceries. Then she went out and brought in the morning paper. She opened the front page and stood there horrified. A picture of an aerobatic plane was nose down in a field. The headline read: "Pilot killed while trying to do aerobatics." Kevin's picture was inserted beside the photo of the plane. Jerry sat down shaking. Could she have done anything to prevent this? Mentally she knew she had told him not to do it, and had warned him of the danger. She had refused to rent him her Aerobat. The FAA had passed him as a private pilot to fly single engine planes. No one could keep people from doing things out of arrogance. What a shame. So many people die needlessly. Jerry could not eat the toast. She just sat for a while, then drove to the airport taking the paper with her.

Maggie had seen the story at home. She was pale and tearful. Cal came in and looked surprised at finding Jerry in the office. Then he saw the paper. "Maggie told me. You tried, Jerry. That's all anyone can do. I'm free until ten. Let me take you to breakfast. I know you haven't eaten. Please."

"I'll be all right. You're right. I didn't have breakfast. Thanks." They left together and Maggie smiled. She had liked Kevin at first then found him to be just the way Jerry had said, cold and unfeeling. Maybe there was a suicide desire inside him to do a darn fool thing like that. She folded the paper, placed it out of her way and went to work checking the day's schedule.

Kevin's death was the talk of the restaurant. Everyone there knew someone with the attitude that no one could tell them what to do. Some of them had paid the penalty; some had made others pay with them. Then the talk gradually returned to the weather. It was hurricane season and none had hit the coast. When they did, all too often they affected them by bringing in days of bad weather. Cal was beginning to know the other pilots and chatted easily with them. Everyone liked him. Especially one waitress, a twenty-year-old brunette looking for a husband. She finally gave up when she noticed the way he looked at Jerry. Back to the drawing board, she thought.

When they returned to the office, Maggie was talking with Mike whose arm was now out of its sling. They were chatting about the cost of fixing his plane and his battle with the insurance company. The phone was ringing and Maggie picked it up motioning to Jerry it was for her. Mike said goodbye and left looking pleased with Maggie's promise for a date that evening.

"Jerry here," she answered. "Richard! How are you coming along?" She listened, then added, "I'm sorry. And Lilly?"

"I'm heading for St. Louis. They have traced a cousin who lives there. I'll call when I learn more, little sister."

"Thank you, big brother. God' speed." She looked at Cal and Maggie. "Richard's brother's child was aborted and the mother disappeared. Richard is going to St. Louis to check out a cousin of Lilly's. He says he'll spend his whole inheritance to find her if need be. Oh, he said he'd like a sister like me and I said I would have liked a big brother like him." She was looking at the paper again and did not see the look of relief on Cal's face. Maggie saw it and smiled as she shuffled papers. "He just inherited forty million dollars. He got it on his twenty-fifth birthday. For the first time he has enough money to hunt for her. His parents let him charge anything but gave him little cash. I think they knew he would look for Lilly. I hope he finds her and his child well even if she is married to someone else. Somehow, I think she's waiting for him to come for her."

Cal smiled shaking her head. "Why Jerry, you are a romantic. Things don't happen like that in real life."

"No. He was going to raise his brother's child, but there is none. That's real life. I can't imagine Charley not helping me if I had needed help when I was just sixteen. Lilly's family took the $50,000 and kicked her out. Alone, sixteen, broke and pregnant."

"My dad might have shot the man, but Mom and Dad would have been by me all the way. Most kids' parents would. I know a few who have been wonderful and are helping to raise their grandchild while the mother goes to college." Maggie sighed. "You have a student at ten, Cal." Cal looked at his watch whistled and headed out to the hangar to prepare the plane.

"I guess I'd best head for home. I need to get some milk. Have fun tonight. I like Mike."

After Jerry put away the groceries, she started laundry and cleaning. This was work she was not suited for but necessary. She hesitated outside Charley's bedroom and turned away. She still could not clean in his room. Somehow she just could not go back into the room. She did not understand it but it was as if a barrier stopped her at the door. Only when she had to get the papers from his flight bag had she gone in there. She turned the vacuum and headed down the hall.

By the end of the day she decided to read a while. A luxury she had been denied for too long. She took a shower and dressed for bed then settled down in the family room with a murder mystery. Tomorrow would be a long day with both Cal and Maggie gone. Maggie worked six days so she could get her flying in more quickly. Arnie took the weekend with his family.

Rosa B. Lane

Chapter 8

For the next week there were no surprises. All was well at the farm and convent, no call from Richard. Maggie showed up a little sleepy one morning. Mike showed up later to see if there was a plane available to rent for an hour. Cal and Jerry exchanged looks.

Cal said, "Maggie, I believe the Aerobat is available. Perhaps Mike would like that. Things are slow today. Why don't you go with him?"

Both young people looked surprised and happy. Maggie looked at Mike. "If it's okay with Mike."

"I'd love that. Will you, Maggie? You can show me where to fly to see the area." That settled, Cal, Maggie and Mike went out to prepare the plane.

When Cal returned, Jerry looked at him and asked, "Who's a romantic?"

"They're nice kids. Now what's up for today?" The question was answered when the door opened and a medium sized man with a moustache turning from brown to grey to match his hair entered.

"I'm looking for Jerry Jackson. She's my niece's mate."

"You're Uncle Andy!" Jerry greeted him. "I'm Jerry and this is my partner, Calvin Morris. I'm so pleased to meet you. Come in, please."

"Where is my niece? And how do I get there?" Jerry told him. "A convent? She's not a nun!"

"No. Uncle Art is a great help to the Church and they are

giving her refuge as a favor to him. I don't have the number, but I'll call Uncle Art. As for getting there I don't know, but you can drive about a hundred miles to Uncle Art's ranch or one of us can hop you over in a plane. He has a runway. I'll phone Uncle Art now."

Flora answered the phone. She called for Art, and he answered. "What makes my favorite girl call me away from my work?"

"We have a visitor here from Australia to fetch Estelle. Her uncle is here. Can you tell her?"

"She's been very anxious to see him. Is he driving?"

"He just got here. I'll put him on." She handed the phone to Estelle's uncle. "Meet Arthur Swenson, Uncle Art meet Andrew Harrison." It was agreed that Jerry would fly Andrew over to Art's ranch. It was a short hop for a plane. From there they could clean up the convertible for Estelle and Andrew to return. Art would notify Estelle to get ready to leave. Jerry and Cal prepared one of the 150s. Andrew had taken a taxi and had left his bags at his hotel. Cal would hold down the fort for a couple of hours. In a few minutes Jerry was off and Estelle's hiding would soon be over.

It was a CAVU day and soon Jerry was lining up with Art's sod runway for a landing. A light crosswind was blowing in from the south, and Jerry automatically put a slight pressure on the left rudder and on the right elevator to slip easily and straight onto the sod strip. She was intent on her flying and did not see the admiration in the eyes of Andrew. She taxied to the ramp where Art was waiting.

"Jerry, my sweetheart." As always, the proficient pilot a few minutes before, Jerry ran to him like a little girl. Andrew watched with laughter. Jerry introduced the men.

"Can't stay, Uncle Art. Cal's alone. We let Maggie go flying with her boyfriend. I hope you find time to come by on the way back. I want to thank you for helping my friend. She's a great kid who wants to be a great woman. I gather the man her mother is planning to marry her to has kids almost her age. Just to combine two great fortunes she would sacrifice her daughter. I don't understand these people. Sorry, I know she's your sister."

"I don't understand them either. That's why I'm the black

sheep. Couldn't take that kind of life. So, when I got my inheritance I packed up and left for the outback and never looked back. I'm not welcome at my sister's house."

"I've got to go." Jerry got into the plane and was off once more with the two men watching and admiring. When she disappeared in the distance Art turned to Andrew.

"Estelle is waiting. I have my men cleaning up her car. It's been stored under hay. My van is ready."

"How did Estelle meet such great friends as you? I know my sister. She keeps her away from real people."

"Jerry dated a lad called Richard Lambert and met Estelle at a dinner dance. They computed as the kids say today." The men got into the van and headed for the convent. "It's about forty- five-minute drive. The convertible will be ready when we get back."

When they arrived, Estelle was waiting. Like Jerry, Estelle ran with open arms to her Uncle Andy. He hugged her and assured her she was safe now and her mother could not touch her. While her bags were put into the wagon, Andrew asked to see whoever was in charge. He disappeared and returned in a few minutes with a smiling nun. She was holding his enormous thank you donation check in her hand.

Art had Flora prepare a special rancher's lunch for them. Estelle hugged Art, goodbyes were said and they were off. Estelle was finally on the way to freedom. She remembered Jerry's warning and in spite of her desire to floor the gas, drove strictly within the speed limit and kept the convertible top up. On the way it was decided that the car would be left in Houston with a company that would deliver it to Estelle's mother after they left for Australia. With giving back the car she would cut the final cord with her mother. Estelle wanted to stop by the airport and tell Jerry goodbye.

Jerry taxied to the hangar shortly after Mike and Maggie had returned. Jerry parked her 150 at the ramp and tied it down. She entered the office and found Maggie beaming.

"He's wonderful! He flies so -beautifully."

Jerry looked at the stars in Maggie's eyes and smiled. "I'm sure he is. Is there anything this afternoon? I had one student who had to go fight with the insurance company to get a new roof after the severe hail damage. I'm still waiting to get repairs I scheduled."

"Cal has the other 150 up now and there was a call for you from the Lambert's lawyer but he'll call back."

"Unless Cal is here too, I'm unavailable. If he gives any guff, hang up. You don't take that kind of talk." Maggie nodded with a grin. She would like to hang up on one of those stuffed shirts.

"A Mrs. Parker called. She left a number." Jerry looked at it and decided not to call until Estelle and her Uncle Andy had time to get here. At least she hoped they would stop by. "You have a student at four. He said he just wants to rent a plane to practice. A David Constock." Jerry nodded. His flight test was tomorrow. He had nothing to fear but, like everyone, he was scared. "That's all. Cal had a cancellation. The student broke her ankle and will not be flying for a while. A Nancy Parish."

"That's a shame. I believe she was doing very well indeed. What happened?"

"She was skiing at one of those resort manmade snow slopes. Just learning how. She was not happy. - Abby called. She wanted to be sure everyone was here. She is coming over in an hour and a half. Actually, about forty minutes now. I think I could smell brownies all the way through the phone. She said she had something for the new baby, too. She made it herself. That's all. I'd better get the mail sorted and the bills need to be paid. I'll have the checks ready to sign in a little while. Thanks for the ride. Cal wouldn't let me charge for the plane, only the gas. He's a real nice man."

"Why do you want to be a nurse when you are so good at business?"

"I don't know. Just the way I feel. I plan to study business too. I like it." Maggie reached for her mail. Jerry got a cool drink from the fridge and went to the hangar.

After so many weeks of no rest she felt a little lost when there were a few minutes of quiet. Cal was coming in for a landing as she left the office. The student miscalculated the height from the runway to pull the nose up for the stall to flare for the landing glide and had to make a go-around and try again. Practice and more practice she thought. On the third try the student made the landing. The plane bounced twice then settled down properly. As they were taxiing to the hangar, Abby drove up. Jerry went to help her with the boxes she was pulling from the back seat. Jerry could smell the brownies.

"Abby, what have you done? I'm going to get fat." Abby grinned at Jerry's question.

"You could use a little meat on your bones. I got some things for the new baby and brownies for the older kids so they won't feel slighted. And some for you all so you won't feel slighted." She piled two large boxes and a small one on Jerry's arms. "If you take these in, I'll go tell Arnie hello." Abby headed for the hangar and Jerry laughingly carried the boxes to the office. Maggie met her at the door.

"I knew it. I smell them. Don't tell my mom but these are the best brownies I ever ate." Maggie took the boxes one at a time from Jerry and put them on the coffee table.

"If you won't tell Ma Brown I won't tell your mom." Cal and his student taxied to the ramp and parked the plane.

The next few minutes were spent snacking on brownies and coffee. Abby dragged Arnie in to enjoy a brownie. As Arnie was leaving Estelle and her Uncle Andy drove up. There were hugs and then Jerry told them Estelle's mother had left a message for Jerry to call. Estelle asked if Jerry would mind if she made the call. She dialed the number and waited a few seconds. When her Mother answered she motioned Andrew to listen and punched the speaker.

"Hello, Mother." Before her mother could answer Andrew greeted his sister.

"Andrew! What are you doing here? Estelle?"

"I've come to take Estelle home with me, big sister. And there's nothing you can do about it"

"He's right, Mother. I told you I wanted something better than what you wanted for me, and I will never marry a man old enough to be my father. You marry him."

"What has come over you? You get home now! Where have you been? I'll destroy anyone who has helped in this-"

"Easy, Essie. She's been in a convent to get away from that unholy marriage. I think you will have a hard time destroying the Church."

"I almost decided to stay. Goodbye. Come visit me sometime after your wedding." Estelle backed away from the phone.

"You're always welcome to visit my humble abode, Essie."

"My name is Melissa! I'll never come there. Don't you dare take my child with you!"

"Haven't you noticed, Essie? Your baby is a lovely woman of legal age to do what she wants. You can't stop her. She doesn't need your money now. I'll take care of her. I hope someday you grow up and realize what you have done. Goodbye." He broke the connection.

Estelle was standing by the door trying not to cry. "Why can't she love me for who I am like you do Uncle Andy?"

Andrew walked over and put his arm around her shoulder. "I don't know. She did the same to me. But we love each other and someday maybe Melissa will wake up and smell the roses. Are you ready to go?" Estelle nodded and after another round of hugs and brownies. They headed for Houston and then to Australia.

The office suddenly seemed empty when everyone had gone but Cal and Jerry. Arnie had picked up the gifts, and Cal and Jerry lingered a while not knowing why. Then the phone rang. Cal answered the phone. It was the Lambert's lawyer. Cal clicked on the speaker and Jerry came over to the desk to listen.

"I'm calling on behalf of Mrs. Lambert. I'm authorized to make a final offer for Jerry Jackson to leave Richard alone." The voice was almost apologetic.

"I'm not bothering Richard. I don't even know where he is." Jerry spoke cold and angry. "You can tell your clients that the last time I heard from him his investigators had tracked down Dale's girl they paid $100,000 to get rid of Dale's baby. She did a week later then disappeared. So they don't have to worry about a grandchild from their late young son. Richard is now looking for Lilly. If Richard contacts me I'll tell him you called. He will be the one to decide if he ever sees his parents again. Is there a message you want relayed?"

"Yes. It's Richard's inheritance. If he will contact me. It's nothing bad, Miss Jackson, but it is important."

"I'll give him your message. Does he have your number?" Jerry wrote the number down.

"Miss Jackson. The offer I'm authorized to make is for one million dollars."

Jerry and Cal gasped. "My answer is still the same." Cal's arm went around Jerry's waist. He bent and kissed the top of her head.

"Do you understand, sir? Please tell your clients we are not for sale." Cal said quietly and firmly.

"I understand. I'll relay the message." The lawyer hung up the phone and said softly to himself, "Good girl."

"I wonder where Richard is now, Cal." Jerry turned in Cal's arms and a feeling of warmth filled her. Without thinking, she put her arms around him and drew his lips to hers.

Rosa B. Lane

Chapter 9

Richard's flight was landing in St. Louis. His investigator, Harry Mc Hugh, was waiting for him at the airport. They had located Lilly's cousin and Richard asked them to wait for him. He wanted to be there when or if Lilly was found. They were not promising anything, but Richard had felt deep inside him that he had to be there. He braced himself for the possibility that this would be another dead end.

Harry Mc Hugh was a middle-aged man with graying hair and a fatherly look. His clothes were of nondescript summer fashion for the St. Louis hot weather. He blended well into the crowds of people waiting for the flight. He spotted Richard at once from the description he had been given. He was a tall well-dressed young man in an expensive suit and carrying only a fine quality leather bag. He walked up to Richard and introduced himself. The two men shook hands and headed for the waiting limousine.

"I was able to get a suite for a week. It seems your family name is well-known here. Do you want to go to the hotel first? Or do you want to go to cousin Joanne's work place first?"

"I've waited eight years. I will go straight to Joanne's work place," Richard's heart was pounding, and he found his hands trembling. This gut feeling was very strong. Harry nodded and gave the driver directions to the office building where Joanne worked.

They found her scrubbing the fourth-floor lobby. She was a thin young woman who would be about thirty. Her worn jeans and tee shirt were damp from perspiration. Her long brown hair was tied back with a faded scarf. She looked tired and faded like her clothes.

"Mrs. Joanne Billings?" Harry asked above the noise of the scrubber. The young woman turned and looked scared as she nodded. "We understand that you are related to Lilly Carsons. Is this correct?"

"I'm not allowed to talk while on duty. I could lose my job." Joanne looked around for her boss with the scared look of a frighten kitten.

Richard stepped forward and spoke gently. "I'm Lilly's Richard. Richard Lambert. I've come to take her and our child home." Joanne shut off the machine and stared at him.

"She always said you'd come for her. I thought she was just dreaming. She's at our place with the children." Joanne brushed a lock of damp hair from her face.

"What's going on here? Get to work! I don't pay you to gab." The demands came from a burly man with a partly smoked cigar hanging from his mouth. Harry stepped closer to Richard and Joanne.

Richard looked at the man and at the frightened Joanne. "Joanne, will you take me to her now?"

"Get to work or you're fired. Jobs for the likes of you don't grow on trees." The man reached out in a threatening movement toward Joanne. Richard stepped in front of him.

His voice was both firm and angry. "Joanne, as of this minute you no longer need this job or any job except to take me to Lilly." Harry looked at Joanne nodding and smiled as he showed his ID as a private investigator.

"I'll get my things. Goodbye, Mr. Drake. You can scrub the floor yourself!" Joanne had wanted to say that for a long time. She led the men to the door of the women's locker room, retrieved her cheap purse, and joined them.

The sleek black limousine parking at the curb of the slum building brought stares from passersby. Richard gasped at the stench from piles of garbage overflowing from cans. "Garbage strike," explained Joanne. They walked up two flights of worn dark stairs. The building reeked of stale cooking and moldy walls. Joanne pushed open the door to the apartment and they stepped into the dark room whose one window opened to show the wall of the next building. The paint was peeling from the walls and the floor was bare of carpet. It was cluttered but clean. The stale odor of the neighbor's cooking lingered here in the hot room. Seven people were living in the two small rooms and a tiny bath. The room they had entered served as kitchen, dining and living room. At the back an open door led to a small bedroom and a bath. Richard was shocked. His bedroom was larger than the whole apartment. At a cheap worn table sat five children. Each had a half glass of milk and half of a peanut butter sandwich. Leaning over supervising them was a young woman thin like all the children. Her blond hair was held back by a worn scarf. Richard recognized it as one he had given her so long ago. She looked up when the door opened. Her large blue eyes opened with joyous surprise.

Richard would have known Lilly anywhere in spite of worn jeans and too big tee shirt. "Lilly, it's me, Richard. I've come." Richard stepped forward. The woman straightened up and smiled.

"Richard. I've been waiting." She walked to him with her arms outstretched. Richard met her and took her into his own open arms. "I never stopped loving you," she said her voice choked with emotion. He kissed her with all the love he had held in his heart for so many years. They were together at last.

"Lilly, my dear Lilly! I didn't desert you. They sent me to England to finish school. I looked for you when I got home but they cut off all my money. Our baby?" Joanne pointed to the table. Richard looked puzzled.

"I never thought you deserted us." Tears of joy tumbled from their eyes intermingling as they held each other close. "Our twins. We had twins. A girl and a boy. They said fraternal twins. I couldn't have made it without Joanne's help. Ricky, Annie, come here. Come and meet your father." Two children dressed in clean but patched jeans and charity shirts came shyly forward. The boy had dark brown eyes and uncut disorderly hair. The girl startled Richard by looking at him with large blue eyes and a smile just like her mother's. The blond hair was carefully braided into long blond pig tails.

"Oh, Lilly, and I couldn't help you." Richard was crying. He knelt as he held out his arms for his children he thought he would never see but could only love in his heart. Now they were here. They were found at last. The boy and girl stared at him.

"Are you our Daddy for real?" asked the boy. "Mama kept saying you'd come."

"Are you going to help Mama get some food? We're hungry, Daddy." His daughter looked at him with expectation on her thin face. Richard sobbed; tears streamed down his cheeks. He remembered the bottles of wine he had dined on. The cost of any one bottle could have bought food for these children for a month. And his babies were going hungry. The girl put her arms around Richard and he held her close. The boy came forward and they were safe in his arms at last.

"Don't cry Daddy, Mama will make the hurt go away." Little Annie wiped his tears with her small hand and kissed his cheek. Harry fought back tears and knew it was times like this that made his job worthwhile. Joanne was weeping with joy.

"None of you will ever be hungry again." He stood up, the twins holding onto his pants. He looked at Joanne and Harry and said, "Gather up all the kids, Joanne. Leave the clothes. Just get what legal papers you must have. Joanne you and your children will come too. No one will ever be hungry again." He took Lilly into his arms and kissed her. All the pain, the longing they had suffered was now over. Richard picked up his daughter and took his son by the hand. "Lilly, my Lilly," he said, looking at her with love. "Come, all of you. We're going home."

Charley's Flying School

Rosa B. Lane

Chapter 10

Jerry was tired when she arrived home. She collected the mail, laid it on the kitchen table and sat down to sort it out. Bill, junk, bill, and a letter from Australia. Delighted, she opened the letter. Estelle was happy for the first time in her life. Her Uncle Andy insisted she go to college. She was starting in the fall. Meanwhile she helped in the clinic where she could and was learning to fly to be able to help Uncle Andy on his flying trips to towns where there were no doctors. His assistant was a nice young man who hoped to run one clinic in a line of clinics being planned by the government to serve the people of the outback. She had been interviewed by a local paper and had an article written about the American niece who came to live with the Doc. She ended by asking about Jerry and Richard. Jerry left the other mail and went to fix something to eat. Her fridge was almost as bare as her pantry, but she fished a TV dinner from the freezer. She shook her head and sighed. She just never got around to making a proper shopping list.

After dinner Jerry showered and got dressed for bed. She went downstairs, paid her bills then reread Estelle's letter and began to answer it.

"Dear Estelle,

It's so good to hear all is well. I love the way you write about your new home. You should study creative writing. I feel as if I'm there. Maybe someday I'll get the chance to really see it. All's well at the flight school. In fact, we have to turn students away for lack of instructors. Uncle Art asks about you. So he'll be happy to know you are fine. The convent appreciated the check.

      I heard from Richard a few weeks ago. He found his Lilly who had been through hell to keep and raise their twins, always knowing he would find them. She has a cousin who helped her even though she had three kids of her own to support. They were living in horrible poverty. Richard said he hates his parents for what they did to Lilly and their children. I doubt if he ever gets in touch with his parents again. Joanne and her three kids are living with Lilly and Richard. Richard has quite a family. He has married Lilly and adopted his own children to make their inheritance very legal. Even got DNA tests to prove beyond a doubt that they were his. This was his lawyer's suggestion when he made out the will leaving everything to Lilly and the twins after providing for Joanne and her children for the rest of their lives. He was surprised to find that he had also inherited Dale's part of the trust fund. He now has almost $100,000,000. I can't imagine anyone having that much money. He's going to send pictures of the wedding and his family. He is so very happy. He told Lilly they would live anywhere she wanted but she only cared if it was with him. Joanne said she always wanted to live in Connecticut so they now have a home there with enough rooms for everyone to have a separate bedroom- except Lilly and Richard. Joanne and Lilly are studying to get their high school diplomas and to prepare to go to college. Joanne wants to study business and computers and just about everything. She's divorcing her abusive husband and freeing herself to start over. Lilly wants to study art and music. The twins are both very talented in music. Joanne's three have shown great promise in a lot of areas. The twelve-year-old boy loves baseball. Richard takes him to summer classes in pitching and stuff. He says Joey has real talent. It seems Joey's abusive father they ran from to save their lives was into sports, including baseball.

      As for Cal and me, our work keeps us so busy we don't have much time to talk about anything except business. I sometimes think he wants to take over my school; then sometimes I think he wants to take over my heart. Can I be falling in love with him? After Angus I'm afraid to commit myself again until I am very sure. I admit I am confused. Oh, Mrs. Lambert's lawyer called with a last offer of

$1,000,000 if I left Richard alone and stopped chasing him. They have the weird idea that I'm pregnant and they need to buy me off too. It was hard to say no to that much money but Cal was at my side ready to pounce if I needed him. I guess they'll be happy when they realize they have made fools of themselves. Well, I'll say goodbye for now. Love, Jerry"

    Jerry addressed the letter and sealed it. She would have to take it to the post office to get a stamp. How much does a letter to Australia cost? Jerry looked at the clock. She stretched and headed for bed. Six came around awfully early.

Rosa B. Lane

Wildfire

I sit waiting. I know today or tomorrow
Someone will toss a cigarette, a match,
Or a careless camper leaves a smoldering campfire.
I sit waiting. Soon there will be a breeze to stir
The embers. I will devour all in my path.
My name is…. WILDFIRE!

Chapter 11

It started as a routine day. Hot, dry forests, and yet humid air. Her first student still froze at the microphone, unable to talk to the control tower. She had taken him to visit the tower after the lesson and he was surprised when one of the controllers admitted that he had been working in the tower for nine years; yet when he started lessons, he found he had mike fright. The young student laughed. Jerry hoped knowing what was going on in the tower would help him get over his fears.

The next student proved ready for her flight exam. She had passed her written but had trouble finding time and money to finish the flying. She was a young mother of two and had to manage to save for the lessons from their tight budget after putting some money into the kids' college fund and some away for rainy day savings. Although her husband made good money and encouraged her flying, it was a difficult money management challenge. The wind had picked up and was gusting unexpectedly but the student had slipped onto the runway with no help from Jerry. Jerry was pleased, and as the student taxied to the ramp told her she was ready for the FAA test. "Just remember you are not finished flying until the plane is on the ramp and tied down or in a hangar."

While Jerry was with her students, a family of four was on their way for a day in the forest. Carl and Lena Felds, their daughter Rachel, and son David were going on a picnic. It was a long drive, but they planned to stay all day and show the forest to their children. It had started with one of their many arguments when Lena wanted to stop at the ranger station for information. Carl refused to stop. "It's only a day outing, for Pete's sake. Are you going to nag all day?" He felt she always wanted to tell him what to do. Lena had not spoken again. Their marriage was beginning to fall apart because Carl always had to dominate and no one but he could make a suggestion. So they headed into the forest. No one knew they were there except his mother who was babysitting their infant daughter.

At the same time the Felds had started on their outing, two young men were deep in the forest farther north. They had been drinking all night and the campfire they built was too big for cooking and illegal. Camp fires had been restricted because of the fire hazard conditions. They clumsily tried to make coffee but the flames leaped around the pot and they jumped back. While the fire burned low, they finished the last of the beer.

"Gotta go get some more beer." One of them staggered to the car forgetting the fire. The other poured the coffee on the fire and joined him. They drove away. The driver lit a cigarette and gave a light to his friend. They talked with slurred words about the night as they finished their smokes. The smoldering butts were flicked out the windows. Behind them the campfire was stirring awake. The cigarette butts tumbled onto dry underbrush and a puff of a breeze fanned a spark.

Ned Hutchens was returning from a flying visit to relatives about noon. He saw smoke edging its way through the trees ahead and reported it to the air traffic controller. The information was relayed to the ranger station.

After lunch Cal had taken fire patrol. Jerry had just returned from refueling the 150 to prepare for her next student when the call came. A wildfire had been reported by a pilot returning home. Cal had verified it. He could see flames licking their way through the brush. A news helicopter was returning from an assignment and in a live broadcast showed film of the fire. While fire fighters were on their way, the wind became stronger and the area was alive with spreading fires.

About 1:30 p.m. a panic-stricken woman called the ranger station and asked about her son and his family. They had gone for an early morning ride into the forest and had planned to picnic. She had seen the fire on the news. The couple had not contacted the Ranger station or they would have been warned about the high fire hazard. From what the son's mother said the family was in the path of the fire. The rangers were calling all the pilots who could to help hunt for them.

"Maggie, cancel my next student. Tell him there's a family with a couple of kids lost in the path of the fire and we've got to locate them. He'll understand. I'm leaving at once." Jerry rushed to the hangar and told Arnie she was taking the 150 she just refueled. Soon she was airborne.

The Felds family had enjoyed lunch, and was getting ready to leave. Their car wouldn't start. Carl leaned over the engine to see what was wrong. Rachel screamed, "Daddy! Fire!" Horrified the four saw the smoke rolling from the trees north of them. A strong wind brought flames to the tree tops and tossed sparks around in the air. Panic-stricken the family ran back into the dry meadow they had just left.

Jerry dialed in the plane to plane frequency and listened for what the other pilots were doing and where they were covering. She used the zig zag pattern for the area she had been assigned. As she searched, she contacted Bob Hardy who was up with his chopper and Carla Wright who had her own chopper searching farther north. Nothing. Cal contacted them and passed their search results to the ranger station. Jerry turned her pattern to the South then caught a glimpse of a road through the trees. The odor of burning pine was stronger here. Jerry could see the smoke blowing from the north then through the smoke burst an explosion of flames. The fire had reached the tops of the pines and was leaping hungrily toward the road pushed by the wind. If the family was in this area, time was running out.

Jerry turned and flew back a few miles to take a closer look at the road. She thought she had seen a dark form at the side of the road and wanted to check it more closely. Then she saw them. Tiny figures running into a meadow waving at her frantically. Jerry circled and let them know she had seen them. What the family on the ground could not see was the fire spreading like spilled orange liquid pouring across the forest. In minutes it would be at the road. The meadow they were in was yellow and dry. A ready meal for a spark. Jerry reported to Cal and the others.

"I see a lake just beyond a stand of trees."

A voice she did not know broke in. "That's Deer Lake. I used to hunt there. There's a game trail leading back to the lake if they can find it. It's on the East side of the lake."

"I can't see it from here. I'm directly over them now. There goes a deer running out the other side. It's only a short distance to the lake and they don't realize it. The fire is moving faster."

"The trail is straight through the trees. About a quarter mile. Just a short walk. Can you herd them to the trail?"

"Herd them? Oh, like cattle. I'll try." Jerry made a steep turn and flying as low and slowly as she dared flew to the spot she thought would be the opening for the trail. The family stood looking up and not moving. The fire was nearing the road. Maybe the kids had a dog that liked to get them to follow it. She turned and once again flew toward the spot this time wagging her wings up and down hoping they would understand. The children were running. Jerry gained altitude and flew back. She saw the running children with the parents close behind them. The small boy and girl stopped pointing excitedly. They had found the trail. Beneath her the family disappeared into the forest. As she flew over the lake and turned she saw the stranded car surrounded with flames from the dry grass. Then the gas tank exploded. Flames and burning debris spewed across the field starting numerous small fires.

"Bob, they're headed through the forest to the lake how far are you or you Carla?"

Carla answered she was at least thirty minutes away. Bob answered he was ten. He could see the lake. Jerry swung the plane around as the small group burst through the trees and onto the sandy beach. They were waving happily at her. Jerry hoped they had ten minutes.

"They're on the beach. I'll circle above them until you get here." Jerry wagged her wings at the group and climbed to 2000 feet, then circled above the lake letting them know she was still watching. Beyond the trees the meadow was in flames and the forest behind the family was starting to burn. As if in slow motion, the chopper came into view. The fire had devoured the meadow, and with a burst of flame leaped closer to the lake as it caught the underbrush. Then the family spotted the chopper. They were screaming and waving with joy. Jerry wagged at them once more and headed for home. As she turned to fly back, Bob was landing on the beach. Jerry smiled. They were safe. The family climbed into Bob's chopper and lifted off just as the ravenous wildfire swept into the trees along the lake.

Bob notified the others of the rescue. The Rangers were now concentrating on controlling the fire. He asked the family which airport would take them closest to home. Soon they were landing at Conroe. Bob refueled and took to the air again with the family thanking him over and over. He had replied in his slow drawl. "It was a team effort. From the pilot who reported it on through to your mother who let the Rangers know you were out there, to a voice I never heard before telling Jerry where to find the trail. We all worked together. Gotta go. My wife is waiting."

Carla Wright returned to the airport and refueled the chopper. This flight counting cancelled students cost her over $1000 in profit. Where would she get the money for her daughter's college fund this month? But the family was safe. She would work it out somehow.

Bob Hardy returned to the airport and called his wife. "Honey, the vacation to Hawaii we've been saving for just went up in flames."

Jerry landed and, after refueling, helped Arnie put the plane away. The wind was getting fierce but it was bringing rain. Cal was making a final swing for the patrol before returning.

Carl and Lena Feilds were picked up by friends. Later that night Lena said quietly, "Carl, you nearly killed us all. For fifteen years I've been treated with contempt and you always have to have your way. I've begged you to go to a counselor with me but you scoffed. I'm going to visit my family in Dallas and I am taking the kids. If you want us back you will have to get help and grow up. If you don't I'm getting a divorce." She moved out of the bedroom into the guest room.

The two drunks had forgotten the fire and their camping equipment. Some miles later they had found the highway and a roadside bar and motel. They had gotten a supply of beer and a room. While the Felds were fleeing for their lives and the wild life were losing theirs, the drunks were sleeping.

The front brought the hoped for and much needed rain. By morning the devastated forest was no longer a threat, yet tired firefighters spent hours looking for possible hot spots. Extra fire patrols were called. Three firemen had been taken to the hospital for smoke inhalation. No human was killed, but the wild life loss was still being estimated. The investigation to find the cause of the fire continued. The news chopper was off to cover a police chase. The fire was old news.

Rosa B. Lane

Chapter 12

Abby was doing the pre-flight inspection by herself now. She had been taking off and landing with no help from Jerry for some time. There were still maneuvers for her to learn, but Jerry had a surprise for her today. When she told Maggie the surprise, Maggie offered to get her brother's professional camera to film Abby as she made her first solo. The surprise was even more than Jerry expected when she got a phone call from the local newspaper wanting to do a human-interest story. The reporter and photographer thought a special report of a first solo was a wonderful human-interest topic. When Jerry told them about Abby, they were elated. They would keep out of sight until Jerry and Abby were gone but would be waiting for them when they returned from a routine lesson. Maggie not only got her brother's camera but her brother came to photograph the flight for a college project.

Abby knew nothing of the pending photos until they were returning to the airport. Jerry told her to land and taxi to the control tower and let her out. Abby looked surprised. "Then you're going to make three touch-and-goes and return to pick me up. You're ready to solo." Abby squealed in delight. "You want to surprise your club? How about a picture? Maggie's brother is going to take a video and the paper wants to photograph you for an interview. You have to approve."

"Wow! What will the girls say to that!? I'm ready and willing." Abby called the tower for landing instructions and made the landing perfect. Then she called ground control and told them where she wanted to go. She let Jerry off at the tower and taxied to the active runway telling the control tower she was going to make touch-and-goes. She was in the air before it soaked in that she was really alone in an airplane with no one to help her. Abby surprised herself. She was not afraid, only busy handling the controls and talking to the tower. There was no time for anything but flying.

Jerry was watching from the walk-in front of the tower along with Maggie, her brother and the news crew. The cameras filmed Abby taxiing, taking off, and coming in for her first solo landing. At first she was a little high, but corrected it and landed with only a slight bounce. The second and third were better. When Abby taxied to the tower to pick up Jerry she was so elated she just hugged Jerry.

"Remember you aren't finished 'til you've got the plane tied down at the ramp," Jerry reminded her as they taxied to the hangar. The photographers were waiting when Abby opened the door to get out. They had her pose by the plane having her log book signed by Jerry. She had soloed! And her picture would be in the paper!

There was one more thing. Maggie produced the scissors. While the cameras rolled Jerry cut a slice of Abby's shirt tail. They then went into the office and Maggie inscribed it with "Abby Norman, soloed 7-14-83". Abby was photographed holding her shirt tail. Then Jerry pinned it on the crowded bulletin board. There were cheers.

Jerry left Abby with the news reporters telling her she needed to review the flight as usual when they finished and went into the class room. Maggie and her brother left to develop his film, and Maggie had a date. Mike would be waiting. They had been seeing each other regularly since the accident. Soon he would be leaving. She would miss him.

When she entered the class room, Jerry saw Cal. Before she could ask him why he was there she heard the sound of Jenny coming in to land. "What on earth! Uncle Art didn't tell me he was coming."

"You don't know do you?" Cal asked. "Will this remind you?" He took a step to her and pulled her into his arms and kissed her gently but completely. "Happy birthday," he whispered. "I've wanted an excuse to do that for a long time. Oh, here's something I picked up for you. Hope you like it." Before the astonished Jerry could answer he handed her a small package. She took the gift with trembling hands thoroughly shaken by his kiss that had sent gentle warm fire through her. This was not lost on Cal for he too had been drowned in the waves of passion that swept over him.

Jerry opened the package a little clumsily. Cal watched her face as she opened the box and saw a simple pair of silver wings. She turned it over and on the back was engraved, "To Jerry with love, Cal." She held the pin in her hand and tears came into her eyes. This was the kind of thing that Charley would have done. "Thank you. I love it." And put her arms around him and kissed him. He held her tightly. Once more she had come into his arms because she wanted to. And he kissed her again.

Uncle Art opened the door and saw the two wrapped in each other's arms, closed it and went to the hangar. It had to happen. They were so much alike and they needed each other whether they knew it or not. With Arnie's help he parked Jenny in the hangar and was laughing to himself when Arnie looked up.

"Need to stay in here a bit. It seems I interrupted a birthday kiss or something." Both men laughed.

"About time. Those two are nice one minute and mad the next. Might as well get married and get it over with. They act like they are anyway." Arnie chuckled. "Abby just soloed. They're going to give her a write up in the paper. That should make good gossip for her garden club."

"She's quite a grandmother. Wonder why she never married again."

"I hear there's lots of women for every man her age. How old are you?"

"I just kicked sixty -five. I was the old guy in the group. "But I always felt the same age. Charley was ten years younger and Rex seven. I guess that made Charley the kid. But we sure had fun. The kid could fly circles around most everyone but Rex and me. Then he started flying circles with us! What a team we made."

"I would have liked to have seen that. Mr. Rex talked a lot about the three of you."

Cal came into the hangar. "Art, Ma Brown says to bring you

over for dinner. She's got a cake for Jerry." Cal's face was glowing and his eyes sparkling. Arnie and Art exchanged muffled smiles.

"Never refuse Ma. Have to go see my favorite girl." Art left for the office. Cal lingered a while still rocking from Jerry's arms and lips. No wind or storm or engine problem had shaken him the way her lips responding to his kiss had.

Art found Jerry in the classroom reviewing the lesson with Abby. "Happy birthday." Art gave Jerry a hug.

"Uncle Art! I had forgotten it was my birthday. See what Cal gave me." She showed him the pin Cal had pinned on her left shoulder over her heart. "Isn't it precious?" Then remembering her manners asked, "Have you met Abby Norman? Abby this is Arthur Swenson my adopted uncle."

"I'm glad to meet you. Congratulations on your solo. I've heard of you wanting to solo to show the gals at the club there's more to life than gardens. Are you going to quit now?"

"I 'm glad to meet you too. No. I'm taking the whole thing and getting my license. I didn't know it was your birthday, Jerry," Abby said. "I really flew alone and did okay. See…," Abby got up and turned to show the back of her tee shirt where the piece had been cut out to label and hang on the bulletin board. "I'll save this old shirt forever."

"I'll go back to the guys and leave you two alone." Art walked back to the hangar. Cal said he was leaving. It was his day off.

"Do you want me to drop you off at Jerry's? Unless you have something here. Jerry will be here all day."

"I'll tell her. She showed me the wings. She loves them." Art went back and told Jerry that Cal was taking him home. He collected his bag he had left in the office and joined Cal. He planned to stay a few days and visit friends. For a change all was quiet at the ranch. They left in Cal's station wagon. It had been repaired and repainted the same red and looked like new.

As they drove to Jerry's, Art said quietly, "All right, son, what's wrong? You need to talk and Rex isn't here." He looked at the young man whose face had a serious frown that had replaced the radiant smile of minutes ago. Cal nodded.

"I love her. I've wanted to marry her ever since I saw her picture with oil on her pigtail. I think she feels for me but there's this idea she has that I'm only after her school. I have to tear down that wall, and I don't know how. Maybe it's still the way she was deserted by the other man. I don't know. But it is between us and until she can trust me, I feel so lost. What can I do?" Cal pulled into Jerry's driveway and turned to Art looking miserable.

"Why did you buy a partnership? Why did Charley sell it to you? This is what is between you. Unanswered questions. In many ways you're still a mystery man from out of the sky, and Jerry can't understand. Come in, Cal. We have all day. Let's talk." The two men went into the house. Art turned on the air-conditioner then got them a cold soda. They went into the family room. Art got comfortable in the big chair. Cal sat on the edge of the sofa holding his soda with both hands and frowning.

"Cal," said Art as he fiddled with his pipe, "Jerry always thought Charley would make her a legal partner. She felt that if she had been a boy he would have the sign read 'and Son' but not for a daughter. When you showed up as a legal partner, she felt betrayed and Charley was dead. There was no way to ask him why. She thought she owned the school. You came in and took charge."

"I didn't mean to do it. She was so despondent and tired. I deliberately made her angry to get her out of the depression I saw was destroying her ability to cope. I knew she hated me for it. But it worked. As for why I bought the partnership. Pride. Charley offered me a job but I wanted to meet her on equal terms not as an employee. And another thing.

I thought I was in love once about six years ago. I was going to ask her to marry me. Then there was a bad flood and I broke a date with her to fly air rescue. That's what I was doing then. This beautiful woman, Sylvia, so intelligent and artistic with a fabulous job was furious. I told her people were dying and I could help save them. Her reply was to let someone else do it. It meant nothing to her. She gave me the choice. Stay and take her to the show she wanted to see and give up my silly flying or else. I was shocked. I stood there and just said goodbye and hung up. I haven't been serious about anyone since. But when I saw Jerry's picture, I knew that she was someone I could love. It was a gut feeling. I had to meet her." Cal stopped and took a breath. He had not talked this much since he came here. "I got here and found Jerry knew nothing about the deal, and she resented me. The thing is we work so well as a team. We seem to know what each other is thinking. One minute she is my partner, the next she is angry and resentful. I'm lost."

"Why did Charley offer you a partnership?" Art fiddled with the unlit pipe. He rarely smoked anymore.

"He said Jerry seemed to have forgotten she was a woman. Charley was afraid she would grow old and so wrapped up in flying she had no other life. Somehow he just understood that Jerry knew she was his partner as well as his daughter even if it wasn't on paper. That's where I remembered my own lost love and left them to take a walk. I think Dad and Charley cooked up the partnership playing cupid or something. Anyway, when I got back, he made me an offer. I took it. Now I wonder if it was a mistake. All I have in the world is tied up in the school. Yet Jerry sometimes makes me feel like a thief in my own business."

"She says you make her feel like an employee instead of partner. Somewhere you two need to make a better communication center."

Cal shook his head, "I wish I knew how." His brows were furrowed with worry lines. "When we fly together, it's as if we know each other's mind. But on the ground- I don't know what happens. She hates me."

"Or maybe she's trying to fight falling in love with you. I don't think she hates you. She respects you as a pilot. That's a beginning. Just wait. The right moment will come. When it does, just tell her what Charley told you about her being his partner. That's all she wants to hear." Art looked at his watch. "I'm hungry. Let's see if there's anything in the house to eat." As they looked in the fridge and freezer they decided to go out for lunch. Cal was feeling better. He had a lot to ponder. They came back with chicken and spent the rest of the afternoon talking.

Jerry looked at the wings pinned over her heart in the mirror and smiled. She still tingled when she thought of his kiss, then she had kissed him. It was as natural as taking a breath to put her arms around his neck and her lips against his. He had been surprised. His response was gentle and so very complete. No one had ever kissed her that way or made her feel like this. For a while she forgot everything but his arms and his lips. Then Rev. Mitchell returned with the Aerobat, and the spell was broken. The time had slipped by so quickly. She had forgotten lunch and it was nearly four.

"How did it go with the kids?" Jerry asked as he came in with the keys. The Reverend looked puzzled, then quickly recovered.

"One of the children died last week of a rattlesnake bite. There was no anti-venom to treat it. The mission had called for help but could not get help in time. The roads are all but impassable but no politician cares about the poor in the back country. I'll have to do something to make them care. But what?"

"Maybe a documentary of living conditions made by a news photographer or even a student might help." She told him about Abby's solo. "If they showed the neglect of those kids and their families on the news I wonder if the people would want it changed. You know more about that than I do, Rev. Mitchell. I met a Senator Stone when Richard took me to that dinner dance. He said if there was ever anything he could do to help me to let him know. It would be worth a try to talk to him. Maybe he would remember my name as a friend of Richard's. Charley flew a charter flight for him once and he remembered him." Jerry did not notice the cold look of fear that flashed for an instant over Reverend Mitchell's face.

"It is worth a try" he said. "I'll check around. I'll see if I can get Senator Stone to listen. I'll drop your name."

"We'll loan you a plane free to go back with one of them if you need it, or one of us will fly them in. That's all I know to do to help."

"Jerry, you're Charley's daughter all right. That's what he would have done. God bless you, my dear. I'll be in touch." As he drove home the Rev. frowned. Things were not working out as they had planned. In her goody two shoes helping, she would spoil everything.

Jerry put the mail aside for Maggie tomorrow. She did not want to foul up Maggie's system. That was something Jerry seemed extra good at doing. She checked her schedule and saw that there were no other students. Mondays and Tuesdays were slow days. She never understood why. She might as well go home and get ready for dinner. She thought of her lovely dress, the only party dress she had, and smiled. Why not dress for dinner? She went to the hangar and found Arnie cleaning up after the day.

"Happy birthday, Jerry. I have everything finished here. The Reverend looked mighty sad. What's wrong with his kids?" Jerry told him. He shook his head sadly. One reason he had come down here was because of the bad area he and his family had to live in back in Illinois after he had lost his job when the shop where he worked went bankrupt. "Will it be all right if I leave now?"

"Of course. I see you have the Aerobat inside. I'll be leaving too. I can't go to dinner at Ma's house looking like this. See you tomorrow. I'll lock up the office and you take care of the hangar as always."

"Thanks. Wear something real pretty. I think Cal would like that." Arnie said as Jerry left. She felt her face flush.

Jerry arrived home and Art was reading the paper. Cal had gone back to Ma's. "I'll have to clean up, Uncle Art. Can't go like this." She was half way up the stairs before she finished. Art looked at her, shook his head and smiled. Ahh, youth, he thought. It was an hour before Jerry finished dressing. She came down stairs and stood in the door of the family room.

"Do I look all right?" Art looked around at her and gasped. Jerry was wearing her blue chiffon dress and her pearls. The only make up was lipstick and a touch of powder to cover her shiny nose. Over her heart was pinned her silver wings. He got up and walked to her.

"For a second it was like looking at your mother. You are beautiful. Give your old uncle a hug." Jerry walked over and hugged Art. "I think you will do just fine."

"Will you drive? I can't do so well in these heels. I guess I'm not used to being a lady." Jerry grinned.

"My dear, you don't need to try to be a lady, you are one naturally just like Elizabeth was. When Charley first introduced us to his wife she had a dress on much like yours. She cloned a daughter." Art took the offered keys and escorted his adopted niece to the car.

When they walked into Ma's house all talking stopped. Jerry flushed at the silence. Ma came over and hugged her. The boarders began to call out "happy birthday" and the truck driver, Hershel Olson whistled. Cal just stood up and devoured her with his eyes. Ma shooed them into the dining room where dinner was already on the table. She had fixed Jerry's favorite dish, baked salmon. There was a bowl of cut flowers on the table and it all looked so special Jerry had to wipe a tear from her eye.

"Thank you, Ma. I'm starved. I forgot to eat lunch." With that everyone took a seat and the feast began. Ma made Jerry sit and not help serve this time. Instead Bonnie helped Ma. After the meal was over and the table cleared, Cal came in carrying a large chocolate cake with blazing candles and set it in front of Jerry. She looked up at Cal and their eyes met in an embrace.

"Blow them all out, Jerry," called Paul Snyder. "Can we forego spanking the birthday girl and just kiss her?"

"How about just singing happy birthday," said Ma. Art laughed and started singing followed by the others. Jerry took a deep breath and blew all the candles out but one. She tried it again. It went out and then flared up again. On the third try it suddenly dawned to Jerry.

"All right! Who's the joker that put the trick candle on the cake?" Everyone looked at Cal.

"I admit to doing it. I did it on my own sister's cake once."

"And what did she do to you?" asked Jerry.

"She just laughed and dropped a water balloon on my head the first chance she got." Everyone laughed.

"I'll think of something you rat." When she said "rat" she had the feeling she was saying something much different, like I love you. "Ma, you get the first piece." She sliced the cake making sure a rose was on the piece and placed it on a plate for Ma Brown.

After dinner Ma and Bonnie disappeared into the kitchen then came back in a minute with a large box. "We all chipped in and bought this for you. Maria made it."

Jerry opened the box and gasped at the contents. She removed a hand crocheted shawl of soft wool the color of the sky on a clear day. "It's so beautiful. Thank you so much." Jerry was crying now. Cal took the shawl and wrapped it around her shoulders. The color made her eyes look like two glistening jewels. Everyone clapped. Bonnie produced a lace trimmed handkerchief and Cal wiped Jerry's tears. He bent and kissed her on her cheek.

"Come on into the parlor," said Ma Brown. "Bonnie is going to play the piano. And we're going to have a sing-a-long." The evening was like the ones Jerry remembered when she was growing up. Uncle Art added his fine voice to the others. Jerry finally realized it was nearly midnight, and everyone had to work.

"Uncle Art, we must leave now. Ma, how can I ever thank you for the dinner and all of you for the cake and my shawl? And you Cal for my wings?" He had noticed she had pinned them on her dress over her heart.

"I'll walk you to the car. You are so beautiful." Cal spoke softly and walked with Jerry to the door. Art started to follow but Ma Brown stopped him.

"Arthur Swenson, you're not that old. Let the young'uns be alone awhile. There's a full moon," Ma turned Art back into the house and closed the door.

Cal took Jerry's arm as she went down the stairs. "Careful. Those heels might catch on the steps." Jerry held onto him playing the game couples have played since time began pretending to need his help. Both knew she was totally independent and capable of going down stairs without help, yet it made Jerry feel like a woman and Cal feel strong and protective. They walked the path and stopped beside the car.

"I wonder what's keeping Uncle Art." Jerry looked up at Cal not caring how long Uncle Art was delayed.

"Look at that moon, Jerry." Cal looked up at the bright moon that lit up the night.

Jerry followed his gaze to the full moon and the stars around it. "It's a magical night. I feel like Cinderella at the ball." She turned toward Cal and found herself surrounded by strong arms. The magic made her put her arms around him, and they embraced. There was a soft warmness in the night flowing around them and making them forget everything except the moment. Jerry felt her desire growing and pressed closer to him. His arms tightened about her.

"Jer, Jer. I love you so much." He could not stop kissing her, and she could not stop responding.

"Cal," the thought was never finished for Art came out of the house talking loudly to Ma Brown to alert them as he said a final good night. Jerry pulled away from Cal as he dropped his arms like a guilty boy caught in the cookie jar. Jerry straightened her shawl and got into the unlocked car. "Good night. I'll see you in the morning."

"Good night, Jer. Good night Art." Cal stepped back and watched them drive away. She nearly said it, he thought as he walked back to the house.

As Jerry and Art drove home, Art told her he had a special present for her. He wanted to give it to her when they were alone. When they reached home he went to his room with Jerry following him. He took a small black velvet box from the dresser drawer and handed it to her. Jerry took it and opened it. In the box lay a delicate butterfly pendant with sapphires, diamonds rubies covering the wings of gold. She lifted it by its golden chain. Tears blossomed in her eyes.

"Aunt Molly's butterfly. Oh, Uncle Art! Thank you! I always loved it so." Jerry hugged him.

"Molly always said it should be handed from mother to daughter. You were the only daughter we've ever had. She would have wanted you to have it." Art's eyes were moist with tears as they both looked at the photos on the dresser. The one with the four of them and Jerry as a toddler was in the old-fashioned frame where Jerry's mother had placed it. Both Jerry and Art were wishing the other three were with them. Jerry kissed him on the cheek.

"Thank you, Uncle Art., I have been so blessed. I always felt that I had two families."

"You had better get some sleep. You're a working girl," Art said as he brushed his eyes with the back of his hand.

"Good night. It's been a magical evening." Jerry hugged the shawl and the necklace close to her and walked down the hall to her room. As she closed the door behind her she realized that the magic was over and she was once again just a girl who had to go to work.

She took off her dress and hung it on a hanger reminding herself it had to go to the cleaners. Her panty hose was dropped into the hand laundry basket. She washed the makeup off her face and put some night cream on not allowing herself to think of Cal. Finally, she got into bed determined to sleep. Sleep would not come.

She kept hearing Cal saying "I love you." And she almost said she loved him too. Did she? She had made one mistake. She could not make another. She got up and put on her robe and slippers and went down stairs, out the back door and sat on the patio looking at the bright moon. The turmoil inside her made her feel that she would boil over and she did not understand why. No one had ever made her feel this way. She didn't want to love him. She was so afraid. Could she trust him? Could she trust herself? Yet the thought of losing him made her ache deep inside until it became a physical pain. She dropped her head into her hands and softly sobbed.

Cal could not sleep. He had told her he loved her. What was she going to say? The softness of her against him, the gentle perfume of her hair, caused a turmoil inside him. He got up, put on his robe and slippers, went out to the patio and sat on a lawn chair. He looked at the moon peeking through the trees and tried to capture the magic of the evening. He could not. He was suddenly afraid he had made another mistake and kissed her too soon. God, how he wanted her. The thought of losing her hurt so much. Cal dropped his head in his hands and softly sobbed.

Morning found Art and Jerry finishing breakfast at the airport restaurant. There was some talk of the fire and the wildlife destroyed. The investigators had determined the fire was started by campers. They found melted beer cans and some debris that they thought may have been camping equipment but they found no signs of any campers. The number of cans made them think it was more than one camper. A search was now on for the missing campers. Jimmy Cole was recovering from his heart attack and trying to get on with his changed life. Everyone sat silently wondering what they would do if it had been them.

Jerry was preparing one of the trainers for the first student when Cal arrived. She smiled as he walked in to check his schedule. She finished with the plane and went in to get the clipboard and key ready. Her student had a job to go to as soon as they finished and she did not want to delay him. She checked her watch and it was 7:45. He would be here at 8:00. Cal was looking over his schedule and looked up when she came in.

"Good morning. Looks like Maggie is first on my list. We're going to be busy today." The business-like tone belied the passion in his eyes when they met Jerry's.

"I have an eight o'clock. Uncle Art has my car and if I need transportation I hope I can bum a ride from you."

"Of course." The look in her eyes said "hold me" but her words were just business. They both were wondering how to handle the emotions that were brought to the surface last night. Maggie arrived. She was bubbling over as always when she had her lesson.

"What plane should I get ready?"

"Come on, Jerry has her student's out and ready. We'll take the other 150. I'll get it out and you get the clipboard." Cal left the office for the hangar so abruptly Maggie looked surprised. She looked at Jerry who was fiddling with the keys to her plane.

"Jerry is everything all right? I felt you two were avoiding each other." Maggie asked her young voice full of concern.

"It's nothing," said Jerry as the phone rang. Maggie automatically answered it, listened and handed the phone to Jerry. It was the mother of her student. "Maggie you can take 316 since it's already out. Tim was rushed to surgery with a ruptured appendix about an hour ago. I hope he's all right. I thought ruptured appendix was a thing of the past."

"Poor guy." The two walked out to the hangar only to find Arnie and Cal conversing over the exposed engine of 236 the other

Cessna 150 trainer.

"Jerry, 236 has to be grounded. There's a noise Arnie can't figure out in the engine. Did you use it yesterday? I had it out Monday."

"No. Abbie soloed in 316. I just used 316 for the other students since it was out. I'll get the records. You and Maggie go on. My student is having emergency surgery. Appendix." Jerry went back in the office and obtained the carefully kept record book for N29236 and took it back to the hangar. Cal and Maggie got on with Maggie's lesson.

"Here's the records." Jerry handed the book to Arnie. He took it and they walked back to the table at the rear of the hangar to study the repair history of the plane. Arnie nodded and smiled. "You know just from the records? How?"

"Well I can't explain it but it's something I just do. Come on I'll show you." Jerry had found an old pair of coveralls she kept in the hangar and pulled them over her jeans and shirt. They walked over to the plane and Arnie started explaining.

The two were still hanging over the engine when Maggie and Cal came back. She looked up and Cal and laughed. Jerry had oil smudged on her nose and chin. It was almost like the first day Cal had arrived. Jerry realized she had to get cleaned up for her next student at ten.

When Jerry returned from her ten o'clock student, Cal and Arnie were in the hangar. She signed the student's log book and went over the lesson with him. He started the stall for the landing glide too soon, as though he was afraid of the ground. Instead of gliding to a gentle landing the plane stalled at ten feet. He had to push the throttle forward while holding the nose down and adjusting the flaps to make a go around. Only practice could correct that. When he left, Jerry took the clipboard and was putting it away when the office door flew opened and a tall thin woman entered. Jerry looked up.

The woman stood in the door for an instant like a mannequin in a department store. Her black hair was cut straight in the latest fashion, short in the back and a long strand half curled around her cheek on one side and cut short like a man's with sideburns on the other. Bangs cut a path across her forehead. The black pant suit she wore was strictly designed for business. Under the lightweight jacket was a shirtwaist top frilled just enough to exclaim "I may be a business executive but I am a woman." On her shoulder hung a small purse supported by a gold chain. Peeking from beneath her slacks were shoes with ridiculously high spiked heels.

"I'm looking for Calvin Morris. I'm told he charters planes." Her voice was both sexy and business like at the same time. Maggie looked at her. She was straight from a fashion magazine. Jerry was not impressed.

"I'm sorry. You were misinformed. We do not have a charter plane here. This is a flying school. We teach flying." Jerry went over to the desk. "I can refer you to a helicopter charter service. You passed it on the way in."

"Does not Calvin Morris own this -"? The look of disdain the woman gave when she glanced around the room made it clear they were beneath her.

"Mr. Morris is my partner. I own half of the school. Maggie, page Cal from the hangar please. If you wish to sit down he will be here in a few minutes. There's coffee if you wish." The woman looked at the vinyl covered chairs and sofa and the coffee pot. Her look of contempt was clear. Maggie paged Cal.

Cal cleaned his hands and went to the office. He walked into the room and stood stunned. Slowly he closed the door. "Sylvia. What brings you to Texas?" His voice was controlled in spite of the inner earthquake he felt.

"She's looking for a charter plane. I recommended Hardy's Charter Service." Jerry did not like the look she had seen on Cal's face.

Sylvia ignored Jerry. "Calvin, dear. It's been a while. So this is where you disappeared to. Owning a flying school."

"I only own half of it. Jerry, this is Sylvia Freeman. Jerry owns the other half of the business." Once the shock of seeing Sylvia again diminished Cal looked hard at Sylvia. This stylish artificial woman standing here was once the woman he thought he wanted to marry. He looked at Jerry so fresh and natural and knew he had found a real woman. He walked to Jerry's side.

Sylvia looked at Jerry and asked, "And what are your duties here, besides bedroom duty." Maggie gasped. Cal's fingers wrapped around Jerry's and she felt he was warning her she was being baited.

"I could never consider our bedroom as a wifely duty," she said sweetly and looked up at Cal hoping she had adoration in her eyes.

"I would never want my wife to consider my bed as her duty, only her joy." Cal put his arm around Jerry's waist and gently kissed her on the top of her head. "What do you want, Sylvia? We don't have planes to charter." Sylvia opened her mouth to reply when the door opened and Art came in with a package.

Uncle Art handed Jerry the package with a grin and said, "Jerry, I stopped by the house and your wedding pictures have arrived." The silence that followed for an instant made Art look at each of them totally perplexed.

"The wedding pictures, Dear." Jerry turned in Cal's arms and hugged him. "I hope they turned out good." She stepped over to Art and took the package. "Sylvia this is my uncle, Art Swenson. He is visiting for a while."

Maggie held out a slip of paper to Sylvia. "Here is the charter list." Sylvia glared at all of them ignoring the paper.

"I have to get to Dallas but I'll be back for a two-week meeting in Houston. I've never let a wedding ring stop me from getting what I want."

"Sylvia, six years ago you made your choice and I made mine. We have nothing here for you to charter." Cal looked at Sylvia then at Jerry holding the package. "Indeed, I have made my choice," he said softly.

Sylvia looked at each of the people in the room. She was not used to being denied. She turned and walked out of the office to the waiting car and driver. She would be back. Silence followed her exit.

"What was that all about?" Art asked looking at the group.

"That was the woman who I thought broke my heart six years ago. She said I had to choose flying or her. I chose flying. She chose

New York with her married boss."

Jerry looked at the package. "Thanks, Uncle Art. These are Richard's wedding pictures of him and Lilly and his family." Everyone burst out laughing. "She wanted to know what duties I had here beside bedroom duties. I guess we kind of led her to think we are married and the wedding pictures came at the right time."

There was a letter in the package. Jerry looked at the happy faces pictured and at the two children obviously Richard's and passed them on to Art. She opened the envelope and pulled out the letter. It was a happy letter. Richard's joy was so great it almost frightened Jerry. Would anyone ever be allowed that much happiness? Then she remembered all the married people she knew. Most had worked at their marriage and had a good life. Richard's family was just beginning to know what a good life could mean. Cousin Joanne and her children were a good-looking group. Lilly and Joanne had a striking resemblance just as Richard's children looked like him and Lilly. She was glad for them. Jerry passed the letter and pictures to the others.

Cal and Jerry were looking at Lilly's beautiful wedding gown. "She deserves the best after the hell the Lamberts put her through." Cal spoke slowly with anger. "No one has the right to hurt others that way."

"He was only seventeen and a minor. They were his parents. I guess that paternity laws don't apply to the wealthy. She was only sixteen. She must be a fantastic woman. Her cousin Joanne looks so thin. Can you believe those two raised five kids on Joanne's minimum wages while Lilly babysat them? I have so much respect for them and I've never seen them." Jerry spoke softly.

"They have invited you to visit them in Connecticut; even offered to send a private jet for you. Sounds nice."

"Cal, I can't go right now; maybe someday. We're just getting things going. We both have everything in this school. I just can't pack up and take a trip. Think of all the money we'd lose. Besides, Sylvia is coming back to 'destroy' our marriage." Jerry looked up at Cal with an impish grin.

"Sylvia could try to destroy our business, but never our

marriage," Cal grinned back. He wanted to - Stop it he told himself. Why did she make him want to carry her away? - Stop it Cal, he mentally scolded.

"Do you really think she could destroy our school?" Jerry looked at him a little frightened. "Charley worked so hard and so have we." Then she felt anger rising. "She might have more of a fight than she thinks. I won't stand by and do nothing while she tries to take away my life."

"And me?" Cal looked at her gravely.

"That would be up to you. I think we both know the answer. We make a good team and work well together." The room was pregnant with emotions. Art motioned to Maggie and they quietly left the office and faced the Texas heat.

"Well Maggie. I don't know what their schedule is, but I think now would be a good time for us to go out to lunch. Can you face a semi-veggie lunch?"

"To get them married I'd eat a hamburger." Maggie followed Art to the hangar where they told Arnie to give the two some time together.

"Might as well come with us to the restaurant and be cool. Too hot here to eat. My treat, Arnie." The three of them headed for the restaurant for lunch.

Cal and Jerry never heard the door close. They stood looking into each other's eyes. "We do make a great team, Jer." At the same time, they stepped into each other's arms.

"Hold me, Cal. I need you to hold me." Jerry held onto him tightly. "I've been so alone since Charley died. Hold me." Cal surrounded her with his arms and his love.

"I'm here, Jerry. You're not alone now. I need you too, Jer. So very much." Their lips met in a passion that they both knew could only end in one way. They both pulled back shocked by the power of their emotions. "Jer, Jer." Cal stepped back as if he needed to protect Jerry from himself. Jerry clung to him. She wanted no protection from him at this moment, but deep inside her a warning light started to flash.

"I-I" she stammered. "What time is it? What is our

schedule?" She was shaken and disoriented by this turn of events. "We- we must get lunch."

Cal smiled his lopsided grin. "We had better do something else than stand here and kiss or I'm going to have a shotgun wedding." Jerry laughed and nodded. They checked the time and the schedule. Art, Maggie and Arnie were nowhere in sight. They assumed they were having lunch, so they locked up and walked to Cal's station-wagon. They both knew that they could not be alone until the turmoil in both of them cooled and became calm. They had reached very close to the point of no return where reason leaves and nature takes over. Dangerous ground for Jerry who was fighting to keep her wall in place. Now Sylvia had punched a hole in it not realizing that by challenging Jerry and threatening Cal she had started the wall's collapse.

As Cal and Jerry walked to the pilot's table everyone smiled knowingly but greeted them as always. To Jerry's surprise sitting by Bob Hardy was a man with a familiar face. "Senator Stone, how nice to see you again. I met you with Richard Lambert at the county club dance a few weeks ago." She smiled as she took a seat by Carla. Cal looked surprised as he sat beside her. The Senator was acting as if he did not know him. "I want you to meet my partner, Calvin Morris."

"Of course, I remember you, Miss Jackson. I'm pleased to meet you, Mr. Morris. How is Richard?" asked the Senator quickly not giving Cal a chance to answer.

"Hello, Senator," said Cal interrupting. "It's been a long time."

"Yes, it has Cal, I hardly knew you." The Senator tried to cover his rudeness.

Jerry looked at the two men surprised at the tension between them. "Richard's well and happy. He's married and his twins and wife are fine."

The Senator laughed. "So, he finally tied the knot."

"By the way, Cal what did you do to that New York gal? She was sure mad. Just because we didn't have a chopper and pilot to charter she claimed we were all in a conspiracy." This came from Bob Hardy.

"She's spoiled with being the big wheel in the fashion industry. Used to having her own way." Cal spoke quietly trying to sound unconcerned. Jerry looked at him playing with his food his jaws clenched.

"She wanted Cal. I led her to believe we were married. She said a wedding ring never stopped her from getting what she wanted." Jerry spoke with a grin.

"She asked Jerry what she did beside bedroom duty for Cal," Maggie said grinning. "Jerry just played her game. Sylvia lost."

No one but Cal noticed the startled look flicker over the Senator's face. "I know her well enough to know trouble when it knocks. She'll be back in Houston in a few days. She's going to be at some kind of business conference for two weeks." Cal said softly as if to himself. Everyone looked at each other. It was as if the same thought occurred to everyone at the same time. Only Cal knew and wondered why the Senator did not say that Sylvia was his daughter.

"God forbid if she teams up with the Lamberts." It was Carla who expressed the thought.

"What could they do?" This question came from Senator Stone. The conversation was taking a most interesting turn.

Calvin answered him. "Senator, I believe you know my father. He owned a small airport in Illinois. Not as big as this one, but my grandfather had started it and Dad carried on. Good farm land around the airport was bought by developers. Then subdivisions starting building up all around us. Eventually we were condemned and put out of business. A VIP resort now sits where our airport was and the hangar we donated rent free to the community for Life Flight and police helicopters is now replaced by a golf course. At least three people died last year, one was a premature baby because they couldn't get her to the hospital. That's what money can do to a small airport. It is happening all over the country." The Senator noted the silence around the table and the look of concern, even fear on the faces of the others.

"But Lambert gave over a million dollars to build the World War II museum. Why would he want to destroy it. And it is dedicated to all the WW II pilots who died and everything on display belongs to all the community in the area. Even the airport is dedicated to the pilots. They changed the name to Memorial in honor of all those who used to fly in and out of here during the war as well as those who were killed. They have a DC3 being restored and a Spitfire. The old Mr. Trenton hoped to make a flying museum like the Confederate Air Force. This airport saw some history made. Not your big stuff, but quiet and important in its own way since it was built. Why would Lambert want to destroy it?" This came from Bob Hardy.

"One million is loose change to people like him. Who knows what a low life like him thinks?" Jerry was angry. She had not thought Lambert would go so far to get at their school because she helped Richard, but she realized the possibility. Now they had the Sylvia factor.

"Oh, by the way, Miss Jackson, a Reverend Mitchell called my office. He said you mentioned I might help him or tell him were to go for help. I was not in." The Senator fished into a pocket and pulled out a card case and handed Jerry a business card. "Do you know what he wanted?"

"He showed up here about two years ago." Jerry told him about the village everyone ignored, the death of a child because the roads were so bad they could not get him out to the hospital or an ambulance in. "Sometimes it's so bad the sod strip is not usable for a plane. Then Carla or Bob take the Reverend in by chopper to deliver supplies. When the runway is useable Charley always loaned him a plane; and now, I do. The church pays for the gas we do not charge for the plane. Nor do Carla or Bob charge for the chopper. I save the Aerobat for him for he likes to give the kids a ride after he delivers the supplies. It's one of the few pleasures they have. No electricity to the homes. They have only wells for water. The mission has a generator that runs most of the time. The church sends a van of supplies once every three months if the roads are passable. The Reverend flies some in each week. All they ask for is a decent road to get their sick to a doctor. They need so much more. You should see the poverty that's on our doorstep. The people live in shanties unfit for livestock even. It appears to be an abandoned ranch with an old farm house that the missionaries use for a clinic. There's a wooded area behind the ranch house and a stream."

"Have the Reverend call me. I'll see what can be done. I don't have much time here today, but can one of you show me this area when my business is finished in Houston? Although I'm not in office now I still have connections."

Jerry nodded. "I'll be glad to give him your message and you a ride." Cal watched him closely. What kind of business was he in now that the government work was over?

"Jerry, we have a student coming in at 1:30." Maggie reminded. Everyone looked at their watches and the group broke up. "It was nice to meet you Senator."

"Nice to meet you, Maggie." The Senator left with Bob Hardy. His ride to Houston was to pick him up there. The waitress started clearing the table.

As the Senator was driven back to Houston, he sat back in his comfortable rented limo contemplating. "A most interesting lunch indeed. The Reverend Mitchell. Well, well. I will have to see what is going on in his poverty village." This and Calvin Morris was a complication he had not foreseen.

When Sylvia Freeman could get no charter at Memorial she told her driver to find another airport. As they drove, she saw the scene once again. Then details swarmed back. Cal had put his left arm around Jerry's waist. No ring. Jerry had covered it with her left hand. No ring. They were not even engaged! She had baited that blue-eyed baby and had stepped into the trap herself. Furthermore, she had made a fool of herself with her anger by acting the way she did in the fashion world that made people tremble. It didn't work in this God forsaken place of common people. She might be down, but she would be back and she wasn't out. She tried to convince herself. But she had never seen the look in Calvin's eyes when he looked at her that he gave to Jerry when he said she would be a joy in his bed. He really loves her. The way Jerry had looked at him was mischievous but with adoration that the girl didn't realize she felt. She loved him too but doesn't know it. Would marriage between her and Cal have been another disaster?

Charley's Flying School

Rosa B. Lane

Chapter 13

It was an excited Abby who called two days later. Abby had made the front page of the local paper. Her picture and a caption saying "local grandmother solos" and a reference to the Local People page.

Jerry had not had time to read it that morning, but Maggie had been full of excitement. There was a very nice story that followed. Abby said the club women had been calling all morning. She was to tell them all about it at the meeting tonight. Jerry was looking forward to hear what was going to happen.

When Maggie answered the phone a few minutes later they received a cancellation. A young man whose father owned a garage in Oxton about ten miles from the airport had to cancel. Jerry listened as he related that a company had bought their mortgage and a number of other small businesses and had called them in early. His father had a job in San Antonio and they were moving. Not only the businesses but many houses were being taken over. Jerry felt cold chills. It was beginning. When Cal returned from his flight she related what the student had said. Oxton was south of the airport. At lunch the news was passed to all the other pilots. They all had similar news. Several real estate companies were doing the business. They left the lunch each with the job to dig as much information as they as they could about these companies. A sense of fear had filled each of them. That night Jerry placed a call to Richard. Did Lambert own any of the companies?

When Richard answered the phone he was delighted to hear

from Jerry. Everything was fine there. Jerry thanked him for the pictures and told him of Sylvia and their arrival which brought a laugh. Then he added, "Is that Sylvia Freeman? She's a devil I understand. She's Senator Stone's daughter."

"Senator Stone's daughter?" Jerry gasped. "I wonder why the Senator and Cal never mentioned that." She stopped for a second then continued, "I called about the land that surrounds the airport being bought. There are a number of companies buying property about ten miles from the airport. They seem to be trying to buy all the surrounding farms. I talked to your mother and she has sworn to destroy us all for helping you. Do you know anything about this? I think we're in trouble." Jerry told him about Cal's father's airport destruction. "It's the same pattern." She heard Richard whistle.

"I don't know anything, but I'll call the law firm that helped me find Lilly to get their investigators on it. I owe you a big one, little sister. If my folks are behind this, they have me to face. I won't let them hurt you. They've done enough. I'll be back to you. Marry Cal!! You are missing so much."

"Thanks, big brother." Jerry smiled into the phone feeling joy knowing that Richard had become so sure of himself.

"I'll get on the research right away. Goodbye."

Jerry hung up the phone. Sylvia and Senator Stone. Why didn't Cal say something? I guess no one had asked, or even thought to ask. She was restless and had a feeling of foreboding that swept over her. She did not want to be alone. She tried to read, but could not concentrate. TV was nothing but ads. She showered and got ready for bed, then went back downstairs. She finally admitted she was overwhelmingly lonely. But she could not make the call. Then the doorbell rang. She knew who it was before she opened it.

"Cal," she said softly. "Come in. I was thinking of you. I need someone to talk to tonight. I need you."

"I couldn't stop feeling that something was wrong and I had to come to see if you are all right." Cal stepped into the house and stood looking at Jerry wondering how she would accept his uninvited visit. "I need someone too. I need your company. No one else can fill the need."

Jerry held out her arms for him and he pulled her to him. They stood there just holding each other feeling secure as if a missing piece of themselves had been put into place and they were complete.

Jerry spoke softly. "I've been so lost tonight. I talked to Richard tonight. Why didn't you tell me Sylvia is Senator Stone's daughter?" She looked at him puzzled.

"I just didn't think it mattered. She is his wife's lover's child. He raised her. Politics I guess. That's all. She's been at boarding schools all her life or with a nanny. He totally ignored her. Why?"

"I guess it doesn't matter. I'm just so confused and felt so alone tonight. I didn't know why. Now I know. I'm lost without you. Ask me to marry you." She looked up at him her blue eyes inviting.

"Will you marry me? I love you." Cal looked at her waiting for the answer.

"Yes. As soon as possible." Their lips met and lingered. Ever so tenderly their need filled them. They were hardly aware when Jerry led him to her bedroom.

The phone ringing woke Jerry from a sound sleep. At first she was startled when she saw Cal asleep beside her. Then she smiled. She reached for the phone. It was Maggie. Cal had not shown up and he had a nine o'clock student. Ma Brown said he had been gone all night. Had Jerry seen him? They were worried.

"Cal is fine. We're engaged and he spent the night. He'll be there, Maggie. You're the first to know."

"Golly, congratulations. I'll call Ma Brown." Maggie hung up the phone then gave a shout of joy.

Cal propped himself up on his elbow listening. "By the time I arrive the whole airport will know we are engaged and I spent the night." He pulled her to him kissing her soundly.

"You have a nine o'clock student and responsibilities now. Off you go to the shower and to work. This is my day off." She stretched, yawned, and lay back down. A pillow landed on her.

"You have to prepare breakfast like a good responsible wife. Get up." They tumbled laughing on the bed, then reluctantly got up. Cal had never been so happy. He could see the joy in Jerry's eyes that said "I'm a woman and loved." Soon they would be married.

When Cal had left, Jerry called Uncle Art and told him the news for which he had been praying. The news for which he was sure that Charley and Rex had conspired. Then she called Rex and Patricia. They were delighted. Of course, the wedding must wait until Pat could get rid of her cast and could walk.

Jerry started her house cleaning with a different feeling. It was not just for her, but for Cal who would be here often. She was surprised at the different feeling she had knowing she was doing for someone else. It was like when Charley was alive. If only Charley were here. For an instant a feeling of sorrow swept over her. Then she knew somehow that Charley knew. She felt alive in a way she had never before felt. When Cal came again, the fridge would have good food and the coffee pot would be ready to brew real coffee. Jerry was in love.

Everyone at the airport was delighted that Jerry and Cal were finally doing what they should have done weeks ago. Otherwise the rumors of land being bought around the airport made everyone worried. Then Carla made her payment on her latest helicopter and discovered a new company was buying the mortgage. One by one the others who owned businesses at the airport had the same thing happen to them. The lunch meeting at the table became tense. A feeling of fear and helplessness invaded the air. What was going on?

On Tuesday Jerry took Abby up for her lesson. Reverend Mitchell picked up the Aerobat as usual and Arnie was busy in the hangar. Today Abby was to do a cross country exercise to start preparations for her required cross-country time. Abby had flown from the airport toward Houston on the usual flight path. Jerry had shown her the sectional, a map showing the roads, towers with their height, and other land marks as seen from the air.

Abby was to find a small airport about 50 miles from where they were. Jerry could see how Abby's concentration was too focused on the ground and, as most students did, she was forgetting to watch the sky around her. They were at 3000 feet and a single solitary small cloud was happily floating in front of them. Jerry waited for Abby to look up but her attention was on the hunt for the airport. It was not exactly the approved thing to do but Jerry had a great and a safe way to imprint a lesson on a student that rarely presents itself. For several minutes Jerry watched the cloud and nothing went in or came out.

Abby was busy searching the ground for the airport glancing at the instruments occasionally to keep her altitude when suddenly everything disappeared. Startled she looked around her and it was only white soft mist. There was nothing to relate to and no way to tell up from down. Abby felt shock and fear for the first time since starting to fly. Jerry's voice was calm.

"Didn't you see that cloud? Now make a 180 degree turn and fly out of it. It has been sitting in front of us for a good while. Watch your instruments."

Abby's hands shook when she turned the plane carefully her heart beating wildly. There was only milky whiteness as she started the turn watching the compass. She made the 180 turn and leveled off, or so she thought. In a few minutes they flew out into the sunshine.

"You gained 300 feet when you turned." Abby looked at the altimeter in surprise. It did not seem like she was climbing. Jerry continued, "You have just experienced spacial disorientation. Non IFR rated pilots do not fly into clouds or weather that obscures the vision. You could have stalled out and gone into a dive. Never be so busy that you don't keep your head on a swivel looking at the sky around you. Always scan your instruments."

"I-I'm sorry Jerry." Abby was visibly shaken. She looked so distressed that Jerry felt almost guilty.

"That's a lesson I don't get a chance to teach so dramatically as a rule. Let's get on with finding the airport. Do you know where you are?" Abby looked around and nodded.

"There it is. Right where it's supposed to be," Abby was so excited that Jerry laughed.

"Now take us back home." Abby turned the plane and carefully looking at the sky as well as the instruments and the landmarks flew them home. She would never forget to watch the sky around her again.

Back at the airport Jerry found Arnie in the hangar. "Hi Arnie. You look worried."

Arnie took a breath then turned to Jerry. "Miss Jerry, I hate to tell you this but I have to take my family back to St. Louis. My wife is so homesick she cries a lot. She's lonely here. The kids are unhappy in school. I have a job offer in St. Louis that is too good to say no to. The company is going to pay for our move. I have only a week. My wife's mother has a big house and says for us to come there. I owe it to my family to try to make them happy. You and Cal have been so good to me I feel awful. But -"

"Your family comes first. I know. I'm sorry we don't have time to hire a replacement, but Charley and I managed and Cal and I can. Thanks for your help. I hope you will be happy." Jerry was feeling betrayed by Arnie. No warning, just walking out. She tried to hide her feelings but her voice was sharper than she intended. "Just clean the tools. I'll have your check ready and you can pick it up tomorrow. Have you told Cal?"

"I haven't seen him since Monday."

Jerry just turned and walked out before she said something she would regret. She liked Arnie and his family, but leaving without notice was unfair. She went to the office to check the schedule.

She prepared for her next student trying to put Cal's disappearance aside. He'd come back. He had to.

When Jerry joined the others for lunch, they all looked worried. More land was being bought. This was a different company. It allowed those who wanted to sell but continue farming to stay. Jeffery had joined them and said there had been an offer to buy the airport but he had refused.

Jerry left them without lunch. What was it about Jeffery that she felt he was lying? Why did she think he wanted to sell but for some reason would not? She headed for home not feeling like eating. When she arrived there was no sign of Cal. She called Ma Brown but he was not there. She tried dry toast and tea but could not. Where was Cal? She went to the phone and called Uncle Art. He had not heard from him. He assured her Cal was probably just shopping. There was a wedding to prepare for. For the first time Jerry smiled. She hung up feeling a little better.

Then she called Richard. He was not there but she talked to Lilly. Lilly was surprisingly aware of everything. Richard kept nothing from her. She would relay the conversation to him. Asking if she could call Jerry her "sister" Jerry was delighted. They hung up with love of family in both their hearts yet they had never met nor were they related.

It was eight that evening when the doorbell rang. Jerry thought it was Cal who had forgot his key. She answered it quickly. There stood a man of middle years carrying two large manila envelopes. "Miss Jerry Jackson?"

"Yes. How can I help you?" Jerry disliked such late unexpected callers.

"Forgive me the late hour, but my client told me to get these to you without delay. I'm Harry McHugh with Stiegel Law firm. Our client, Richard Lambert says we are to be at your service in any way we can. May I come in?" Surprised, Jerry stepped aside and let him in. "I was with Richard when he found Lilly and his kids. He's a mighty fine young man. These are very important, Miss Jackson."

Jerry took the packages and led him into the breakfast room and placed them on the table. "May I get you something cool to drink?" He shook his head and seated himself at the table while she opened one of the envelopes. One by one she read the sheets of paper with a look of astonishment. They were the mortgages of all the airport businesses paid in full. She looked up at the smiling man.

"A present from your 'big brother' he said. But there is more. Not good news I'm afraid." With trembling hands, she opened the second envelope. Her blood ran cold as she read the documents. She looked up at him frightened.

"Statements made by a drunken driver with a previous record. He says he was offered $5000 to kill me. He had $2000 on him. Someone wants to kill me. Why? Why would anyone want me dead?"

Harry shook his head. "I think you may be treading on someone's toes and they are afraid you will see who it is. What about your partner?"

"I wonder where Cal is?" Jerry froze as the thought hit her. "Cal has been gone all day. It's not like him not to call. Can he be in danger too? Mr. McHugh, I'm frightened."

Harry leaned over and patted her hand. "My client said to

protect you. I'll have a man watching you 24 hours if you wish. I'll get someone looking for Cal if he doesn't show up tonight here or at the rooming house. We have female agents. Do you want one here tonight?"

"No. He'll come home." But Jerry had a sinking feeling that he would not. "Do you know where Sylvia Freeman is? She made some threats when she was here, and Cal let her know he loved me. What's going on? What did they do to the drunk?"

"They kept him as long as they could. As it says, when he sobered up, he denied everything. He explained the money as a gambling win. They finally had to let him go." Harry saw the look of disbelief on Jerry's face. "I don't know, but I think there is more here than a spurned romance. Something -just a feeling. Are you sure you don't want a woman here tonight? That man is still out there. But he's been printed and mugged and he knows if anything happens to you he's first in line for the accused."

"Cal should be home soon. Thank you. I'll get these papers to the airport tomorrow."

"This is much bigger than a jealous woman. I'll report it at once. I'll have a man watching your house 24/7. You have my card there. Call me if anything unusual happens. Be careful driving. I guess that's all. Oh, put those documents in a safe place just in case. Good night, Miss Jackson. Please call us at once if anything else comes up." Jerry walked him to the door. Across the street there was a strange black car. As McHugh left he gave a slight wave and a nod to the driver.

Jerry made sure the doors and windows were all locked and went back to the breakfast table. She reread the papers still not believing this was happening. Harry must be right. Why kill me? Where to put these papers? She walked to Charley's door hesitated a moment then went upstairs. She would leave all the lights on tonight. She finally decided to put them in the laundry hamper under the clothes and talk to Cal when he came home. But he did not come. She finally went upstairs and got ready for bed. Something was terribly wrong. Where was Cal?

The alarm went off unnecessarily since Jerry had slept little hoping Cal would come home. She got dressed and went to the airport taking the documents with her. At the restaurant everyone was trying to figure out what was going on. She took a seat then pulled out the envelopes and read off the names handing each one their paid mortgage. "Compliments of Richard Lambert. There's something more going on here. Read this." She handed Bob Hardy the other envelope. He turned pale.

"My, God Jerry! Why would anyone want to kill you? What in the hell is going on?" He passed the papers to the others. All were dumbfounded. "What does Cal say? Where is he?"

"I don't know. He didn't show up this morning. Ma Brown hasn't seen him, and I haven't since I said goodbye yesterday morning. He's gone." She burst into tears. Carla was at her side at once. She knew what it meant to be betrayed.

"Jerry, you can stay with me. I'm alone and have plenty of room. You shouldn't be alone."

"Why don't you go to Art's farm? You'd be safer there. Just close the school for a few days." Jeffery Trenton suggested. There was something in his voice that made Carla look at him. Does he know anything about this? She shook her head puzzled by the feeling Jeffery knew more about this than he was telling. It was her imagination.

"He'll be back. I'm sorry. But they can't get your mortgages. I've lost Arnie. His wife and kids were unhappy here and he had a better job offer in St Louis. So he is taking them back home. I now have to be our mechanic again." She collected her envelope and left with no breakfast.

At the office Jerry called Ma Brown only to find Cal had not showed up there. Then she called Uncle Art. He was on his way to her in less than an hour. Jerry was wondering what would happen next when Maggie and Mike entered the room. They took one look at the empty coffee pot, the pale Jerry, and no planes out to know something was terribly wrong. Jerry looked up. She had walled back the grief as she had done before. How fleeting happiness was.

"Cal hasn't shown up for two days. No one knows where he is. I've had to cancel his lessons and Arnie had to quit. He's moving back to St. Louis to a better paying job that's waiting for him. And someone wants to kill me. You're not safe here, Maggie. They might hurt you instead of me."

Maggie and Mike stared at her. "I don't scare that easily," declared Maggie in a firm voice. "There are real estate companies who have been trying to buy out everyone in the area. I think it's oil. Or maybe a development company wants to build here."

"It may be some big government project worth millions. But why kill you?" Mike pondered. "What do you know that could hurt them?" Jerry was astonished. It had not occurred that it might be something she may not even remember.

"No, it can't be that. I know nothing that is that important."

"That Sylvia woman," said Maggie. "She threatened you. Jerry, you can't stay alone. Mom can scoot someone over. You can stay with us."

"Dad has an empty room. You're welcome at my house." Mike offered.

Jerry looked at the two with love and gratefulness. "I'm not alone with friends like you. Uncle Art is coming. He's driving since it's supposed to rain again. Richard has sent an investigator to help us. He's having the house watched. Please don't put yourself in danger for me. But thank you."

Charley's Flying School

Rosa B. Lane

Chapter 14

Cal stood up to leave. Senator Stone cautioned him one last time, "You are to tell no one what you have been told. This is a multi-million-dollar deal and the firm would not be happy. It is not to leave this room. Not Jerry, not even Art. Understand?"

"I worked with the government and you years ago. That was official. Now you have no official capacity to order me, Senator. I won't do this. I have a business and a fiancée. I feel you're not telling me everything. If I find out this is illegal, I will have to turn you in. I spied for my country. But what you are asking is to research private incomes. To be no more than a snoop. I won't do it."

"I think you will help me and be silent. Your woman can always have an accident." The Senator's voice was cold and Cal felt anger building inside him. "You will do as I say." The Senator did not see the look of horror that flitted over Sylvia's face.

Cal stepped toward the Senator grabbing the Senator's shirt front and pulling him forward. "You'd better pray nothing, I mean not even a stubbed toe, happens to Jerry. If it does, I'll find you and I'll kill you. Do you understand? I will not help you." He let go of the Senator throwing him against the desk.

"She'll think you spent the last two days with me and you did." Sylvia walked up to him.

"Not the night. You lost Sylvia. You had your chance six years ago. I was going to ask you to marry me the night I had to fly the rescue chopper for the flood. You wanted me to give up my life to be a puppet for you. I would not do that. Thanks for keeping me from making a big mistake." He started to leave. Sylvia stepped in front of him.

"You're sure you want a child or a woman?" Sylvia looked up at him. She looked cold and shallow.

"What I want is what I have, Sylvia. Look at yourself." He turned her around so she had to see her reflection in a decorative mirror on the wall. "What I see is a too thin woman, over painted and cold and only wanting a man to toy with. You make me think of a hollow chocolate bunny. All fancy on the outside and nothing on the inside. What I have is warm, soft woman who wants to have my children and whom I want to be the mother of my kids. She's more beautiful without makeup, with oil on her nose, and hot and sweaty from hard work than you could ever hope to be. What do you want in life anyway? Just business? I have found more than that. She's waiting for me. I have to go."

"You care that much about her? How will you explain your absence?" Sylvia said what Cal was wondering. How would he explain to Jerry? He knew he could not lie to her. How could he explain his absence from the flying school?

He had left Tuesday to buy Jerry an engagement ring in Houston. While at lunch, he bumped into Senator Stone and Sylvia who asked him to come to his office and discuss a business deal. He consented as soon as he had done his shopping. In his pocket he carried Jerry's engagement and wedding rings. The business deal had lasted through dinner, but the Senator had told him virtually nothing and refused to answer any questions. Cal refused the job. He was going home but was persuaded to come in the next morning. He stayed in a hotel room that night.

"I don't know," he answered honestly. He turned to walk from the room thinking, "I don't know what you're up to but I'll have no part in it." Then he stopped and looked back at Sylvia. "Sylvia, I believe inside you there is a real woman if you will only let her come forth and be your real self. Whatever is going on, don't be a part of it." He left the room.

Sylvia watched him leave shaken at what he had said. Cal had changed. He was a stranger she did not know; a strong man, no longer the infatuated boy she had spurned. She looked at herself and saw the reflection as Cal had seen her and hated it. She turned from the mirror.

"Well, Sylvia," Senator Stone said quietly. "I'm sorry I have not been a better father to you."

"You have never been a father to me. Maybe because you know that you're not my blood father. My birth father didn't want me either. My mother deserted all of us. My half-brother, you and me. You got stuck with her bastard. But as a good politician you kept me to save your own face. Who was the man that should be on my birth certificate as my legal father instead of you? I've always wondered. You sent me away to educate me. Never denied me anything except what I wanted most. The love of a father. That I'll never have. I'm the product of two people using each other. You were "honorable" enough to raise me. I'm here because I owe you for that and the education that has given me the knowledge to become a business woman and wealthy in my own right." Sylvia turned her back to the Senator to keep him from seeing the tears that wanted to spoil her perfect make-up. The Senator got up and walked to her. He put his arm around her shoulder for the first time in his life. Sylvia felt chills at his touch and wanted to push him away.

"Sylvia," the words were choked and seemed hard to say, "I'm so sorry. I ask you to forgive me. I never saw you as a person with the same feelings as I have. I have been such a fool. I would be honored to be called your father. I'm so ashamed." He stood by her seeming to not know how to handle this stranger who was his legal daughter if not his biological daughter. A woman he seemed to no longer be able to control. He would have to watch her. He needed her a little longer. Then he would never have to see her again.

Sylvia turned and looked up at him. "Tell me who my biological father is."

The Senator walked to his desk and then turned to her. "Are you sure you want to know?" Sylvia nodded. "He is Harvey Lambert. That S.O.B. is your biological father. I'm to blame for your unhappiness. I don't deserve forgiveness, but I'm begging you for it."

Sylvia looked at the Senator. He was a really good actor.

Something in his eyes was cold and cruel. I'll play your game Senator.

The Senator continued, "I'd be proud to try. When this is over come home for a visit. I know a good fishing hole." Sylvia nodded. She picked up her purse and left the office. The Senator watched her leave and wondered if he had been good enough to make her believe him

As Sylvia drove back to her apartment she wondered if the Senator had thought she really believed him and trusted him. She had worked with him before but this was not the same. He admitted it was not official government work. They had all left government service years ago. There was something she did not quite trust. Some instinct was throwing up a caution signal. Whatever is going on, I've had enough of it. I'm getting out.

Chapter 15

Calvin drove back to the airport in the late afternoon traffic. He could not lie to Jerry, nor could he tell the truth. To tell her would endanger her life. He knew the Senator meant the threat. He had meant his threat too. He drove up to Charley's Flying School and parked by Uncle Art's car. He went into the office and said, "Hi, Art. What brings you here?"

"It seems someone wants Jerry dead," he said accusingly. "You should have been here. Arnie's quit. I hope you had a good time." Art turned his back on Cal and leaned over the map. Cal stood looking at them in shock. Was this the work of the Senator? Who else would do such a thing?

"Arnie quit? Why?"

"He had a better job offer in St. Louis, and his family wanted to go back."

"I cancelled your students for today. Will you do the honor of teach the class tonight?" Jerry glared at him. "Uncle Art came to help me. This is a business, Cal. You can't go off with another woman whenever you wish. It's best I find out now. I'm finished for the day with my students. I'm leaving. Maggie, if you have Arnie's check ready you can leave too." She turned to Cal, "It's up to you to cancel the class tonight or to teach it. I don't care. You own half the school. It's your money and honor too." Jerry turned and fled from the office.

"Art," Cal started but Art was gone and Maggie was leaving. Cal stood alone. He reached for the phone and started dialing students to cancel the class. He would go to her house and stay until she listened to him.

Jerry was in the kitchen when Art let him in the front door. Cal walked into the kitchen. Jerry glared at him and asked angrily, "What are you doing here? Get your things and get out. When you are ready to tell me where you have been, we will talk. Until then go back to your room at Ma's."

"Jerry, I can't tell you except I have not cheated on you. I have seen the Senator and Sylvia only on business. You must trust me."

"I see. I thought we shared everything. I'm supposed to blindly trust you as to where you disappeared for two days without any word, but you don't trust me enough to tell you where you've been." Jerry took the coffee she had made for dinner last night and washed it down the drain. She cleaned the pot and prepared it to make some fresh. Art turned to Cal.

"It takes both people to trust each other in marriage, Cal. Where were you? Jerry's life is in danger. Your place is with her." Art had never interfered with anyone's quarrels before but this was his Jerry's life that was at stake.

"I cannot tell you, Art. I will say that I was with the Senator. Just like you, Dad and Charley used to meet with him and do your 'aerobatics.' And that is really too much."

Art's face blanched. "You too?" Jerry looked from one to the other.

"I refused to work with him. I have said too much already." Cal looked at Art and their eyes met. He's been contacted too! And he has refused.

"Jerry," said Art. "Trust him. Don't ask any more questions. He can't tell you."

"Jerry is untrustworthy." She said angrily feeling alone and shut out. She needed to be in the air and feel the friendship of her plane. Sobbing, she turned and ran through the utility room grabbing her flight bag, purse and keys to her car. The men stood as if paralyzed as she backed her car out of the drive narrowly missing Art's car and backing onto the grass to get by Cal's wagon. She bounced over the curb and skidded around headed for the airport. She forgot a cardinal rule not to fly when you are upset or ill.

"Stop her Cal. She'll get the Aerobat and this weather–. Stop her!" Art cried in alarm as Cal ran to his car. Then Art picked up the phone and called the police. He was lucky. Jerry's friend Jeb was on duty. He reported her speeding and asked him to have her stopped. Jeb had the dispatcher call the police chopper and the patrol cars that were in the area then he got into his car and followed Cal. The clouds were dark and forbidding and the wind had picked up.

Jerry realized she was going seventy in a fifty-five-mile zone and started to slow down. An eighteen-wheeler was coming up behind her fast. She pulled to the far right to give him plenty of room to pass. The deep drainage ditch along the road was wicked so she was careful to keep on the pavement. She checked the rear-view mirror and saw the truck coming directly behind her not making any effort to pass her. He's going to ram me, she thought.

Cal had arrived at the highway and had to wait for an eighteen-wheeler to pass before he could turn. He floored the gas to catch up with Jerry when he heard the sound of a chopper above him. The truck was catching up with Jerry very quickly. Cal had a cold chill. He's going to ram her!

Above them the police chopper called the dispatcher that he had spotted the yellow speeder. Then he realized the truck was going even faster and called in the report. "He's so close, he's going to ram her. I'm going down to try to slow him down."

Jerry knew there was a turn off road that led to a farmer's fields a half mile ahead. She could see it from the highway. If I only had an airplane, she groaned, but she would try it. The road was near. The rear-view mirror showed only headlights. Jerry braked and made a sudden sharp right turn into the side road just as the truck hit the right end of the rear bumper whirling her into the field. She threw her arms over her face. The car slammed the passenger side into a tree growing at the side of the farm road. There was a jarring and horrible pain. Everything went black.

The police chopper reported the hit and run, called for an ambulance and settled down in a clearing. Grabbing the first aid kit the police officer ran to the car. Cal had seen little except Jerry's car sailing into the tree and the truck speeding off. He pulled into the farm road and parked clear of the road for the ambulance he knew had been ordered. He joined the police chopper pilot and ran to Jerry's car terrified at what he would find. With the help of the police pilot, he wrenched open the car door. Jerry was bleeding badly from a head wound and cuts on her arms. She was unconscious. The odor of gasoline filled the air as it poured around the car.

"Help me get her out" Cal said, the calm of his voice belying the terror he felt. They removed her from the battered car and Cal carried her away from the fire hazard laying her gently on the grass. The police put a pressure bandage on the cut and a temporary splint on her left arm.

Art made his call and then followed after Cal and Jerry. He arrived as Jerry's limp bloody body was being lifted into the ambulance. Art was numb with shock. The ambulance was returning from a false alarm in a nearby subdivision when it had been sent to the accident scene. As soon as the ambulance left, the chopper was in the air trailing the truck.

"Cal, is she-" the word would not come out of Art's mouth.

"She's alive, unconscious, but badly hurt. I'm getting her purse and flight bag from the car. Come see if there's anything she might need." Cal went back to the car and pulled Jerry's things from the front seat. There was nothing in the back seat. The trunk had sprung open and Art took the tools from it. Cal emptied the contents of the glove compartment into his pockets. "Let's go, Art. This is my fault if she dies." His voice was a failed attempt at control. Senator, if you did this, I'll kill you. He threw the bag and purse into the front seat of the wagon. Art dumped the tools in the back of his car. The wind was blowing harder, but the much needed rain had not come.

When they arrived at the hospital, Jerry was still in the emergency room. The admitting desk asked if they were relatives. Cal said he was her fiancée and her business partner. Art said he was her godfather and that she had no living relatives.

"What insurance does she have?" the admission clerk asked.

Cal looked in her purse. He did not know why he had carried her purse and flight bag with him to the ER. He found her new insurance card of the company that the school had only recently bought into. The clerk looked at it and frowned. "I'm sorry, we do not handle this company." She handed the card back. "You will have to go to another hospital." Art and Cal looked at each other unbelieving.

"My fiancée is unconscious, in critical condition, and you are going to throw her out. No way."

"Someone must pay the bill. It's not my rule." The phone on her desk rang and she answered it.

"We'll see that it is paid." Art and Cal said at the same time.

"Never mind. It's taken care of. She'll go to the VIP suite on the 4th floor. There will be round the clock nurses. She must have a friend in high places."

"Who?" Asked Art.

"They didn't say. You may have a seat." The tone of the clerk was that of coolness as if disappointed that she had been over ruled. She motioned them to the waiting room chairs to make room for the next patient.

"What's going on?" asked Art as they were seated. "Who would know we're here?" Cal shook his head.

"As long as Jer is taken care of, I don't care who pays the bills." A nurse wearing scrubs came out of the ER room where Jerry had been taken.

"Are you her husband?" she asked Cal. "We need a treatment authorization signed for her to have treatment."

"I'm her fiancée. She has no relatives. I'll sign." The nurse hesitated.

"I'm her godfather. I'll be responsible." Art looked at the nurse. "She's like my own child."

"We've been together. If she is pregnant, it is mine. I have the right to see that my expected child is taken care of." Cal's voice was angry and full of fear. The nurse looked surprised. "Only a few days, but there's the chance."

"I'll take your consent," the nurse handed him the clipboard and Cal signed it. She then noted on the page that there was a possible pregnancy. This might make a difference in medication that would be given. "We have the bleeding stopped, and her left arm needs a cast. She will need stitches. She may have other injuries we will have to treat. We'll let you know when she will be transferred to her room." The nurse looked at the men and said, "She'll be all right." As she left she tried to tell the same thing to herself and believe it.

Jerry felt pain. Blackness and pain. She heard voices. Cal and Uncle Art were saying words she could only partly comprehend. "She's got to make it–get him-love you." She could not move her left arm. Someone was holding her right hand. They think I'm going to die. Willing it to happen, she opened her eyes. Her right eye would not open far. Everything seemed blurry, then slowly things came into focus. Cal was kissing her fingers. An IV needle was in her hand. Uncle Art was looking grave. Her lids fell shut again in spite of her attempt to keep them open. She refused to die.

"Don't leave me, Jer. I couldn't live without you. I love you so." Jerry tried to squeeze his hand and failed. It was hard to breathe. She heard someone moaning and vaguely realized it was herself. Finally, with all the effort she could muster she said, "Cal", and forced her eyes open. "I hurt." There was a flash of white as the nurse bent over her hand. In a few seconds the pain lessened. She went to sleep.

"She'll sleep for a while. I'll order some dinner for you. There's coffee in the other room." The nurse pointed to the second room of the suite with a bed, sofa and small dining table and chairs. Coffee was already on the table. "You can rest on the bed. It's for relatives to stay the night if they need to."

Art touched Cal's arm. "Come, son. Let's get some coffee. We'll be right back." He led the reluctant Cal to the other room. It was complete with another bath room and shower. Above the sink on a shelf were shaving items, hotel soaps, lotions, shampoo and all the accommodations of a first-class hotel. Art shook his head. "I didn't know they had rooms like this in a hospital. She has a private bath too." The two sat down at the coffee table, Art pour two cups and they settled in for a long wait.

Jerry opened her eyes painfully. Cal was at her side his unshaven face showed fatigue. "Cal." She tried to tell him to go home and sleep but her lips seemed swollen and her face stiff. She couldn't move her left arm. "Cal."

"I'm here, Jerry." Cal kissed her fingers. Her poor swollen

face he dared not kiss for fear of hurting her.

"Where am I?" Jerry looked around and saw the nurse, the IV, and said, "I hurt everywhere." The nurse stepped over to the IV and once again Jerry felt better. This time she stayed awake longer. "I love you." She reached up and touched his unshaven cheeks. "Go home and rest. They can't kill me so easily." Her eyes closed, and she slept.

"Mr. Morris, why don't you go lie down? I'll call you when she wakes up again. She is stable now and doing well. You can't help if you become ill yourself. You didn't touch your dinner or your breakfast. She doesn't want you so tired." The nurse spoke gently. She was a middle-aged woman whose life had been spent doing special duty for many desperately ill patients. She knew the pain of a hurt or an ill loved one. All her training could not save her husband. She had never left his side either. "I put your juice and milk in the refrigerator."

"Thanks, Mrs. Page. I think I will lie down a bit while she's sleeping. When Art gets back, have him wake me. He's bringing me some clean clothes." Cal got up and the nurse nodded. He still had on the bloody shirt he had worn when he carried Jerry from the car. He went into the other room and stretched out on the bed. The nurse closed the door behind him.

Arthur Swenson had called Ma Brown to pack some clean clothes for Cal. He went to the airport and checked on the planes. Nothing at the office appeared to be disturbed. When he went to Ma Brown's she insisted on feeding him. Art took Cal's clothes and stopped at Jerry's where he showered and changed clothes then returned to the hospital.

Jerry opened her eyes. This time it did not hurt so much. She looked around the room and saw Uncle Art sitting next to her. "Cal?" she asked. She could breathe better now. Her head hurt but the awful pain she had felt before had lessened. Her face was not so stiff. "Cal?"

"Cal will be back. He had to go to the bathroom." Art looked at the beloved daughter of his best friend and felt a little relieved. The black eyes were now clearing up and the swelling was less. They knew she would make it. Cal came back and Art relinquished his chair. Jerry smiled for the first time.

"Cal. You've shaved. You look better. You'll miss the class

tonight." At the puzzled look on Cal's face then his smile, she asked, "What day is this?"

"This is the 28th. You've been in and out of consciousness for a week. You gave us all a scare." Cal kissed her fingers.

"The school?"

"I closed it for a few days. But it's fine." Cal said. "Jer, I'm so sorry. This all my fault."

Art filled in, "Richard learned about this and called his father. Mr. Lambert wants you to know he had nothing to do with this and has hired an agency to work with the police to find out who did it. He apologized for the way his wife insulted you."

"How did he find out?" Jerry spoke through a haze of pain.

"It seems the police reporter for the local TV news had the accident as a live special report before you got to the emergency room. Then the six o'clock news had scenes of the car wreck and a follow up story of the attempted murder. It then made national news and Richard saw it. He came as soon as he could. Your news reporter friend Tillie made a scoop." This brought a smile to Jerry and it hurt her stiff, sore face.

"My face? It's so sore." She reached up to feel her head, and Cal caught her hand. "Is it that bad?"

"You have an IV in your hand, two black eyes and about six stitches in your head. You had stitches on your arms and your left arm is fractured." Cal looked grave as he continued. "They are keeping you here because you had internal injuries." Jerry's eyes met his. "They are waiting for more x-rays."

Jerry looked at the nurse. "I'm due to start today." The nurse nodded and went to the chart and made a note. She knew what the two wanted to know.

"He left out a couple of fractured ribs. And the fact he donated all the blood they would let him. It seems you are compatible in every way." The nurse grinned as she spoke.

"They caught the driver when he tried to ditch the stolen truck. He's afraid to talk; but also afraid that if you die, he'll go up for murder. He swears he only meant to scare you. The police found an envelope with $10,000 in it on him and there were smeared fingerprints. They are trying to find who they belong to but it appears hopeless. Richard and Mr. Lambert have brought in the best detectives. I think the man will break. The police respected Charley and they loved his pigtailed kid. They'll get who is behind this." Cal added realizing he was talking too much. He saw it in Jerry's swollen eyes that she knew he was not telling everything.

"What has happened that you are not telling me?" Jerry demanded and tried to turn to Cal. She cried out in pain. The nurse was there and before Jerry could stop her injected the IV with another dose of pain medicine. Cal shook his head. Jerry lay back and closed her eyes. Will I never stop hurting?

"She reads me like a book. I can't hide anything from her." He was angry with himself.

"But then she knows you were never unfaithful to her. She was only angry that you would not tell her where you had been." Art looked at Cal. "Why don't you go home and take your laundry, and I'll stay here until you get back? Sarah said she did your wash for you. But not to expect it after Jerry gets well."

"You haven't left this room since she came in, Mr. Morris. You need to get outside and stretch your legs. She is out of danger now." Mrs. Page spoke gently. Cal looked at her and nodded. He relinquished his chair to Art, went into the guest room, and got the keys to his station wagon. Cal reluctantly left.

When he was gone, Art looked at the nurse and opened his mouth but was stopped. "Mr. Swenson, I've been briefed on what is going on."

"You aren't a police woman by any chance?" he asked. "You sure sound like one."

"I have had police training. I work undercover for a detective agency. Now I'm going to get a cup of coffee. May I bring you one?" Art shook his head no.

Cal had been surprised to learn they had all been contacted and they all had refused. What was the real "business" of the Senator? Did it have anything to do with the airport?

Jerry was standing in the bathroom looking at her face now turning green and yellow. Nature let her know she was not pregnant leaving her both glad and sad. At least Cal was free to pursue Sylvia or whatever he was pursuing and not have any guilty feelings about her. Once again, she was angry. She was permitted to walk about the room with the nurse near her. A hospital terry cloth robe covered the ugly green gown split down the back. She wanted to go home.

"Miss Jackson, you have a visitor downstairs if you wish to receive him. A Mr. Richard Lambert." Her nurse waited for her to answer. Jerry nodded yes and found a seat in a comfortable chair. In a few minutes Richard appeared at the door. He held two boxes that the guards had orders to open and make sure they were safe. Jerry had not realized she was under guard.

"Richard!" She was so happy to see someone else for a change. She had been in the hospital for two weeks and should have been home by now. He walked over to her and kissed her on the head, the only place that seemed free of bruises.

"Wow! Those eyes must have been lulus when they were fresh. Lilly and your friend, Carolyn decided you must be tired of ugly gowns and picked you out something pretty and a robe. Carolyn said she would keep them clean for you. Sorry, the guards had to check them out." He handed her the boxes which she opened with his help. In it were several shorty gowns of blue, green, pinks and floral. They were designed so her cast had no problem going through the sleeves. Jerry felt the silky satin fabric trimmed with lace holding it against her cheek and relishing the luxury. The robe was short and multicolored so it would match each gown. To keep her arms warm in bed there was a bed jacket to match. They were accompanied with a pair of matching slippers.

"Oh, Richard they are beautiful. Thank you. Lilly is here? I have to meet her. Did you bring your children? They have to let me go home. I can't wait to hug her and the kids."

"Cal said that you had internal injuries they were watching closely. Don't be too hasty, little sister. Enjoy while you can. Yes, the kids are here and anxious to meet 'Auntie Jerry'."

"This is partly business to check with my lawyer on my inheritance. Here," he pulled the morning paper from his pocket and handed it to her. "I just picked it up to read while I waited. I was afraid

I'd find you very ill, but you look pretty good considering what your car looked like."

"They won't tell me anything, Richard. I'm scared that something bad has happened and I'm responsible for it. I can't help but feel somehow all this is my fault."

"Dad said he wanted you to know he had nothing to do with this and we are working together to find out what is going on. He's really sorry Mom was so nasty. I think he's changed. He seems kind of nice now."

"You saw your parents? Lilly?"

"Jerry, I wish you should have been there. We went to see them and she looked them straight in the eyes and said, 'Hello, Mr. Lambert, Mrs. Lambert.' My folks just gasped at this beautiful young woman who stood before them waiting for an answer. I stepped close to her and put my arm around her and said 'Meet my wife, Lilly.' Where there had been a frightened teen, now stood a woman of grace and elegance. The teen who had been thrown out to the wolves had survived raising their only grandchildren with the help of charity and Joanne. Then she smiled at his cigar and said, 'The price of that cigar would have filled the empty bellies of your grandchildren for a couple of days. They were always hungry. My cousin Joanne who had three kids of her own helped us. With the charity of others, we survived, while you lived in luxury. I'm not sure I will let you see them. You may be a bad influence on them and we are trying to raise them right.' I thought Mother would have a stroke and Father started laughing. 'By god girl, you've got guts. I'm sorry I missed judged you. You're probably right about a bad influence. Arrogance has caused us a lot of pain. That Jerry Jackson, she told us off too. Welcome home Richard and Lilly.' And Lilly said quietly, 'We have our own home, we just came to visit Jerry in the hospital. I wanted to meet the people who wanted to murder my babies. Here is a picture of them. I always had faith that Richard would find us and he did. Now my babies aren't hungry and cold any more. And we had DNA tests done to verify they are Richard's.' She handed the picture to him and turned and walked out. I said I'd be in touch and left with her."

"Good for her. I'm anxious to meet her. Are your children

doing well? And how's Joanne's college?"

"Yes, for all five of them. I have two nannies. They make sure the kids get their homework done so when fall comes they'll not be left behind. Joanne soaks up knowledge like no one I've ever known. She's into business and has been dating a professor of math. Her divorce will be final soon. And you and Cal?"

"I love him, but he is pushing me out of things. I don't know what to think. He was gone from Tuesday to Wednesday afternoon and refused to tell me where. I do know that Sylvia Freeman was with him. Is that a good basis for marriage? Uncle Art is on his side. Some big hush- hush project they won't tell me about. I feel so alone. And scared." Jerry stopped then smiled, "That's about it. I won't be flying for a while. My car is wrecked, and I just today felt like calling the insurance company. They're trying to get out of paying for it. I just feel too tired to fight right now, but I must."

"You get well. Let big brother fight for you. If they give me a hard time, I'll sic Lilly on them." At that Jerry laughed. Richard added, "I don't want to tire you." He bent and kissed her on the head and took his leave.

He wanted to go by the airport and check on it. After all, he now owned most of the land around the airport and someone was not happy with him. He planned to build a WWII flying museum if it was feasible. Yet the farmland it would be built on would be ruined forever. He had a lot of environmental research to do. Meanwhile the farmers would continue to grow food and raise cattle.

Cal arrived at Jerry's room that evening. He was surprised to see her sitting at the table in the guest room having tea with her nurse. She was dressed in a beautiful gown and robe.

"Jerry, you look marvelous," he said smiling. He bent over to kiss her head and she looked up at him and smiled sweetly.

Then Jerry stood up suddenly. "Why are you here? Where's your beloved Sylvia? She is so important she can know everything, and I am told to trust you. This is no basis for a marriage. Tell me or get out. I won't start married life like this."

"Jerry, we've been through this. I can't tell you." Cal said taken by surprise at Jerry's attack. Jerry whirled and took a step toward the bed. The room kept whirling and she stumbled forward in a black haze. She felt Cal's arms around her catching her and his cry of "nurse" then all went black.

Cal laid Jerry on the bed. "Jerry. Jer," he cried, then looked at the nurse filled with fear and guilt. "What happened?" He stood there trembling and feeling lost and helpless. "If anything happens to her," he fought for control. The nurse took over. She dialed for the doctor.

"Mr. Morris, the hospital room is no place for family scenes. She nearly died in the accident. You know that. She is still very weak. Her being upset by you was just too much. Doctor Shipman is coming up. You can talk to him. He's the one on call tonight. I personally think it would be best for you to leave and stay away for a few days till she calms down. You can call her regular doctor tomorrow." Nurse Kelly was firm and unsympathetic with Cal. She was new at nursing but not at the kind of feeling Jerry had of being shoved aside like a child. "She's right, you know. Marriage takes a lot of work. Better to find out before than after if both are up to handling it. Communication is all important."

"I won't leave until she is all right." Cal stood by Jerry's bed looking at her pale face. The door opened and Doctor Shipman came in. He was a average looking young man about Cal's age. The beard he was sporting, which seemed to be the 'in' thing with doctors currently, hid most of his face. He nodded to Cal and went straight to Jerry.

He examined her as the nurse told of the angry exchange between them not explaining Cal's attempt to explain to Jerry his side. When the doctor finished, he turned to Cal and motioned him into the other room. The doctor shut the door.

"I started to order a sedative for this evening but she is already on one, though I think it is rather strong. I understand you're her fiancée. At least were. Right now, she blames herself for all that's happened. You're a lucky man. She is still very weak. Whatever the dispute if you can resolve it to her satisfaction it will be a big help. Until then perhaps if you stayed away a day or two until she calms down it would be better." The men shook hands and the doctor left thinking, "If they split up, I hope I'm around to help her pick up the pieces."

When the doctor left, Cal returned to Jerry. She was sitting up in bed and telling the nurse she was sorry. Then she saw Cal. She turned her head and looked away from him. He was totally shut out. He felt lost. Then it struck him that this was the way Jerry felt when he shut her out. "Jer," he said, "I'll be gone when you get home. I love you very much and hope someday you'll understand. Get well, and then we'll talk things over." He turned without giving her a chance to speak and walked out. Cal still carried her wedding rings in his pocket and felt the box with a heavy heart.

Charley's Flying School

Rosa B. Lane

Chapter 16

Cal did not want to go to the empty house to get his things. This was entirely his fault. Somehow, he should have handled it differently and the accident would never have happened. He drove to the airport and was passed through by the night guard. Once in Charley's Flying School office he could not keep his grief and guilt of what he had done to Jerry from exploding. He had finally found the one woman he loved and he had destroyed his chance. He placed his arms on the empty desk and the sobs came out in spite of his attempt to control them. He laid his head on his arms and cried. He did not hear the door open.

Richard had spent the afternoon at the airport meeting the business owners who were surprised by the visit from their benefactor. Their suspicions were put at rest when he talked to them about his plans to build an air museum at the airport if it was feasible. Little by little, he found out what was going on. It was getting late and he called Lilly to tell her he would miss dinner and explained why. She asked about Jerry and he told her. Tomorrow he'd see if they could visit. He ate at the airport, and was allowed to visit the control tower. He asked if he could bring his family before they left and got permission. Then he drove by Charley's Flying School. It seemed a long time since he had kissed Jerry, and she had slapped him. He laughed at the memory. How much water had flowed under the bridges of their lives since then? He saw Cal's station wagon parked at the office. He hoped he would get to meet Calvin Morris. He parked and went into the office.

"Mr. Morris?" He asked before he realized the man was sobbing. "Are you all right?" He walked to the desk as Cal looked up, embarrassed, and wiped the tears on the back of his hand.

"Yes. We're closed." Then Cal recognized him from his pictures. "Richard Lambert? I heard you were in Houston. Sit down. How can I help you?"

"Is something wrong with Jerry? I was there earlier and she seemed fine. What has happened? I care for her too. Like the sister I never had." Richard still stood by the desk looking down at Cal's tortured face, his own suddenly full of fear.

"I'm a fool." Cal got up and walked around the desk and held out his hand to Richard. "Let's sit." He went to the sofa and sat down. "I got her upset and she passed out. She broke off our engagement. She hates me. And she's right. That's what hurts."

"Jerry calls me the big brother she never had. Could I be a friend who understands a little of what may be going on?" Cal looked at him surprised. "I know Senator Stone. I've had business dealings with him. Nothing hush-hush. I know about the time you spent away from Jerry with him and Sylvia. I'd be mad too if I were Jerry. Why don't you explain?"

"I refused to help Senator Stone since he has no official orders or standing in the government now. He threatened Jerry if I would not work with him. I refused him. I felt I could protect her. She won't accept the fact that Sylvia was there too. And she thinks I cheated on her. I would never do that. That's why she left the house like a maniac and had the accident. I stopped to wait for that damned semi to pass before I turned on the highway. If only I had taken a chance and pulled out in front of him. It was my fault she is hurt."

"She loves you and that is why it hurts her so much when she feels she is shut out of your life."

"I'm not shutting her out. I was trying to protect her. Senator Stone threatened her life if I told anyone what he had told me. I think he's into something illegal. But I don't know. I'm sure he has not told me everything." Cal looked at him miserably. Richard raised his eyebrows questioningly. Cal could not answer the look.

"Cal, may I call you Cal?" Cal nodded. "I owe everything to

Jerry. When I was trying to impress her and apologize for my bad behavior of kissing her, she and I talked. She was the one who gave me the courage and helped me find where to start looking for Lilly. If I can help her, I want to. I do know that the Senator is into some sort of a business deal. But I'm not sure I trust him completely. Maybe he kind of reminds me of my dad, jovial on the outside but ruthless on the inside. At least the way Dad used to be. Something about the Senator is not completely right." Richard stopped and took a breath. "How well do you know him?"

"My father, Art and Charley worked with him when they were young before they married. Their aerobatic show was a good cover. They were on official government work. I worked some when I was flying air rescue. But I had official orders from the government. I got into places not normally allowed. We spotted illegal operations and stopped some drug deals. This time there is no official order. I think he wants to use me. For what I can only guess. That's more than I should say. I can't tell Jerry. Come to think of it, I really don't know him at all outside of credentials. I'll kill him if he did this to Jerry."

"And because of this you are losing the woman you love. Don't let it happen. What I'm saying is that I almost lost my family because of my parents. I did not fight back. Don't let it happen to you. Tell Jerry what you just told me."

"Richard, I can't make her understand me." Cal shook his head in despair.

"Then you must try to understand her and do what you would want her to do if the situation was reversed. Will you let me be your friend?" Richard held out his hand to Cal. Cal took it and the two men clasped hands in a friendship that would last for the rest of their lives. "Where do we start?" The door opened. They looked around to see who it was.

Sylvia stood there. Cal frowned, then smiled. Her stylish hair that swirled around her cheek was gone. The show girl makeup was gone and in its place was a soft natural look. She still wore her fashionable suit and spike heels. Cal looked at Richard to introduce them but instead gasped, "Good lord, you look like twins. Sylvia Freeman meet Richard Lambert." The two stared at each other. Their black hair, their eyes, and cheekbones showed them as obvious blood relations.

"Well, Richard Lambert I'm glad to meet you. We have a lot in common. Our father." Sylvia looked at Richard with anger flashing in her eyes.

Richard looked at her and shook his head. "I don't understand. Please explain. I know Father played around but didn't think he left any evidence."

"My mother had an affair with your dad and I am the unwanted result. Since my mother was Senator Stone's wife, she put his name as my father. Then deserted us all, my older brother who is now somewhere with the Marines, me and the Senator. The Senator had too much political face to save to give me away. He hired a nanny and as soon as I was old enough sent me off to Swiss schools. Out of sight and out of mind. My brother thinks I'm a disgrace to the family, and I've not seen him for twenty years. I came back to go to college and made a bad marriage. I worked for the Senator for a while then started my own fashion business. I'm good at business and have done fine." Sylvia paused, "Until I joined him with this job. I don't know what the Senator is up to, but I'm getting out. End of story. I guess you are like that bastard of a father we have, too good for the unwanted child." She spoke as if Richard was as much to blame as his father.

"Well. You sure sound like him too. I lost a younger brother to social snobbery. To find I have a sister one minute and lose her the next would be too much. Sylvia are you my big sister or baby sister?" Richard gave his charming grin that challenged Sylvia's unwarranted anger.

Sylvia looked at him perplexed. Then suddenly it seemed funny. She laughed. "I'm twenty-eight. And you?"

"I just turned twenty-five, big sister. Come give me a sisterly hug." He held open arms out to her. Sylvia stared in complete surprise. No one had ever wanted to just hug her because they wanted to be her friend. She hesitated and for the first time since he had known her Cal saw the woman of iron disappear as she stepped into her new found brother's arms. "Cal, I've got a real sister. And you Sylvia have a sister-in-law and a niece and a nephew. We're a family." He gave her a big tight hug.

"I was so mean just now," she said taking a deep breath to keep from showing too much emotion. "It was uncalled for. Cal, I have a new brother."

"And I have a friend," replied Cal. "What brings you here Sylvia?"

"You, Cal. I thought-well, maybe that," she stopped. "I was wrong, wasn't I?"

"I told you that it was over. We both know it would have been a mistake. But Jerry has broken the engagement because she thinks we spent the time together as lovers not the reality of the business. I can't blame her. You know I couldn't tell her the truth. Did the Senator order the accident like he threatened?" Cal took a deep breath and tried to continue but could not. He turned his back to them struggling for control.

"I don't know about the accident. But I do know that Jerry is very wrong. I'll talk to her. No one told me not to tell. Everyone, as usual, just takes it for granted that I'll do anything they want. I'll see her tomorrow. I'll take her something every woman needs. A silver mirror, comb and brush set. Richard, no, I'll call you Rick, when do we face the lion in his den? It's time he met one of the results of his adultery."

"How about meeting your new family first? Then we'll see Jerry. Cal, don't pay any attention to those doctors. Go see her. Crawl if you have to, but don't let her slam the door. She doesn't want to, I'm sure. I need to get back to Lilly and my kids. I hate being away from them even a minute." Richard took his leave followed by Sylvia. Cal was alone again. This time he felt better. He reached for the phone.

Chapter 17

Cal was surprised when Jerry answered "Don't hang up. May I come over? It's very important." He waited, not daring to breathe.

"Cal, what's wrong? I didn't mean what I said. I love you. My luxury suite has a guest room. Come on over. I'll tell the guards you're coming."

"Thanks, Jerry. I need you. I love you, and I was so wrong." Cal's heart ached to know she forgave him. "I'll stop at Ma's for some things. I love you so much."

When he arrived at the rooming house he found Ma in the kitchen making sure everything was in order for breakfast. She scowled at him. "Kind of late for dinner."

"I guess I'll have to go hungry. I have to go pack an overnight bag." He looked at her with the lopsided grin that made him look like a mischievous boy.

"I reckon I can find a sandwich for you." Cal bent down and kissed Ma's cheek. "Go on now." She grinned. He reminded her of her youngest boy.

When Cal returned, a sandwich was on the table. Ma placed a beer beside his plate. "Now if you get arrested, don't tell them I gave beer to you," she said.

"Thanks, Ma." Cal hastily gulped down the sandwich and his beer. "Have I said 'I love you' lately?"

"Go on now. Where ever you're going, remember Jerry."

"I'm going to the guest room in Jerry's fancy suite. I miss her, Ma."

"No hanky-panky, young man."

"She's got a guard called a nurse on every shift. Can't get away with anything. Good night."

When Cal arrived, the guards were expecting him and passed him through quickly. Jerry had refused her sedative until he was safely in the room and in her arms.

"I didn't mean it." Cal shushed her.

"Nurse Kelly, we need to be undisturbed and there will be no hanky panky since Ma Brown has given me orders." The nurse stopped her protest and laughed as he led Jerry into the guest room and locked the door. Jerry giggled. It sounded like Ma Brown. When they were alone, Cal took her in his arms and gently kissed her. "I was so wrong, Jerry. Forgive me. I was offered a job by the Senator and I refused. I think what he's doing is illegal. He threatened to kill you if I told anyone. I was trying to protect you. Sylvia was there, but I stayed alone in a hotel room. Richard came by tonight so did Sylvia. It seems that Sylvia and Richard have the same father. She wants to see you and tell you we were not together except for business." Jerry stayed in his arms while he told her. Jerry looked at him with love.

She went to the bed and sat on the edge. "In my heart I never doubted. I don't know how I could have acted so crazy. This is all my fault. What's he doing? The Senator."

"I only know that Art and Dad refused just as I have." Cal talked softly and told her all he knew. Then said, looking at Jerry's tired face, "We've had a long, day. We both need to get some sleep. I wish it would be in your arms, but Ma's and the doctor's orders." Jerry unlocked the door and turned and said, "Good night. Don't worry about the car. Richard is taking care of the insurance company." She kissed him and went to her bed and like a good patient took her medication. "I've got to get out of here," she thought. Cal shut the door to the guest room and went to bed.

The next morning Cal was already up and dressed before Jerry knocked on the door. "Breakfast, darling. Rise and shine." The nurses were changing shifts and were conferring outside. They were momentarily alone. As soon as Cal opened the door Jerry was in his arms. Cal finished packing his bag as the day nurse, Mrs. Page, came in with one tray and a guard with the other. Cal thanked them and told them to put the trays on the table. Jerry and Cal enjoyed breakfast together. Jerry ate very little. She wanted to go home. Cal kissed her goodbye and said he had to go to work. They did have a flying school to run. He'd be back tonight. As he started to leave Jerry stopped him.

"Cal," she said. "They have a chapel here. Let's get married now. I can do without all the fuss. I just want to be your wife."

"Are you serious? I thought you wanted a church wedding with all your friends and our folks. My mother still can't travel. Have you called Art?"

"I only want you. Carolyn is bringing the dress she picked out for my approval. I told her to bring shoes and everything. Can we somehow by pass the red tape? I don't want to go home without you." Jerry did not say what he knew she was thinking. Mrs. Page read between the words too. Jerry had almost died once. The killer was still out there. She wanted to be Cal's wife at least for a while.

"I'll look into it. I love you." Cal reached into his pocket and pulled out the small box he had been carrying for weeks. "This is supposed to go on your left-hand Jerry," he said as he opened the box and removed the engagement ring. Jerry held out her left cast encased hand then her right hand. He placed it on her right finger and took her in his arms. Mrs. Page turned her back and fiddled with her chart while Cal said a final goodbye to Jerry.

When he was gone, Jerry turned to Mrs. Page and holding out her right hand and looking at the sparkling diamond, said with a quiet smile, "I guess it's bath time."

On the way home Cal stopped at a public phone and called his mother.

"Cal! How are you? Have you got the wedding plans underway?" His mother was awake and glad to hear him.

"I'm fine, but the accident stopped the plans. Is Dad there?" He waited.

"No. Your father has been in California on business. Something to do with the farm. He left last week. What accident?"

"Mother, I just wanted to know how you were."

"What accident?" she demanded. Cal told her. "Oh, dear God. Bring her here out of danger." Cal's mother was alarmed. "Come home, Cal. Marry her, and come home."

"I love you, Mom. I am going to marry her as soon as we can. I wanted you there. But as it is, we're going to cancel the church wedding and make it just a simple one. We'll get some pictures for you. Jerry has her left arm in a cast and her cracked ribs are still healing. So the honeymoon will have to wait until the doctor says we can have it." Cal heard his mother laugh.

"You want to bet?" she said covering her shock with the joy for her son.

"I love her, Mom. I think you would lose that bet. No way will I ever hurt her again. I blame myself for her accident. I have to go."

"Wait. Give me Art's phone number. I should have it. In case of an emergency." Cal's mother requested.

"Got a pen?" He gave her Art's number.

Charley's Flying School

Chapter 18

Sylvia Freeman stood in front of the Senator's desk. The file cabinets had been emptied and the empty safe stood open. In her own office all her files were gone. "So, he's just skipped out to where ever he has put the money. Cal was right. This time it was illegal. My debt to him for raising me is paid in full. I'll do what I can put him in prison." One slip of paper had fallen on the floor and landed under the desk unnoticed. Sylvia picked it up and smiled as she put it in her purse. She walked to the elevator and headed to her apartment.

Sylvia called Jerry's room to see if she could see her. Jerry consented. Cal had asked her to please see Sylvia, so she did for him. When Sylvia arrived, the guards opened the gift package that had been elaborately wrapped apologizing for doing their job. The nurse let her in the room. The two women looked at each other for a moment.

"Come in Sylvia. I understand you found a brother. I'm happy for you. Sit down and let's talk." Jerry motioned to the small sofa. She was relaxed in the comfortable overstuffed lounge chair. Sylvia looked around at the huge room and shook her head.

"It's like a suite. Is this another room?" Sylvia walked to the door of the guest room.

"Yes. Why don't we go in there? I had refreshments brought up. If you are like I am when I work, you live on coffee. I thought I might entice you to have a goody. It gives me an excuse to eat extra, too." Jerry struggled to get up, and the nurse helped her. "I still am off balance with this cast." She led Sylvia into the guest room and the waiting table of refreshments. "I'm so spoiled that it will be hard to go back to scrubbing floors and doing laundry when I get home. But I almost enjoy it."

"Almost?" Sylvia set her gift on the table. "This is for you. I wanted to see you in person to tell you what an ass I was to you that day and to apologize."

"You did shock our secretary and make me angry. But it wasn't too far from the truth. The night we became engaged I took him to my room. I hoped I would get pregnant. Three days later I ended up here. But I'll be all right as soon as my cracked ribs heal. I want to get married right away. It's a feeling I have I can't explain. I love him so much. I'm sorry." Jerry talked as she opened the box. "Oh, Sylvia, it's beautiful. Thank you." Jerry picked up the mirror and smiled at the initials. J. M.

"I'm glad you like it. I am sorry to rush out, but I'm meeting Richard at one. You know, these pastries do smell good." Sylvia picked up a dainty morsel and sipped some of the coffee Jerry had poured for them. "Richard and I are meeting the old lion in his den. I'm introducing myself to my birth father. It's time he meets one of the by-products of his adultery."

"Sylvia, I really disliked you that day. But from what I see here today you've changed. I would be honored to be you friend." Jerry held out her hand to Sylvia. Sylvia took it.

"Thank you, Jerry. It would never have worked between Cal and me. I have to go now." Sylvia got up and Jerry walked with her to the door.

"I should be home. They keep telling me they have to wait for tests to come back. I feel like a prisoner. A spoiled one, but a prisoner. Good luck. Keep in touch." They hugged goodbye and Sylvia left. For the second time in her life someone had hugged her as a friend. It made her feel warm inside. Maybe life was worth living after all.

Jerry stood in the door and waved goodbye to Sylvia and Sylvia turned to return her farewell. Dr. Shipman was reading his chart as he came down the corridor. The two collided. Sylvia lost her balance and toppled over breaking the stiletto heel of her left shoe as her ankle twisted. She let out a yelp of pain as she hit the tile floor with an unstylish thud, her short skirt flipping too high to be lady like and high enough to be interesting to the astonished young doctor. Dr. Shipman caught his balance then hurried to Sylvia's side.

"Are you hurt?" he asked looking at her twisted leg.

"I didn't yell because it felt good! I'm sorry, I wasn't looking where I was walking. My ankle hurts and my heel is ruined. These are designer shoes, too." She looked up at the doctor and his full bushy beard and giggled. "Sorry. I just can't get used to men who look like pioneers in Alaska. Please help me up." Sylvia reached her long slim hand to him and he clasped it firmly. As she tried to put weight on her left ankle, it gave way in a flood of hot pain. She clutched at him and his strong arm went around her waist.

Jerry hurried to the aid of her friend with the two guards following and the nurse calling her to stop. "Sylvia, you're hurt. Bring her into my guest room, Dr. Shipman." Dr. Shipman stood with Sylvia clinging to him in obvious pain. With one swoop he lifted her in his arms. Sylvia laid her head on his shoulder making muffled little moans. He smelled the soft floral perfume that seemed to envelope her and which filled his senses with feelings a doctor carrying an injured patient is not supposed to have. Escorted by the guards to the door, Jerry led him into the guest room and Sylvia was laid gently on the bed. Mrs. Page hurried Jerry to her own bed and ordered her to stay put for a while. She then went to Dr. Shipman's aid.

"It's only a twisted ankle. No need to make a fuss." Sylvia objected unconvincingly as she flinched as the doctor felt her ankle.

"I agree, but I'm going to order an x-ray to be on the safe side. I'll take you myself. Mrs. Page, please get a wheelchair."

"I haven't time. I have to meet my brother. We have an important appointment." Sylvia was trying to hide the pain so she could get on with her appointment.

"I'll call him, Sylvia." Jerry had ignored her nurse's orders and stood at the foot of the bed. "Where were you supposed to meet him?"

"At the airport. He wanted to see Cal about something. Thanks, Jerry. I apologize for the unkind remark, Doctor," Sylvia flinched as a pain shot down her ankle.

"I'm going to give you something for pain. I'll take you to x-ray myself." Mrs. Page called the floor supervisor and told her of the doctor's order. Dr. Shipman continued, "We'll use Miss Jackson's wheelchair. I'll have to go to the desk for the x-ray form and pain medication. I'll be right back." Mrs. Page was amazed. Doctors sent nurses on errands; they did not go themselves. Then she saw the look in the eyes of the young resident doctor and shook her head. Young residents have no time or money for romance.

"Doctor, a nurse can take her. I'll call you when she gets back." Dr. Shipman's eyes met Mrs. Page's twinkling blue eyes. "I'm sure you are very busy."

"On the contrary, I was just going off duty and the accident was my fault. I'll have a ton of papers to fill out anyway." He looked at Mrs. Page and she nodded, silently laughing. She had seen this many times before. She walked Jerry back to the bed.

"You have some medicine to take and it will make you drowsy, so please stay in bed. I don't want to do a ton of paper work if you fall." Jerry smiled and nodded. She took the offered medicine as she picked up the phone and called Charley's Flying School.

Maggie answered the phone. "Maggie, is Richard Lambert there?" Jerry was beginning to feel the medicine's effect more quickly than she thought.

"He just came in with Cal. I'll call him. Do you want Cal too?" Jerry said yes, and the call was relayed to Richard and Cal.

"Richard, I'm calling for Sylvia. She's in my guest room. She has fallen and twisted her ankle. She has to have x-rays and can't make the meeting. The doctor gave her a pain shot and she'll be here a while. My wedding dress is being brought for a fitting. May I have them bring a pair of walking shoes for Sylvia?" The answer was yes, they would bring anything she needed. Richard said he'd be right over. "I want to talk to Cal." Cal came on the line.

"Jer, what happened? Richard left here in a rush." He grinned at Jerry's description of the collision. "I'll be finished here in a couple of hours. I love you." What Richard had told him had him wondering. There was a Zebra Company that was separate from the other conglomerate of over a dozen businesses. The conglomerate's mother company was owned by Angus Hampton's father-in-law, Donald Vaugh a well-known real estate developer. What had this Zebra to do with the airport, if anything? Was this another developer wanting to close the airport? He shook his head and prepared for the next student.

Jerry sent Mrs. Page to get Sylvia's shoe size and tell her a new pair of shoes was a treat from her brother. She then called Carolyn and relayed the shoe size and asked her to bring some for Sylvia to try on. Sensible heels that could be used with crutches. She was feeling drowsy and could not think clearly anymore. She lay back on her pillow and Mrs. Page fussed with her pillow and pulled her sheet over her and Jerry dozed. "I'm not taking any more of this stuff," she told herself as she closed her eyes.

When Jerry awakened, Mrs. Page was admitting Carolyn who was carrying a load of boxes. Another one of the employees from the store had come along to assist her. "My gown!" Jerry was wide awake at once. She swung her feet off the bed before her nurse could stop her.

"Miss Jackson, your slippers. Be careful you might lose your balance." She rushed around the bed and ushered the barefoot Jerry to a chair. Before she could put on her slippers Carolyn handed Jerry a pair of white satin pumps. Jerry put them on and stuck her feet out before her. They fit. Jerry got up and with Nurse Page holding her arm did a test walk across the room.

"They are beautiful! My wedding gown?" Carolyn opened a large box that she had laid on the bed. She pulled away the tissue layer by layer and lifted out a beautiful white satin gown, simple, sleeveless with an A line skirt shorter in front and gradually longer in back to form a short train. "Oh, Carolyn. You know me so well."

When Sylvia returned from x-ray a few minutes later, she and Dr. Shipman opened the door to find Jerry standing in her wedding gown. She turned around with the nurse holding her arm to show them the back.

"Jerry, you look beautiful. Now my good news is that I have no break and can go home with crutches and my word not to walk on my left foot."

"Carolyn brought you some shoes to try if the doctor approves the style. And some designer elastic bandage for your ankle."

"What!" Asked both the doctor and the nurse at once. "Who ever heard of designer elastic bandages?"

Carolyn handed him a roll of elastic lace bandage. "We had another client that decided she would not wear any kind of bandage on her sprained ankle. So we canceled her order. My boss said it's free to you if you like it. It works well with any of the shoes. Jerry, hold out your cast." Carolyn took from one of her boxes a long sleeve of material that matched the gown and slipped it over the cast. It looked like a fingerless glove. "We thought it would look better than a plaster cast." Jerry held up the elegantly covered cast.

"Now if only I could get the red tape cut and get a license today, we could be married day after tomorrow. The chapel is available at 11 am Saturday. The hospital chaplain will do the sermon. Anyone know any big shots?'

Dr. Shipman sighed. "While it is against my better judgement to let a pretty woman slip into matrimony with someone else, I might be able to help. Ever hear of Judge Arleen Martin?" Everyone shook their head no. "She's my mother. Kept her maiden name for her profession. If you will hand me that fancy bandage, I'll see if it will work. Then I'll call Mama and ask for help."

Sylvia held out her lace covered bandaged foot and the shoes that had straps with Velcro fastenings that could be adjusted to fit over it. They were both stylish and fit well. "Did you want that pair?"

"I want all of them. The white, beige and black. Don't you think, Dr. Shipman?" Her voice was soft.

"Mrs. Freeman, I'm a man. Men, if they are wise, do not mess with the fashions of wives, mothers, sweethearts or patients. I'll make my call from the other room while you ladies get dressed." With what dignity he could muster, he walked into the other room. Jerry and Mrs. Page came back in and shut the door.

When the doctor finished his call, he informed Jerry that Cal could pick up their license at the city hall that evening or tomorrow. "The judge has waived the red tape under the circumstances. Mom's a romantic."

"Mrs. Freeman, I'll release you to go home as soon as you get the crutches from occupational therapy and are shown how to use them. Just keep off your foot for at least a week. You have the pain medicine if you need it. If you have any problems, call the hospital. I'm here." He started to leave, but stopped and turned. For a long moment Sylvia and Dr. Shipman looked into each other's eyes. Both knew that the feelings between them were not allowed. "Ships passing in the night," he thought. Sylvia said goodbye softly as he left. She sat there looking at the door until Jerry came out of the other room at the same time the therapist appeared. It was with an empty, lonely feeling she took her first steps with her new crutches.

When Richard came, he was delighted to see Sylvia had only a severe sprain. More good news followed when he learned about the red tape slashing. With Mrs. Page's help, the chapel had been reserved for 11 am the day after tomorrow. The hospital was going to have a free buffet lunch special for the guests to be served in the board's meeting room. This was a first for the hospital.

Jerry had called the office. Cal was notified that all was cleared to get the license. Maggie and Mike were invited to come as were the friends at the airport who could get away. Maggie spread the word, especially to Abby. Jerry called Ma Brown and Lilly herself. Along with her dress, Carolyn's employer had sent Cal and Jerry a gold chain to hold the wedding ring around Jerry's neck. There was no way to put the ring on her left finger with her arm and hand encased in a cast. Richard and Sylvia left to keep their appointment with Mr. Lambert and Carolyn and her assistant went back to work.

Jerry tried to call Uncle Art. No one answered. After several attempts, she gave up and called Cal and told him. Maggie would keep trying. It would not be a proper wedding without Uncle Art. Jerry and Mrs. Page were alone when lunch was served. Jerry was very tired. More than she expected. The nurse did not have to coax her into bed for a nap after the lunch she barely touched. She was asleep at once.

Richard had taken Sylvia to her apartment for her to change clothes and get some things she needed. Her car was still at the hospital so they arranged to have it delivered to her hotel. They then headed for the Piney Woods Estate to face the lion in his den.

When Richard was ushered into his childhood home once

again, he was surprised at how strange it felt after having his own home and family. He realized it was no longer home. He and Sylvia were alike. Both were guests of their father. Both were unwanted guests of Richard's mother. She had not forgiven him for marrying 'beneath' his social class. In reality, Lilly was so far above the 'social class' he had grown up in he was grateful he had been able to reach high enough to find her.

"Hello, Father." Both spoke at the same time as they walked into the office of Harvey Lambert. He stared at the two as they stopped in front of his desk. "Father meet my sister by way of Senator Stone's wife. Sylvia Freeman. She's three years older than I am." Richard was speaking. His father just stared.

"I thought it was time you met the results of your adultery, Father," Sylvia said through clenched teeth.

"Damn, if you don't look like twins." He laid his cigar in the tray with shaking hands.

"You seem surprised. You see my mother deserted me when you deserted her. The Senator put me in a school and forgot me. Paid my bills, but did not want anything to do with the bastard you gave his wife. You did not want anything to do with the bastard you sired. So here is the bastard in front of you. I never saw my mother. Have no idea who or where she is. I don't want to know. But after meeting my brother Richard, I wanted to see the man who could pay to have his grandchildren aborted and desert his pregnant lover. That's why I'm here. I don't want your money. I have my own. I earned it. I rather pictured spitting on you, but what a waste of good spit."

"Well, I'll be damned. You've got spunk. Sound just like Jerry Jackson and Lilly. I like them, too. Well, girl, I've done a lot I'm ashamed of just to make my wife happy. I went to your mother for comfort I could not get at home. I cared about her. She told me goodbye and I never saw her again. I didn't know about you until this minute. Honest to God, I knew nothing about you. No matter what you think or were told, I did not desert your mother. She left me. I went time and again to our apartment but she never showed up. She took her jewelry and left her clothes. That's the last I heard from her. I tried to find her but it was as if she just disappeared. I even called the Senator's house and was hung up on each time by the help. I drove by but never saw her." Harvey looked down at his desk to keep the emotion he felt from showing. "I loved her." He spoke quietly.

He looked at Richard and continued, "Richard, I am so sorry for the way I treated your wife. If she can forgive me, I would like to come see my grandchildren. The boy looks like you. Got your wife's chin, but he looks like you. The girl, she's got eyes like her mother. Looks like her too. What I did to them." He sat there shaking his head. His cigar smoldering in its tray unheeded.

"Dad, Sylvia came to see the man who sired her, but I came about the Zebra company. Have you found out anything about it? The big conglomerate is something else, and they have been buying the land. But I've been buying some of it too. Some of the farmers don't want to sell. I tell them if anyone tries to force them to call my lawyer. What are they up to?"

"You know as much as I do. I've gone over maps again and again and see nothing. It was arson that started the fire in the forest near the lumber mill. Jerry spotted the smoke. I guess she saved the place. The fire was traced to a couple of men I fired for smoking in a no smoke area. I think it was just revenge." He looked at Sylvia. "You know anything about this?"

"Now that you ask, I have been working for the Senator. I agreed to do one more job for him to pay him back for raising and educating me. I did not trust what he was telling me. Some papers I had worked on in my files for the project were missing when I checked earlier. He emptied the office of all papers and just left without telling anyone. He shredded everything or took it with him except this. I found it on the floor. Can we go where there is privacy and a big table?" The two looked at her with surprise. Harvey led them into a large conference room. From her tote bag that Richard carried, she withdrew several large envelopes and a slip of paper. She handed the paper to Richard who passed it to his father.

"This is a duplicate check for a million dollars to the Zebra Charities president Alphonso-. I can't read the rest. A donation to a charity."

"One day the Senator left the intercom on accidently. I heard him and a visitor he called Alphonso quarreling. The Senator said it was the last blackmail money he would get. Then the intercom clicked off. I grabbed my purse and left fast through my private door and went to the ladies room. When I got back, the Senator was yelling for me. I went in apologizing for leaving to go to the ladies' room. I think he believed that I had been gone a while. Then, when I was waiting to take his orders, I saw a personal account book he kept locked up. He was at his files, and all I could read upside down was "Alphonso one mil - paid." Whatever the Zebra is, it is this Alphonso's private blackmail charity."

"He was being black-mailed out of the money he was embezzling from the conglomerate." Everyone laughed.

From one envelope she pulled a folded map. It was a map of the United States. She spread it out on one side of the table. From the other envelopes she took maps of various states and one sectional she had bought of the area around the airport. She spread them out. She pulled several colored marker pens from her bag. "Now," she said, "This is what I saw while I worked for the Senator. He doesn't know I have a photographic memory. I recall everything I see. If he did, he would kill me. I do not know what the dots are for, but I will put them in place where I saw them. I do not have all the maps; I did not get a good view of part of the country. Maybe one of you can tell me what they mean."

She proceeded to mark black dots all over the map she had just laid out. Then she did the same with a blue marker. Next she used a yellow marker and finished with red XX's. One X was on the lumber mill and one on the airport. Others were scattered over the maps. The men stared at the maps.

"My god, you've marked oil refineries, nuclear power plants, and natural gas fields all over the area. In fact, all over the West." Harvey Lambert had to sit down. "But many of these seem to be in the middle of nowhere. Just forest. Like my mill." What the meaning of this was, he could only guess.

"I couldn't see the East Coast and some of the Midwest. I tried to find the maps and almost got caught. So I decided not to try for more."

"What is going on?" Richard frowned as he studied the maps.

"Sylvia, what was your job?" Harvey was light headed and weak at what he thought he saw.

"I was to interview workers and see if they had certain needed qualifications that the Senator gave me. I was told it was a top-secret job to track down terrorist groups that were forming across the country. I also was a fetch and carry girl, much to my disgust. But anything I owed him is paid. The interviews varied. One a computer expert, a chemist, an engineer, a mechanic," as she listed the workers, she felt cold chills. "One was a bomb expert fired from the police. I recommended he not be hired, but he was. I had only a small part of the whole." Harvey bent over the map the cigar now dangling from his lips. The ashes fell on the map covering it with dirty grey. The three stared at the map and at each other as a thought formed so fantastic it seemed impossible.

"You've just dirty bombed my map," said Sylvia putting her thoughts into words.

"A dirty bomb? No, bombs aimed for the energy areas of the country. They'll never get away with it." Harvey shook his head. "This can't be. What were the men you recruited told?"

"I don't know other than what I told them at my interview to see if they qualified. From time to time I was told of a success in secret raids. Somehow, I always felt this was just a pacifier so I wouldn't ask questions. Cal refused to be a part of this. I heard him refuse. But what has this to do with Jerry and the airport?" The pain shot was wearing off and Sylvia's ankle was beginning to hurt. "I have to sit down." She tried to maneuver into a chair and almost fell. Her father caught her. With Richard's help she was seated. "I guess I don't have the hang of crutches yet. May I have some water? I have some pain pills, and I need one. They are in my purse."

Richard went for a glass of water. When he returned, Harvey had propped Sylvia's feet up on another chair and was putting a cushion under the injured one. Richard smiled. He had never seen his father being tender with anyone. He handed her the water, and she swallowed the pill.

"Have you told anyone else of this?" Harvey asked.

"No. Who is there to trust? Something is wrong. I was told it was a government ordered project. Cal said he had no orders. The Senator admitted it was his own. I think he was collecting money by the millions from some real estate investors and skimming millions off the top. And this Alphonso is black-mailing him. Who is this Zebra man?"

"I'll find out if I can. We must guard you and Jerry," said Harvey. "Is she guarded?"

Richard responded, "Her nurses are hand-picked police trained for undercover work for the detective agency. They are all armed." Harvey sighed in relief.

Richard continued, "It's getting late. We'd better get Sylvia home. Sylvia, will you stay with us tonight? There's still a couch. I'll work it out. I won't feel right leaving you alone."

"Are you sure?" Sylvia asked, "I'm not concerned and I don't want to be in the way."

"We'll love having you. I'll feel better if I know you're safe." Richard smiled at his new sister and she nodded consent. No one had ever worried about her before. It was a nice feeling.

"Will you stay for dinner? If Laura doesn't like it she can eat in her room." Harvey Lambert sighed. "I'm too old to worry about what someone who has not been my wife for years cares about. It has always been her society, not mine. That's why I like to go to the mill. As for the mill, I must pay a visit to the back buildings we plan to tear down. After dark. I know it's fine during the day. If anything is going on it will be after my workers have gone. I have to check on the night security."

"Dad, no. Not alone! They'll kill you if something is really going on. Why not have a power failure or something and close the plant for a few days for repairs? Then take a small army, and go over the place. You can think of something, but we need you. I have something to ask you. If you don't want to try, say no and that's fine. It's personal, and I'm butting in where I shouldn't. Jerry and Cal are getting married day after tomorrow in the hospital chapel at 11 a.m. Art can't be reached. Cal has asked me to be best man. Jerry has no father substitute to give her away. Will you offer to walk her to the altar and give her to Cal? She may say no and cuss you out, or she may start to cry and say, 'Thank you. Yes.' And they may get hold of Art. I don't know." There was silence. Then Harvey picked up a phone and dialed a number.

    Jerry was surprised when Mr. Harvey Lambert offered his arm to walk her down the aisle. "I -I thank you. I will be honored to have you substitute for my late father." And so the wedding party was complete. Carolyn was to be matron of honor. Cal would be coming soon. They were going to have dinner served here for the two of them privately in the guest room. Tonight, Miss Kelly would have to eat alone in the hospital room.

Rosa B. Lane

Chapter 19

The next day was a very long one for Jerry. While Cal carried out the flying school responsibilities, Jerry walked the floor. Her hair would be done early tomorrow morning. Carolyn was coming to help her get dressed, and a beautician was coming to cover her red scars with makeup to make them less noticeable. Today she was told to exercise very slowly and easily. She was told not to get too tired; but that order was in vain. She shoved aside the ache that Charley was not there nor was Uncle Art. Where was he? It was not like him to just disappear. This hurt the most. She had seen the hidden pain in Cal's eyes too when he called to check on his mother. His father was gone on business too. Aunt Margaret said Patricia was feeling better. Cal tried to hide his concern, but Jerry felt it in her heart. That night when he held her and kissed her good night, Jerry had a sudden feeling of chill. She clung to him not wanting him to leave her. He promised to call her when he got to Ma's. He had not moved into Jerry's house yet. Ma insisted he stay so she could feed him properly. She took her pill only after he had called and was safe.

Jerry was awakened early hardly able to comprehend this was her wedding day. Still no word from Art. The lab technician took her daily blood sample, wished her happiness and the nurse took her to the shower. After breakfast her hair was done and Carolyn showed up looking lovely in her matron of honor dress of soft pink satin. The bride was dressed and by 10:45 she was taken by wheelchair to the chapel. There she waited until Harvey Lambert came to walk her down the aisle. When the music started every head in the full chapel turned. There were patients as well as students and her colleagues from the airport. She made her nurse help her from the chair. She would walk down the aisle as a bride should.

Harvey Lambert took her arm and looked at the beautiful bride beside him. "I've a strong arm, Jerry. Just hang on." And they started down the aisle. Cal stood in his place and watched his dream come true that the pig-tailed kid would someday walk into his arms.

Jerry was getting tired sooner than she thought and held tightly to Harvey's arm. "Almost there, honey. You can do it." Harvey told her softly and took a firmer grip on her arm. Then he was handing her over to Cal. She felt weak and tired. But she looked up at her lover with such love that he hardly believed his own good fortune.

Cal saw her pale lovely face and was a little frightened. Her hand was cold and trembling as he took it. He looked at the minister and down at her then put his left arm around her waist to support her. "I have you, Jer."

The Reverend Bradford looked at the bride and smiled. "We are gathered here to unite this man and this woman in holy matrimony. If anyone has reason to object speak now or forever hold his peace." All was quiet. "Due to the long illness of the bride, I will not preach a sermon on love." His voice was far away to Jerry struggling to listen when her body wanted to collapse. Then Cal said "I do" and Jerry said "I do" and they were pronounced man and wife. Cal kissed her gently and whispered, "Forever" and swooped her up in his arms. Carolyn caught up the trail of Jerry's dress and tucked it safely out of Cal's way and he carried his bride from the chapel. Jerry tossed her bouquet over Cal's shoulder to the guests. Maggie leaped high and caught it in the scramble.

The banquet hall was only a short distance down the corridor. With Mrs. Page and the crowd following them, Cal walked into the room. There he finally accepted the wheelchair Mrs. Page had been pushing behind them. He sat Jerry gently into the chair then rolled it to the table. A large wedding cake in shape of an airplane with the bride and groom as wing walkers sat on the table. Mrs. Page brought Jerry a glass of punch and handed Jerry her noon pill. Then with cameras flashing and cheers the bride and groom cut the cake.

"Mr. Morris, I believe you should take your wife back to her room. Why don't I have a tray prepared for you and extra cake for you to keep? She's so tired." Cal consented.

He raised a toast to Jerry and told everyone to enjoy the buffet. "My wife needs to go to bed." He explained with a smile. Everyone laughed and he pushed a blushing Jerry back to her room. A tray with the bride and groom and one wing of the cake along with punch and food from the buffet was delivered to her room.

"At last," he said. "I've wanted this since I saw the picture Charley gave me. For a while I thought you hated me." He kissed her.

She leaned back on her pillows and said "For a while I thought I did. Then I got angry because I had to admit I was in love with you. You're my husband. I'm Mrs. Calvin Morris. I love you." He bent and kissed her.

"You must rest now. Will you mind if I go back to our friends, or they won't believe you're really tired?"

"Go. Give them my thanks and love. Come back soon. I'll miss you." She reached for him, and he kissed her again wanting to stay and make love, but he left.

Rosa B. Lane

Chapter 20

Mrs. Page looked at Jerry's chart and once again at the doctor's orders. Who was Dr. Zorak? She had worked in this area for many years and never had heard of him. He had ordered pain medication long after Jerry did not need it. She realized this and simply asked Jerry if she needed something for pain when the three hours rolled around and when she started saying no, Mrs. Page had written on the chart that medication was refused. The drug given in the amount Dr. Zorak had ordered would lead to addiction. Then he ordered a stiff routine of sedatives that Jerry did not need. He had kept her in the hospital to get daily blood work done that was not necessary and could be done as an outpatient. The blood count he made such a fuss over was low, but with exercise and a good diet would correct itself. So would the low blood pressure which was not really very low. In fact, her own normally about the same as Jerry's. Why? She picked up the phone and called her employer, Harry McHugh.

Jerry opened her eyes after a short nap. She was still in her wedding gown and Cal sat by her side. Mrs. Page stood at the end of the bed. "Mr. Morris," she said. "I must speak to you and your wife. Now that she has someone legally on her side. I think it is time for you to get a second opinion of Mrs. Morris's condition from another internal medical doctor. All the other doctors, GYN and orthopedic specialists cleared her to go home over a week ago. Dr. Zorak works for the hospital and is new here. After Mrs. Morris no longer needed pain medicine, Dr. Zorak became very angry when I charted I was giving it as necessary only. He wanted to continue an addictive drug that was not needed. Remember, Mrs. Morris?"

"Yes," Jerry nodded. "I thought his anger was uncalled for and told him so. He glared at me and started writing on the chart."

"He ordered a very strong sedative three times a day. It should be given only twice and no more. In fact, the dose is more than necessary. I did something that I have never done before and could lose my license over. I gave you half the dose and I did not give you the afternoon dose. What you are getting at noon is the vitamin pill Dr. Whalen, your OB specialist, ordered to help build your strength for that baby you want. I am now telling you that you do not need any sedatives and should have gone home at least a week ago. All you have to do is to refuse the sedatives; and, I cannot give them to you. That's why you are weak and groggy. I called the orthopedic doctor, and he is surprised you are still here. I asked if he would order physiotherapy for you to help get you in condition. He is starting you tomorrow. Easy and slowly." Cal stood staring at her and at Jerry. "Here is a list of clothes she will need to exercise in. Don't forget good exercise shoes."

"You're only a nurse," he said. Mrs. Page smiled.

She reached inside her white smock and from a pocket on her shirt she pulled a card holder. She flipped it open. It contained a nurse's license, a doctor's assistant license and a private investigator's license. "I am more than a nurse. I've had some training in drugs in my job as a police woman and as an investigator. I have the feeling that for some reason the doctor wants Mrs. Morris to become addicted to drugs. I won't permit it nor will her other nurses who also are private investigators. We were hired to protect as well as nurse you. We feel you need another really good well- known internal medicine specialist to give a second opinion. Meanwhile, I recommend you take no medicine without questioning it and no sedatives. I also recommend your husband stay in the guest room at night and visit as much as possible. What purpose could he have to cause you to be addicted?"

"I would lose my pilot's license and could never teach again. It would mess up my life and my husbands. Who would want that? I just don't know."

"Here is a list we three made out of specialists in the area. If you have trouble getting an appointment, I recommend you contact Mr. Lambert. Now I think Mrs. Morris will be more comfortable in her nightgown so I have laid out one for her and I have to go to the desk for some forms and would appreciate it if your husband would help you get into bed. Your wedding dress will be ruined if you sleep in it. Oh, I will be gone about twenty minutes. Only a little hanky-panky. After all this is your wedding day. The real honeymoon will have to wait. This is a hospital. Lock the door behind me." She picked up her chart and a sign reading "Do Not Disturb" and left.

Cal and Jerry looked at each other with loving smiles and she reached for him. They were alone for the first time since they became husband and wife.

Rosa B. Lane

Chapter 21

Sylvia and Richard had joined Mr. Lambert in Sylvia's suite at a hotel in Houston. They were discussing the maps and dots coming to the conclusion that it was like a kid's treasure map. "But suppose it is for real? I don't want my company to be caught up in something like this. I should have been more attentive to the mill. I guess I'm getting old and tired. My foreman is very reliable old stock Texan. He comes from a family of Texas Rangers but couldn't get in because of an injury leaving him with a bad leg. He would know if anything was wrong. At least during the day. But we have shut down the plant as you have suggested. Would you believe that I was called and told by some unknown voice I was going to be raided? So yesterday I called in the Rangers and asked for their help to find out what was going on. They and I went in at night and found another raid going on. Had quite a time making the Feds realize we were Texas rangers. Apparently after the plant closed at night the place was being filled with another crew, this one was of terrorists. They were using the old buildings. The Feds and Rangers found a lot of stuff that was being used to make bombs. Fortunately, no one who worked with me was in the bunch they arrested. I never saw them before. It seems that none of the bombs had been completed because they were waiting for some supplies. I found out that this was only the tip of a country wide raid. I didn't know what was going on! I may be a lot of things, but I'm not a traitor!"

"I wonder if they have them all? Did they get the Senator?" Sylvia asked the question. "I wonder where he is?"

"Let's see," said Richard. "Charley and Art worked together with him flying didn't they? Maybe Art knows something." He looked at Sylvia. She shook her head.

"I think that Art has a ranch somewhere west of here but I don't know where. Cal and Jerry would know. But this is their wedding day." Sylvia picked up the phone and dialed information.

Cal left Jerry to go get her clothes. He returned in about two hours with boxes of new clothes Carolyn had helped him pick out. "Cal, we can't afford these. I have clothes." Jerry was alarmed that the school had been closed due to the wedding. "But thank you. You're spoiling me." Cal kissed her. "I'm going to get dressed for the rest of the day. I'm tired of gowns. They just make me feel sick and I'm not." She selected a comfortable three piece outfit and Cal grinned at Mrs. Page's look as Jerry started to undress.

"I'll do my book work in the other room. Young lady, you have no modesty." Mrs. Page laughed as she went into the guest bedroom. "I gotta get those kids home!" She shut the door and went to the phone to call Harry McHugh. Harry had found some interesting information. He could not find Richard to tell him, but felt she should know it. Dr. Ivan Zorak seemed to be practicing with his license revoked for over prescribing controlled drugs. He was using fake papers. Someone at the hospital who hired him was in trouble. The door opened and Jerry stood fully dressed in light weight sweats and cotton tee shirt with sport shoes and socks.

"Now I feel like a human again," declared Jerry as she spun around much to Cal's dismay and he hurried to catch her. "I'm not dizzy without those pills. Thank you, darling. And thank you, Mrs. Page. I'm going to walk down the hall. Will you come along in case I get tired?" She asked her nurse. "I'm not going to be held prisoner any longer." She took a deep breath and started for the door.

"Wait, Mrs. Morris. Don't overdo it. Slowly, it takes a while to get back in gear. I have no orders for you to walk down the hall." The conversation was cut short when the door opened and Dr. Zorak appeared. He was shocked at seeing Jerry fully dressed.

"What's going on? I did not dismiss you" He turned to Mrs. Page and realized Cal was in the room. "Who is he?" He was angry and turned on the nurse. "She should be in bed. Where's her chart?"

"I won't go to bed. This is my husband," Jerry responded with cool anger at the doctor's attitude.

"Dr. Zorak, I'm Calvin Morris, Mrs. Morris's husband. We were married in the hospital chapel. I have concerns about the slow recovery of my wife. What is the reason for all of the addictive drugs you have ordered? You have not explained to her why she is still here. I think it is time for a second opinion." He turned to Jerry and added, "While I was out I contacted a specialist in Houston who will see you tomorrow as a consultant." He looked at Dr. Zorak and demanded, "I want to know what is wrong. All the other doctors discharged her nearly two weeks ago. Why have you kept her here?" Cal had taken control of the situation very quickly.

Dr. Zorak felt sick in the pit of his stomach. "They told me she had no relatives and would be no problem." He had to answer something and fast. "I have to finish my rounds. I will be glad to explain to you if you make an appointment to see me in my office." He turned and left.

Cal started to reply but the doctor disappeared out the door. He turned to Mrs. Page and said, "How does one fire a doctor?"

"Why not wait until the consultant sees her, and then compare the two diagnosises. As yet Dr. Zorak has not written a diagnosis except low blood pressure and low blood count both of which are generally treated by diet, supplements and exercise at home. In fact, my blood pressure always ran 90 or 100 until I gained twenty pounds. Now it's 110 -120. Some people just normally run low pressure. I suspect your doctor will recommend you be discharged and go have a honeymoon. If that doesn't raise your blood pressure I don't know what will." She was grinning the same charming grin Jerry had grown to like so much.

"Mrs. Page!" said Jerry laughing, "You have no modesty at all. Do we walk down the hall?" The three of them and a guard walked down the hall until Jerry began to get tired.

The next morning Jerry had returned from her physiotherapy session, showered and dressed when the consultant from Houston arrived. Cal had made it a point to be there. The introductions were made and Cal was asked to wait in the guest room while Dr. Davis examined Jerry. He looked her chart over when he had finished.

"All your tests have shown you are fine. The other specialists have discharged you. I am concerned as to why you have been ordered so many narcotic drugs. You were wise to refuse them. So far as I can see you can go home and enjoy your new husband. Continue the vitamins that Dr. Whalen ordered and eat a diet of green leafy vegetables and iron rich food. Keep increasing your activity gradually so you don't get too tired. Mr. Morris will have to help you or hire help for a week or two. I'll write my opinion that no narcotic drugs are needed, and you can be discharged at once. But remember, I understand it was an attempt to murder you. Please be careful." As he started to leave, Dr. Zorak came into the room.

The two men looked at each other. "Hello, Zachary. I thought your license had been revoked. What are you doing here?"

"This is Dr. Zorak, Dr. Davis. He's been taking care of Mrs. Morris." Mrs. Page introduced them.

"Oh, I know who he is. I worked with him in Nevada when he was called Zachary Jones. He nearly killed a man by overdosing him, and did kill one woman. How did he get a job here? His license was revoked and he was jailed for ten years. I will have this investigated. You have my recommendation to be discharged today, Mrs. Morris."

"You must be mistaken, Dr. Davis. I have my papers." Dr. Zorak was pale, "We can continue this in my office. Mrs. Morris, I advise you against going home, but do as you wish." He turned around and left.

Mrs. Page called security to stop him and hold him in his office. Then she called the police.

"I'll be going home. Thank you, Dr. Davis. Cal let's get out of here." Two hours later, Cal and Jerry were standing in Jerry's home alone at last.

Charley's Flying School

Rosa B. Lane

Chapter 22

Cal told Jerry to go sit down while he brought in her things from the station wagon. Jerry went into the living room and relished the familiar surroundings. Old, worn but loaded with memories. Then she looked around the room again. Cal came in arms loaded with boxes of night gowns, new workout clothes, her bridal gown, and the special dresser set and the bag of medicine and instructions from all the doctors. He set them down at the foot of the stairs and heaved a sigh, then went back for the flowers and plants. These he set on the kitchen table.

"How in the world can a woman arrive at a hospital with only her purse and flight bag and come home with enough stuff to start a department store?" Cal exclaimed looking at the heap. He heard Jerry laughing and went into the living room to her.

"My darling husband. You've a lot to learn about women and I intend to teach you." She held out her arms as she stood up. He gathered her into his embrace and held her close. Then Cal sat down on the sofa pulling her onto his lap. She snuggled up to him, laying her head on his shoulder. "Oh, Cal, I finally feel safe again." Her arms went around him and he kissed her long and lingering. He held her close. His cheek against her tumbled curls, his eyes closed with the powerful emotion he felt of holding her soft body against his. His jaws clenched as he remembered pulling her bloody unconscious body from the car. Unbidden, tears slipped from his eyes. Jerry reached up and kissed his cheek.

"You're crying. What's wrong?" She was suddenly full of

fear.

"I was thinking how close I came to losing you forever. That I would never feel you in my arms or make love to you again or hold our children. I love you so much."

Jerry wiped the tears away with her fingers. "When I woke up and saw you looking so tired, your eyes so red and you unshaven I wanted to tell you to go home and sleep but I was so glad you were there. All I could say was 'I hurt.' I tried to say 'I love you'."

"You did. But the nurse put you to sleep again. I just want to hold you and love you." For a long while they sat clinging to each other absorbing the scents, the feel and the wonder of each other and at being alive and together. Their souls joined silently as their bodies had and they were united by more than words. They indeed were one, yet two.

"Let's go upstairs." Jerry got up and held out her hand.

"It's too soon. I don't want to hurt you." He took her hand, and she led him to the bedroom as she had once before. The honeymoon began that lasted the rest of their lives.

She awakened and leaned over Cal who smiled. He had been so careful so afraid of hurting her. "We're shamelessly immodest. Making love in the afternoon." She leaned over and kissed him. "I've needed you so much these weeks away from you. I love you very much."

Cal held her close. "We'd better get up and get some dinner. I haven't prepared for your homecoming. How does pizza and salad sound?"

"I'd rather stay here, but if you insist," she smiled and got out of bed quickly, then sat down surprised. The room whirled and she was off balance.

"Jer." Cal was at her side. "What's wrong?" He was holding her.

"I got up too quickly. Mrs. Page warned me about doing that until my strength got back." She reached to him. "Here help me up." Cal pulled her up slowly and she leaned against him looking up with mischief in her eyes as she snuggled closer.

"Okay, young lady. To the shower or we'll starve to death on love." He kissed her and walked with her to the bathroom.

"Cal, my plastic cover for my cast is in the bag from the hospital. I have to have it." Cal told her to stay put and ran naked out of the room and down the steps coming up with the bag. Jerry was howling with laughter. "You look so-so -well, I've not seen you running around nude before. I don't want any other woman to see how handsome you are." And she was holding him again, her breasts burned like fire against his chest and his passion stirred.

"What am I to do with you? You are a siren, and I don't want to stop feeling your call. But I think we had better wait." He took a deep breath and she smiled filled with joy that he wanted her so much. "Here's your stuff. I'll bring the rest up after we get dressed. You've had enough excitement for the day." Jerry took the bag and pulled out the cover. Cal helped her to fasten it over her cast. Then they went into the shower together.

"Let's just stay home alone. Call out for food and then tomorrow I'll call everyone and tell them we're here. I want to be selfish tonight. Just you and me." Jerry held her arms out to him. "I can't get enough of you." The warm water fell over them as their lips met and the joy of love overwhelmed them.

Rosa B. Lane

Chapter 23

In the morning Cal looked at Jerry beside him. She opened her eyes and smiled, "I feel so fulfilled, so complete."

He kissed her and replied, "It's the way I always thought it would be if I found the right woman. Then I found you."

"I'm going with you and have a big breakfast at the airport. I've had healthy food for three weeks. Now I want good junk food." They had dressed and Jerry looked around the small bedroom. It was not made for two people. She had lots of room growing up alone, but now they needed a bigger room. She turned to her new husband and said, "It's time to pack Charley's things and redecorate and furnish the master bedroom for us. I want a new bedroom outfit, ours only."

"If you're ready, Jerry. We'll go shopping when you feel able. Another week and you'll be fine. Not that you're not now," he added eying her.

Jerry went downstairs and looked at her dresser set box and started to lift it. "Stop, I'll get it. No lifting." Cal was at her side and as he picked up the box stole a quick kiss. "Where do you want it?"

"On the table." Cal smiled and carried the box over to the table.

"Being in love does make me hungry. And I want you to take me up flying. I know I can't fly, but I'll be a passenger and back seat pilot."

At the airport restaurant they were greeted with happy welcomes. Everyone moved over to make room for the newlyweds. They ordered the ham and eggs special. Jerry asked in a straight forward fashion that was hers, "What's going on here now?" There was silence, and then Carla spoke.

"Things are getting back to normal. Word has gotten out that the Lamberts are taking an interest in us."

"The Lamberts?'"

"Richard and his father have joined forces and are buying the land around the airport." Suddenly things got quiet.

"Cal why didn't you tell me?"

"Because, my dear, you were in the hospital under sedation. Remember? Any way I didn't want to worry you." He looked at her then at his breakfast.

"Are you planning to keep secrets from me all our lives?" Jerry felt hurt and left out. There was a ripple of laughter around the table. Jerry blushed. They were acting as if they were married. She laughed too. Cal looked at her and saw that all was forgiven.

"Kiss him," ordered Carla. Jerry leaned over and gave Cal an orange juice kiss and received one tasting of ham. Their audience clapped. "A toast," said Carla raising her coffee cup, "to the bride and groom. May all their disagreements be settled so quickly." The others responded with "Cheers!" It was a lovely reunion but Jerry realized she had learned little. Now they were on their way to the hangar, and Cal was going to take her flying.

When they reached the hangar Cal opened it and pulled out the Aerobat. "We'll do a loop to celebrate," he laughed. Jerry felt helpless when she had to watch. Maggie and Mike drove up about the time Cal had finished the pre-flight.

"Jerry," squealed Maggie. She ran to the plane and hugged Jerry. "We really missed you. You know I'll be leaving at the end of August. I have a scholarship for the hospital near Mike's college, and we'll be seeing each other often. Mom and Dad finally agreed. How long 'til you can fly again?" Maggie was breathless.

"After my cast is off, I'll need to strengthen my arm. So, several weeks. Depends. Cal's taking me up, but he treats me like a baby."

"Enjoy it," said Cal walking up behind her. "All ready to go. Bathroom? We have no ladies' room on this flight."

"No, Daddy," said Jerry in a little girl voice. "See you when we get back. I'll have to be briefed on your work. At least I can do that." Jerry walked to the plane with Cal, and he helped her into the plane. She had not realized it would be so hard with only one hand. Cal buckled her in and went around to the pilot's side. Soon the memorized check list was gone through and Cal called, "Clear prop" and started the engine.

The plane rolled forward as instructed by the control tower to the active runway. Jerry's heart was pounding. A smile flowed into place and her eyes sparkled with joy as the plane rolled down the taxiway and to the active runway for takeoff. She felt like a flower opening up to full bloom as the plane lifted into the sky. She was home again.

"Thank you, darling," Jerry said into the intercom mic. It was an exalting feeling to be flying that always swept over her and her soul soared as the plane lifted toward the blue sky. It could have been so different. But she would not think of that now. Only the sky above, the earth below and the joy of flying. She reached out and touched the control wheel in front of her with her right hand but her cast prevented her from properly holding the throttle.

"I'll help you," Cal told her. Jerry took the controls gently as she did when she had a student in the pilot's seat. Cal was handling the throttle and monitoring the instruments following her carefully with his left hand on the controls in front of him. Jerry was elated. She had been away for three weeks and now she was back. What a wonderful understanding man she had married. She looked at him with such love and worship that Cal felt his heart leap with happiness. He shuddered at the thought of how tragic the accident could have been.

Jerry watched the plane climb 1000, 2000, 3000 feet and in the distance she saw black thunder-heads from which rain poured onto the earth many miles from them. Above them small puffs of clouds happily drifted in the wind, the kind of clouds that could in a few minutes gather into giant cumulus clouds or could just sail away and disappear. Below them the earth was like a checkerboard of colors from greens to brown.

In the spring these fields looked like blue lakes; but, they were really fields of bluebonnets or red splashed fields of Indian Paintbrushes. It was such a wonderful world the human race had been given.

Jerry began to tire and looked at Cal who understood and nodded taking the controls. "We do make a great team, darling." And he grinned back, "Forever, Jer. Forever," and turned the plane for home.

As they flew over the airport Jerry spotted a strange car by the office. "Looks like we have company," she said as Cal parked the plane at the hangar. He reached over and unbuckled Jerry's seatbelt planting a kiss on her cheek. "I'll help you out," he said softly. Jerry waited while he walked around the plane. She had opened the door and held her arms out to him. Easily, he lifted her to the ground. Jerry's face was glowing with happiness. He held her close.

"Thank you, Cal, my husband. I needed to fly so much. I love you."

"I understand. Flying is a part of us just as an artist must create and writer must write. Without it no matter what other success or personal happiness one has without flying something is missing. People like us need to fly as much as we need to breathe to be really alive. I know. I've had to stay away, too. I could feel your need as I felt my own. Now, did you make a grocery list?"

"I was too busy making-something else." She looked at him reminding him of a mischievous imp her eyes crinkling with her grin.

"Then go ask Maggie for some paper and a pen and get busy, woman." He gave her a loving pat on her rear. She laughed as she walked to the office. She was tired, very tired. It was a good tired. The kind that made her feel happy and fulfilled.

Charley's Flying School

Rosa B. Lane

Chapter 24

Sylvia and Harvey sat in Sylvia's comfortable apartment with the maps before them. They had marked the areas around the airport owned by Richard in red, the others in blue, and the still private in green. There was not enough land in the blue to hurt the airport. It was surrounded by farms that would not be sold.

At least for now the airport was safe. But where was the Senator? What was he up to?

"There are terrorists planning something, and I don't think it is connected to oil or gas. Not nuclear power plants. But what?" It was then that she saw the smoking cigar. "Who might want revenge or to destroy a particular segment of our country. The X points are near large cities. Cities have huge populations, hospitals, colleges, sports arenas as well as industry. Wait. The forests! Not the cities. The forests. Look! All the points where the bombs were being built are in the wilderness. What would happen if forests all over the country were on fire at the same time? Chaos! There would not be enough of anything to fight them. But why? Pollution? Or just plain terrorism? Who would do that?" Sylvia looked at her father. He was staring at the map.

"My forest would be ruined for years to come. But it would not destroy me, only the workers and the people who need my lumber. People who must import lumber as well as domestic. It would be the worker who would be caught. Then it would add to the already millions of jobless people. People would need the government to give them social services. There would not be enough."

"When there are enough hungry people in a country we know what that means. Revolt. Who would benefit from an uprising of jobless people? Communists? Islamic Terrorists? Rogue Nations? I guess I'm imagining things." Sylvia shook her head. "I still don't know why anyone would want to hurt Jerry. She's not political. Nor rich. Everyone likes her."

"Someone who wanted to destroy her life doesn't. Maybe Richard knows of someone." Harvey Lambert was dialing his son.

Richard's reply was, "Only Angus. Otherwise, I don't have the faintest. I'll get in touch with Jerry. She's home now. I had planned to take the kids and Lilly to see her. I traced her to the airport and she's up flying with Cal. We are headed over there now. I'll be in touch. Bye."

They were waiting in the office when Jerry came in. "Welcome back, little sister." Richard hugged Jerry. "These angelic children are my twins and this is my beautiful wife, Lilly."

"We finally meet. I'm so glad to see you Lilly. And this must be Rickie and Annie. Hi, kids. How do you like the airport?" Jerry clumsily hugged the three.

Before they could answer the phone rang and Maggie cried, "Uncle Art! We've been so worried. Jerry just came in. She's home now." Maggie handed the phone to Jerry who took it to the sofa and sat down.

"Uncle Art. What's wrong on the ranch? We were so concerned not to get an answer from you."

"Didn't you get my message? I called your home and the office and couldn't get an answer or the machine. So I left word at the restaurant that I was going to a cattle auction. Flora is with her daughter who is having her third baby and Grandma is babysitting. I just got back. Jeffery said he would be sure to let you know."

"He never said a word. I'm so sorry you missed the wedding. Cal and I were married in the hospital chapel. Harvey Lambert gave me away. I was so hurt that you never answered any of our messages. Then we got scared something was wrong. Cal was going to fly over as soon as he could. We'll have a real celebration when you get here."

"You finally did it! Congratulations! I am sorry I wasn't

there! I'll be a few days. While I was gone we lost some cattle to a pack of wild dogs, and I'm going to join the other ranchers on a hunt. There's been more than a dozen killed on the ranches. There's a lot of territory to cover. Well Mrs. Morris, I think this is what Charley wanted and I congratulate you. I know it's what I saw as inevitable. Now you take care. I love you, Jerry."

"I'm so glad everything is all right. I love you too. We have a lot to catch up on. Good-by." Jerry hung up as Cal walked in. "Uncle Art is okay. He left a message with Jeffery to tell us he would be gone to buy some cattle. Why didn't Jeffery tell us?"

"Maybe he forgot." Cal suggested. "But the airport nearly shut down for the wedding. Surely he would have remembered then. I'll have to ask him. Today he said nothing. I know he saw us."

"Jerry, Dad wants to know if you have any idea who is mad enough to want to destroy you. I suggested Angus. From what I know of him he isn't beyond revenge of some sort. Can you think of anyone?"

"No, not really." Jerry stood up and walked to Cal.

"I'll shoot anyone who hurts you, Auntie Jerry," little Rickie declared.

"Rickie! We all love Jerry, but we don't shoot people," said Lilly. "We let the law put them in jail."

"Auntie Jerry, can I -oops- may I sign your cast?" Annie looked up at her. "Mama has some pretty colored pencils."

"Of course," said Jerry. Cal helped her remove the sling and she went back to the sofa. After a brief quarrel between the twins over who would go first, they proceeded to decorate the white cast. Annie made a big smiley face and signed it "Annie" then Rickie drew a red airplane and signed it "Rickie." Jerry held her arm out for all of them to see. "How beautiful it is now. I shall hate to have it removed."

"That's all right. We'll mail you some more pictures," said Annie. "Mommy can send you one too. She used to sell some to help us get food. Now we ain't-aren't hungry since Daddy came." She walked over and reached her arms up for Richard. He bent over and scooped her into his arms grinning with pride.

"Aren't my kids wonderful?" he said.

Lilly looked at the three of them and said softly, "Thank you, Jerry. Thank you."

The phone rang and it was Carla. "Jerry, what have you done to make Jeffery mad? When you and Cal left he stood in the kitchen door and looked daggers at your backs. It was pure hate. I felt chills and thought I should tell you. He then went into the kitchen and we could hear him yelling at Sophia, the cook. She's been here for 15 years, and she walked out. He's had tantrums before, but nothing like this. That's why he has such a turnover in help."

"I have no idea. I hardly know him. I was just a kid and he lived with his mother after the divorce. I rarely saw him when he visited here. He didn't like it. That's why I was surprised when he took over the airport when his father died. Thanks for calling." Jerry turned and looked at the others. "It seems Jeffery is angry at me for something. I wonder what. As I was saying, since I've been home everyone has been so nice."

"How about a student? Any who got angry that you wouldn't pass them?"

"I've never had to fail a student if that's the right word. I've had them leave for money reasons, for family and health, but only Kevin was angry. I refused to rent him the acrobatic plane because he was intending to 'stunt' in it without training. I told him to get training first. He got a plane from someone else and died trying to 'stunt fly' without knowing how."

"How about his parents?" Asked Richard.

"I called his parents and warned them of his intentions. I said I was not qualified to teach aerobatics but there were several in the area who were. Suggested he find a really good instructor. That's all. Then I saw that Kevin had crashed."

"Think about it and let us know if you can come up with any one at all. Even the slimmest possibility from years ago or college. The kids need to get back now. How about you and Cal being our guests at the dinner dance at the club next Saturday night? Lilly needs someone to help her face the lionesses."

"We would be happy to go. Will Sylvia come?" Said Jerry.

"Yes. She has sold her business and is staying in Houston. Dad put her up in his apartment." Richard started to leave then Jerry stopped him.

"Wait. When I was in college I helped a friend escape from an abusive boyfriend. She insisted on moving in with him and then he started beating and threatening her. One day when he was at work I picked her up and took her to the home office for abused women and they took her to the secret safe house until her parents came for her. I haven't seen her since. We decided it best if she did not correspond. I have no idea where she went."

"Did you have your yellow car?" Cal asked. "If you did maybe he knew you if he was a college student. What was his name?"

"She called him her 'Man' at first, then just "him". I don't know anything else."

"Was 'Man' for male or a nickname?"

"I have no idea." Jerry frowned trying to remember some little thing. "But I'll think on it. Cal what will I wear?" Everyone laughed.

"Then I'll call Mother and tell her I've invited three more guests." Everyone said goodbye, and Jerry leaned back inspecting her pretty cast.

When Richard told his mother that there would be Sylvia, Jerry and Calvin for dinner, his mother hit the ceiling. "Absolutely not! It is enough to please your father and have-," Richard stopped her sharply.

"Fine." He hung up and called the club and reserved his own table for six at 7:00 p.m. Then called his father. "Dad, Mother doesn't want my guests at her table Saturday and I have reserved a table for Sylvia, Jerry, Cal, Lilly and myself. I hope you will join us." He waited holding his breath.

"I'd be pleased to. My family together. Your mother and I have had separate lives for most of our marriage. The togetherness has been only social and financial. I'll see you at the dance." Harvey Lambert walked into his wife's study. "My dear, Laura, I am joining my son and his family at their table Saturday at the club. It seems you have made our daughter-in-law and my daughter as well as my son's friends unwelcome. I have had my fill of your social crap. These dinners are your idea. You do it your way. I will attend no more of them. You haven't been my wife for years. I know about the abortion in Japan when you took a vacation there. Richard was about eighteen months old. I had found out about you and your lover. You came back and I hoped in vain that we could be like it once was. But Dale was born and you turned away completely. You acted so high and mighty against my daughter Sylvia when you didn't even face the pregnancy of your adultery. I don't know who he is and I no longer care. He can have you. I will be talking to my lawyer about a divorce. I'm finished." He turned and walked out before she could comprehend what he had said. He whistled a tune as he went back to his office. Laura Lambert stared at her husband, then smiled as he left the room. He would not dare. But this time she was wrong.

Saturday, Richard's limousine delivered Jerry and Cal to the country club. Richard, Lilly and Sylvia were waiting. As they joined Jerry, Harvey Lambert arrived and joined them. The six were seated at a reserved table near the Lambert's long elegant table. Mrs. Lambert presided in her husband's place. There were three empty places. The society crowd gasped at the three beautiful women and the handsome male who accompanied Richard and his father.

Jerry wore the same gown she had worn before. She was the only woman wearing a dress that had been seen at the club before. Lilly looked like a fashion model with her hair swept up in the latest style. Sylvia made all eyes sweep from her to Richard then to their father. No doubt about the relationship. Sylvia who was a fashion model and had owned her own fashion business stood out in a room full of designer dresses and elegant women. Mrs. Lambert's social companions had been led to believe a bunch of trash would be with Richard. Instead they saw a gracious group of ladies and gentlemen. The women envied the way Richard and Cal took such loving care of their wives. The men wondered if the dark beauty was available, then sighed and glanced at their wives or dates. Laura Lambert fumed. For the first time she realized that it was Harvey who had carried the dinners along. It was his laughter that overshadowed her arrogant stiffness. For a moment she felt lost. Then she put on her best fake smile and played the warm hostess.

The six at Richard's table were amused at the stir they had

caused. "So this is how the 'other half' dines," Cal said with a laugh. "These are the 'beautiful people' I've heard so much about." He shook his head in amusement. "They're just like the rest of us. Only they dress better and their fish is cooked fancy instead of on a backyard barbeque."

Harvey Lambert's laugh was loud and hearty. "That's about the way it is. Just their imagination that the wealthy somehow are more moral in their adultery than common folks who wear work clothes. Now, Sylvia has come up with a thought. What's the possibility of destroying so much of the forests of the U.S. that it could cause economic as well as environmental disasters?" Cal whistled softly.

Cal shook his head. "That would be impossible if there was rain in parts of the country. However, right now California has several dozen fires caused by lightning, Florida has been so dry they have a large fire that is still out of control, and we had one here a few weeks ago that Jerry helped with. But the rain came here. In all these fires, every state goes to help its neighbors. I would say the chance was slim."

"Suppose these all came at the same time all over the country started by terrorists. Would there be enough help to control them? And others would pop up as fast as the first ones were put out. In other words, keep the fires so widespread and frequent in hundreds, maybe thousands of places burning continuously all over the country. The oil fields, gas and nuclear plants are too well guarded. The forests are not."

"About six percent of the fires we have in Texas are caused by careless smokers, more by careless campers as was our last one. Many are caused by home owners who live in the forests burning trash. One person with a pack of cigarettes could cause a bad fire. Terrorist cells across the country could do a lot of damage. If it didn't rain, people would die and so would wildlife. Homes destroyed. Forests ruined for years for commercial use. But nature always comes back," Jerry said thoughtfully.

"Here comes our food so let us enjoy it since my son is paying for it," Harvey said. They all laughed.

"I can't help but think we're overlooking the obvious." Jerry sipped at her iced tea and tasted the shrimp cocktail, "This is good!"

"Has any one heard where the Senator went?' Sylvia questioned. "I believe he is in way over his head. Someone he knows just walked in and took over. By what means I don't know. Maybe blackmail. If he gives the millions back the big conglomerates may not kill him. Did you know Mrs. Lambert gave him $10,000,000 to have a part in destroying the airport? Anyone know who Alfonso is?"

"I knew she gave him money, but not what it was for. It was her money. That's all she has now, money and society. She has destroyed her family. I'm getting a divorce." Harvey Lambert looked at his son. "I just want to live with someone who likes me or live alone. I have neither now. Being with my family and friends for the first time in years makes me realize there's not much time left for happiness and peace."

"You're welcome to come live with us, Papa Lambert," said Lilly. "It's a quiet lovely place. At least when the five kids are in school or asleep." She smiled at Harvey.

How could I have been so insensitive to this beautiful child who only wanted to love my son and bear his child? He wanted to blame his wife but, in his mind, and heart he knew he was equally to blame. He had only understood money then. Harvey Lambert felt the shame of what he had done to both his son and daughter-in-law deeply and painfully. He had changed his will to make Richard, Sylvia and Lilly equal heirs in his estate. Laura got nothing but a valuable painting that they had bought together when they were married. "Thank you, my dear. Right now, I have a mill to run and many other things to do. But I will come to see you for the holidays if I'm welcome."

"You'll always be welcome, Dad. I only wish Mother would change too. But it's her choice." Richard spoke wistfully then sighed with resignation. Lilly reached over and gently touched his hand.

"I've been thinking that everyone at college knew my car if they knew me. Dad gave it to me when I went to college. I loved it. Could it be possible that 'My Man' was a student or a new grad who lived nearby and recognized the car from the neighbor's description?

I had forgotten that. But I haven't the faintest idea who he was. As for Alfonso the only one I know is Alfonso Mitchel. Reverend Mitchel." Jerry laughed.

"Maybe Harry McHugh can find out. He loves a mystery." Richard chuckled as he finished his wine. "Harry will want to question you. May I send him over tomorrow? I will have him call first." Jerry said yes as the coffee was served. When dinner was over, the others wanted to stay and dance. Jerry was not supposed to, and she was tired. Richard's limo took them home.

At home Jerry once again stood in the living room enclosed in her husband's arms. "I'm so confused. It seems there are so many facets to this and yet I feel there is a common factor. What is it? I think I'm ready for bed. It's been a long day. I know it's early for the rich and famous. Coming?"

"I have an early student. So I'll join you." Cal held out his hand and this time he led Jerry to the bedroom. They fell asleep in each other's arms. Cal realizing his dream had come true, Jerry feeling safe and knowing she had found a new and wonderful life she had never dreamed was possible.

Rosa B. Lane

Chapter 25

Jerry was in the kitchen trying to wash the dishes with one hand when the phone rang. It was Harry saying he could be there at nine if it was convenient. Jerry agreed. She had put her shower cover over her hand with the cast and tried to get the dishes rinsed and in the dish washer before the Texas roaches found them. The pest control had been here a couple of months ago and it was time to call them back. She had grown up with the sneaky bugs and she knew no food or crumbs could be left out or they would somehow find their way in to them. One of her neighbors from the north said it was a disgrace up north to have a pest control van in front of your house but in Texas it was prestigious. Charley had said they were here before man came and would be here after man left. Maybe they were the meek that would inherit the earth.

At nine the doorbell rang. Jerry greeted Harry McHugh warmly and offered him a fresh cup of coffee. She had just made it since there was not much she was allowed to do for a week but drink coffee and read or watch TV. She escorted him into the breakfast room and poured a cup of coffee and produced well-covered cream and sugar for him and poured a cup for herself. She opened the tightly covered bowl of Danish rolls and offered him one. Then they got down to business.

"Richard told me of the help you gave your college friend. Is 'Man' a nickname or just man?"

"I always thought it was just her way of saying he was her 'man' but it could have been part of his name, like, Manuel or something. I just don't know. Not much to go on." Jerry sipped her coffee. "I think her folks lived in Montana, but the college would know. She was afraid. Said he threatened to kill her and them if she left him. Then he would say he was sorry and beg for another chance. She finally felt he would kill her someday if she stayed. I helped get her to a shelter until her folks came for her. I don't know where the shelter was. The workers at the office took her there and brought her to the office for her folks to pick up. That's all I know."

"And you drove your yellow car. Did she associate with any other students?"

"Not that I know of. She studied most of the time in the library. She was ashamed to admit that she was a victim and had been wrong in moving out of the dorm. She finally confided in me because-well - I insisted she go to the student clinic when she came in one day pretty badly bruised and her eye swollen shut. From there we arranged to get her home. There's not much more to tell."

"What do you know about the people at the airport? How well do you know them? Dr. Zorak keeps saying 'they said she had no relatives and it would be easy.' Sounds like more than one and at least one knows you. Anyone else in town or at the airport you may have made angry?"

"I've known most of them for years. Not the workers but the business owners. Jeffery Trenton took over after his father's death. I don't really know him. He lived with his mother so I just saw him once in a while when we were kids. I never paid any attention to him. He didn't like to be here and was not very nice. Uncle Art left a message that he was going to be out of town and Jeffery said he would give it to me, but he talked to us and said nothing. Carla said Jeffery looked daggers at Cal and me. I haven't done anything to him to make him angry. Carla Wright and Bob Hardy I've known for years. Grew up around them. I played with Carla's daughter when she was visiting. We are about the same age. As for the help I really don't know them except to say 'hi'." Jerry sat silently while Harry took notes. "I'm frightened, Harry. Why would anyone hate me so much? How could I have made anyone so angry without knowing it:"

"I think that Angus is mad enough and I think the girl's "Man" is mad enough for revenge. There are a lot of sick people out there, Jerry. You don't look too good. I think you're overdoing it. Why don't you go up lie down for a while and rest?" Harry looked at her tired face. "Here you are doing dishes, and I'll bet your doctor said not to." He grinned. "That's what my wife did when she was fresh out of the hospital."

Jerry agreed and she went upstairs to rest. She fell asleep. When she awakened, she saw Cal sitting on the bed. "I got worried and closed shop and came home." He said and bent over and kissed her. "I stopped by the store and got some stuff for a non-nutritional lunch when we get hungry."

"Harry called you. I'm sorry. I just suddenly felt so alone and so afraid, Cal. We can't afford to keep the school closed. We'll have to start over again."

Cal laughed. "Look outside. Nature closed the school. There's a front that intends to stay a while. I'll go back this afternoon if you feel better and check out the planes. And to think you were doing everything alone. I did not realize how much courage you had. I love you so much, Jer. Right now a thunderstorm is not the best time to be handling metal tools. At least when you have a pretty wife at home waiting."

"I didn't even hear the thunder. What time is it?" Jerry sat up feeling much better and realized she had done too much too soon just as she had been warned not to do. "I just got so tired. I feel better now. I just overdid it. I love being Mrs. Morris." She held out her right arm for him. He took her in his arms and pulled her close to his heart.

"It's noon. If you're hungry I'll toss a mean sandwich - both mustard and catsup. No extra charge for onions." Jerry laughed.

Cal was glad to see her laugh. While he fixed lunch, she went into the living room and looked at the sofa and chairs. Suddenly she wanted the whole house redecorated just for the two of them. It was her childhood home, but now it was her marriage home. She would put the curtains her mother had made in a room for their daughter. Until then they could go with the spread into her cedar chest. They would have everything new. She grinned as she wondered what Cal would say when she told him. Most husbands groaned and then nodded yes wondering how it would get paid for. She would wait until the bedroom was redone to spring it on him.

Cal came into the room and set a tray on the coffee table. "Jerry, I was thinking that maybe we could redo the whole house. Would you like that? It's up to you, but Mom said we should get everything new for us and I agree." He looked so surprised when she started laughing.

"Am I never going to get to pull a wifely surprise on you? I was just thinking that." Cal grinned and shook his head. He could not believe how they seemed to read each other's mind. But that was something that had always been between them. They were a team. "Now let's solve the mysteries of life. Which is first?"

"How about finding some news on the TV or radio? I've been a little preoccupied and have missed the world." Jerry turned on the TV and went through the channels finally finding the noon news. She felt a cold chill and turned to Cal. He looked at her as if the unbelievable was believable. The newscaster was saying the fires in California from lightning strikes and careless campers had reached over a thousand isolated fires. Nevada had a huge fire and Florida's fire raged unchecked. The resources of these states were strained. The National Guard was being sent to help fight them. Prisoners were offered part of their sentences reduced if they volunteered to help. Hospitals were crowded with smoke inhalation victims and towns were being evacuated in the path of the fires. Hundreds of people were homeless. The smoke from the fires was drifting over the nearby areas making people stay indoors. In many towns businesses had come to a standstill. "That's what Sylvia was talking about. And this is only a small part of the country. Suppose it hit all the forests all over the country. Cal," Jerry looked at him frightened as if he could stop it. He just sat for a moment staring at the pictures. The phone was ringing and he went to answer it. "And this is from mostly natural causes." Jerry added to herself.

When Cal returned he said that it had been Sylvia. "She said that Harvey Lambert wants all of us to meet at the airport tomorrow and have a conference. She suggested the small airports near forests could be used for starting fires from the air. Will you feel like coming tomorrow? I won't leave you alone."

"I'm sorry to be such a baby. I'll be fine. I need to go. Have you heard from your dad? Art is still on a wild dog hunt with other ranchers. You make a mean sandwich and pour a fantastic glass of milk. Thanks for being home."

"I love you, Jerry." Cal kissed her gently on her hair. What a honeymoon they would have someday!

Maggie had already opened the office when they arrived the next morning. It was a clear and beautiful day. The Lamberts were waiting in the classroom.

"What about the 10 o'clock student?" Maggie asked looking at the appointment book. Cal said he would take him. He was almost ready for his check ride with the FAA inspector. They all went into the classroom for the conference. The other business owners at the airport had been invited. By nine o'clock they were all sitting in mild disbelief as Sylvia explained what she thought. The Forest Rangers had been informed and were to pass the possible idea to the appropriate government agency.

Carla said shaking her head. "In a drought it would really mess up the country. And then the terrorists would take credit. The people would panic. There would be no safe place to go especially if the fire spilled over into Canada and Mexico. Panic and terror is what the terrorists want. They know they can't win a face to face war, but they can wreck the country's morale and hurt us economically. What can be done?"

"I don't know." Harvey shook his head. "We felt you should know why small airports are being bought, at least a possible reason. We can prove nothing. It is up to the big guys in Washington to figure this out. If they only believe us."

Carla looked at Jerry and asked, "Are you all right?" Jeffery sitting beside her took a deep breath. Carla looked at him and was startled that he was looking at Jerry again with a flash of pure hate then he smiled weakly. Carla looked at Jerry who was looking down at the map.

"I'm fine. Thanks, Carla."

The crowd had dispersed all but Carla. She looked around and made sure Jeffery was gone. "Jerry what have you done to make Jeffery so angry at you? He was glaring daggers again."

Jerry looked at her shaking her head. "I haven't the slightest idea. We have hardly spoken."

"I saw a look in his eyes of hate that gave me chills. I've never seen that look in anyone's eyes before. Not even my ex when he had to pay child support and alimony." Carla tried to make it a little light when she saw the color drain from Jerry's face.

Jerry looked at her and asked, her voice shaky, "Does he have a wife? What's his middle name?"

"He said his wife left him about five years ago; at least that's the gossip. I have no idea what his middle name is. Why?" Jerry told her about her college classmate whom she had helped escaped a brutal boyfriend. Carla raised her brows. "You know some of the help quit because of his abusive ways. I've heard him yelling at them once or twice. He seems very impatient. Not at all like his father was. I'll ask Bob if he knows his middle name."

"Thanks, Carla. I'll see what I can find out too." Carla went back to her helicopter business and Jerry asked Maggie to start filling her in on the procedures she had so successfully implemented. They were engrossed in the procedures when Cal returned from his flight.

"You're ready to take your test. I'll get you an appointment for next week," he was telling his student as they came into the office. Maggie with her efficiency had the bill ready for the student. Jerry was amazed as she learned Maggie's work rules. She shook her head. It was so much easier to fix an engine!

"Cal, I need to talk to you for a minute in private. Only a minute." Cal nodded. Jerry would not ask this at a time when he would be debriefing a student if it weren't very important. When they were alone, Jerry explained what Carla had noticed. "I'll call Harry Mc Hugh and see if he has found out anything more." She left the classroom and went back to Maggie's lessons in how to be a secretary and file clerk.

Harry checked in with her before she could call him. Dr. Zorak had decided to make a deal. He had named names of those who hired him. Not to kill, but to destroy Jerry's life. Jerry was shocked. She sat down and with shaking hands called for Cal. "Why?" She kept saying over and over as he took the phone from her hand. He clicked on the speaker so Jerry could hear.

"Harry, what's going on? Jerry's as white as a sheet. She keeps saying 'why'." Cal listened while Harry explained. "I'll kill him."

"No, Cal. Let the police handle it. Please. Angus and Jeffery. Where did they meet?" Jerry shook her head. Harry was still talking and Cal smiled nodding.

"The police are on their way. Angus has been picked up already. It seems that the two were college fraternity brothers and have kept in contact. Angus told Jeffery of your engagement ring and Jeffery told Angus of his girl. It was Jeffery Mansfield Trenton who was the abusive boyfriend. He recognized Jerry's car when she got out of college and came home. The two talked to each other and Angus already was acquainted with Zorak by way of Angus's illegal drugs, so the rest was easy, so they thought. Then someone played into their hands trying to kill you in the accident. They did not count on our trio of nurses and a husband. Tell Jerry it's safe to go for a ride with you and do loops. It's almost over."

"Almost?" asked Cal.

"We still don't know who was blackmailing the Senator and where he is. We'll keep looking. The Feds are on it now. They don't like drug dealing. I'll be in touch with you."

"Thanks, Harry." Cal hung up the phone. "I guess that's all for the drug business." He took Jerry by the hand and added, "I think I'd like a cup of coffee from the restaurant. I think I'll ask Bob and Carla to join us. Is that okay, Jerry?"

Jerry smiled and nodded. Calls were made and the two friends joined Cal and Jerry at the restaurant a few minutes later. They had just been served coffee and doughnuts when the police arrived.

Jeffery glared at Jerry as the police cuffed him and led him out. The hate was there. "What will happen to the airport now?" The others shook their heads. One problem solved and another steps in to fill the void.

Rosa B. Lane

Chapter 26

A week later Jerry had her cast removed. She was shown a routine of strengthening exercises to do at home. Now she was looking for a car. The insurance company had stopped arguing when Richard talked to them and sent Jerry the proper settlement. Cal went car hunting with her when they were both free. She settled on a medium sized passenger car in a blue-green. It was not unique but a rather popular color and car. At the same time the airport was sold.

Jerry was working with Maggie to get her last lesson in and office work finished since Maggie was heading out for nursing school in a few days. This was her last day. She was now a private pilot single engine plane. Jerry had planned a goodbye party for her at the office after work. Mike had already left for college; but, Mike's mother came with a cake she had insisted on baking. Abby showed up with brownies and Cal brought soda. Maggie's mother had sent her son over with fresh baked Danish rolls. The airport business owners showed up with farewell gifts. Everyone had grown very fond of the red-haired girl and her romantic meeting of her boyfriend. Uncle Art appeared all spruced up. He had driven to the airport. Except for the closed restaurant things were almost normal. The fuel pump had remained open and was filled as usual. The boy who supervised the pump continued to take care of the customers. However, he said the new owner had not started the payment system. Since there was no place to pay, the customers each kept track of their bills. No one knew who was running the fuel supply. A few travelers left "I Owe You" tabs with their names and addresses but most had enough fuel to get to another airport.

The party was a big success and everyone wished Maggie the best. She promised to write to Jerry. As the last of the guests were leaving, a limousine drove up and Harvey Lambert walked to the office. They all greeted him warmly.

"What brings you here?" asked Art as he shook his hand.

"Well, since I own the airport, I thought I best see what has to be done," said Harvey in his best Texas drawl.

"You bought it? I thought Richard might have something to do with it, but didn't think of you." Jerry was smiling.

"I stopped at the restaurant and it's going to need a complete renovation. It's pretty out- dated. We'll get it going again. You folks and the visitors need food, and the museum will be fixed up too. We're going to have a memorial for our boys to be proud of. I had little trouble making a deal with Jeffery. Seems he needed money to pay his lawyer. The previous offer he turned down was withdrawn because the owner decided to build his subdivision elsewhere. I see you're out of your cast. Are you flying yet?"

"No, not without my instructor." Jerry smiled at Cal. "It'll be a while until get my strength back in my arm. How's your Connecticut family?"

"Fine. All set for school. Richard is enrolled studying business as well and Lilly majoring in art. Joanne is engaged. She went to school all summer and will get her degree in half the time. She's a smart lady. She's marrying her math professor. He's got a couple of kids. His wife died two years ago. That's all the news. I had to pry it out of them with several phone calls. Finally, my grandson answered and told me all the news. He's mighty smart. And little Annie, she took the phone away from him and told me all about art and business and how she was going to be a pilot like Aunt Jerry."

"I'm glad everything is working well for Richard. How's Sylvia? I couldn't reach her to invite her to the party. Has she gone back to New York?" Jerry was cleaning up the coffee pot getting it ready for the next day.

"Yes. She gives you her best wishes. She has some business

to finish up and plans to come back and live here."

"Things seem to be getting back to normal. They found the Senator. He was trying to leave New York. I think some of the people he embezzled money from caught up with him. They dumped him on the court house steps during the night. He's recuperating in the prison hospital. He never thought he might get caught. We still don't know who was the head of Zebra Company and was blackmailing him. I think he will talk." Cal looked at the others. "I keep thinking we are missing the obvious. Any of you heard what the police are doing?" Everyone shook their head. "Locally they are doing nothing except watching the airport and making it mandatory to have permits to go into the forests. That's all. Oh, have you found the Alphonso? Know of anyone by that name around here?"

"No. Only the preacher, it couldn't be him." said Jerry more to herself than to the others. "We never connected Angus and Jeffery. Who else might be connected to the Senator and the Zebra Company and Jeffery? A common factor."

Chapter 27

That evening Cal came home early to find Jerry had an old-fashioned country dinner waiting for him. After dinner she served coffee and brownies which she admitted were not as good as Abby's. As they ate the brownies Cal frowned. "What do you really know about Rev. Mitchell? He seems nice but in a false way. I guess I haven't seen much of him and somehow I don't trust him."

"I only know he showed up here a two years ago asking for help to get supplies to a village in the hills. He leads some kind of fundamentalist, unorthodox church I never heard of. I don't know anyone who goes to it. Maybe Mike's father would know. Why?"

Cal shook his head. "I guess I've gotten to the point that I am too suspicious. We've had so much happen. I was ready to believe the Senator and look what happened. I wanted to beat Lambert to a pulp for the way he talked to you. Now we are friends." He looked up at Jerry. "Is anything around here real?"

"Our love is. Our marriage is. We are, and so are the others at the airport. The offers to buy up the farms have disappeared. Where is the other shoe I keep waiting to drop? Zebra Company is still out there. It's connected to the Senator somehow."

"The Feds have broken over a dozen plots to start fires. But the borders are open. Anyone can sneak across." Cal held out his arms to her and she settled onto his lap. "Something is missing."

"Rev. Mitchell will be gone Tuesday. Abby and I will take the supplies. He's been gone a lot lately. But Abby was happy to get in some free flying time."

"Where's the grocery list? Back to reality of filling the larder." Cal smiled. "My wagon can pull that boat, and Lake Conroe is a nice place to fish they tell me." He sighed. "We'll have to give it a try some time. Off to get the groceries. Let's go my love." He reached down and pulled her up. "Now, none of that," he said trying to be firm as Jerry hugged him. "We are serious people."

"I'll just put on my fancy jeans and tee shirt and I'll be ready to go." Jerry picked up the grocery list and her purse. "I'm ready." They both laughed as they headed for the wagon. She wondered if they would ever have a few hours alone much less a honeymoon. Jerry looked at Cal's relaxed grin.

Something was still nagging at Cal about the Reverend. Jerry had thought of him as a good man, but she really did not know much about him. She pushed it aside as nonsense. Everyone had helped him deliver the boxes of supplies. Everyone trusted him, didn't they? Actually, it had never been discussed. They arrived at the grocery store and their thoughts returned to the here and now.

The next day was very busy and Jerry tried to help with the servicing of the airplanes. Little by little the strength was returning in her left arm. Jerry decided to work on Monday to try to catch up on paper work. Cal had a number of rescheduled classes keeping him in the air all day. Both were quite tired when the last student had left.

Jerry was cleaning up the coffee pot for Tuesday and Cal was reviewing the students he had scheduled on his day off to try to catch up when the door opened. They both looked up as a woman stepped in and closed the door quickly. She smiled and looked at them with assurance. Her short brown hair was windblown and her face tanned. She had the bearing of an athlete. Tall, broad shoulders, strong arms and well-tanned she smiled broadly showing white teeth.

"They told me you needed help. I need a job." She spoke simple and sure of herself.

"I can sure use a secretary. Paperwork is not my best skill," Jerry said. Before she could say more the woman interrupted her.

"Oh, I'm not a secretary." She looked at their surprised faces. "I'm an airplane mechanic. They said you needed one." She added looking unsure for the first time. Cal looked at Jerry grinning. Jerry smiled. "I grew up around airplanes. I had my pilot's license as soon as the law allowed, but I could fly long before that. I helped my dad and uncle fix cars and airplanes all my life. They sent me to school to get a degree. Here are copies of my pilots license, mechanics certifications, and references. I've worked on all kinds of planes. I'm sorry. Paperwork is not my cup of tea either."

Jerry smiled as she reviewed the young mechanic's documents. "They were right. Our mechanic quit. He and his family returned to St. Louis. I'm Jerry Morris and this is Cal Morris my husband. We can't pay much right now. But we could use the help if you are qualified." Jerry set the coffee pot down. "I'm in charge of the mechanics and Cal the flying school. We both teach flying. Right now I can't do either for a while. Shall we go to the hangar, and I'll see what you know?"

The girl sighed. "I understand the trouble that has been here. But people don't want to hire a woman mechanic. My dad isn't working now because of Mom. She's getting treatment at Baylor." The girl's voice quivered. "We need the money. My uncle had a stroke and had to give up flying so they sold their charter business. Dad, Mom and I came to Houston to get Mom treated. I don't have the skills for anything else but planes and flying." Her smile had faded to a distressed look.

"Come on, I'm the same way." Jerry held out her hand to the girl. "What is your name?"

"I'm sorry. I'm Ramona Seabens. Dad calls me Mona. She held out her hand and took Jerry's in a firm handshake. Jerry told her what they could pay. Ramona nodded agreement. They walked out to the hangar. Jerry showed Ramona the planes and they went over what needed to be done. When they inspected the Aerobat, Ramona spotted some oil on the floor under it. "I think it has a leak. She's a beautiful plane. How does she handle? I haven't had a chance to take one up."

"You're right. It will be down for inspection. I have a tag in the office and will put it on the clipboard with the key. It needs gas, too. So I'll leave it until we find the leak." Ramona left whistling a happy tune. Jerry smiled and watched her walk away knowing that

Ramona was the highly qualified mechanic that the school needed.

When Jerry went back to the office, she told Cal that Ramona would start work Wednesday. "She is right. She knows each nut and bolt of the planes. She spotted a possible oil leak in the Aerobat so we can't use it till it's serviced. She's not an Arnie yet, but in time she'll be as good or better. I'm still disappointed in Arnie leaving, but his wife and kids missed family and he was concerned for them. Abbie is coming in to fly the supplies. I'll go with her. She's a real good pilot. Shall we close up and go get some dinner?"

"I'm ready," replied Cal. The two turned off the air-conditioner and locked the door. When the hangar was secure they headed for home. Tonight they would take home Chinese. They were both exhausted.

Charley's Flying School

Rosa B. Lane

Chapter 28

Tuesday morning found Jerry and Cal at the flying school early. Cal prepared a Cessna 150 for his own student and the other 150 for Jerry. To assure that the plane was not overloaded, Jerry supervised the loading of the carefully weighed boxes marked clothes and food into the 150 she would use to make the flight for the Reverend. She could not get over the poverty in the all but forgotten hill country village. Some help the Senator had been, she thought. She shook her head remembering the big show Senator Stone had made when he said he would help. Now he was in prison because of fraud. Who had tried to kill her? They were all still hunting for answers. Jerry did not know the other shoe was about to drop.

Abby arrived on time and went straight to the loaded Cessna 150 that Jerry had ready for Abby's preflight. With the preflight inspection finished Abby went to the office to do the flight plan. Jerry gave her a sectional with the flight plan marked. They went over it together and Abby filed the flight plan with Flight Service. Soon they were flying toward the village.

"Look at that big truck coming. Isn't that the direction of the village?" Abby asked.

"It is, but I have no idea if it came from the village. This is a busy road sometimes. The only main one out here." They flew over the truck and left the main road and followed the dirt road. Soon the small sod runway of the village came into sight. "There's usually a cross-wind, so you'll have to be prepared to compensate. You'll be making a short field landing. It's a sod strip."

Abby nodded and looked at the battered windsock lined up with the right end of the runway. There was no one in sight. No excited children. No happy women. None of the missionaries to greet them. It was not until they had landed and taxied to the turnaround did anyone come forth. One woman, a thin mother of six, came rushing to meet them followed by several men as Jerry and Abby climbed from the plane.

"Miss Jerry. It's dangerous here. Can you take the children? Those awful men took everything away from the clinic. They said they were coming back to blow up the village. Help us," the terrified woman was crying.

"Natalie, what men? Where are the missionaries?"

"They were never missionaries. I think, they only pretended. We could tell for they never said their prayers." Jerry opened the door of the luggage area and the men unloaded the supplies. "We are grateful, but you must help us save the children."

"We can carry only two passengers. The pilot and one more. We'll have to come back with a bigger plane. What's going on here?"

"The Reverend came yesterday. He loaded all the stuff from the clinic and warned us we would be destroyed. No one must be alive to tell he said. The truck was a Zebra Company truck only they covered it with paint before they left."

"Reverend Mitchell?" Jerry was shocked! The other shoe had fallen.

"He was mean. He made the men work to keep the road and runway good. He beat the men. His men were worse. The Reverend said he would kill any of them if they touched a woman. He shot one man who tried to rape one of the little girls. That was the only good thing he ever did." The men and women confirmed the speaker's story. They added their own stories of extreme hunger and the threats of death that they received as prisoners.

"The airplane rides? Didn't he take the children for rides when he came?" Jerry was feeling stunned and angry.

"No one ever got to ride. Please help us get out of here." Jerry's disbelief turned to fury.

Abby walked to the clinic. Jerry followed. "I know clinics," said Abby, "my uncle was a doctor. This is hardly even basic. Look-the radio has been destroyed. Jerry, we need the police."

Another woman showed up carrying a small very sick child. "Help me please. Take my baby."

Jerry turned to Abby. "Abby, can you find your way back? When you're air-borne call the air traffic controller and tell them we need help. I'll send the mother and child with you. I'll stay here. Can you do that?"

"Yes. I'll call for an ambulance to be waiting. And for Cal if I can reach him. I'll get the police and anyone else I can reach. Jerry, be careful. I don't want to leave you. Let me stay and you fly."

"Abby, I can't handle the plane fully yet. My arm isn't strong enough. Are all the packages out?" The men nodded. "Let's get back to the plane and get this mother and baby out of here."

Abby and Jerry led the woman and child back to the plane. When they were buckled in, Abby took off and turned the plane toward Memorial Airport.

Jerry turned to the women. "Now let's get organized. Where are the children?"

"We hid them back in the brush by the trees and the lake."

"Then gather up water and food. Bring only things for the children that are needed. We mustn't carry anything to tire us. It's a long way to town."

Abby was in the air and on the radio. Cal was listening to the air traffic control with his student when he heard Abby's call for help. He felt cold chills.

"Melvin, we have to go back. My wife is in danger. I'll give you a free lesson next time." The student nodded and Cal took the controls. He put out a May Day call to all choppers who could carry passengers. The number who answered surprised him. He told them the situation and directions. Most of them were locals and knew the area. Cal landed at Memorial only a few minutes behind Abby. An ambulance was waiting and the mother and child were sent to the emergency room.

Cal called the sheriff and immediately the sheriff's chopper was in the air. He prepared the 182 with its capacity to carry four passengers and was soon in the air heading toward the village. Carla canceled a student and called for Bob Hardy but failed reach him. She readied her four-passenger chopper and headed for the village.

At the village Jerry was organizing the group. "It's a long walk, but we can get out of here away from the danger." On an impulse she started opening the boxes. There was food and clothes on top but under them were hidden small pieces that looked like parts of a machine. "Are all the "charity" boxes like this?"

One woman shook her head in surprise. "They were taken to the clinic. The missionaries unpacked them and gave us the clothes and food. We never saw them opened before. There never seemed to be much food for so many boxes. We asked, but we got no answer. They would not let us leave the village. They said we would be arrested and our children taken away. Many of us came as illegals. We were afraid. What is it?"

"I'd say its part of whatever was going on in the clinic. We must save a piece or two to show the police."

"We have to stop these people," the words were spoken by a middle-aged woman called Mayor Ida. She was thin, tall and showed signs of once being a handsome mixed Native American Indian and Mexican woman. Now, like all the others, she was half-starved. She appeared to be the head of the village. Two pregnant women looked full term.

Jerry heard it first. A low drone then it became louder. They all hurried out to look at the sky. Coming into view was one helicopter then two. Soon the sky was filled. With them the familiar 182 came into sight. "Cal", she cried. "Help is here! Everyone, get the children, the sick, and the pregnant women to the runway. Abbie came through. She did it! My husband is here." Jerry was close to joyful tears. Cal. I love you.

Then a cry went up from one of the older children. "Mama. They're here to kill us." All eyes turned to the road. The truck was coming back. Jerry stuffed the piece of metal she still had in her hand into her pocket. They all ran to the runway.

The first to land was Cal followed by the police helicopters and civilians. Harvey Lambert in his business chopper landed last. As

Charley's Flying School

the pilots loaded the children and women, the truck from Zebra Company came closer. Chaos followed. Harvey Lambert leaped from his chopper and before anyone knew it was organizing the chaos into order. The pregnant women were loaded onto his large business helicopter along with their four children. The police rescue team was loaded and gone before the truck stopped and the shooting started.

Shielding his employer, the pilot of the Lambert chopper took a bullet and fell. Cal turned to Jerry. "Are you all right? Can you take the 182 back? I'm the only other chopper pilot." Jerry looked at the choppers leaving with their victims. Carla had gone earlier with a load of children. All agreed to deliver everyone at Memorial so the families could be reunited. A cry gave Cal his answer.

A frightened woman ran to Harvey. "She's in labor! Hurry!"

"Go, Cal. I'll do it. Harvey, I'm not strong in my left arm yet. Can you help?"

"I have a strong arm, Jerry." He turned to Cal. "Get my pilot to the hospital with the women. I'll get Jerry home safely." Cal nodded. He ran to the chopper and helped the pilot into the cockpit. He made sure the pregnant women in the backseat were strapped in safely, climbed into the pilot seat and lifted off.

Jerry told the men she could only take two of them and asked for volunteers to stay behind. The children and women had all been evacuated. A police swat team arrived and the truck had left speeding fruitlessly trying to escape. The attack had been met with unexpected return fire from the air for which they had no stomach. The truck went into a ditch and exploded. Two of the men had jumped to safety and simply surrendered with no fight left. Others were crawling from the burning truck screaming for help.

Jerry's plane was the last to leave, except for the police helicopter. She had given the captain in charge her mechanical pieces she had found and told him where the rest were. He examined them and nodded and whistled. "Let me know what it is. I have to go now."

Soon she was in the air. She had tried flying the 182 yesterday and could not hold the controls when she landed. Cal had landed it for her. Her arm was still sore but Jerry tried to ignore it. Harvey watched her closely. Once in the air with the plane on course, she took the controls with her right hand to rest her left arm. If the weather stayed easy she could do it. "Cal, I need you." she thought. Her eyes swept across the instrument panel constantly monitoring the gauges. She watched the sky for weather, tall signal towers, and birds.

The flight was only about an hour. All went well. Jerry accepted the pain in her arm and settled back concentrating on flying. It was when they neared the airport, the tower told her a stiff cross wind had developed. She looked at Harvey. He nodded. His hands gently took the controls to be ready. The cross wind hit the 182. Jerry automatically made the correction to slip into the flight path. Perspiration broke out on Jerry's forehead as the pain shot up her arm. Her left arm with its injured muscles began to tremble then simply gave out. With her arm shaking she felt her grip on the controls slipping as her arm weakened.

"Harvey," she called. "I'm losing it" she added to herself. She felt the controls lighten as he took the force needed to bring the plane into a stall landing. Jerry guided the plane telling Harvey what pressure to use as if he were a student. The plane landed with a bump, then settled into a taxi with Jerry guiding it to the ramp.

She looked back when the props stopped and the grinning young men started applauding. "We knew you could do it, Jerry," they praised her as they unbuckled. Jerry sat for a second. Her face was pale and she felt the numbing pain slicing her arm and shoulder. Harvey got out and went around to help her.

"I have you, Jerry. Well done."

"Without you I'd have failed. My arm just gave out." She looked up at him shaking her head to make the faint feeling go away.

"I think you would have made it. But let's get you inside out of this heat. This way men. Your families will be at the restaurant."

"You can use my car, Harvey," said Jerry. "The keys are in the office."

"We'll walk. It's not that far. Be there before you are." The young men took off anxious about their families.

Abby was waiting in the office. She smiled as they entered. "The ambulance was waiting, and the little girl is in good hands."

"Abby, you were marvelous! Every one of the women and

children and most of the men got out before the truck got back. How can we ever thank you?" Coming from Harvey Lambert this praise brought a blush to Abby's cheeks.

"Anyone could have done it. Remember I was taught that if you can fly from A to B a short distance you can fly anywhere like driving on a trip. I've been sorting your mail for you. Hope you don't mind. I had to keep busy."

"Abby, I love you," Jerry gave her a hug. "I'll just find a couple of aspirin and sit a minute." Jerry would never admit she was feeling faint. She found the bottle of aspirin in the bottom drawer and Abby had water waiting.

"Come to the sofa and sit. You look pale." Abby gently guided her to the sofa. It did feel good to Jerry to lie back and close her eyes. "Do you want a cool soda?" Jerry shook her head no.

"Just to relax a second. Harvey you can take my car if you want to check the refugees. The keys are in the top drawer."

Abby smiled. "I hope you don't mind, but I called my club president and the mayor's wife. They were going to call the Red Cross, Salvation Army and any other local programs to help. I wouldn't be surprised if everything is well controlled. Oh, we are also finding families who have extra rooms if we need shelter. The mayor is trying to get legal permits for those who were being held prisoners."

"Prisoners?" asked Harvey. Abby nodded and filled him in. Jerry added what she had learned. Harvey was enraged. "Promised jobs and a home and then held in slavery. I'll take your car, Jerry. I have to take care of them."

"It seems they were brought to the village to work on a farm. But they found the conditions worse than what they left behind. The women and children had to grow food and carry water from the lake for everything because the well went dry last year. The drought has ruined the crops. It was awful." Abby added. "The men were forced to work in the barn behind the clinic making stuff they did not understand. They dared not ask about it. One young man did and was beaten so badly he died. I guess with women and children there were 20-25 people held as slaves."

When he was gone, Abby sighed. "I hope they find the

Reverend and throw the book at him."

"They will. The Reverend has made Harvey Lambert mad." Both laughed.

Jerry had finished looking at the last of the mail when she heard her car return. Instead of Harvey Lambert it was Cal. With long strides he was at her side. "Are you all right? Harvey told me about the flight. Abby, how can we all thank you? You and Jerry are the heroes of the day. The Red Cross is taking names and getting families together. Some who have local relatives are already leaving with them. Others are having bus arrangements made to go to their relatives out of town. The Salvation Army is feeding everyone and the woman's club and the mayor's wife have arranged local shelters for those left. I've never seen such organization so fast!"

"The President of the Woman's Club is a natural. She and the Mayor's wife have the whole town organized. They are responsible for kicking butts and getting a disaster plan worked out. I figured that we all worked together, and everyone is a hero including all those who volunteered to fly to the rescue."

"You're right Abby, but you are the one who saved a child and got us help. Then called the organizers to get here. You have my vote." Jerry smiled. "And there are the police who were shot and Harvey's pilot who saved Harvey's life." Then she added. "I'm glad you're back, but what about a car for Harvey?"

"You know Harvey. A phone call and a driver and car are on the way. He plans to stay in Houston tonight. Since we had to cancel everything, how about me taking both of you to dinner at the steak house?"

"Oh, I've got plans for tonight," said Abby, "but thanks. If you don't need me, I think I'll go on home. It's been quite a day. I wouldn't want to make a living with this much excitement. All I started out to do was give my club something to talk about." She shook her head and sighed. "The best laid plans -" Abby collected her purse and headed for her car. I loved every minute of it, she added to herself as she drove away. Never in her life had she felt so alive.

"Shall we close shop and head for home?" As Cal spoke, the door opened and Tillie the reporter hurried in.

"Wow! What a story. I scooped them all! Where's Abby? She called me." Tillie's eyes were sparkling with excitement as she scanned the room for Abby.

"She went home. She has plans for tonight. I guess it is quite a scoop. How can we help you? We were getting ready to leave." Jerry asked the excited woman.

"Sorry. I wanted to interview you three. Just a few questions. Please. I've interviewed some of the refugees" Cal sighed and Jerry smiled and nodded. An hour later Tillie finished her interview and left. Jerry and Cal quickly followed before anything else stopped them.

They stopped for a moment to check with Harvey who was amazed at the well-organized "operation rescue" that he had found. Family by family, the villagers were being sent to relatives or sent to shelters. Jerry and Cal left quickly. They were not needed.

Chapter 29

The morning was clear and warm with white cotton clouds scurrying across the sky. Jerry and Cal arrived as usual in their separate cars to give each other the freedom to leave at will and not strand the other. As scheduled, Ramona arrived looking excited and dressed ready to start work. Jerry took her to the hangar and told her what needed to be done. "If you need a break, just come in and cool down and rest. I forgot to tell you to bring a lunch. We have no restaurant."

"I gathered that and brought one. I hope I can use the fridge."

"You can, and help yourself to a cold drink if you wish or coffee. I need to go back to the office. I sure miss Maggie." Jerry left Mona to her work and went back into the office. The phone was ringing. It was her friend, police officer Jed.

"Jerry, they got the Reverend at Houston airport. Had a ticket for Brazil. We raided his apartment and the so-called church and found among the church records a few items he forgot to shred. It seems he is the head of the Zebra Company. A Donald Vaughn and the others had plans to turn the farms and the airport into subdivisions and a shopping mall. The Reverend was blackmailing Senator Stone when he found out about the embezzlement. It seems they knew each other before. The Reverend is being held in Houston. He was making incendiary bombs and selling them to terrorists. I find it hard to believe that he really is an ordained minister who has been defrocked for questionable behavior. He always seemed so nice."

"I know, Jed. We all trusted him here and his congregation

gave hard earned money to help the poor village people. The scum should have to pay it all back. So, he is the head of Zebra. The Senator and Reverend Mitchell were in this together." Jerry shook her head sadly.

"I hear you were a real hero yesterday," said Jed grinning.

"Not me, Abby was." Jerry told him what happened. "Then we were right, they really were making some kind of bombs for terrorists to destroy their own country. Thanks, Jed. I'll let Cal know when he gets back. Goodbye. Give my best to your wife."

It was a few minutes later that Ramona came in. "We'll need some major work on the Aerobat. It can't be flown until I get to the oil lines and we need to know why it's leaking. There's very little oil left. And it's got about half an hour of fuel."

"Let's look at it." The two went to the hangar and Jerry got lost in the engine diagnosis. "Looks like it will be more of a job than I thought. Can you do it?" Ramona nodded. "First check out the 182. Cal has a student for it at 1:00. I'll help you all I can. My arm is still a trifle sore."

"I read about that. I missed all the fun." Ramona grinned mischievously. She brushed her short hair back and started to work.

Jerry returned to her desk and groaned. Then she sat down and started to blunder once again through the mass of paper work. The one thing she could do was to pay bills. The morning went well. She scheduled lessons and gave information on the flight school to several potential students. One signed up for the next class when it started. One did not know that classroom work was necessary. He thought all he had to do was to fly. Shocked at all that had to be learned and a written exam passed he decided, he really wasn't the flying type. Jerry smiled and shook her head.

Cal arrived with his student and after the briefing; Ramona joined them in the office for lunch. The 1:00 student was all that was left until the night flying student. Cal would teach the flying class; and then, his student would join him in his first night flying experience. The world was different at night. The old timers used to hang something dangling from the ceiling so they could tell if they were right side up or flying upside down. It was going to be a long day, they decided. Ramona returned to the hangar and Cal's student arrived. Soon Jerry was alone once again. Then the phone rang.

"Charley's Flying School, Jerry speaking." She looked surprised. "What's wrong, Jed? You wouldn't call again unless it was business."

"You're right," Jed replied. "We don't know how it happened, but the Reverend killed a guard and stole his gun. He took a police car and is headed your way. I have men on the way."

"Dear God. How could he get away? Cal's with a student. My new mechanic is in the hangar. I'll have to send her to safety. Thanks, Jed. I think it is the Reverend who wants to kill me."

"Our men will be there in a few minutes. Lock your door and go home."

"Not and leave Cal and the student. I'll get Mona out of this." She hung up and ran to the hangar. Mona was finishing her last 152.

"Hi," she called. "You take good care of your sky babies. So far no nuts or bolts are loose. Only the Aerobat."

"Ramona, you have to get out of here now." Jerry blurted it out. "The Reverend killed a guard and they think he's headed this way. Go now." Ramona was staring beyond Jerry to the hangar door. Her face drained of color.

"She stays." Jerry froze. She turned and was looking into a police gun held by a wild looking Reverend Mitchell. His eyes were blazing with hate and fear. "Now get the Aerobat out and I'll be off."

Ramona looked at Jerry. Jerry looked at him and asked, "Why did you sell bombs to terrorist against your own country? Why did you put a hit out on me?"

"GET THE DAMNED PLANE OUT AND NOW." Jerry nodded to Ramona. "That's better. Money. That's all. They kicked me out of the church. I was penniless and had to do something. So, I met these terrorists who pay well. I put the money in safe overseas accounts and I'm out of here. That stupid Senator was skimming millions from the real estate company and I took it from him. He supplied me money I needed to make millions supplying the terrorists. You were going to let the news know about the village and it would have spoiled everything. I had to stop you." The women rolled the

Aerobat out of the hangar.

"I think you should -," Jerry started to tell him the plane was not in condition to fly.

"One more word and you're both dead." He pointed the gun at Ramona and continued. "Let's go get the key." They walked quickly to the office and Jerry handed him the key. "Now, out of here. Into the hangar." The women complied. "Lay face down on the floor if you move, you're dead." They heard the plane start and taxi for takeoff. Then they got up.

"My guess is the engine will overheat and freeze and he'll go down in less than fifty miles." Ramona said in a shaky voice.

"Unless he runs out of gas first. Here come the police. I thought for sure he would kill me. If he stays over the fields, he might be able to land it. But if he gets over the trees no way." The police cars parked and the men hurried to the women. "He stole a plane and took off. He wouldn't listen when I tried to tell him it has an oil leak and not much gas. He did no pre-flight check. He knows we always have our planes in ready to go order. But this time the plane was down for repairs. He'll go down somewhere within about fifty miles. He turned south." Then she laughed. "Enough excitement, Mona?"

"I'm glad I missed the rest." Mona answered. The color had returned to her tanned face.

Jerry turned to the officer in charge. "Come in and we'll look at a sectional and estimate where he might come down if you think it will help. One thing you need to know. He is a very good pilot. But, today he was in a hurry and did no pre-flight. He also has a rather stiff crosswind that will slow him down."

This information was relayed to the police. The police helicopters covering a wide area were soon in the air. Cal and all pilots listening to the controller heard the message. He turned to his student who nodded.

"I wonder if any student ever gets to finish a lesson at this airport" said student with a chuckle as Cal turned the plane heading toward home and Jerry. "I heard all about all the cancellations yesterday."

He grinned and said, "I hope they do soon. I can't afford all these free lessons. Thanks, Tony. I have to know if my wife is safe. It seems we have lost our aerobatic plane and a part of our business we were just getting started."

Cal arrived shortly after the police left. Jerry met him and he folded her in his arms. "Jerry, are you all right?"

"He said he did all those horrible things to those poor people for money. Just money. Oh, Cal I just can't understand that. How can money be so important?" She clung to him feeling safe in his strong arms.

"I guess no sane person can. Look at what the Senator did. We just have to face the fact that there is pure evil in the world. Evil, like Hitler."

"Cal, Mona had found a leak in the oil line and I had not filled the gas tank yesterday. The engine will go out or he will run out of gas in about half an hour. The police are putting out a dragnet of about 50 miles. And yes, you can go search. That was your business wasn't it?"

"You read me like a book. I'll call and see where I can be the most help. I love you." He gave her a big kiss and picked up the phone.

"Let's go." At Cal's surprised look Jerry added. "Four eyes are better than two. I'm coming with you."

"Mona, see how she bosses me. He has a gun, Jerry." Both Jerry and Mona laughed.

"We are aware of that since he threatened to blow our brains out if we didn't get the plane out. He wouldn't let Jerry tell him it was not safe to fly. I don't like looking into the business end of a gun. I'll never go deer hunting again," declared Mona.

"I guess you can go home, Mona. We'll lock up before we leave."

"I can fly too. I've been on search parties with my dad before. Dad was a member of the Civil Air Patrol. If you'll loan me a plane and tell me where to look." Cal shook his head and reached for the phone. "Women! Are there no sacred jobs for us men anymore?" Both women smiled and shook their head no.

The police found the wreckage of the plane in a wooded area about fifty miles away. The Reverend was dead. A local farmer working in his fields saw the plane go into the trees and the pilot fly out of the door. In his haste the late Reverend Mitchell had neglected to fasten his seat belt and lock the doors. The Zebra Company was out of business.

Charley's Flying School

Rosa B. Lane

Chapter 30

Tillie's story splashed not only over the local news, the international news media picked it up as well. Abby called and said the rescued children were doing well. With time and proper care, they would all be in regular classes. Harvey helped with the immigration problem and kidnapping charges were added to the arrested men. The few villagers who stayed in town found homes and jobs. The restaurant was open again. Slowly everything returned to normal. Jerry was back to her flying. All they needed was a secretary to make things perfect.

The secretary came one Monday morning. Jerry and Cal had forgone their days off to keep things rolling. Cal was flying and Jerry was at the phone. The door opened and Jerry looked up. A grinning young man of medium height and neatly combed red hair walked to her desk. He was built like an athlete and dressed like a business executive. Jerry smiled back at him.

"How can I help you?"

"I heard you needed help," he answered.

"I'm sorry, but I have hired a mechanic."

"Oh, I'm not a mechanic. I'm a secretary. I'm planning to go to college and get a business degree and I need a job." His blue eyes sparkled with delight when Jerry looked surprised.

"Well, we can't pay much right now. I can sure use some help." The man looked at the jumble of papers on the desk and laughed.

"I don't fly," he announced unasked. "I'm a good organizer.

A friend recommended I see you."

"Who?" asked Jerry.

"Maggie. She said if you haven't found help by now you would be in a "gawd awful mess" for you are no file clerk. I'm her brother, Hank Dawson." Both laughed.

"Maggie! How is she? I haven't heard from her." Jerry was delighted.

"Very busy. I went with my folks to visit her when Mom got worried because she didn't write. With her classes and her fiancée, she's about forgotten her family. Mom set her straight. Gave her stamps and stationery and said 'Write to us.' Sis won't dare not write."

"If Maggie sent you, and the pay is satisfactory, then you're hired." She looked at the desk and asked, "When can you start?"

"Maggie said you would say that in a forlorn voice. I came prepared to start now."

"Good," Jerry got up. "I'll show you around first. Come to the hangar and meet my mechanic." Hank followed her to the hangar.

"Mona, I've just hired a secretary. Meet Hank Dawson. Hank, Ramona Seabens."

It was Hank's turn to be surprised as Mona stood up with oil on her face and smiled the most beautiful smile he had ever seen. "Pleased to meet you," he stammered his composure shaken.

"Pleased to meet you, Hank Dawson. Yes, like Jerry, I was raised fixing airplanes. Don't look so surprised." Jerry stifled a chuckle. "Jerry, I have an order list I was going to bring in. Let me get it." Ramona walked with grace to the workbench at the back to retrieve it. Hank watched the gentle sway of her hips that Ramona was totally unaware of. Jerry watched Hank. She half expected him to whistle.

"Good. We'll get these things ordered. You'll join us for lunch at the restaurant when Cal gets back?"

Mona grinned and nodded. "I'll be a while here." She turned to Hank and added "This is a nice place to work if you like guns in your face." Mona gave a mischievous grin and handed the list to Jerry.

"I heard about that. My sister, Maggie met her fiancée here. He crashed landed and they rescued him. Glad to be where the excitement is. We'll have to talk about what happened to my sister over dinner one evening."

"That would be nice. I'd like that, Hank. Got to get back to work."

Jerry took the list and Hank back to the office. "She's a good mechanic, Hank." She showed him the file cabinets. As Maggie had predicted, they were in confusion. She told him about the mail and said she would handle it and pay the checks. Hank smiled. This was exactly what Maggie had predicted.

"I can do that, Mrs. Morris. All you will need to do is to look at things and sign the checks. It may take a while to sort out the files."

"Just like Maggie warned you." Jerry smiled. "I have no students booked til tomorrow, so I'll get you started and get back to the hangar." By the time Cal returned he found a strangely familiar young man at the desk and Jerry in the hangar helping Mona check tires.

"I'm Calvin Morris," said Cal. "Who are you?" He smiled at the young man. "You look familiar."

"I'm Hank Dawson, Maggie's brother. Mrs. Morris just hired me. I'm a secretary. I hope to get a business degree." Hank stood up and offered his hand to Cal. Cal grinned.

"Of course. You look like Maggie! How is she? Please sit down. I have a student to debrief, but we really love your sister. Please excuse me." He took the student into the class room and Hank looked at the files, shook his head and started his new job.

Hank soon had the office in order and Jerry and Cal were able to concentrate on students. The insurance company finally paid off on the Aerobat and a new one was ordered. It would be a while before it was ready for delivery. Things seem to fall into place at last. Cal and Jerry had quiet evenings at home discussing the school and Uncle Art visited them when he could. The airport was back to normal.

It was a Saturday that Sylvia showed up unexpectedly at the school. Jerry was free for a while so they retired to the classroom. "What is it, Sylvia? You look like you can't wait to tell a secret." Jerry asked smiling.

"I like to travel. I always keep a journal and take films. But I'd like to go on the back roads and meet the people who work and live there and see their own special parks and fishing holes. I've been to a lot of places but only got to do a few tourists things and never really got to eat where the regular people eat or see where they live. It was all work. I quit my job and am going to study professional photography and be a free-lance travel photographer. I've always wanted to do it. Now I am. Dad and Richard think it's a great idea. Dad even said he would try to take some time off and go with me." Sylvia was smiling and excited. "I came by to say goodbye."

"Great. You have enough money. Go for it. For me it's always been flying. Nothing else. It sounds like a great experience." Jerry sat across the table from Sylvia. Sylvia looked up with a sparkle in her eyes Jerry had never seen before. They said goodbye and Sylvia left. What a different woman than the first time I met her, thought Jerry.

When Cal and Jerry got home that evening a letter from Estelle was waiting. She was doing well in school and helping her uncle on week-ends. She loved Australia. She hadn't heard from her mother or any friends except Jerry. After dinner Jerry wrote her a long letter telling her of the Senator and Reverend Mitchell. She said all was quiet again. I hope it stays this way, Jerry thought. Life being what it was, she knew it would not.

The weather was getting cooler. Up North the winter snows had already started. Here some trees had turned fall colors, but the pines remained green and elegant. Fronts were coming in every few days. Today they were warned of a storm coming in tomorrow. Jerry wondered if it would ground the airport. They had just begun to get the house redecorated, and she hated more loss of work.

As predicted. The morning came in with dark clouds bringing rain. Cal and Mona were washing the airplanes in the hangar. Jerry had just gone into the office when the hospital called. Hank handed her the phone. The hospital was searching for a rare blood type for a very ill patient who had been in an accident and had found some. The patient was a new mother. The hospital's chopper was down for repairs and they could not get help from the National Guard due to an emergency in Houston. They wanted Jerry to fly to a small town south of them to pick it up. "A new mother's life depends on it." Jerry said she would and rushed to the hangar to get the 182 ready. Cal looked up and asked what was going on. When Jerry told him, he looked at the sky with storm clouds rolling in. The wind had picked up considerably.

"Jer, I'll take it. I've flown this kind of weather many times. You've not had a lot of storm experience." He walked over and helped her pull the plane out of the hangar.

"Cal, I know the area well. You don't. I can handle it fine."

"This is a bad storm. You need more experience than you have. Normally you would never fly in this weather."

"I know the way, you don't." The rain was starting.

"I know the weather. You don't."

They ducked into the hangar out of the weather. Then at the same time they looked at each other and smiled. "I'll navigate," Jerry said. For a long moment they looked at each other. Cal placed his hand under her chin and looked into her laughing eyes. He bent and kissed her.

"I'll fly. You file a flight plan and I'll do the pre-flight." Cal was waiting at the hangar door when Jerry returned from filing the flight plan with the keys and maps. Cal reached out and Jerry took his hand. "Come on, we have a life to save." For a moment they shared a look of love deep and forever. Then hand in hand they ran out to the waiting plane to face the coming storm together.

My Mother was a cloud,
My Father the roar of an engine.
I have wind for my hair and sky in my veins,
And when I die just bury me
Where the music of the airplanes will my eulogy be
I am a Pilot.

Rosa B. Lane

The End

Rosa B. Lane

ABOUT THE AUTHOR

The Writings of Rosa B. Lane: A Word from Rosa

I am a ninety-year-old widow, mother of two adult children and grandmother to one adult grandson. I grew up in a working-class family of eight, that included my mother, father, grandmother, three bothers and older sister, in Wood River Illinois, a small oil refinery town along the Mississippi River on the Metro East side of Metropolitan St. Louis area.

My Dad, Pop Veach, was a man who had the biggest heart one could imagine, had the best recipe for vegetable soup in the world, and had a knack for never meeting a person he did not know and like. My Mom, Ma Veach, worked hard to keep us kids in line, manage a house hold in the depression, and in her later years, to serve her church as a very devote Christian. Even with the help of my Grandma, keeping my three brothers, sister and me in line was a tall order for both Mom and Dad!

Rosa B. Lane

I graduated from East Alton Wood River Community High School where my English teacher Ms. Hart really made us think about quality writing. I have written stories since I was age six; and, I have been writing all my life. In high school I even learned some valuable life lessons and experienced some real heart ache "ghost writing" stories for my friend's English assignments!

As a young girl I love airplanes and the idea of flying among the clouds. I kept a scrap book of all the latest fighter planes, bombers, and transport planes; and, when I graduated from high school, I decided that being a nurse was to be my ticket to flying. I earned my three-year Registered Nurse diploma in the 1940's through the United States Cadet Nurse Corps in order to be able to become a flight attendant and soar into the sky. On my 90th birthday I flew a Cessna 172 under the watchful eye of an instructor, high above the fields and clouds of Champaign, Illinois.

I practiced nursing before being married to my husband, Bob, who was a mechanical engineer. Bob and I shared many interests, camping, scuba diving and flying. We flew all over the United States and loved every minute of it. I have been painter, sculptor, fisherman, camper, scuba diver, and a private pilot. My interest in the arts led me to earn an Associate's Degree with honors in Fine Arts from North Harris Count College, Texas. I continued to read about writing, attended a number of Elder Hostiles, including a week long Creative Writer's Workshop, and of course, I continued to write. In short, I have lived a wonderful and full life with my late husband and all of my family and friends.

I write because I must! The characters demand to be born and their stories simply must be put into words. I love meeting my characters and trying to bring out the thoughts and feelings of each. While I work hard to provide sufficient detail to the stories, I also try to leave room for the readers to use their own imagination.

Readers of my writings can expect certain standards to be met in each book. The writings of Rosa B. Lane will always contain the perspective of strong, capable, intelligent and caring women who face the significant challenges that life presents to them with a stubborn grit and determination. They find romance and eventually love as they work through these significant every day, and as only fiction allows, not so every day, challenges that life brings to them. The reader will not find torrid, explicit sex or rough language. Instead, the reader will find a journey of self-discovery and earned mutual respect. While my stories certainly do imply the fact that women and men to become close and do, when the time is right, share intense intimacy, I want to recognize that sex is a part of life, is all around us, and, at its best, is the product of a true love and mutual respect that develops over literally hundreds of shared experiences and mutually respectful interactions. My writings will always be clean and wholesome.

    I have always loved writing and I have been writing all my life. "Charley's Flying School" is my second novel, following "Connie" is my first serious attempt to publish online. "Charley's Flying School" and "Connie" will be joined shortly online by my third work, a novella "The Sermon". Hopefully, two more novels that I am currently working on will follow those three. All of these are romantic stories featuring strong, independent women who through the challenges that life brings to them find lasting love with equally strong and caring men. Like I said earlier, I write because I must! I want to share my story with others, give the readers a few hours of joy, and hopefully, something interesting to ponder. I sincerely hope that you enjoy "Charley's Flying School"!